Kyona
Jiles

Copyright © 2024 by Kyona Jiles

1st Edition

All rights reserved.

ISBN (eBook): 979-8-9898052-6-6
ISBN (Paperback): 979-8-9898052-7-3
Library of Congress Control Number: 2024901677

No part of this book may be reproduced in any form or by any electronic or mechanical means, including information storage and retrieval systems, without written permission from the author, except for the use of brief quotations in a book review.

Title Production by The Bookwhisperer

Cover Design by Sandy Robson

Michael
1977-2019
Friendship shouldn't have a time limit. You were taken from us too soon and my heart is broken. Thank you for being my Rachel and Kinsley rolled into one.
I love and miss you every day. ♥

Darrin, you have given me new faith in unconditional love. I didn't know Soul Mates were real until you. Thank you for being the port in my storm of emotions and the second half of my soul.
I love you!

For my dad, Fred
1947-2021
You gave me the love of all things science fiction and supernatural. You told me I could be a writer. You're the reason I'm where I am today. Thank you for the sacrifices you made for me.
I love you and I miss you so much.

Chapter One

WHEN I DIE, I hope I can stand on my own two feet, staring down whatever monster is about to kill me.

I know, kind of dramatic. When did I become a drama queen?

If I were normal, I'd picture my death at one-hundred-something with my children, grandchildren, great-grandchildren, maybe even great-great-grandchildren, hovering around me. Unfortunately, I'm not normal so I don't plan to die an old lady in my bed.

None of that is in my future.

When I found out I was a Shadower, my life changed forever. When your destiny is to protect good vampires and destroy evil vampires, you don't get to have the white picket fence and raise the two-point-five kids. You die killing a monster.

When I die, I hope I can be as brave as my parents. As brave as my Aunt Marie.

Because just like them, I know I'm going to die.

Chapter Two

"WHO REALLY THOUGHT it was a good idea to name a town Ecstasy?"

Raven stood gazing over the Pacific Ocean, her short black and hot pink hair moving like Medusa's in the coastal wind. The sun was coming up, giving the water a silver tint. The late September breeze was cool off the water and gave me goosebumps.

"I think it's kinda cute," said my best friend with a smile. That was Rachel, the eternal optimist. Her long blonde hair was braided and tucked under a wide-brimmed, white hat. "Of course, it could have been a group of perverts," she added with a laugh. Eternal optimist with a twisted sense of humor.

"No, really," Raven persisted. "What group of founding forefathers thought it would be a good idea to name their town Ecstasy?"

Electricity seemed to move from the bottoms of my feet to the top of my head. I stood for a moment and absorbed the current, realizing what it meant.

"No," I said slowly. "A cadre of vampires named the town."

Raven narrowed her eyes.

Rachel jumped up and down, clapping her hands. "I knew it! I knew Marie would be here!"

"Just because I can feel the electricity I think indicates vampires doesn't mean Marie is here with Isaac."

"Sure it does," Rachel said with a shrug. "Since you're a Shadower, you can *feel* when a vampire is near."

"Well," I said, "I think I can tell. It would have been nice to be trained for real." My parents were supposed to train me, but they were killed. I have a legacy to carry on and I don't even know what it entails or if I want to.

"Can you feel Marie or Isaac?" Raven asked.

Thinking of Aunt Marie with that evil vampire made my skin crawl. Having been his captive for four days and seeing the scars he'd given Marie the last time he'd held her captive, I didn't even want to think about what could be happening to her.

I shook my head.

Raven growled. Sometimes I forgot she was a cougar since she spent most of her time in human form being my friend and bodyguard.

"I hate being a plain ol' human," Rachel said. "I could be more helpful if I had superpowers like you two."

Lately, I wished I was just a plain ol' human, too.

"When Scott wakes up from his pain pill nap, he might call Beck and Nathaniel," I warned the girls.

Scott used to work with my parents killing vampires. He's just a regular human, too. Beck and Nathaniel are my non-human friends, bodyguards, and who knows what else. In only a few months, my life had become quite complicated. My twenty-first birthday brought huge changes. Not only did I learn about the existence of vampires and shapeshifters, I learned many of the things we see on TV and read in books aren't true. Ha! That's funny. Of course it's not true. Not many people know vampires are even real. Needless to say, my vampire education from movies was pretty much worthless.

Beck is a vampire, college professor, and the hottest guy I've ever met. Well, one of the hottest guys. There's also Scott. Hence, my moral dilemma.

I realized yesterday I think I'm in love with both men. Maybe not *in love*, in love. I'm not sure I know what it means to be in love with someone. But I knew I was willing to lay down my life for both men and they were willing to do the same for me. That's got to be some form of love, right?

Yes, I really want to find Marie because her kidnapper is a sick vampire son of a bitch. But I also had to get out of Seattle and away from the magnetic pull of both Beck and Scott. I felt like a floozy because I wanted both guys. What was wrong with me?

This is how I had become a drama queen.

"Hell-o, Kinsley!" Rachel's voice broke through my tumbling thoughts. "You're blushing. What were you thinking about?"

I think her comment made me blush more because she laughed.

"Scott won't call Beck unless he has to," Rachel said, fighting a smile, reminding me what had started my thoughts.

Rachel was right; Scott and Beck didn't like each other. Okay, that was an understatement. They hated each other. Yet, I needed both their expertise and had to find a way to make them play nice together. Of course, getting them in the same room without bloodshed was my first goal. It helped they were trying to work on it themselves. It only took me being kidnapped and almost drained of all my blood.

"We need to find the house," Raven said with a hint of exasperation in her voice. Technically, she worked for Beck. She was probably worried about the ramifications of letting Rachel and me talk her into skipping town to go halfway down the Oregon Coast without telling anyone what we were doing.

Marie had been with Isaac for almost four days, and I needed to find her. Beck and Scott could be as angry as they wanted; Marie was my priority.

"She didn't write the address down. We're going to have to wait for city hall to open so we can get the records." Now Rachel sounded annoyed. Apparently, six straight hours in a car throughout the night had taken its toll on all of us.

Rachel was fairly sure she knew where Isaac had taken Marie. About eighty years ago, he had bought her a house on the Oregon Coast. We thought we had the key, we just didn't know exactly where the house was.

"Let's get a hotel room, coffee, and showers. By that time, City Hall should be open. I don't care how small a town is, it should be open by eight." That's me: the reasonable, logical one.

Rachel and Raven's eyes both lit up at the word coffee. It was a little after five and that gave us plenty of time to become human.

Human. That was kind of funny.

I was glad I still had a sense of humor.

We piled back in the car and pulled away from the lookout. A few miles later we passed a faded wooden sign.

WELCOME TO ECSTASY, OREGON.
WHERE THE DAY MEETS THE NIGHT.
POP. 1042

"'Where The Day Meets The Night'? What the hell does that mean?" Raven asked.

Rachel and I shrugged.

We crested a small hill and Ecstasy came into view. It

resembled a picture-perfect fishing village. Boats were moored at docks, and we could see people scurrying around, pulling lines, and setting out into the open ocean. Other boats were just specks on the horizon, already out starting their day. The houses were all Victorian era with fresh paint, white picket fences, manicured lawns, and trees lining the sidewalks.

"Is it creepy, or is it just me?" Rachel asked, poking her head between our seats with a look of disgust.

"Creepy?" Raven said. "I don't think it's creepy. I think it's cute."

Rachel and I looked at her with raised eyebrows. This was the woman who didn't like small towns because she either needed to be in the middle of a city or hiking in the mountains.

"You think it's cute?" I asked in disbelief.

Raven ignored me, pulling the car over in front of a particularly gingerbread-looking house with a Bed and Breakfast sign.

"I've always wanted to stay in a Bed and Breakfast!"

"Now you're just scaring us," I said.

"I was expecting some run-down ghost town," Raven said. "This place is beautiful! I know we're here for a serious reason, but I'm glad we don't have to sleep in the car and worry about being attacked by vampires."

I kind of understood her relief. I hadn't been sure what to expect of Ecstasy, either. But I still thought she was acting weird.

I was getting ready to say just that when power flowed over my skin. It was stronger than the usual electricity feeling. I looked at my arms and saw my hairs standing on end.

"Ooh! There's another Bed and Breakfast across the street! Which one do we pick?" Rachel bounced in the back seat.

They left the car, each going to different inns.

"Hey! Wait! Where are you guys going?" I yelled at their backs.

Neither one answered as they went into the buildings. The car was still running and their doors were open. What the hell?

Knowing Raven could take care of herself, I took the keys from the ignition, then closed and locked the doors. I jogged across the street to the inn Rachel had disappeared into.

As soon as I touched the screen door handle, electricity shot through my arm and threw me backward onto the porch. I landed with a whoosh of air from my lungs, pain radiating up my spine.

From the doorway, an old woman who looked something like the witch from Snow White smiled at me. Then she slammed the door.

"Hey," I yelled, climbing to my feet. "Open the door!"

Through the window, I saw the little old lady standing with her hands on Rachel's shoulders. In a split second, she was leaning in to kiss her! Before I could pound on the door again, Rachel leaned in to meet the old woman's lips.

"Screw this," I said.

I ripped the screen door off its hinges and tossed it into the yard. I placed my hands above and below the doorknob of the main door and shoved. Wood splintered as my Shadower strength ripped the door open.

A shimmer of iridescent rainbow covered the old woman as her white hair turned chocolate brown, her skin tightened as if from invisible Botox. What was once old had become new again as Rachel crumpled to the floor.

The beautiful woman turned to me. "Ahh, Shadower. I could feed from you for days."

"What?" I asked, blinking as my brain tried to catch up.

The woman glided toward me, rainbow shimmer in her wake. I backed up until my butt bumped the broken door.

What had I gotten us into now? I glanced at Rachel's still form on the floor. I couldn't tell if she was breathing.

A popping sound startled me for a moment. I'd only heard that sound once before. A flash of light gave only the briefest warning before the sudden and dramatic arrival of Beck. Damn it.

"Lilith!" he yelled, stepping between the woman and me.

"Oh, Beckford." She ran a finger down Beck's cheek and jealousy reared its ugly head in my gut.

"You know this... this thing?" I asked.

Lilith, if that was her name, hissed and swiped her hand at my face. I only had a moment to register her fingernails were longer than normal before pain knifed my cheek. I raised a hand to my face, wiping blood.

Beck's nostrils flared and he grabbed the woman by the neck. He flew her back until she slammed against the far wall, still held in his grip.

She laughed, a rich sound that had me stepping toward her. I shook my head to clear it.

"Still like it rough, I see," she purred.

"Enough," Beck said, his power filling the room.

"They came to me, Beckford. You know I demand payment. I'll take you or the Shadower. You can have your human and cat back."

I looked across the street to the Bed and Breakfast Raven had entered. Had the same thing happened to her?

"You will not touch my Shadower."

"That's how it is, hmm?" Lilith asked. She didn't seem worried she was pinned to the wall by a pissed off vampire. In fact, she seemed to be enjoying it. When her legs wrapped around Beck's waist, I stepped forward.

"Stop, Kinsley," he said.

Wait? He was telling me to stop and not the psycho slut who had her legs wrapped around him?

"What?" I asked, truly perplexed now.

"You brought Rachel and Raven to the House of Lilith. Now the price must be paid." He closed his eyes and lowered his head, dark hair brushing his shoulders.

"What does that mean?"

Lilith laughed, a sexy melodic sound that crawled across my skin and made me shiver. What *was* she?

"Allow me to transport the women away, then I will come to pay the toll."

"Oh, no no, Beckford. You might not come back. I've waited centuries to taste you again. I'm assuming I get you. You don't want me to touch *your* Shadower." She glared at me.

My cheek pulsed and throbbed, and I was thankful for my healing Shadower ability. I was debating if it was worth it to attack Lilith. Probably should wait until I knew what I was up against.

"What are you?" I asked.

"Kinsley," Beck warned.

Lilith removed her legs from Beck, pulling herself from his grip without a struggle. She was on me before I knew what was happening. One minute I was standing, and the next I was on the floor covered by Lilith's body.

Her silky hair sent erotic waves of pleasure over my neck and down my body. I moaned as the pulses made me feel things I'd never felt before. I arched into her, rubbing my breasts against hers.

Wait!

I closed my eyes and said through gritted teeth, "What the hell *are* you?"

Lilith made a sound I couldn't distinguish. I opened one

eye to see her face scrunched in pain as Beck tried to pry her from me.

Lilith shrugged from Beck's hands, pushing herself against my thighs. I moaned again.

"I, my dear Shadower, am Queen of the Succubi."

Then she kissed me.

Beck growled and ripped Lilith away, throwing her against the wall. Pictures fell to the floor in a shower of broken glass.

"I tire of playing games! Give me the Shadower or I get you!" She strode from the room, uninjured.

I lay on the floor in shock. Dear lord. A succubus? The queen? No wonder her name was Lilith.

"Beck—"

"What the hell are you doing in Ecstasy?" he demanded.

"How did you know where to find me?"

"Will you never answer a question?"

"You're one to talk!" I said, gently pulling myself from the floor. My skin was tingling and my knees were weak. Maybe Rachel was just passed out from ecstasy. Wait. "Is that why this town is called Ecstasy? Was I feeling succubi instead of vampires?" I slowly made my way to Rachel.

Her skin was sallow and wrinkled. "Did that bitch steal Rachel's youth?" I knelt, feeling for a pulse. It was slow but steady.

"She will recover because you interrupted. It will take time, though."

I glared at Beck.

"Do not argue with me. It is your fault Rachel and Raven are hurt! If you do not trust me, then maybe this arrangement is not going to work."

A fist grabbed my heart. Was he dumping me? I mean we weren't a couple but we were. . . what were we? I needed Beck to help me find Marie. I needed him to help me understand what it meant to be a Shadower. I also needed him to help keep my friends and me safe.

Damn. No wonder he was so angry. I'd kind of taken advantage of him. Who did I think I was? Xena? Buffy? Wonder Woman? What in the world made me think I could find Marie without anyone getting hurt?

I opened my mouth to apologize. Beck cut me off.

"You will get Rachel in the car then get Raven. I will pay Lilith and we will go home."

"What do you mean *pay* Lilith? What do you pay her?"

"She is a succubus. What do you think she demands as payment?"

I swallowed. I wouldn't sleep with Beck. How horrible was it I didn't want him to sleep with anyone else?

A knowing smile lifted his lips.

"Stay out of my head," I said quickly.

Beck narrowed his eyes. "You have already told me not to take your thoughts. I can tell you are jealous without reading your mind."

"I am not jealous!"

He raised an eyebrow.

We were bonded. I had no idea what it meant. He liked to refer to me as *his* and he could read my thoughts when he was in my head. He could track me and do his little *popping in thing* I really needed a name for.

Rachel moaned and I ripped my gaze from Beck's, happy for the reprieve, relieved she was okay.

"Could you do something for once without arguing, please? Take Rachel to the car, get Raven, and send Nathaniel to pick me up around noon."

"Noon? You're going to be with her for six hours?" Really, I wasn't jealous. I carefully picked Rachel up and moved to the door. "Why does Nate have to come back and pick you up? Can't you just pop home like you got here?"

"I will not have the energy to *pop* home. Six hours of sex with a succubus of Lilith's power will drain much of my energy."

I almost dropped Rachel.

"Sex?"

Lilith appeared in the doorway. "What did you think the payment was, Shadower?" She was completely nude and I felt my face heat as I turned to leave with Rachel in my arms.

"Can I, uh, just go get Raven?" My voice cracked.

"She's so precious, Beckford. Can I have her? Give me one hour and all will be even."

Beck growled and I heard him push her back in the room and slam the door.

I put Rachel in the back seat of the car. Squaring my shoulders, I headed to the door of the other house to get Raven, trying not to think of Beck and Lilith. Naked.

I cautiously reached for the doorknob, remembering the shock from the other house. Nothing happened when I grasped the cool metal. I wasn't sure what to expect when I swung open the door.

I gasped and four sets of eyes locked on me. Two old women and two younger women surrounded Raven. She was spread eagle and naked on the floor. Her eyes were open but glazed over.

I barreled through the door. "Lilith said I could have Raven! Get away from her!"

The women moved away as I approached. Raven's clothes were shreds of fabric surrounding her on the floor. I grabbed a blanket from a couch, wrapping it around Raven as I picked her up.

"I've got you."

The women watched like we were prey. I suppose we were, but not today.

"I couldn't overpower them; why?" Raven whispered.

"They're succubi."

"That explains why they destroyed my clothes." She tried to laugh.

I backed toward the car, the women crawling along the sidewalk and grass, ready to pounce. I carefully put Raven in the front seat.

"Why don't they affect you?"

"I don't know. The Queen of Sluts who entranced Rachel had some pull over me, though." I shivered when I thought of the power that had flowed over my skin like a thousand seeking fingers.

"Queen?"

"Yeah, umm, Beck's here and he's pissed," I said as I started the car.

Raven groaned and closed her eyes.

"I'm supposed to take you and Rachel home and send Nate back to get him around noon. He's *paying* the," I wasn't sure what to call her. I liked Queen of Sluts. It fit. But it wasn't very nice. "He's paying the Queen of Sluts in sex." Nice was overrated. Besides she'd attacked Rachel and me and was, right this moment, attacking Beck. The latter bothered me more than the former. No time to think about that now.

"We're leaving? We just got here!" Raven pulled the blanket tighter around her.

"I said Beck *told* us to leave. We're not leaving."

Chapter Three

I DROVE twenty miles before pulling into Newport. I'd never been to this town, and I wasn't quite sure why I was there now. Instinct maybe? Something made me turn off the main highway. A small itch on the back of my neck followed by a feeling of calm when I stopped in front of a one-story brick house.

Raven opened an eye. "Really? You think stopping again is a good idea?"

This place *felt* right. I wasn't sure if I could explain it to Raven. She probably didn't care right now anyway.

"Just let me check things out," I said.

Energy tickled my feet as I made my way up the concrete steps. It didn't hurt like Lilith's energy had. Is this why I'd come here? Was there something that would help me?

A small figure stood in the shadow of the screen door. As I moved closer, the outline of an old man took shape. His green sweater seemed bright against his white, spiky hair. Brown corduroys held up by rainbow suspenders made me smile.

"What's so funny, girl? You got injured friends and a vampire pissed at you. Don't think you really have much to smile about." His gravelly voice held anger.

I stared into his piercing blue eyes, my smile slipping. "How do you know about my friends and the vampire?"

"I know almost everything about you, Kinsley Preston. I know your hardheadedness almost got your human friend killed. What the hell were you thinking?"

Raven, always the bodyguard, was slowly making her way toward us. She wasn't really limping, but she was having trouble lifting her feet to make it up the steps.

"Kinsley, you okay?" she asked.

"Not sure yet," I said.

"You're fine," the old man replied with a grunt. "If you knew how to use your powers, you'd be able to tell I'm harmless."

I raised an eyebrow. "I'm pretty sure you're the opposite of harmless."

A smile tickled his lips, then he clamped it down. "Maybe you're smarter than I thought. We'll see."

He pushed open the screen door. "Get Rachel in here. She needs fluids and rest. We're going to need to restore her aura."

"I'm not going anywhere until I know who you are, how you know so much about us, and *what* you are."

He finally smiled, revealing crooked, yellowed teeth. "Now you're acting like a Shadower." He stepped on the porch, leaning heavily on a cane.

"How do you know about Shadowers?"

Raven made it next to me. I put a steadying hand on her arm. Her skin was clammy.

"What made you come here, Kinsley?" the man asked.

"It felt right," I said.

Raven looked at me with a raised eyebrow. She turned her gaze to the little old man of no-fashion-sense. "Who are you and why should we trust you?"

That's why Raven is the bodyguard. She went straight for

the important stuff instead of holding a dumb conversation like me.

"Ah, pretty cougar. You'd give your life for her, wouldn't you?"

Raven stiffened and growled. She sounded more like a weak kitten than the fierce animal I knew she was.

"I'm not going to challenge you. Smell. I'm human."

Raven leaned in to take a whiff. Stepping back, she wrinkled her forehead. "He *is* human."

"Which means Kinsley can kill me if I try to harm any of you."

He sounded so reasonable, it made me suspicious. But he was right. I could kill him. I was faster and stronger.

He said, "Okay. How about if I show you some pictures?"

"What?" I asked.

"I forgot to tell you the most important part. Silly me." He smacked his forehead with one gnarled hand.

It was so much like Marie, I almost broke into tears. That alone was enough to have me walking through the screen door.

"Kinsley, wait," Raven said.

I stopped. Sheesh. What was up with me? It was like this place had some kind of pull on me like Ecstasy had on Raven and Rachel. Oh man. Was this little old man an incubus? Wasn't that the male counterpart to a succubus? Was he going to try and attack me? I shivered.

"Get your scrawny butt in here, girl. I've been waiting a long time for you to come. Your dad and I had a falling out years ago. Tom wanted to keep you girls protected."

My dad. He knew my dad?

Raven shook her head.

"It's okay. Wait by the door. If something happens, get Rachel out of here. Can you drive?"

Raven adjusted the blanket and held out a shaky hand. "It wouldn't be safe, but I'll do it if I have to."

"You can go get Beck if I can't."

The man shouted from inside, "You're as suspicious and wary as your mother. I guess with everything you've seen, I can't blame you."

I stopped, a chill whipping up my spine. My palms started to sweat. "My mother?"

"Get in here and look at these pictures," he said again.

I walked through the door into 1970. Green shag carpeting covered the creaky floor, and dark brown paneling graced every wall. Golden crystals tinkled from the lights as the breeze wafted through. The appliances in the kitchen were the lovely yellow that went so well with green and yellow diamond linoleum. Puke.

"I'm Floyd, by the way. Maybe I should have started with that and the pictures. It's hell getting old. I forget the dangdest things. Sometimes I walk into a room and forget why I went in there. Now I have Mei to help keep me in line."

My mind couldn't keep up with what was going on. He acted like I was supposed to know who he was. What was I doing? "I don't understand."

He stopped and waved his hand, gesturing around him. Pictures covered almost every wall. I turned in circles taking in the photos, black and white and color.

My eyes were drawn to faces I recognized. My parents and Marie. The poses varied. Some were of the three of them and other people with weapons and dead vampires. Others were more family oriented.

I took in a history of a life my parents never shared with me. My feet moved across the carpet, the swishing sound loud in the hush of this time capsule of a home. This was the side of them I'd never known. It looked like they'd lived in some kind of commune.

"Are you here?" I asked Floyd, my voice cracking.

He pointed to a good looking man with his arm around Marie. There was another one with my mom and Marie both sitting on his lap.

I glanced from the smiling young man in the picture to the wizened old man behind me.

"I know," he said. "The rest of us got old while Tom, Claire, and Marie never did. I don't think we completely understood what it meant that they were Shadowers."

Floyd pointed to a picture of my parents with a group of young women covered in vampire bites and Marie standing off to the side. "This was the year we rescued Marie from Isaac. I wanted your parents to kill her. She'd been his blood slave. I'm glad they didn't listen. Marie was one of the best things to happen to me. I like to think I'm one of the best things to happen to her, too. I was twenty and thought I knew everything." He shook his head slowly, tracing his finger over Marie's face.

I fell to my knees. When would the surprises stop? Just when I thought I had a handle on my life, I realized I didn't know anything.

"Hey, girl, don't go losing it now. Your friends and Marie need you," Floyd said.

Raven came to my side. I looked up at her with tears. "We never should have come here," I said.

"Yes, we should have," Raven argued. "You need someone to tell you all the things you don't know. I guess that's going to be Floyd."

"Why can't Marie tell her?" Floyd said.

"How is it possible you know everything going on, but you don't know about Marie?" Raven asked.

SECOND CHANCE

"Because I didn't tell him," a voice said from behind us.

Raven growled, this time sounding more like herself.

A girl stood at the end of the hallway. She was smaller than Raven, if that were possible. Well, she was taller than Raven, because everyone is taller than Raven, but her body was smaller. On closer inspection, I realized she wasn't a girl at all. She was a young woman with Asian features and long black hair.

Raven growled again, and the woman growled back. Shifter.

"Is there going to be some kind of weird cat girl fight?" I asked. Then I started to laugh. Hysterics were threatening.

"I could kick this cougar's ass and eat her for breakfast."

"Stupid leopard," Raven growled, a ripple tripping across her skin.

Suddenly I could see the people in the room with halos of color surrounding them.

"Hey, Floyd, you said something about auras. What do they —"A scream stopped me.

"Rachel," Raven and I said together.

I struggled to get to my feet. "I'll go get her."

"Mei," Floyd said. He pointed his cane toward the door. "Go help the girl."

Raven growled again. "I don't want that leopard anywhere near her."

"You're still weak," Floyd said, "and you don't have any clothes. Let Mei bring Rachel and your stuff in here. You can trust her as much as you can trust me."

"We don't know we can trust you," I said, finally standing.

"I don't know whether to find your sudden backbone admirable or a pain in the ass," Floyd said.

After some more arguing, Raven supervised while Mei brought Rachel, then our bags, into the house. I called Nate and quickly explained where we were and where he was supposed to find Beck. It wasn't a pretty conversation. Especially when I told him he couldn't talk to Rachel because she was *tired* from her run in with Lilith the Slut.

"That was fun," I said, ending the call.

Floyd laughed. "Damn, I wish I was twenty years younger."

Mei raised an eyebrow. "Twenty? More like fifty, old man. You wouldn't be able to keep up with these guys even when you were thirty years old." She winked at me.

It shouldn't have been enough to make me trust her, but it was a start. She had been so gentle with Rachel and I could tell by the way she fussed over Floyd she cared about him.

Within the hour, Rachel was sleeping on the couch, Raven had changed into new clothes, and Floyd was in a rocking chair. It all looked so cozy, but I was on edge, pacing the room.

"Maybe someone should give me an abbreviated version of what's going on?" I said.

"Floyd doesn't do abbreviated," Mei said, putting a tray of drinks on the coffee table. "He's an old windbag who goes on and on and—"

"They get the point, you little pain in the ass," Floyd said.

With Mei's help and the pictures covering the walls and various photo albums, Floyd regaled us with tales of his youth and my parents. With some of his stories, I could picture my mom, dad, and Marie with movie like clarity. Other stories? I couldn't fathom my mild-mannered, schoolteacher mom using a semi-automatic rifle or a silver sword cutting down entire cadres of vampires.

It was almost too much to take in, but I needed it. I needed to know what their lives had been like.

"And then you were born," Floyd finally said. He had a picture of him holding me at birth. "That was when your dad said he was done. No more Hunting. He couldn't put you and Claire in danger like that anymore." He turned his head.

"I told him he was a dumb-ass and that's not how the world worked. You would be the most powerful Shadower any of us had ever seen. The blood of Tom and Claire?" Floyd covered his face with his hands.

I didn't know what to say. I didn't understand why he was suddenly emotional.

Dropping his hands, he whispered, "I kidnapped you."

"What?" Raven, Mei, and I said at the same time.

The noise caused Rachel to stir.

"Hey," I said quietly to her. To Floyd I said, "You have about five minutes to gather your thoughts and explain."

While I tried to fill Rachel in on where we were and what had happened, Mei pulled Floyd into the kitchen where they started a heated argument. Raven was listening to them, and I kept getting distracted talking to Rachel because I was watching Raven's facial expressions.

"So," Rachel said slowly, "we're in Newport, I got attacked by the Queen of the Succubi, Beck is having sex with her right now, Nate is on his way, and you were kidnapped by the old man in the kitchen when you were born?"

Once again, I was in awe of Rachel's ability to just take everything at face value. But it sure made explaining the unexplainable so much easier.

"Basically," Mei said as she brought a red-eyed Floyd back to the living room.

"And you're a leopard," Rachel said.

Mei smiled. "That doesn't faze or scare you?"

Rachel shrugged. "My boyfriend's a cougar."

"God damn it!" said Floyd. "I need to tell you. You have to understand."

"Tell me what happened?" I asked, rubbing my temples.

"Marie convinced me to take you. That you had to be trained."

"You said earlier you and Marie were the best things to happen to each other. You were in love, weren't you?"

"You're a smart cookie," said Floyd. "Yes. In love. At least that's what I thought. She was nuttier than a fruit cake and sometimes didn't make a lot of sense. But I was the only person, besides your parents, who she let touch her. Who she could hold semi-normal conversations with. She said we had to take you and I didn't even think twice."

When Floyd broke into tears, Mei picked up his story.

"They made it two days before your mom and dad found them. As I'm sure you can imagine, your dad wasn't happy."

"He kicked my ass," Floyd said, tracing a jagged scar on his temple. "I'm surprised he didn't kill me. I was basically an old man then. I knew we'd made a mistake five minutes after we left with you, but I couldn't deny Marie anything."

I knew exactly what he meant. Marie had a way of getting people to do things. I don't know if it was the way she seemed so innocent or because she had the moments of lucidness and made perfect sense. Whatever it was, she could bend the will of whomever she set her sights on. Floyd would have been putty in her hands.

"Were my parents mad at Marie?"

"Well, of course they were. Until she started to cry and explain why we took you. It sounded perfectly reasonable coming from her. You had to be raised and trained as a Shadower. You needed to fulfill your destiny. Blah, blah, blah. Instead of killing me, your dad took me to a hospital. He made me swear to stay away. He said he never wanted to see me again. My broken ribs, nose, and arm were enough to make me agree.

"I didn't even get to tell Marie goodbye. But I kept my

promise. I discreetly kept tabs on you all for a while. I wanted to know you were okay. I'm your godfather."

Slowly exhaling, I sat on the edge of the couch and closed my eyes. More surprises.

"I was so proud when you went off to college. I wanted to contact you, but I knew I couldn't. You didn't know anything about the life you were supposed to live. And now I'm just an old man. I can't train you. I can't offer you anything."

"That's not true," Rachel said. "You've given her history and her past. That's more than anyone else has given her."

Opening my eyes, I stared at Rachel for a moment. She was right, of course.

I nodded and Floyd wiped away a few stray tears.

"I'm so sorry. I should have come to you when your parents died. Then you wouldn't have been alone. Maybe I could have helped you with Marie."

"Well, you're here now," I said. "You can explain things I don't understand and you can help me find Marie."

"I haven't told him that part," Mei said.

Floyd scrunched his face.

"You wouldn't have been much help if you had known she'd been taken. I wouldn't have been able to get you to calm down."

"You damn cat! I'm tired of you only telling me the things you think I can handle! You don't get to decide what's best for me! When Parker finally calls back, I'm going to give him a piece of my mind!"

Floyd kept rambling while pacing the room and swinging his cane at Mei.

"That's the second time you've said you didn't tell him something," I said. "How do you know what's going on?"

Mei cocked her head. "I *see* things."

"What do you mean?" I asked.

"It's hard to explain. I get little visions. It's not a complete picture, but it's usually enough I can fill in the blanks."

"Cool," Rachel said.

"Fill in the blanks, my ass," Floyd yelled. "You guess most of the time from what I can tell. And you can't see Parker and where he is or if he's even *alive*."

"Will you shut up? I want to be here about as much as you want me here. I don't know why I can't see Parker. You think that doesn't bother me?"

"Who's Parker?" Raven asked.

"No one," Mei said at the same time Floyd said, "My grandson."

Mei glared at him.

"Okay," Rachel said. "One problem at a time."

"Start with Marie," Mei said.

"I'll do anything I can to help you," Floyd said as Mei walked into the kitchen. He was still glaring at her.

"We need a plan," said Rachel.

"Our last plan didn't turn out so well," Raven said.

"Sure it did," Rachel said. "We found Floyd and Mei."

"And the Queen of Sluts," I said.

It took another ten minutes to tell Rachel about Lilith and the other succubi in more detail. She kept interrupting, of course.

"So, Beck is angry?" she asked.

"That's an understatement," I said.

"You said the feeling of succubi was different than vampires?" Raven asked.

"Yes. Energy, but different. I'm not sure how to explain it. It's incredibly sexual."

"Auras," Floyd said from the kitchen.

"Tell me about auras," I said. I had a general idea, but I wasn't really sure.

Floyd and Mei came back to the living room to sit with us.

"Every living creature gives off an energy signature," Mei said. "Take your time and concentrate on the electricity feeling. You can tell the difference between the energies."

"I can't believe I haven't had you try this," Rachel said with a sigh.

"We've been a little busy," I said, squeezing my tired eyes shut.

"Think of the energy as different flavors," Rachel said. "I bet vampires, humans, and shifters *taste* different."

I opened one eye and gave what must have looked like a strange expression.

"What?" She sounded offended.

"*Taste* different?"

"You know what I mean." She glared at me.

The scary thing was I thought I knew what she meant. I closed my eye again and tried to relax. I took some deep breaths and concentrated on the electric current tingling in my feet. I stood and used a yoga stance to try and center myself. I knew yoga would come in handy one day.

My mind conjured colors to go with the electricity. A rainbow haze filled my vision, their own clouds. I could *taste*, to use Rachel's word, the energy on the back of my tongue. It was the weirdest thing. Kind of like the electricity I felt with Beck, but smaller, not as emotional.

Raven put her hand on my shoulder. I knew it was her because I could taste her energy and see her energy color. She was red. I don't think I could have explained to anyone what it felt and tasted like, just that I knew it was Raven.

"Raven," my eyes popped open and met hers. "I could taste you."

"Told you," Rachel said.

"How do you even know any of this?"

"Do I need to remind you I'm the one who spent the time translating that book with Marie and Beck?"

"What did you sense?" Raven asked.

"You *taste*. . ." I needed to come up with a better description, "like, well, like *you*. Your energy color is red in my mind."

"Did you see any other colors?" Rachel asked. "What am I?"

"I saw blue, yellow, and red. I don't know what you are."

"Hold my hand." Rachel extended her hand and I closed my eyes to try again.

She was sweet on my tongue, like cotton candy, totally Rachel. I smiled.

"What?" she asked.

"Shh," I said with a chuckle.

I had to concentrate hard to see her color. It was almost like my brain automatically picked out the supernatural and not the humans.

"You're pink," I said quietly.

"Pink? Cool. Hot pink or pastel?"

I opened my eyes. "Hot pink, of course." I turned to Floyd and Mei. "Floyd, you're pale blue and Mei, you're bright yellow."

Suddenly, Mei crouched in the cat attack pose I was used to. A second later, the energy rolled over me.

"Beck," I whispered.

Chapter Four

NO WAY it had been six hours. How had Nate gotten here so quickly? I looked at the clock ticking on Floyd's wall. Yep, it had been six hours.

Before I could mentally deal with the fact Beck was here, Nate came rushing into the house. "What in the hell is the matter with you, Kinsley?" He dropped to his knees next to Rachel, pulling her into his arms.

"Nathaniel," Beck said.

"No, he's right," I said.

Rachel comforted Nate while he tried to comfort her. "I'm okay." She kissed his forehead.

Nate glared at me. "How many people do you have to put in danger?"

Before Beck could verbally attack Nate, I held up my hand. "First of all, I haven't knowingly put anyone in danger. We came to find Marie since no one else was doing anything. Second, I don't make Rachel do anything she doesn't want to, and you know it."

Rachel nodded.

Nate closed his eyes. "You're right. I'm sorry I yelled at you. I was just so worried." He buried his face in Rachel's neck.

"What do you mean no one was doing anything to find Marie?" Beck said. "You up and left without consulting anyone. You *did* knowingly put everyone in danger by coming here without us."

Part of me knew he was right. However, the last time we'd been together he'd muddled my head with talk of being a couple. He'd never come on to me like that before and I wasn't sure how to act around him.

"And Raven," Beck turned his anger to her. "There will be consequences for your actions."

Raven's body trembled slightly. I thought back to when everything had first started to fall apart, or maybe it was when everything first started to come together. When I had hurt my knee arguing with Nate and Scott Masters. Nate had cowered in the hallway when Beck yelled at him.

I wasn't going to have anyone living in fear. We had enough problems and other creatures to be afraid of. I walked over and punched Beck in the shoulder.

Everyone stared in shock, especially Floyd.

"I was going. Would Raven be in more trouble if she had let us go alone?"

Beck's power seemed to fill the room and push down on us like a blanket. Floyd fell to the couch and Mei moved to a corner, fear in her eyes. Rachel began to hyperventilate, and Raven's eyes closed in pain. Electricity made the hair on my arms stand up as small shocks rippled through me. I'd never seen or felt Beck's power affect anyone else before.

"Humans, vampires, and shifters are afraid of me; cringe in fear when I am angry. But not you. Why?"

"Because I'm a Shadower!"

"*Precisely*! It is time you remember that and act like it!"

"Sir," Nate said cautiously.

Beck didn't turn away from me. I'd never been scared of

him before. Okay, maybe once before. The night he'd seemed to have been controlled by the Monarchs and he'd attacked Scott. What did I really know about Beck? He'd shown me nothing but kindness, but what had he gotten out of the deal? Me possibly *bonded* with him. I didn't know what it meant, but it didn't sound good when I knew a Shadower family was food for its vampire counterpart.

"Sir," Nate said again.

"What?" Beck yelled. When he finally looked at Nate, some of the power in the room seemed to dissipate.

Nate nodded to Rachel and then Floyd who were both trembling and struggling to breathe from the flood of energy. Beck was obviously much more powerful than I'd ever imagined.

I was pulled toward him slightly as a small tornado ripped his energy back into his body. A light blue electrical current came away from my arm and then snapped back to me like a rubber band.

"You're bonded," Floyd said, breathing heavily. He struggled to pull himself from the couch. Mei quickly came to his side. He slapped at her hands, and when he was upright, he swung his cane toward Beck.

"What's wrong with you? You can't bond with her!" To me he said, "You gave him your blood?"

When neither of us responded, Floyd swung his cane at Beck again. Beck grabbed it and yanked Floyd to him.

"I do not know anything about you, old man. You do not know anything about me. I suggest you stand down before you get hurt."

"When did you become such a bully?" I demanded as I pulled Beck's hand from Floyd's cane. "You can be mad at me all you want but leave everyone else the hell alone!"

"Perhaps I have always been a bully, as you call it. You do

not really know anything about me, do you? Maybe it is safer for you that way."

Yeah. Safer for my heart.

During our staring contest, power began to fill the room again. A faint sound of the song "Baby Got Back" broke the tense silence.

Rachel giggled. "Scott is calling you. I might have changed some of your ringtones when Beck got your new phone after you'd been kidnapped."

Nate groaned and stood. He used the distraction to try and talk Beck down. I continued to glare at him as I pulled the phone out of my pocket.

"We need to talk, little girl!" said a deep male voice tinged with anger.

Yep. It was Scott. Not long ago he'd called me sweet thing. We both seemed to have a penchant for nicknames. He called Raven a garden gnome the first time he met her.

Beck hurt my feelings. Scott just pissed me off. Downgrade me to little girl? I don't think so. Asshole, there's a nickname.

"I'm great, Scott. Thanks for asking. How are you feeling? How's your leg?"

I was met with silence. He obviously didn't know how to respond to polite sarcasm.

"Where the fuck are you?" he finally said.

"Maybe if you wouldn't talk to me like I'm a child, I'd have a real conversation with you."

Mei laughed.

"I'll talk to you any goddamn way I please. I wake up and you're not here. Some dude named Kevin is in my living room watching soap operas. Where the fuck are you?"

I ended the call and put the phone back in my pocket.

"Men," I said, shaking my head.

"I hear ya," said Mei.

"You women are no picnic," Floyd said. "You're just as annoying. This bonding issue is a great example."

"That is enough out of you," said Beck. "It is time for us to leave."

"No," I said. "Floyd knows more about my parents than I do. Mei has visions of the future. I'm staying here and then I'm going to find Marie."

"You are the most stubborn person I have ever met!"

"Well that's good because you are the most stubborn person *I've* ever met!" I said.

"*My anaconda don't want none unless you got buns, hon!*"

"Except for maybe Scott," I said, ignoring my phone.

"Hey, guys," Rachel said, "with everyone in this room, we should be able to find Marie."

"We do not need the old man and the leopard. We can handle this on our own," Beck said.

Floyd laughed. "You just don't want me talking to Kinsley."

"Is that true?" I asked Beck.

"Again, you know nothing of the situation. You do not know anything," Beck said to Floyd, ignoring me.

"He knows more than you think," Mei said. "And he knows where the house is."

"What house?" Beck asked.

"Is Marie there?" Rachel and I said at the same time.

"That, I don't know," Mei said. "I'm sorry."

"Tell me what is going on!" Beck demanded. I *felt* him try to get in my head. It was like little fingers poking in my brain to get the information he sought. Oh, hell no!

"Get out of my head! You promised!" I concentrated hard on closing my thoughts. He pulled back mentally and physically as though I'd smashed his fingers in the proverbial cookie jar. "I don't like your new, bossy attitude."

"I do not enjoy you putting yourself and others in danger. Someone *will* tell me what is going on."

"Floyd, let's talk in the kitchen while someone fills Beck in on the details," I said.

I left the room amid Beck's protests. Floyd and Mei followed me to the kitchen.

"Why in the hell did you allow yourself to be bonded to the vampire?"

"Isn't that what I'm supposed to do? The Book of Protection says Shadower families bond with a Monarch. I don't even know what it means to be bonded. The Book didn't explain it. My Shadower manual needs a manual."

"The Book of Protection? That's what you have? Where is the Shadower Journal? The Book of Protection is just generalized information for Shadowers and Protectors. Your family should have a Shadower Journal. Actually, there should be two. Your dad's Preston Family Journal and your mom's Kinsley Family Journal."

"I have no idea what you're talking about," I said, mind racing. I didn't see anything that looked like a journal when we packed the house.

"Marie doesn't have them?"

I tried the best I could to explain to Floyd how messed up Marie's mind was. He had mentioned earlier he knew she was crazy, but as we compared stories, it sounded like she'd gotten worse after I'd been born.

"So, she let herself be taken by Isaac and he flew away with her," I said, wrapping up the last few months of my crazy life. "Rachel thinks he might have brought her to the house he bought. That's why we're here."

Floyd scratched his chin. "She let herself be taken because Isaac told her to do it. That's part of being bonded. He can *make* her do things if he's in close enough proximity. That's why her family moved around so much in the beginning. They were trying to keep as many miles between them as possible. She gave him her blood of her own free will. Lots of blood.

"How many times have you given the vampire your blood? How much has he taken?" Floyd directed his laser stare on me.

"Only a few drops the first time. I helped him break a bond with the Monarchs. Then, when I was Isaac's prisoner, Beck took Marie's blood and my blood. I let him feed so he would have more strength."

"Did he feed from Marie?" Floyd asked.

"I don't know," I said. "Why does it matter? Wait. If he fed from Marie, is he bonded with her too?"

"This is where it gets tricky and I don't even understand all the rules. Since your parents never bonded with a Monarch, everything I know is just what I can remember after fifty-plus years. We need those journals."

Beck came to the kitchen. He looked a little calmer than he'd been fifteen minutes earlier.

"I am not bonded with Marie," he said. "She would not allow me to feed from her and I did not want to. Karlof extracted her blood and I consumed it."

Consumed it sounded so clinical but I suppose it was. A small part of me was glad he hadn't fed from Marie. Considering it had been the most erotic experience of my life, I didn't want to picture him feeding from my aunt. Or anyone else for that matter.

"Well?" I asked Beck. I didn't know what I would do if he wasn't willing to help look for Marie.

He looked at me for a moment. I expected to feel him prying in my mind again. Instead he closed his eyes and nodded.

"Where do we start?" he asked looking to Floyd for guidance.

"Talk to her," Floyd said, pointing his cane at Mei. "She's the one who knows everything."

"I don't know everything!" Mei said. She couldn't have been much older than me. Right now, she looked like a scared thirteen-year-old.

She covered her eyes. "I don't even know what most of my. . . *visions* have meant since I got here two weeks ago. I don't recognize the people or the places. Usually the visions involve people I know."

"You've only been here two weeks?" I said. "How long have you known Floyd?"

"Two weeks," they said at the same time.

"I thought he was your grandfather. Who's Parker?"

"Parker is my grandson," Floyd said. "He's in the military. He fancies himself in love with the girl and brought her here for me to keep watch over."

While Floyd's manner was gruff, I could tell by the way he looked at Mei he had come to care for her in the short time she'd been in his home.

"Watch over me?" Mei said. "I'm the one watching over you! Who's cooked all your meals, done all your laundry, and cleaned this time-warped house for you?"

Floyd scratched his chin again. This was obviously his thinking face. "Well, looks like the boy duped us both. He told me to watch you and told you to watch me."

"This family history is all very touching, but we have work to do," Beck said.

"What flew up your ass?" I asked.

He glared. "You and your scheme did. We should have planned all this together. If you had come to me to begin with, we would not be in Ecstasy and Lilith would not know anything about you or where I have been."

At the mention of Lilith, I stiffened. I'd almost forgotten about her. Too much was going on.

"You can scold me later. Let's figure out what to do with the little information we have."

While Mei excused herself to whip up a quick lunch, we went back to the living room. Raven appeared recovered from her run-in with the energy stealing succubi. Rachel was still moving slowly, but she'd regained some color. Eating helped them both feel better as well.

We decided Raven, Nate, and Rachel would still go to City Hall to look up records. Beck, Floyd, Mei, and I would go to where Mei thought her visions were taking place. That meant we were going back to Ecstasy. I was worried about Lilith, but Beck assured me she could not demand payment again as long as we stayed away from her.

Nate brought Scott's Hummer so he, Rachel, and Raven took that. Beck drove the Mercedes with Floyd, Mei, and me.

Mei rode up front with Beck so she could attempt to direct him using the landmarks from her visions. I sat next to Floyd and asked questions about my parents. I was still having trouble picturing them in the stories he told.

"What about you?" I finally asked.

"What about me?" Floyd said.

"What did you do after you got out of the hospital and my parents were gone with Marie and me?"

"I was devastated. I'd been with your parents for a few years before we found Marie. When you were born, I'd spent over thirty years with them and by that time I was in my fifties. Hunting is a young man's game. I didn't know what to do with myself at first." He wiped at a tear.

Beck glanced at me in the rear-view mirror. I tried to ignore the need to reach for him. I couldn't run to him every time I got emotional. Especially with how he'd been acting since he got here.

"I tried to find our original group of Hunters," Floyd said. "Most of them had been killed. I was able to find a few who were left. I wasn't a saint when I was younger. I found out I had a son."

This time, Floyd didn't try to hide his tears. "I made so many mistakes over the years. I'd gotten a woman pregnant and taken off. I didn't know she was pregnant at the time, but that doesn't excuse my behavior. I guess none of that matters now, anyway.

"She named our son Tyler. I missed out on his entire childhood while I was off hunting vampires and shifters with your parents and playing house with Marie. Tyler's mother died of cancer when he was fifteen. He tracked me down and wanted to become a Hunter. I didn't want him anywhere near the life I lead because it was too dangerous."

Floyd pulled out his wallet and handed me a wrinkled, faded picture of him, a young man I assumed was Tyler, and a pre-teen boy.

"Even though I didn't raise him, Tyler had my stubborn streak. He refused to go away and found me every time I tried to hide from him. So, we brought him in and trained him. He got married to another Hunter and shortly after, they had Parker." Floyd pointed a gnarled finger to the young boy.

"Tyler and his wife, Jen, were killed not long after this picture was taken. Parker became my responsibility. I changed our last names and moved. But you can never fully get out of the life once you're in. Hunters use our house as a safe zone. Parker was still in the thick of things."

I handed back his photo.

"When he was eighteen, he joined the military. That was over ten years ago. He's a different type of Hunter now."

"Why did he bring Mei to you?" Beck asked.

"Parker has finally been able to convince some of the higher ups in his SEAL unit vampires and shifters are real. They're in the process of creating a clandestine military unit for hunting the unknown," Mei said. "We met almost a year ago and we're in love. I care about him more than anything or anyone in this world. But when I found out his military unit is setting up this plan, I freaked."

"He doesn't know you're a shifter, does he?" I asked quietly.

"Nope. He came home from meetings about a month ago and said he needed to tell me something important, that it was going to sound crazy, and how he needed to keep me safe. He showed me pictures and videos of shifters and vampires his team had captured. They're doing experiments on them to figure out how to kill them. I don't know if any of the people they had were good or bad vampires and shifters. I didn't know what to do without exposing my secret to Parker. So, I ran."

"Well, obviously, he found you," I said.

"Yes. I went to my brothers, Blaze and Blade."

When I tried to cover a laugh, Mei finally smiled.

"Their names; I know," she said. "We're natural born leopards; our parents are both shifters. They wanted the boys to have *American* names. I think something was lost in translation."

"They're unique, all right," I said.

"Let her finish the damn story," said Floyd.

With a shrug and a smirk, I said, "Sorry, go on."

"Parker found me. Rather than letting my brothers rip him to shreds, killing the man I love, and exposing our family secret, I came with Parker here." Mei waved her hand toward Floyd.

"He knew what I was the minute I walked through the door. I'm still not sure how."

"It's your aura," I said. "I can't explain what it looks like, but there's this tinge of something when you're not human."

"Exactly," Floyd said.

Mei sighed. "Long story short, Parker is off trying to capture and kill what he thinks are monsters and I'm one of them."

"I'm telling you, girl, he loves you. You can tell him and he'll still love you."

"It does not always turn out how you hope," Beck finally said.

"That's what I'm afraid of," Mei said. "Have you ever heard of a human and a supernatural being having a relationship?"

"It usually does not work," Beck said.

"What about Rachel and Nate?" I asked.

"They have only been together a few months and Rachel is quite open-minded and accepting."

"What do you think he'll do, Floyd?" I asked.

"I honestly don't know. But I know he loves her."

"I don't know what he'll do either," said Mei. "So, I'm just continuing to keep my mouth shut."

Mei was using the *Kinsley tactic* for dealing with difficult situations: Ignore it and maybe it will go away. I should probably tell her it didn't work.

We were coming into Ecstasy.

As we entered Ecstasy, Beck said, "Mei, do you think you can remember where the house is?"

"I never knew exactly where it was. I just saw the outside of it and saw Marie. I didn't even know who she was until I saw her in the pictures on Floyd's walls."

"Tell us what you do know," Beck said.

As Mei explained her vision, I sat quietly with Floyd. At some point he started holding my hand.

"It's like trying to find a needle in a haystack, isn't it?" I asked him with a small smile.

With a soft scoff, he replied, "At least we know where the haystack is."

Chapter Five

HALESTORM WAS SINGING "HERE'S to Us" and it took me a second to realize it was my cell phone. "Did everyone get a special song?" I asked Rachel when I answered.

She laughed. "Of course! I had time on my hands while you were kidnapped. I knew you were coming back and I needed something to do besides translating that damn book."

I wondered what Beck's ringtone was. It's not like we needed to use cell phones.

"Anyway, I digress. Shocking, I know," she laughed again, her voice tinny through the speakerphone. "How's it going?"

"Mei is trying to describe what she remembers of the house from her vision. You might find something before we do."

"Okay, I'll keep you posted. Love ya, chica," Rachel said and ended the call.

"You said Floyd knew where the house was," I said.

"Ummm. Well, Floyd, where is the house?" Mei asked slowly, turning to look at Floyd.

"It's in Ecstasy," Floyd said.

Beck growled.

"He knew Isaac bought Marie a house, but that's it. I

wanted to make sure you brought us with you. Sorry," she pleaded quietly.

"No apology needed," I said. "I understand you wanted to come with us. We would have brought you because of your visions. I demand, for safety, we all have to be completely honest with each other from here on out. Deal?"

"It would be nice if you would adhere to that demand as well," Beck said, meeting my eyes in the rear-view mirror.

"You're right." I wasn't going to apologize for coming without him, though.

He raised an eyebrow.

"So, Mei, what can you tell us?" I said, ignoring Beck.

She closed her eyes. "I can't just conjure a vision. I either have them as dreams or they catch me by surprise during the day. When they're dreams, it's more difficult to tell if they're real visions or just normal sleeping dreams. Does that make sense?" she asked as she opened her eyes and turned to look at me.

"Yes," I said. I'd dreamed about Rachel being attacked by a vampire and found out it had happened while I was dreaming it. I hoped I never had another *vision* like that again.

She scrunched her eyes shut again and slowly said, "The house is old and two stories. The furniture is covered by sheets and everything has a layer of dust. The windows are either boarded over or have dark curtains."

"No one lives in the house currently?"

"I don't think so." She opened her eyes and shook her head.

"That might make this easier." I sent Rachel a text letting her know we were probably looking for a house that was abandoned or maybe for sale. "What else?" I asked.

She looked over her shoulder at Floyd.

"We can take it, whatever it is," he said.

"In the vision, Marie was lying in a coffin. She looked dead."

I sucked in a breath and Floyd dropped his head into his hands.

"That doesn't mean she's dead," Mei said quickly. "It's not like I could check her pulse."

I knew she was right, but my mind still conjured all kinds of horrible thoughts. What if we were too late? "Did you see anything else?" I asked.

"No," Mei said shaking her head. "I'm sorry I'm not more help."

"You were incredibly helpful," Beck said. "We know the house is abandoned and she is in it. That is more than we knew before." He put his hand on her arm and squeezed gently. "Think of your vision again. Could you see anything out the windows?"

"No. They were all covered or boarded up."

"Concentrate. Could you see between the boards or between where the curtains came together?" he said.

She closed her eyes again. "Umm, no. Wait! Yes! I can see between two boards. The ocean! I can see the ocean. The house is on a hill! I can see a lighthouse, too!" Her eyes popped open and she smiled at Beck.

"Excellent job, Mei. Kinsley, can you look up a map on your phone? There are historic lighthouses all along the coast, however, I believe there will only be a few which also have a house near them."

I was glad Beck was here to help make decisions. He was right. I never should have tried to do this on my own. I let down the guard in my mind a tiny bit and reached out. I didn't say anything and I didn't actually let him in, I just wanted to see if he'd notice. He, of course, did. Our eyes locked in the mirror and he nodded slightly.

I opened the map on my phone and zoomed into the coastal area of Ecstasy. I saw a few lighthouses but only one had a structure next to it.

"Mei, how close was the lighthouse? Did you see it across the water or was it like, right there?"

"It was right next to it."

"Bingo! I think I found it!" I had Mei put the coordinates in the car's GPS so I could call Rachel.

"Rachel, I've got an actual address I want you to look up in the county records."

As I explained how we used Mei's vision to narrow things down, Rachel searched through microfiche files. The clerk told her they hadn't moved their records to the computers or Internet because they didn't like technology. I told Rachel I thought it had more to do with vampires and succubi.

"Yes!" Rachel shouted with glee. "You were right! The house is owned by Dr. Gabriel Finch!"

"Is this too easy?" I asked.

Everyone in the car, and Rachel over the phone, said yes.

"That's what I think too."

"Ask Nathaniel and Raven to meet us at the location," Beck said.

"What about Rachel?" I asked.

"I do not want her there in case it is a trap. But I also do not want her alone."

"Agreed," I said.

"I'll keep an eye on her," Floyd said.

"No offense, Floyd, but you're old and out of practice," I said with a shrug.

Floyd crossed his arms. "I'm not useless."

"No, you're not. I just don't want you to get hurt."

"I'll be fine, damn it! Now let's get going!"

It took us twenty minutes to find the house. Nate was

parked at a padlocked gate at the bottom of the driveway that led up the hill to a dilapidated house and lighthouse.

Beck broke the padlock and we drove through.

As we got closer, I tried to search for auras or any kind of energy. "Beck, I feel you and everyone else. I can't tell if there's anyone or anything in the house, though."

The fact I couldn't sense Marie scared me. Was she even here? If she was here, was she dead?

"We will go inside and see. Just because you cannot feel her does not mean she is dead," Beck said.

We parked facing away from the house and gathered at the back of the Hummer. Rachel's face was pink and bright instead of so pale; she looked almost back to normal. I wrapped her in a hug.

"I'm okay, chica, just tired," she said. "I also know you're worried about this being too easy. Maybe he left her here because he didn't think there'd be any way in hell we would find her?"

"Yeah, maybe. But I can't sense any energy except all of you guys."

"Kinsley, try something for me, would you?" Floyd said. "Concentrate on us. Map us out."

"What do you mean?" I shrugged.

"You just started trying to read auras today. Maybe you need more practice. Map all our locations in your head and see if you can pinpoint an energy that isn't one of us."

"Okay," I said. Floyd was brilliant. Instead of just randomly searching for energies, I would specify everyone and see if anything was left over.

I thought of the map I'd looked at earlier on my phone. Once that was in my head, I put a name to every energy color standing around me. I had Floyd's light blue, Mei's yellow, Raven's red, and Rachel's hot pink as little dots on my *map*.

Nate was green with a tinge of pink. As I concentrated more I noticed Nate, Raven, and Mei all had a halo of orange but the others didn't. Maybe that was a sign of shifters? Did Nate have a tinge of pink because that was Rachel's color? I was going to need to practice this more and write everything down.

"Kinsley," Beck said quietly, touching my shoulder.

His aura wasn't there. Well it was, but it wasn't. He was a blob of black. I could also see a halo of gold, almost like his eyes. And there was, of course, the electricity that only flared with him. I trembled as the energy moved over and into me.

"Stop," I whispered.

He pulled away. "I did not mean to do that."

"Do what?" Mei asked.

I heard Floyd whisper, "They're bonded. That means Beck has a special connection with her. She'll be able to sense him more than any other being. It's probably bordering on erotic."

"Whoa, really?" Rachel asked. "We'll need to discuss this later, chica."

"Will you all please be quiet and let me concentrate," I snapped. But Rachel was right. As soon as I could get Floyd alone, I was going to ask more about this bonding thing.

I sent my mind toward the house, the colored spots on my map acting as anchors. That's when I noticed the other black dots in the house. At least fifteen of them. And one pale pink dot. Was that Marie?

"Beck, I think vampires are black and shifters have an orange tint to whatever their aura color is. If I'm right, there are fifteen vampires in the house."

"Fifteen?" Rachel screeched. Her hand flew to her neck and she turned into Nate's arms.

"What about Marie?" Floyd asked.

"There's one pale pink aura. I'm hoping it's her."

"What do you think, sir?" Nate asked.

"It will depend upon how old they are. If they are newly changed, they will be no match for us," Beck said with confidence.

"Is there any way to tell how powerful they are?" I asked.

Floyd said, "Compare Beck's aura to the ones in the house. Does one seem bigger or stronger than another?"

I tried to concentrate only on Beck and the black dots in the house. If there was a difference, I couldn't find it. "No," I sighed.

"What if we try together?" said Beck.

"What do you mean?"

"Perhaps if we look into the house together, you will be able to see better."

"Look together meaning I drop my mental doors and let you in my head?" I whispered.

He nodded.

"No."

"I thought you wanted to save Marie," Floyd said. "Who cares if the vampire roots around in your head a little? This is about Marie!" He waved his hand at the house.

Floyd sounded so much like me. Do whatever it takes to find Marie. Yet, here I stood, afraid to let Beck in my head for fear of what he'd find and wondering what this continued emotional connection was doing to me.

"Fine. But I want it noted I'm doing this under duress."

"Duly noted," Beck said with a smirk, taking my hand.

As soon as he touched me, the electricity shot up my arm and straight to my head. His energy blew away my mental shields. He could have looked in my mind whenever he wanted, yet, he hadn't. Was he being a gentleman or just playing games with me?

"I am not playing games," he said quietly.

Shit. I had already forgotten he was in my head. I needed to quit thinking. What would I do if he knew I had feelings for both him and Scott?

"Both of us?" Beck said with wide eyes.

Shit. Again. Turning off all the thoughts in my mind was way harder than I ever imagined. "Can we please just try this and you promise to ignore my babbling brain?"

He squeezed my hand. "Yes. I apologize."

"Do I just do what I did before and show you everyone's auras?"

"Please." He nodded.

I sent out my searching brain so Beck could see my map. As I looked at each color, I told him who they were. This time I could see myself. "That didn't happen before. I could only see all of you."

"I think since we are looking together, you are also connected to what I see," Beck said slowly.

"What color are you, Kins?" Rachel asked.

I was silver. A bright, blinding, moving mass of silver. It reminded me of mercury.

I ignored Rachel's question and concentrated on the house.

"*Silver Shadower,*" Beck's thought drifted across my brain before I felt him slam his mental doors shut.

"What—"

"Concentrate," he said quickly.

There were always more questions than answers. When Marie was safe and we were home, someone was going to start telling me what I was. Hopefully Floyd and Mei could help.

I felt Beck direct my mind to continue to the house. I showed him where each of the dots were.

"*Try to compare my energy to the energy coming from the other vampires,*" he said in my mind.

I concentrated on Beck's warmth then reached out to the black dots in the house. They were cold and the energy was more like a freezing, stinging sensation than the flow of electricity. I wanted to *taste* Beck and compare him to the others. His flavor made me want to moan. He was like chocolate caramel. Was I making flavors up or is this what they would taste like to others?

"Floyd," I said, "I meant to ask, do you *taste* the auras too, or just see the colors?"

"I was gonna comment on that earlier, but we got interrupted," Floyd said. "I've never heard of flavors going along with the auras. I just see the colors. But I suppose anything is possible."

I tried to tamp down my growing anxiety. My future was in the hands of a book that wasn't actually for me, nucking futs Marie, and ancient Floyd who knew just enough about my life to make me need more that he *didn't* know.

"Check the pink one," Rachel said.

Thank god she was thinking rationally. I was too busy salivating over Beck's decadent aura.

"*I find you just as decadent,*" he whispered in my mind.

The electricity moved over my body.

"Stop it!" I said through clenched teeth.

He chuckled and the electricity became more charged.

"What?" Rachel said.

"Not you. Sorry."

I went to the pink dot. The scent of Marie's perfume filled my senses.

"This is amazing. I have never witnessed such a thing in all my years." The awe in Beck's voice filled me with pride and scared me a little. He'd been alive for over seven hundred years and he'd never seen something like this? Like me?

"How are we going to do this?" I dropped Beck's hand and shut the mental door between us.

"Nathaniel and I will go in while you all wait here."

"No. That's stupid and you know it. Raven, Mei, and I can all fight." I put my hands on my hips.

"I can fight, too," Floyd said, waving his cane.

"Floyd, I need you out here protecting Rachel. You have to admit we are stronger and faster," I said.

"I can hold my own if I have to. I want to help save Marie."

"I'll be distracted if I'm worried about you and Rachel. Please, Floyd? I'll feel better knowing you both are out here."

"We'll sit here with the big guns and kill anything that tries to come out the doors. How does that sound, Floyd?" Rachel said, rubbing her hands together.

At the word *guns* Floyd lifted his head and smiled. He adjusted his suspenders and straightened his shoulders. "Silver bullets?"

"Of course," I said. I nodded to Nate who opened the lock box in the back of the Hummer.

Nate gave Rachel and Floyd each a pistol and extra clips of silver ammo. I reached in and grabbed my favorite silver dagger and two newly cast silver swords. I secured the dagger to my thigh and the swords went in a special harness on my back.

Before he'd been hurt, Oliver, one of Scott's bodyguards, had taught me how to decapitate with the swords. I'd only practiced on mannequins and I wanted to try them out on the real thing. I paused from securing my hip holster in place and shook my head. I was excited to go in and kill vampires. Well, maybe excited was the wrong word. No time to analyze it now.

While I'd been strapping on my personal arsenal, Raven, Nate, and Mei had transformed. Mei was a beautiful leopard, a little smaller than Raven's cougar, her spots almost symmetrical. I hoped she was as dangerous as she looked.

Beck chose not to have any weapons. He hadn't said how weak he was after *feeding* Lilith and I didn't want to give him blood. It was selfish, I knew, but unless he had to have it, I wasn't sharing. I hoped my selfishness wouldn't get us killed.

Was I being stubborn and stupid? What if my blood made the difference between winning and losing? What if Marie died because I wasn't willing to do something Shadowers were born to do? Okay, yes, maybe I was being stubborn and stupid.

"Do you need blood?" I asked quietly.

Beck whipped his head around. "Are you offering?"

"Only if you absolutely need it."

"I had Nathaniel bring blood since I was not sure what kind of situation we were walking into nor how long we would be here. Your blood would make me more powerful, but I do not believe we will need that since there are five of us."

"Yeah, but there are fifteen of them," Rachel said. "Just let him have blood, Kins, this is to save Marie."

I looked to Floyd for guidance.

"Don't look at me," he said, "you've done it before. Stopping now would be like closing the barn door after the horse was out."

Rachel laughed, "I like you more by the minute, Floyd!"

Floyd was right. I still wasn't sure where all this concern about Beck taking my blood was coming from. Mostly, I supposed, because I had no idea what it meant to be bonded to each other. However, it had been incredibly helpful to speak to each other in our minds when I'd been kidnapped and when I needed to call him when I was fighting with Mya and Isaac. Not to mention what we had just done together to see how many vampires were in the house.

I held out my wrist. "I'm going to do this, but you have to promise to talk to me about being bonded as soon as there is time."

He took my wrist gently in his hands and kissed the pulse

beating there. My heart rate sped up as he held my gaze and gently pierced the skin with his sharp fangs and began to suck.

Oh, holy hell. It felt amazing. Not as erotic as when he'd fed from my neck, but pretty damn close. I locked my knees to keep from swooning and tried to think about it like it was a medical procedure. Not his sexy mouth or the suction of his mouth on my skin.

After about fifteen seconds, he licked the small wound closed. "Thank you for trusting me."

I closed my eyes and watched his black aura with a small ring of gold change to a ring of silver. My blood changed his aura. I got the feeling we were all treading in new waters. Was this about me being the Silver Shadower? Was it about Beck and I being bonded? Both?

I'd let Nate have my blood when we'd been captured. I wondered what his aura would look like with my blood.

"Kinsley? Are you ready?"

My eyes popped open. Beck had been talking to me and I was, once again, on a field trip in my own head. Now I knew how Marie felt.

Speaking of Marie, time to bring the Crazy One home.

Chapter Six

RACHEL WAS SUPER DISAPPOINTED we didn't need the key. We walked right through the front door, and no one was waiting to jump us. The inside was just as Mei described.

Sending out my mental feelers into the house, I felt every nook and cranny for auras. "Okay, they're all below us. I'm guessing a basement. It looks like they have Marie surrounded."

Mei bumped my knee and walked to a door in the kitchen. She lifted her head and sniffed. Raven and Nate sniffed, too. The three of them took attack stances. My heart rate picked up as I moved to open the door, pistol in hand.

As I went to turn the knob, the door splintered and a body crashed through, knocking me to the floor. My pistol was knocked from my hand and slid across the linoleum. Cold, putrid breath on my neck had me swinging my arm up to protect myself. I connected with the vampire's head just as Mei bit its arm and dragged it off me.

The three cats ripped the vampire to pieces before I could even register what it had looked like.

I didn't have much time to recover or even think before another vampire sprinted up the stairs. Beck grabbed him around the neck and ripped his head off in one smooth motion, finally tossing the body and head to the glistening, quivering pile of bodies our cats had started.

I jumped to my feet as a third vampire dashed up the stairs. I drew my swords and cut off her head as she cleared the door.

And so it went, one vampire after another came up the stairs and was quickly dispatched. If we hadn't just killed them all with methodical precision, it might have been funny. Yet it seemed much too easy.

Beck, as always, knew what I was thinking even though he wasn't in my head. "They were all newly turned. They had no idea what they were doing."

"Maybe Marie isn't down there," I said. Hell. What if she wasn't here? A tremor of fear wracked my body. I organized my weapons back into their holsters to hide the shaking of my hands.

Beck's voice interrupted my troubled thoughts. "Raven and Mei, keep watch. Nathaniel, follow Kinsley and me."

Beck led the way down the stairs. It was damp and dark. The smells reminded me of when I'd been Isaac's captive. I missed a step as my brain took me back to being weak and scared. My hands reached for Beck automatically.

His strength was my strength, and I drew on his calm. I was no longer that weak person. I took a deep breath and let his stability soak into me. He squeezed my hand, and I nodded in thanks. He slowly pulled away to continue down the stairs. I sent out my thoughts to see who or what was left in the basement. The fading pink aura was all I encountered.

Just as Mei had said, Marie lay in a coffin in the middle of the room that was less a basement and more a root cellar. The floor was dirt with shelves of long forgotten jars of food lining the walls.

"Marie!" I ran to her, but stopped mere inches away, afraid to touch her.

Her long black hair had been braided and her hands rested on her stomach. She was dressed in an old-fashioned white lace wedding dress, veil, and shoes. When I finally touched her hand, she didn't move and her skin felt ice-cold.

"Beck?"

"She is alive," Beck said with a carefully neutral expression. "However, her pulse is weak." He lifted her carefully. The back of the dress was saturated with blood and more blood covered the white satin lining of the coffin. He held her while I searched her body for injuries.

Her throat had welt marks where previous wounds had been healed. I slowly started to move the soft, lacy folds of the dress and then froze. "Her thighs," I said, struggling to keep from crying. Breaking down now wasn't going to do us any good. I took a deep breath and settled my nerves. "That's what he did to her when he had her before. He'd feed from her thighs and not heal it."

Beck laid her limp body on the ground next to the coffin. I knelt and pulled up the skirts of the dress and, sure enough, her thighs were a mass of old scars and new slices and tears that wept blood. I'm pretty sure she would have bled out if we had gotten here later. But there was no time for those thoughts.

"I don't understand. Why did he take her only to leave her here to die?" I asked.

Beck and Nate both scented the air. "Do you smell him?" Beck asked Nate. The large cougar moved his head from side to side. "I do not either. So it has been hours since Isaac was here, if he was here at all. It does seem as though she was left to die."

"Or left to be found?" I asked. I gripped the side of my head with my hands. "Why?"

With a nod from Beck, Nate began to bathe the wounds

with his healing saliva. When the open skin was all healed, I rubbed Nate's head, fell back on my butt, and pulled Marie's upper body into my lap. Rocking her gently, I could no longer hold back the tears. She was alive and in my arms.

"Kinsley," Beck said, "we must go."

With a desperate whimper, I fought Beck as he tried to take Marie from me. I felt like I had to keep touching her or she'd disappear. I had to save her. I had to save *me*.

Nate pushed at me until I let go. I wrapped my arm around his neck and sobbed. It wasn't until Raven yowled at me from the top of the stairs that I stood. Beck was halfway up the stairs, Marie limp in his arms.

I followed slowly, my feet as heavy as my heart. Where was Isaac? Was Mya still alive? Would Marie wake up?

By the time I was at the top of the stairs, Beck was going out the front door.

Steeling myself once more, I turned to Nate and Raven. "Get dressed and bring the gas can and torch. We need to burn these bodies." Business as usual, right? Everything is perfectly normal here.

Raven rubbed against my hand before they both left. I stood in the kitchen surveying the carnage we'd created. These had been regular people just days ago. Isaac didn't care who or what he destroyed. Not that I was surprised anymore, but seeing it all in vivid color before my eyes in this moment, I was struck with a fiery anger.

I would kill him if it was the last thing I did.

A few minutes later, Nate and Raven were back with Mei and what we needed to destroy the newly turned vamps for good.

"Is it always like this?" Mei asked.

"Well, to tell you the truth, this is only the second time I've really fought vampires. I've never been up against this many. Nate? You have more experience at this than me."

After a brief pause, Nate answered, "No. It's never this easy. I don't understand any of this either."

"It's like he didn't care if we found her," Raven added.

"I've fought against other shifters in animal form, but I've never fought against vampires. My brothers didn't want me out fighting," Mei said. "In most parts of China, the shifters are still the majority and the vampires are the minority, so they stay away from us."

"How did you end up here?" asked Nate.

"Parker," she said with a longing sigh.

I put my arm around her for a brief hug. "It will all work out. You'll see."

Mei hugged me back but dropped her head. "Yeah. We'll see."

We doused the bodies with gasoline and I lit them with the torch. By the time we were back to the vehicles, flames were leaping from the kitchen windows.

Rachel had taken the blood-soaked dress off Marie and wrapped her in a blanket. I ran to the porch and tossed the dress through the door.

"You lost, you sick bastard!" I yelled to the sky. I didn't know where Isaac was or if he could hear me. It didn't matter; yelling made me feel better. "You'll never have her!"

Beck put his arm around me and walked me to the Hummer. He put me in the backseat with Floyd and slid Marie in so her head was in my lap and her feet were on Floyd's lap.

Dried blood coated Marie's legs. Floyd absently tried to wipe it away. "She's always been so beautiful," he said. "So beautiful and perfect, just like the day I first saw her. Except I'm an old man now." A few tears slid down Floyd's face.

I reached out and squeezed his shoulder. I didn't have any

words for him. I couldn't imagine how he felt or how much he hurt to see Marie again after all these years.

What was Isaac's plan? My mind went over so many scenarios and none of them made a bit of sense. Isaac went through so much trouble to kidnap Marie. Why would he leave her to bleed to death? He couldn't have known we were here, could he?

It didn't matter now. Marie was alive and she was with us. We would deal with the rest as it came.

"Kinsley," Floyd said quietly as we pulled up to his house. "I know I have no right to ask you this. You just met me today—"

"Yes," I said. "You're coming home with us when we go back."

He blinked back his surprise, but I could still hear it in his voice when he asked, "How did you know that's what I was going to ask?"

"Because it's what I would want. And to be honest, I'm being a little selfish. If you're around, I can learn about my parents and Marie. Maybe you can help me figure out where the Shadower journals are."

He sighed in relief. "I figured you'd kick Mei and me out at the curb and drive away."

"Of course not! You're family, Floyd. As soon as I saw those pictures, I knew my parents cared about you. And I can tell how much you love Marie."

"I don't even know what to say to her when she wakes up." Floyd stared off into the distance for a few seconds, then said, "She's basically a twenty-something and I'm a geriatric. It's not like we can have a romantic relationship again."

My heart ached for him. I thought I couldn't imagine what he was going through, but maybe I did know. Another reason I couldn't fall in love with Beck. Eventually, I'd start to age. I didn't know when that would be, since Marie was apparently over one hundred years old, but I couldn't bear the thought of watching myself become an old woman while Beck stayed young. And if I was with Scott, he'd age like Floyd and I'd stay young like Marie. Neither scenario seemed like a future I could live.

Marie didn't move when Beck carried her into Floyd's house. He put her on the couch so we could keep an eye on her while we discussed what to do. Beck, Rachel, and Raven seemed to be completely healed from their run-in with the succubi. That was yet another thing I was going to have to find out about. Would we be dealing with demons and angels along with everything else? How many more folklore/myth/legend creatures were out there? Would they be friends or enemies?

Floyd and Mei went to the kitchen and were having what sounded like another heated discussion. My hearing was better than a regular human, but I still couldn't quite make out what they were saying.

Beck, Raven, and Nate, on the other hand, could hear every word.

"What were you thinking?" Beck demanded. "You told Floyd to come home with us without even talking to me?"

"I was going to talk to you!"

"We know nothing of the human or the leopard. You just want to bring them into our world?"

"*'The human and the leopard'*? When did you become prejudiced? They're *people*. Floyd is *my family*!" I waved my arm at the pictures on his walls. "He can tell us things, damn it!"

I pushed myself into Beck's mind. He staggered back at the intrusion, widening his eyes in surprise. I caught a trail of his thoughts before he slammed his mental doors shut. *". . .do not want to share her with anyone else. . ."*

"Do I need to be worried about this stalker, protective streak you seem to have developed?"

Beck grabbed my arm and pulled me out the door onto the porch. I was caught so off guard I didn't protest.

"I bared my soul to you yesterday. I have not sought a relationship with a woman in hundreds of years. You ignored me and ran away. You want to know why I have suddenly become possessive and angry? That is why!"

Obviously my ignore tactic had backfired. Again. "What do you want from me?" My voice shook and I was going to be angry if I started to cry.

"I want to know how you feel about me!"

"There are too many secrets, Beck! I don't know how I feel about you because I don't know anything about you!"

"I suppose you know all you need to about Masters?"

My face went hot. "Scott doesn't have anything to do with this!"

"Of course he does! You think you have feelings for both of us."

"I don't know what I think or feel right now! I'm so confused about everything. So I concentrate on what is important and try to take care of that first."

Though his face remained unchanged, he pulled back slightly and I felt a shift in the energy around us when he asked, "You do not consider me, us, important?"

Frustration bubbled in me. I didn't know what I felt, how could I explain it to him? "I can't do this right now. There are more important things to worry about."

He threw his arms in the air in frustration, something I don't think I'd ever seen him do. "And that is yet another reason I am so angry. I have put you first every time. You! Before the Monarchs, before the shifters, before my jobs at both the

University and Screamers. I have always put you first. You have always put me last."

"I haven't put you last!" Had I?

"Yes, you have!" He dropped to the chair on the porch and held his head in his hands. It was such a human action, like throwing his hands up. Defeat, despair, heartache, perhaps. I'd never seen Beck appear defeated.

I really couldn't deal with this right now. How could I make him understand?

"Can we please set aside *us* for now? Floyd and Mei proved themselves today. We need to get Marie back and have her examined. You have to go back to work. There is so much to do." I paused to take a breath. When he didn't interrupt, I continued. "Then, tomorrow or the next day, I will sit down with you and try to explain what I'm feeling and going through with you and Scott."

He was silent for so long, I turned to walk back in the house. When I grabbed the door knob, he finally spoke.

"I agree there are more important things right now than my feelings. I will try to leave you alone until tomorrow."

"I didn't ask you to leave me alone! I need your help."

Uh-oh. Was I using him and sending mixed signals? No! I had never once acted like I wanted a romantic relationship. Had I? Great, I was going to end up over-analyzing everything I said and did around him and Scott.

"What do you want from me?" He threw my earlier words back at me, but there was no heat or anger, just sadness.

"I need and want everything you've been. A protector, a confidant, a friend. You are all those things to me, Beck."

He stood and grabbed my wrist. "But I am not enough to be your lover?"

When the word *lover* left his lips and his skin touched

mine, images began scrolling through my mind. My body quivered.

A dark room, candles flickering. I was naked on a bed of silk sheets and rose petals. Beck's naked body lowered onto mine, kissed my eyelids, my cheeks, my neck, my lips. The kiss went on and on until my legs wrapped around him and I dug my heels into his lower back, trying to pull him into me. He moved down my body, licking and sucking each of my nipples, his tongue darted into my belly button. I gripped his hair and thrashed my head in erotic agony as his tongue swiped over the most sensitive part of my body. He gripped my hips to pull me into his mouth. I screamed—

"What the hell?" Nate said.

What was Nate doing in bed with us? No. I wasn't in a bed. I was on a porch.

I fell to my knees, my whole body shaking on the verge of an orgasm. Beck still stood, bracing himself against the door frame and Nate was in the doorway.

"Why did Kinsley scream? Are you okay?"

I couldn't talk. Couldn't get the image of Beck and me out of my head. "Damn you, Beckford Alexander!" I wanted to yell it at him, but my voice shook as much as my body, and it came out as a whisper.

"I did not give you those images. You gave them to me."

I looked up at his wide eyes and shaking body. He seemed as off balance as I was.

Again, my face went hot and I was suddenly feeling very exposed. "I did not! I wouldn't do that!"

"I did not do it either."

Mei came to the porch and put her arm around me, lifting me so I could stand. "I think you had a vision," she said.

"What?" Beck, Nate, and I all said.

"This is how I usually react when I have a vision."

"So, like, what I just saw is going to happen?" I wrapped my arms around my middle and bent over trying not to hyperventilate.

"That's how it works with me. Has this ever happened before?" she asked.

"I had a dream about Rachel that came true."

"Well, this is the same, you just had it while you were awake."

I straightened and turned to Beck. He didn't say a word but his face showed need, want, and longing. My stomach quivered with the same longing.

"What did you see?" Nate asked.

"Nothing." I pushed my way into the house on shaky legs. I had things to do and didn't have time for a sex dream or vision or whatever the hell it was.

"I don't want to talk about visions right now," I said to Mei. "I'm guessing you and Floyd were arguing about whether or not to go to Washington with us."

"Yes."

"Parker will be able to find you. That's what cell phones are for. Besides, he's a Navy SEAL."

Mei's tone was guarded when she said, "That's almost exactly what Floyd said."

"So, you'll come with us?"

After a brief pause and a long sigh, she replied, "Yes. Because I don't know what else to do. My brothers and parents are still in China. They're protective. They told me I had to choose between the American human and my family."

"That's pretty harsh," I said wondering how I'd handle having to make a decision like that.

"Ancient Chinese and shifter customs run deep." It sounded like a rehearsed response, but I felt there was something much deeper than the words hinted.

Maybe Scott had an empty house in the development. I turned my phone on to see how many nasty messages I had from him. I'd gotten tired of hearing "Baby Got Back" ringing constantly so I'd shut the phone off. Kind of childish, I know.

Seven voicemails and twenty-two texts. The man was persistent. He wasn't happy with me, and I didn't really blame him. With a badly broken leg, he was stuck at home. I knew it wouldn't keep him down for long, but it hadn't even been a week since Isaac had broken it. If I had told Scott what we were hoping to do he would have either wanted to come or tried to talk me out of it.

I didn't want to actually talk to him so I sent a text. Less than ten seconds later Sir Mix-a-Lot started to serenade me. I so had to figure out how to change my ringtones.

"Before you yell, please just listen," I said.

"Where are you and are you okay?"

I suppose I owed him that much. "We are in Newport, Oregon and I'm fine. We found Marie."

"What the hell were you thinking? How did you find her? Where was she? You were in a fight, weren't you? There's no way Isaac just handed her over."

I attempted to explain things as quickly as possible so I could appease him and get to asking about a house for Floyd and Mei.

"It was all too easy, I know," I said, wrapping up my story. "But the point is, we have her and I'm bringing her home."

"I should have been there for back up," he said.

"There wouldn't have been anything for you to do. You have to heal."

"I hate feeling useless and weak." I heard his sigh through the phone and pictured him staring at the ceiling in defeat.

I lowered my voice. "I know you do. But you're not useless and you're far from weak."

"Are you telling the truth or just trying to stroke my ego? Because I can give you something else to stroke," he said, the tone shifting to something much more playful.

"Please don't," I said turning away from my audience of listeners, hand over my eyes.

Beck growled. With everyone's super hearing, they knew what Scott said.

"Do you have an update on Oliver?"

"I love how you change the subject when you're embarrassed. No change in Oliver's condition as of a few hours ago. Beth is keeping an eye on him and promised to call me if anything changed."

Dr. Elizabeth "Beth" Chavez was also a vampire. I trusted her more than Dr. Karlof and planned to call her as soon as I was off the phone with Scott.

"Okay. We met two people who I'd like to bring back with me. Don't you have an empty house in the development?" I asked.

"You're bringing home strays?"

I huffed at him in frustration. "I don't have time to explain right now. Do you have a place for them or not?"

"Of course I do. Bring 'em home."

"Thank you. We'll be back sometime tomorrow."

"Okay, sweet thing."

My eyes narrowed and I said slowly, "Why are you being so easy?"

"Because you're back under my roof tomorrow. Kisses."

I sighed and ended the call. Tomorrow was going to be a long day if I was going to have to deal with both hard-headed men and sorting through my feelings.

I called Dr. Beth to explain Marie's blood loss and possible coma. I wouldn't talk to Dr. Karlof if I didn't have to. I also wanted Marie moved to Scott's so I didn't have to leave her alone in Karlof's medical facility.

Beth agreed to have everything ready at Scott's when we arrived. She said Marie probably didn't need a blood transfusion because Karlof had a blood sample and they had checked on cell regeneration. More than likely, Marie's blood had already repaired the blood loss damage on its own.

I was angry Karlof had experimented on Marie's blood but conceded it was helpful to know how Shadower blood worked. Once again, I was back to warring with myself and my conscience. I needed to wrap my brain around the fact I couldn't have things both ways. Our blood was different and important, and we needed to know how it worked.

I also had to figure out everything with Scott and Beck. I wanted to learn about my parents' past so I could embrace my future. I had to find out if the prophecy of the Silver Shadower was real and, if so, what it meant. I needed to know what it meant to be bonded with Beck. I had to figure out what I was capable of.

Once again, I needed to embrace the obvious: that I was not quite human.

Chapter Seven

IT HAD TAKEN us about six hours to get to Ecstasy in the first place, but we had stopped a few times. According to Beck, the drive back to Bellevue should only take five hours and we'd be rolling in by the time the sun was coming up. Though we could have slept at Floyd's and left in the morning, we all agreed we needed to get Marie home so Beth could do a thorough examination.

I also wanted to be as far away from Ecstasy and Lilith as possible. Not to mention the fact Isaac and Mya had to be somewhere nearby, didn't they?

After packing all of Floyd's pictures and anything related to being a Hunter, we ordered takeout and sat in the living room. As we ate our last meal in Floyd's home, he told stories about my parents and his life as a Hunter after my dad put him in the hospital and told him to stay away. We laughed, I cried, it was wonderful and emotional. And while it opened some old wounds and maybe made some new ones, it was helping me heal and come to terms with my parents' secrets.

Marie slept through it all, and Beck kept staring at me out of the corner of his eye. I made sure we didn't accidentally touch. I couldn't handle another vision-induced orgasm. In fact, I didn't want to ride home with him, but he put his foot down about that. I didn't put up a huge fight, mainly because I was already mentally and physically exhausted.

Once we had everything cleaned up and put the boxes and suitcases in the Hummer, we locked up Floyd's house and split into our driving groups. Beck driving the Hummer with Mei, Floyd, Marie, and me. Nate driving the car with Rachel and Raven.

I made Mei sit up front so Floyd and I could hold Marie like we did before. I wanted to be right there if she opened her eyes. I felt so helpless. I was tired but didn't think I'd be able to fall asleep.

"Floyd," I said in the darkness of the backseat, "What do you know about the Silver Shadower Prophecy?"

He rubbed his chin. "Everyone thought it was your mom. Her eyes sometimes looked silver and she was one of the best Hunters I'd ever met. Everyone we did jobs with agreed she had to be the Silver Shadower."

"But?"

He shrugged. "But she never bonded with a Monarch and then she and your dad disappeared."

I sighed. "It still could have been her." My tone was whimsical and full of unattainable wishes. If it was her, then it couldn't be me.

"Yes, I suppose it could have been," said Floyd, although he didn't sound convinced.

"Isaac called me the Silver Shadower. There's no way it's me. From the sounds of it, I'm not even half the Hunter my mom was."

Without warning, Mei's head slammed back against the seat and her whole body began to shake.

"Beck!" I yelled, sitting forward. "What's wrong with her? Pull over!"

"She's having a vision," Floyd said. "It's almost like a small seizure." He didn't sound worried.

Before Beck could pull over, Mei went still. I reached forward and put my hand on her shoulder.

"The Silver Shadower shall emerge and call down Zeus. All who stand in his way will perish," Mei said in a monotone voice.

The car swerved as Beck turned to me. Those were the exact words he said at dinner almost three weeks ago; the Silver Shadower Prophecy.

"Mei," I said, "are you okay? Can you hear me?"

"Whoa," she said, shaking her head and rubbing her hands together, "that one was intense."

"Did you see anything?" Beck asked.

"I was in an old house, almost like the one we just burned down, but different. People live in this house. We walked upstairs and moved a panel from a hidden door. Inside the hidden room were more hidden panels in the walls. Shelves. I saw books and weapons."

I sucked in a breath.

"Kinsley?" Beck asked.

"My house," I said softly, "Well, my old house in Paradise. The hidden room." Of course the hidden room would have more stuff hidden in the walls. My dad wasn't stupid, but apparently I am. We'd packed the house and sold it but I hadn't thought to look for hidden panels in the hidden room.

"I think I know where the Shadower Journals are. We have to go to Paradise." I looked down at Marie. "We have to go to Paradise *after* we get Marie to Beth."

I started mentally calculating how many hours it was going to take. We'd be lucky if we got to Paradise by the end of the day tomorrow. I looked at the clock. At least it was almost 'tomorrow'.

"What's Paradise?" Mei asked.

"It's the town I used to live in with my parents and Marie. There's a hidden room upstairs, kind of like a panic room. I think that's what you saw."

She nodded. "Sounds like it."

"That means we are going to be getting back in the car almost immediately. You should all try to sleep," Beck said.

I snapped my fingers. "Can't you jump us to the house?"

"Jump?" he said, the word drawn out.

"You know. How you pop in, teleport, whatever it's called."

"It does not work that way," he said.

"Teleport?" Floyd asked.

"Yeah. Beck was able to show up where I was twice. There's a popping sound and a flash of light and then he's there."

"It has to do with the bonding," Floyd said. "I've never seen it before but I've heard about it. He can track you." His head whipped back and forth between Beck and me.

"Really?" Great. More bonding stuff I didn't understand. "He can't just jump anywhere he wants to go?"

"I have not tried it yet," Beck said.

"You've never done it before?" I asked, my voice going high.

"Floyd is correct. It is the bonding. I had never done it before that day I came to you at the construction site."

"When were you going to mention that little tidbit of information?" I could hear my heart pounding in my ears. I needed air. I blindly reached for the window controls.

"We have not had time to talk, have we? You ran away."

"I didn't run away!" I managed to find the button and roll the window down a few inches. This was not the time or place to have this conversation. I closed my eyes, breathing deeply.

Beck's voice was strained. "More things to discuss when alone."

"Don't mind us," said Mei, humor in her voice. "'This is fascinating. I'm learning more about vampires and it makes me think my life isn't as screwed up as I originally thought."

I tried to laugh, but it came out strangled. Finally, I said, "Go to sleep."

I WOKE as we pulled into Scott's housing development. The sound of Beck entering the numbers on the keypad seemed loud in my sleep-fogged mind.

"Wow," Mei said, as the wrought iron gate slid open and we drove through.

Marie looked roughly the same as she had hours ago. At least she no longer resembled a corpse; some pink stained her cheeks. Beth was right, Marie's blood must be regenerating itself. That was good, right?

Floyd was still asleep, his head lolling to one side. I was uncomfortable; I could only imagine how much Floyd's old body was going to ache.

Beck parked outside Scott's house, Nate right behind us. A black van sat in the driveway. Scott's door opened and Beth came out. Even at five in the morning she looked stunning. I didn't know if it was because she was a vampire or because she had been beautiful before she'd been turned.

"Are we here?" Floyd asked groggily, wiping at his eyes.

"Yes," I said.

"My entire body hurts. I haven't slept in a car in I don't even know how many years. I hate being old."

As Mei helped Floyd out of the Hummer, Beck talked to

Beth. Scott made his way off the porch to me, struggling with the crutches.

As Scott moved to try and hug me, Floyd's cane flew between us.

"Who are you?" Floyd demanded.

"Who the hell are *you*?" Scott stood as tall as his crutches allowed.

"I'm Kinsley's godfather."

"What?" Scott said, glancing from me to Floyd and back again.

"So, um, this is Floyd and this is Mei," I said holding out my hands to point at them. "Floyd used to hunt with my parents and he was in love with Marie. They kidnapped me when I was born so my dad disowned him. Mei is a leopard from China. Her brothers are assholes, and the man she loves is a Navy SEAL who doesn't know she's a shifter." I took a breath. "Does that about cover it?"

Floyd burst out laughing, and Mei nodded.

"The trouble you can get yourself into in one day is beyond amazing, sweet thing," Scott said. "Nice to meet you both." He shook their hands then pulled me in for a hug.

It was awkward with his crutches, but he managed.

As soon as his arms were around me, my vision started to blacken.

"Mei," I said, "help."

A dark room, candles flickering. I was naked on a bed of silk sheets and rose petals. Scott's naked body lowered onto mine, kissed my eyelids, my cheeks, my neck, my lips. The kiss went on and on until my legs wrapped around him and I dug my heels into his lower back, trying to pull him into me. He moved down my body, licking and sucking—

I was sitting in Scott's yard practically on Mei's lap. Scott was staring open-mouthed at me, and Floyd was yelling for Beck.

"I'm fine," I said, standing on wobbly legs as Beck came to my side. I was careful not to touch him.

"What the fuck just happened?" Scott asked, anger and confusion making his face scrunch up.

"What was the vision you had with him?" Beck asked, trying to grab my hand.

At the same time I said, "Nothing," Scott said, "We were in a dark room with candles and rose petals."

"The same room? The same vision?" Beck asked, stepping back before touching me.

"Same room as what? What vision?" Scott asked, looking back and forth between us, his brow furrowed.

"Kinsley, are you okay?" Beth asked as she came toward us.

Wasn't this exactly what I needed right now? More people crowding around me asking probing questions. "Yes, I'm fine. I'm just really tired. I haven't gotten much sleep the last few days." An obvious lie, but I was still reeling from the vision.

Standing slowly, careful to not take any help from Scott or Beck, I wiped my clammy hands on my pants, then smoothed my hair. Honestly, my hair didn't need smoothing. I just didn't know what to do with my damn hands. I didn't want anyone to notice how bad they were shaking.

Why in the hell was I having the exact same vision with two different men in the starring role? Maybe they weren't visions. Maybe it was my sex-deprived subconscious. I was going to have to talk to Mei about how her visions worked.

After a few calming breaths, I decided to focus on something other than my own mess. Plenty of time for my own drama later. I couldn't process right now. With a wave of my hand, I guided Beth to the Hummer and Marie.

"She hasn't moved at all?" Beth asked. She eyed me as though I was going to fall on my face at any moment.

Happy for a distraction, I touched Marie's hair. "No."

Beth directed two men from the van to move Marie. I followed behind, worried and anxious. When we came through the door, Scott's family room looked like a mini-hospital. It had been split in half by plastic sheeting. His bed was still in there, but now the half cornered off with plastic held a hospital bed and medical machines. The men put Marie in the hospital bed and began hooking up the monitoring equipment. Within moments, the heart monitor was beeping a slow but steady rhythm.

Beth brought me in and explained what she was doing as she drew blood from Marie, set up an IV, and took her vitals.

"After I check her blood, we will determine if she needs a transfusion, but I don't think it will be necessary."

"Thank you for doing all this here. I know it would have been easier to do it at the medical facility."

"We made it work. I'm going to have Jared stay here to keep an eye on things. He's one of my assistants. I'll be back in a couple of hours. Will you still be here?"

I looked to Beck.

"Yes," he confirmed. "Everyone needs rest, food, and showers. The books have been hidden in the house for years; a few more hours will not change anything."

"What books? What house?" Rachel asked as she came in, tossing her bag and coat by the door.

"I'll explain in a minute," I said. Turning back to Beth, I shook her hand and added, "Thank you, again, Beth. I'll see you when I get back."

"Always an adventure with you all," she smiled and released my hand. "Beck, walk me out?"

He nodded and they slipped silently out the front door.

Scott crutched his way to the living room and his recliner. The rest of us followed.

"Well," he said, dropping into his chair, "you found Marie and brought home your godfather no one knew about and another kitty for the collection, huh?"

Mei growled.

"Don't be an asshole please," I said. "Without Floyd and Mei, we wouldn't have been able to find Marie."

He puffed up his chest. "You and I could have done it."

An eyebrow raised, I asked, "When would that have been?" I held my hands out, palms up. "Five weeks from now when you get your cast off?"

"You shouldn't have been out there by yourself!" He smacked his hand on the arm of the recliner.

Anger flared inside me and burst outward in a heated string of excuses. "I wasn't by myself! I had Rachel and Raven!"

"Who you managed to get attacked by a succubus," Nate said.

"What?" Scott yelled.

"You're not helping, Nathaniel," Rachel said, kissing his cheek.

"Things could have gone south fast," Nate said. "Kinsley and Raven can take care of themselves, but you're just human."

"Which means I can't take care of myself?" Rachel stepped back, her face stern.

Nate closed his eyes. "That isn't what I meant."

"Well that's what it sure as hell sounded like."

He opened his eyes and ran his hand through his hair. "You're fragile compared to the rest of us. So is Scott." Nate pointed to Scott's broken leg. "It has nothing to do with being a female. This is about being human."

I stepped to her. "He's right, Rach. In fact, I said almost the same thing to Beck the day Isaac kidnapped Marie. You, Oliver, and Scott got hurt."

"You and Beck were hurt, too," Rachel said.

"And we were completely healed by the time we got to the medical facility."

"And then you took off a few days later and put her in danger," Scott scoffed. "I guess I shouldn't be mad you don't listen to me when you don't even listen to yourself."

I hated he was right, and he knew it.

My mind bounced through ideas like a BINGO wheel. "We need to come up with better plans for hunting and when we are attacked." I walked a small circle, hands moving in circles as well. "Floyd and Scott, since you both worked with my dad and you're Hunters and human, I'm going to put you in charge of the game plans. You know the best ways to do things.

"Raven, Mei, Rachel, after you've rested, I want you to add what you've experienced."

"What about you and me?" Nate asked.

I stopped pacing. "We're going to Paradise with Beck."

Scott sat up. "What the hell for?"

"Why?" Rachel asked, shaking her head.

"Mei had a vision," I said.

Floyd, Mei, and I explained about the other journals and the hidden shelves. Just as we finished, Beck came back in the house.

"Nathaniel will stay here with the others." Beck's tone left no room for argument. "It will just be Kinsley and me traveling to Paradise."

So, of course, Scott argued. "Bullshit," he said. "I'm going with you."

Beck stared him down. "No. You are not."

"Scott, you'd be more of a hindrance and you know it," I said, trying to keep the peace. "Nate will go with us."

Beck said, "I need Nathaniel here with everyone in case Isaac decides to come claim Marie. The more people who can fight, the better."

Beck made a valid point. Damn it. I didn't want to ride more endless hours in the car, especially just the two of us. He'd make me talk to him.

"I'm not an invalid," Scott said, rubbing the thigh of his broken leg.

"Just because you do not want Kinsley and me alone together is not a reason to go to Paradise. You will need to stay here to make sure Floyd and Mei get settled. It is, after all, your home area they will be living in."

Once again, Beck's words left no room for argument even though Scott looked like he wanted to continue the discussion. He got out of his recliner and crutched himself to the front door.

"Well, since the rest of us aren't good enough to go to Paradise, we may as well get you set up here."

Mei nodded to me. Floyd kissed my cheek, murmuring, "be careful." Rachel and Raven both gave me a hug. Nate took Rachel's hand and followed everyone out.

The air in the room felt tense, like it was pressing on me. A headache was trying to push its way into my brain.

Beck cocked his head. "You should rest first."

I shrugged. "I should. But I wouldn't be able to sleep. Give me thirty minutes to shower, change my clothes, and eat. That would be fantastic."

"As you wish."

I walked to the plastic walls of Marie's temporary hospital room. Jared stepped out and shook my hand. Vampire, but he reminded me a little of Ian with his shaved head and stocky build, and my heart ached for the werewolf who had been murdered by Mya. So much death and destruction, and I was at the center of it all.

I went to Marie's bedside. Well, *we* were at the center of it all. I took her hand, tears welling in my eyes. She was still so cold.

"Marie? Can you hear me?"

She, of course, didn't answer.

"I'm so sorry I haven't kept you safe." I wiped my tears then gave her a kiss on the cheek. I took a deep breath and squared my shoulders. One problem at a time.

I left Beck and Jared in the family room and ran upstairs to get ready for the inquisition that was sure to be my car ride to Paradise. Beck had questions I didn't have answers for. He also had things to say I knew were going to make me uncomfortable.

Of course, I was going to have to talk to him at some point. If we were all supposed to work together and live together, boundaries needed to be set and things needed to be out in the open. He owed me explanations about being bonded and I owed him explanations about my feelings for him and Scott. Then I was going to have to have the same talk with Scott.

It made my head hurt and my stomach clench.

I took a quick shower, got dressed, and packed an overnight bag. The shifters kept a change of clothes in almost all Beck's vehicles. I was going to start doing the same.

In the kitchen, I ate a quick breakfast and made some sandwiches in case I got hungry on the drive. Since Beck wouldn't need to stop for food, I was going to try and make it the whole way without stopping. The sooner we got there, the sooner I could get my mom and dad's Shadower journals.

I was nervous about that, too. What if Mei was wrong and the journals weren't there? Or what if she was right? It would hopefully give me answers to so many of the questions I had. But it was going to be emotional to read my mom and dad's secrets. I was still angry they had never shared any of this life with me.

And if they had been such amazing Hunters, why were they dead? How could I expect to keep myself and those I loved safe when I'd been a Shadower for barely four months?

Enough.

I would deal with whatever Beck threw at me on the drive. I'd also be ready with questions of my own.

Time to go back to Paradise.

Chapter Eight

WE HAD ONLY BEEN DRIVING on I-90 for ten minutes before Beck started in. I was actually glad because those ten minutes had seemed like an eternity of uncomfortable silence. It had never been like this between us; I felt awkward and fidgety.

"Tell me about your vision with Scott," he said. The tone was almost demanding, but there was something else flowing underneath I couldn't quite place.

I wanted to say it was none of his business, but if I was going to expect him to be honest with me, I needed to be honest with him. I sighed. "It was the exact same vision I had with you. Except Scott was in it."

Beck's hands tightened on the steering wheel. "I see."

I threw my hands up. "You can't be mad at me for having a sex vision of Scott. It's not like I had any control over it. In fact, if I had my way, I wouldn't have another vision ever again. What if everyone I touch gives me a sex dream vision?" I shuddered.

"Did anything happen when the others told you goodbye?"

"No."

He had no physical response, no facial expressions when he

answered, "Then I do not think you are going to have sex dream visions with everyone you touch."

"Why would I have the same vision with both of you?"

"I do not know. Maybe it is because what I saw in your mind earlier; you think you have feelings for both of us. Maybe it means you have not made a decision."

"There is no decision to make!" I gripped the sides of my head.

"What do you mean?" He glanced at me.

"What do you mean: *what do I mean?* I'm not choosing either one of you! Can you imagine how horrible things could turn out?" I touched my chest. "I've never even had a real relationship. I don't want to try and navigate that along with being a Shadower! I care deeply about both of you. I suppose it's its own form of love. But I'm not going to become romantically involved. It can only end in disaster. If I choose you," I pointed at him, "I could lose Scott's friendship and everything we've built with him to become a successful hunting operation.

"If I choose Scott," I pointed out the window behind us, "you and I will always be uncomfortable, and if we really are bonded, that would lead to mistakes and possibly shifters and my human friends getting hurt because we wouldn't work as a fluid team anymore. I also don't know how I feel about us being bonded, what that means, and I'm still confused about sharing blood with you."

I paused to breathe. Verbal outpouring? Check.

"You have put much thought into this," he said slowly.

I threw my hands up again. "Of course I have! It's my life and my future and my friends' lives on the line if I make mistakes!"

Beck took one of my waving hands. "I apologize. I was not thinking beyond my own selfish needs. I had not taken the time to consider how a relationship between you and me would affect others."

"You're apologizing?" I almost slammed my head back in the seat, I was so shocked.

"Yes. Why do you find that so hard to believe?"

"Well," I pulled my hand away, "you've been kind of an ass the last few days. You were acting more like Scott than yourself."

He chuckled. "That is the other reason I am apologizing. As soon as you were back with Scott, I realized I sounded like he would when he does not agree with decisions you make. I do not wish to come across as a chauvinistic jackass."

I laughed without humor. "So now you're going to play the game where you constantly point out everything annoying about Scott so I'll see you in a positive light?"

Beck put his hand on his chest. "Moi? I would never do such a thing." Then he laughed.

And just like that, things were back to normal between us. This time when he took my hand I didn't pull away.

"Will you finally tell me about your past?" I asked, almost a whisper.

"I do not wish to. But I will because you were honest with me about your feelings. What would you like to know?"

"Start at the beginning. I want to know about before you became a vampire and how you became a vampire."

He sighed. "I will do my best. I honestly have not thought about my early years much because it was not an enjoyable time. I was born in the early-1200s. Our family had a title and money. I learned later, my father bought a title of European nobility from blood money earned as a mercenary. My father was cruel and unfair to the peasants who worked our land. He was also cruel to my mother, brothers, and me. I hated him for it.

"I had all these ideas of how to change what he was doing when I was called upon by the King to fight in the Crusades."

It was a living history lesson. I wished I had paid more attention in high school so I could better picture what he was describing.

"After four years fighting a Holy Battle I did not believe in, I returned home to find one of my brothers dead, I believe at the hands of my father but I had no proof, my other brother just as cruel as my father, and my mother a weak shell of herself. The abuse had finally broken her. I was to marry the neighboring nobleman's daughter." He paused and squeezed my hand. "It is not like it was a surprise; that was how things worked in those days. But I thought my father would want my input. Naturally, he went for the most lucrative business deal. More money and more land."

"Oh my." It seemed so barbaric; fathers basically selling their children into marriage. But it was the thirteenth century.

"Her name was Isabella. She was young and naive; not at all who I would have chosen for my bride. Fighting in the Crusades changes a man. I needed someone who would not shy away from work, or from me, when I lost my temper."

"You told me before you were only together a few years before she died. What happened?"

"Childbirth. She and my son died right after he was born." He dropped my hand and changed the radio station, as though he needed something to do.

I pulled his hand to my knee and cradled it in both of mine. "I'm so sorry. I can't even imagine the pain you must have felt."

"I was never madly in love with Isabella, but I grew to feel affection for her. Especially when I learned she was with child. All I ever wanted was a family of my own so I could raise a child differently than my father raised us.

"It was the loss of my son which set me on my path to

damnation. I never emotionally recovered. You do not realize how much you want something until it is snatched away from you." He gripped my fingers. "I became the worst sort of cad. Drinking, gambling, visiting establishments of ill repute." He cleared his throat. "I hope you do not think any less of me."

I reached over to touch his cheek. "Of course not! Your wife and child died!"

"Well, had I shown more restraint and better judgment, I never would have become the monster I am."

I cocked my head. "Is that really how you see yourself? As a monster?"

He put both hands on the steering wheel, severing our physical connection. "I have been alive eight hundred years, food and drink have no taste, I am supposed to live at night by the shadows, and I must consume human blood to survive. Yes, I consider myself a monster. And I was worse in the beginning."

Trying to let him work through his anger, I pushed on. "How did it happen?"

"Many gambling establishments quit allowing me to enter because I always won. When you have nothing to lose and no emotions, gambling is easier. I had to find new locations. I was told of a high stakes game on the outskirts of town. When I arrived, one woman and six men sat at a table playing. I would think back later and realize something was wrong the minute I came through the door." He sighed.

"No pig roasted on the fire, no women serving ale, no other groups of men gambling. What I should have done was turned and left. What I did was sit and ask the stakes."

"Were they vampires?" I didn't want to rush his story, but I felt the need to know right then if this was when he had been turned.

"All but the woman. She came to me and sat on my lap. She

was beautiful and clean, so different from all the other women I had been bedding. That should have been another clue things were not right. I lost all thought and reason. All that was going through my mind was how I needed to have her right then. How good she would feel. Sound familiar?"

I wasn't sure what he was asking, then it hit me. "She was a succubus."

"Not just any succubus. The Queen."

"Lilith?"

"Yes. She was often the distraction for the vampires in those days. While random men and women were under her allure, the vampires were able to make the victims do whatever they wanted. For every four she brought them, she was given one to keep her young and beautiful. A succubus will kill you if they feed off your energy long enough."

Shaking my head in confusion, I asked, "Why didn't you kill her yesterday? She's the reason you were turned."

"I spent many years trying to kill her. Then we came to an agreement."

"Which was? I can't think of anything that could make up for what she did."

"Things are not always black and white, you know that. I will tell you later. I wish to finish this sordid tale."

I let it go. For now. I pulled his hand off the steering wheel and back to me, gently rubbing his palm.

"The men were all Monarchs. They took turns feeding from me while Lilith kept me," he paused, "while she kept me distracted."

"Distracted? I bet I know what that means." Once again, jealousy I had no right to feel took control.

Beck cleared his throat. "Yes, well, it is not hard to distract a drunkard who cared not about living or dying."

Some of my ire leaked away when I remembered the pain Beck had been in back then.

"I lost all track of time. When I woke, my entire body ached and light hurt my eyes. I was naked in a bed with three women whom I did not remember getting into bed with. They all had bite marks on their bodies and were dead."

I covered my mouth and fought the urge to throw up. My overactive imagination had been playing a movie in my mind. I pictured him with Lilith while the vampires had fed on him. Now the thought of what had been done to those three women was in Technicolor.

Noticing my reaction, Beck pulled his hand from mine and gripped the steering wheel. "I was worried if you knew of my past, you would think differently of me. I never should have told you these details."

"Yes, you should have. It makes you who you are. You know almost everything about me. I deserve to know. I won't think differently of you."

He scoffed.

"I won't!" I pulled his hand back to my leg and held it there. "I'm picturing what you went through. You were young, scared, all alone."

He glanced my way, and when he saw I wasn't looking at him in revulsion, he relaxed.

"I was scared and afraid I would be found with the bodies. I went home to my mother hoping to get my wits about me and recover from whatever poison I was sure I had been given.

"After two days of not being able to keep down real food and not sleeping at all, I realized I could see and hear things better than ever before. I did not need a candle to walk in the dark; I could hear the heartbeats and whispered conversations of the servants.

"My father came home from a hunting trip and wanted to

know what I was doing in his home. He hit my mother when she tried to explain I was sick. In rage, I hit my father, and he flew twenty feet across the room and slammed into the wall. As I tried to process what happened, I smelled the blood. I had not eaten in days because nothing satiated my hunger. His blood was all I could see, smell, and think about."

"Oh no," I whispered.

"Yes. I ripped out his throat and fed. It was the most horrifying and amazing feeling."

I closed my eyes. Beck's father had not been a good man, but knowing Beck, he would have been angry at himself.

"My mother was, of course, screaming and crying. The servants came running. Their whispers over the days had been that I was a demon. When they tried to kill me, my mother intervened and was stabbed. She died in my arms. I wanted to kill them all. Instead, I took her body back to where it all began." He closed his eyes for the merest of moments and took a deep breath.

"The building was empty when I arrived. I yelled and broke every table and chair until the six men were standing with me. I tried to attack them, but I was nothing compared to their strength and power.

"I gave up and begged them to kill me. Instead I was whisked away and my life as a vampire began. It took weeks of explaining by the Monarchs, but I came to understand I was now a demon of the night, the monster from people's nightmares. In those days, feeding meant killing. And the flood of power from feeding during orgasm and then the fear that came when the prey realized it was going to die—" He stopped and glanced out the driver's window before returning his eyes to the road.

"That was how it was done, and I did not know any differently. Because the Monarchs had created me, each fed from me and I from them, I was theirs to control. I lived that way for over a hundred years before I learned of people with different blood. Blood that made us stronger and we did not have to kill to gain that power."

"Shadowers?"

He nodded.

We rode in silence for ten minutes. I made small circles with my thumb on his hand. Slowly, his posture relaxed and he squeezed my fingers. I could almost see the burden of carrying his story leave his shoulders.

"The relationship between Shadowers and Monarchs began thousands of years before I was created. Since there were only ten original Shadower bloodlines, not many Shadower families remained. Only two original Monarchs existed who still remembered the old ways. The Sovereignty was becoming more powerful. I had been told, and the Book of Protection stated, over a thousand years earlier, some were killing Shadowers to gain the ultimate power. They split from the Monarchs and the Sovereignty was born.

"By the time I joined, Shadowers were almost gone. Each higher-ranking Monarch bonded with a family and took them to Greece. Lower-ranking Monarchs scoured the rest of Europe and Asia to search for more Shadowers, me included. I ended up in England. We still needed to feed regularly, as you know, but the Shadowers demanded Monarchs never kill innocent humans if they were going to rebuild their relationship."

In all the information he threw at me, one detail stuck out like a blinking neon sign. Lower-ranking Monarchs?

"You're a Monarch?"

"Yes."

"Is that why the Monarchs want me? Because there aren't any Shadowers left?"

"They wanted me to take from you the night they made me attack Scott. They can control me since they created me."

I thought back, tilting my head. "But you didn't attack me. I gave you my blood of my own free will, which is apparently a big deal."

He nodded. "I wanted to explain it to you before it happened, but I could not. They were too powerful."

"I think I get it," I was starting to shake. "If you had attacked me, you would have been able to control my mind and take me to Greece. Because I gave you my blood by choice, I started the bonding process."

"Yes. They cannot control me anymore. You set me free from the Monarchs."

"But made myself what? Bound to you like you used to be to them? You make them sound horrible! I thought they were the good guys!" I was trying hard to not lose it. Beck was helping me understand and he was baring his soul.

"They are better than the Sovereignty, better than Isaac. But you need to remember they are still the top of the food chain and will do whatever they need to survive. To the best of my knowledge, they do not randomly kill people anymore."

"To the best of your knowledge?"

"I have not been in Greece for a long time. I do not agree with all their ways. And now," he pulled his hand from mine and motioned between us. "And now, they are unhappy with me for starting the bonding process and making you mine."

Making me his. I closed my eyes. There was so much to being a Shadower. I hoped like hell the journals were hidden in my old house. But if my parents had never bonded with a Monarch, would I learn anything from the journals?

"What are you thinking?" he asked slowly.

"Us. Bonding. Monarchs."

"I told you I killed people, killed my own father. Do you fear me?"

I shook my head. "What happened almost eight hundred years ago can't be changed and doesn't matter anymore. Like I said earlier, your past made you who you are; you did what you had to in order to survive. I haven't seen you hurt anyone but Scott and I'm sure you showed restraint."

He smiled a predatory grin. "I did."

"It makes my heart hurt to know about your past and I'm glad you shared it with me; it helps me understand where you're coming from. Now we need to focus on the present. We need to talk about the bonding and what we both know. You've said twice now we *started the bonding process*. Does that mean we can stop it?"

He glared at me. "Stop it? Why would we stop the bonding process? It makes us both more powerful."

"We don't even know what it means to be bonded!"

"We know we can share each other's thoughts, I am no longer under the control of the Monarchs, I have more strength to do things like teleporting to your location, and I have more control over the shapeshifters."

"What do I get out of this besides you in my head? Everything is a benefit to you. Did you know all those things when you had Nate tell me to share blood with you?"

"I only knew it would break the immediate connection with the Monarchs. I honestly did not know it would break their complete hold over me. I hoped it may."

"But you had to have known there would be some benefit to being bonded. What's the point if there's not a benefit, right?"

He waited a moment before answering. "I am not sure what you want me to say."

"You haven't shut up for the last hour and now you don't know what to say?"

"I will admit the Monarchs wanted me to watch you and earn your trust. However, as I got to know you and how amazing you are, I knew I would never just turn you over to them. You did not ask for this life. You do not deserve this."

"No, I don't. The more I learn the less I want to have anything to do with it." I pulled my hand away and immediately felt like a pouting child.

"I want you, you know that."

I started to protest and he squeezed my leg.

"Please let me finish," he said.

I took a deep breath and waited.

"I want you. But I want you to be safe, happy, and protected more than I want you sexually. Had I left you alone, they would have sent another Monarch. He would have just seduced you and controlled you. I could not allow that to happen. I am sorry it seems like I tricked you. I did what I did to protect you. I also did it so I could break free from the Monarchs."

I knew there hadn't been time to explain before. He had been on top of me ready to attack. There wasn't time for a lengthy conversation.

I put my hand back over his. "I have one more question about the Monarchs and the Shadowers."

"I will answer if I can. No more lies, no more secrets, no more evading." He met my gaze briefly.

"You said there were ten original Shadower families."

"Yes."

"And six higher-ranking Monarchs bonded with Shadowers when you were turned."

He nodded.

"So, at some point, my mom's family and my dad's family, and apparently all the other Shadowers, left their Monarchs. Why? If this is such a great relationship between Monarchs and Shadowers, why would I be the last living Shadower, besides Marie?"

"I do not know," Beck said, shaking his head.

"How can you not know? I mean, obviously they're dead. How did they die?"

"I do not know."

"You promised not to lie to me anymore!"

"Kinsley! I know what you know. I will prove it."

He dropped his mental shields and threw his thoughts into my head. It slammed my body back in the seat. His fear for me was the first thing I felt. Then I saw his entire life; the story he had just told me came through in fast-forward clips.

As I saw everything he knew, lived, and felt, it ended with his overwhelming love for me.

Love and fear. Probably not a good combination.

And then, blackness.

Chapter Nine

I WAS DROWNING.

Cold, black water surrounded me and I didn't know what direction was up. I tried to float so I could get to the surface and breathe. The blackness started to clear. Beck was to my right but swimming away. Out of the corner of my eye, I saw Scott swimming away on my left. Which way did I go?

As I floated in the nothingness, I struggled to keep holding my breath. I tried to swim up, but couldn't. I had to choose right or left; Beck or Scott.

When I didn't choose, the water rushed into my nose and mouth.

Drowning.

I was drowning.

I CAME TO, gasping for air.

"Kinsley?" Beck's voice was troubled, his hands cupping my face. "Breathe. Please breathe."

My head throbbed as though I had been hit with a baseball bat. I was supposed to be doing something important, but I couldn't remember what. The dream came back to me in a wave of relentless pounding. My lungs ached as though I had been holding my breath.

"What happened? What did you see?" Beck's panicked voice pulled my eyes to his.

We were stopped on the side of the freeway; vehicles whooshing by caused our car to shake.

"How long?" I rasped out.

"How long what?"

"How long have I been out?" I squished my eyes closed and took a deep breath in through my nose and out through my mouth. I opened my eyes.

"It took about ten minutes for you to go through the visions I put in your mind. Then you seemed to be sleeping. I did not mean to throw it at you like that; I am new to this. I am sorry."

I put my hands over his, still trying to slow my breathing. "It's okay. I know you wanted me to see you were telling the truth." I averted my eyes. I didn't want to talk about the love and fear he felt for me. "How long did I seem to be sleeping?"

He stroked my cheeks with his thumbs until I looked at him again. "A few hours. We are almost to Spokane. But then you stopped breathing. I tried to wake you but you would not answer me, so I pulled over."

"It was a bad dream."

"Was it a dream or a vision?"

I wasn't sure, so I opened my mind and showed him. His eyes opened in astonishment, but he let the vision come to him.

After a few moments, he let go of my face and sat back in his seat. "It is obviously not a vision; if you were drowning, neither Scott nor I would swim away from you."

"That's true."

I could finally breathe normally. My head was still pounding so I dug in my purse for Tylenol. Beck watched me for a second to make sure I was steady then slowly merged back on the freeway.

Settling back into my seat, I closed my eyes. It had been a stupid, Freudian-subconscious dream where my mind was trying to tell me I had to choose one of the men in my life.

I sent that thought to Beck. He chuckled.

"I could get used to this. It's much easier than explaining everything," I said, eyes still closed.

"Are you okay?" He reached over and took my hand.

"I think so. I must have fallen asleep like you thought."

"We will be getting off the freeway and heading north. Would you like me to stop at a gas station?"

"Yes, please. I need to stretch and eat something."

We were both obviously going to ignore the *Pick a Man* dream. Fine by me.

Beck stayed in the car while I went in. I knew he could be in the sun more and more lately, but he didn't hang out in it if he didn't have to.

I stared at my reflection in the bathroom mirror. I felt like I should look different. Everything else had changed, why hadn't I? The circles under my eyes proved I needed to try and get some sleep tonight, but that was the only difference in my appearance.

I splashed water on my face. It made my heart race as I thought about my drowning dream. That wasn't anything I ever wanted to experience in real life.

I bought a soda and bag of M&M's to go with the sandwiches I had packed. Caffeine and sugar were my new friends along with my endless need for protein.

"Are you okay?" Beck asked as I climbed in the car.

"Peachy." I reached in the ice chest for a sandwich and saw blood bags. My appetite immediately went away. "Do you, ah, need some?"

"Is this going to be a problem?"

"I guess it bothers me more than I thought."

"I could go see that woman pumping gas." He pointed to a petite blonde.

"Really?" I rolled my eyes.

"Well, those are your choices, my dear. I can continue to consume blood from the blood bank or I can take humans. I chose the one I thought you would find the least repulsive."

He was right. I shrugged and rubbed my face. "I'm sorry."

"No. I was crass. I will not put it in with your food next time. I did that when we left because I was angry with Scott. I should not have been holding it against you." He pulled back out on the highway.

I said, "If his leg wasn't broken, I would have asked him to come along."

"I would have as well."

In response, I simply raised an eyebrow.

"I would have," Beck insisted. "I expect when he is healed, we will begin working like he and your dad did. I have been considering submitting my resignation to the university."

I shook my head. "Resign? You were just named department head."

"And I worked one day and had a grad student take over because Marie was kidnapped. Being department head will require even more responsibilities to the university. I need to set my priorities."

I laughed without any humor. "Yeah, me too. I have a feeling I won't be enrolling this winter. I figure something will always pop up and I'll never make it to class anyway."

Everything that had happened since last spring rolled through my head. The part bothering me most was not getting my college degree. Teaching was out because I couldn't put students at risk, but I had thought maybe I could finish my degree. Priorities screwed up? Yep, that was me right now. I found out vampires and shapeshifters were real, my parents were dead, Marie was in some kind of coma, and I was upset I couldn't graduate from college.

"We will deal with things as they happen. Right now, it is Shadower Journals and working with Scott."

And that was Beck. Logical and reasonable.

"All I know about what my dad and Scott did was it involved strange incidents in businesses. What about regular people who have security problems?"

"When we get home, we will sit down with Scott and his other employees and get detailed information. I agree with you we may need to see if we can expand our services to individuals as well."

"Do you mind if I call Scott? Checking in with him will be good for his ego and I can tell him what we just discussed."

Beck nodded.

My phone was buried in my purse. I had a few missed calls from Scott not long after we left. He didn't leave any messages. He sent two texts three hours ago. The first one just said: *call me*. Four minutes after that he sent: *please*.

The *please* made me smile. For Scott, that was a grand gesture of trying to be polite.

He answered immediately, voice tinted with fear, "Are you okay?"

"Of course I'm okay. Why wouldn't I be?"

"Because I haven't heard from you in almost five hours and you're alone with Alexander."

"Knock it off," I said, rolling my eyes even though he couldn't see. "We were both just saying how you'd be with us if your leg wasn't broken."

As I expected, he didn't know what to say.

I forged on. "Since I don't know if we'll be back late tonight or early tomorrow, we were wondering if you'd be willing to set up a meeting with all of us and your employees in the next couple days. I think it's time I knew what your business really is and what you and my dad did. Beck and I are on board."

"What?" Scott said slowly, dragging out the word.

It was mean of me, but I almost wished I could see the look on his face.

Slowly, like I was explaining rocket science to first graders, I said, "After Marie went missing, we all agreed we needed to get along. Well, you and Beck agreed you needed to get along. It's almost been a week and you're back to bickering and not trusting each other."

"Your little disappearing stunt didn't help things any!" Scott almost shouted.

"You're right, it didn't. That's why I want us all on the same page. I'm also hoping my parents' Shadower Journals really exist and are hidden where Mei thinks they are. Those would help us too, I think."

"You both really want to work for me?"

Beck, of course, could hear Scott's end of the conversation. Shaking his head he said, "Tell him we plan to work *with* him."

"No one is going to work *for* anyone, Scott. We will work together as a team. We realize you are the expert right now because you've been doing this for years and we want to learn. But this needs to be a group effort."

"Okay. I'll get things rolling. Do you really think this will work?" Scott sounded hesitant yet hopeful.

"We're going to make it work," I said with conviction.

Silence again. Then, "I'll try." When I snorted, he added, "I'll try harder than I have been."

"That's all I can ask. We're almost to Paradise. I'll call you again when we're on our way home."

"Good luck, sweet thing. Kisses."

"Thank you." I put my phone back in my purse.

"Kisses?" Beck said.

"He's a shameless flirt. We're both going to have to get used to it."

"Indeed."

"At least we have a plan when we get home." I tried to shift brain gears. "So, what exactly is the plan when we get to Paradise and my old house? Am I just going to knock on the door, introduce myself as the woman who used to live there, and ask to get in the secret room upstairs?"

Beck chuckled. "I was thinking about it while you were sleeping. We have a few options. You can do that, but I am not sure how they will react. Do you know anything about who bought the house? Do they have a family? I am not sure many people would let strangers in their home, especially if they have kids."

I shrugged. "I don't know who bought it. I honestly didn't care at the time. The less I knew, the better, because I didn't want to think about someone else living in my home."

He nodded. "We will drive by and see if they are even there. We can wait for them to leave, we can also wait for them to go to sleep, or I can go in silently."

I raised my hand. "I'm going in. Once we're in the secret room, they won't even know we're there."

"And then how do we get out?"

Damn Beck and his logic.

"I don't know! Can't you brainwash them or something?" I asked pointing at my temple.

He glanced at me. I swear he frowned but it crossed his face so fast I couldn't be sure. "Brainwash them?"

"You know, go all Star Wars and Obi-Wan on them. *These aren't the droids you're looking for.*" I slid my hand in front of me like Obi-Wan. "Aren't vampires supposed to be able to control humans?"

He shook his head, laughing. "I am not Obi-Wan. However, depending on how many live in the house and how strong their will is, I may be able to put some suggestive thoughts in their minds. I did not think you would want me to manipulate the humans."

"You're the one who said things aren't black and white anymore. We won't be hurting anyone. Maybe you can just make them take a nap? We can go to the room, see if there are hidden shelves, get what's there, and leave."

"We will park and watch the house first to see if anyone is there."

"It's out of town on fifteen acres. The neighbors, although not right next door, will notice if we just park and stare at the house."

"What do you suggest?"

"We're going to have to park somewhere and walk in from the back. Luckily I know every inch of that place since I lived there for twenty-one years." I paused to breathe through the hit of pain to my chest.

We drove through Paradise and I directed Beck to turn down my old road. The emotions and memories that hit me were unexpected: riding the school bus, learning to ride my bike, walking down the road with Rachel and my mom. I needed to hold myself together if we were going to go inside the house. A tear rolled down my cheek and I pretended to rub my eye so I could wipe it away. Another one fell.

Beck put his hand on my knee and squeezed. I knew he was trying to help, but it made me cry harder. "I'm sorry. I never thought I'd come back here. I'm sure I should be stronger and less emotional."

Rubbing my leg, Beck quietly said, "One thing I never want

you to feel like you have lost is your emotions and your humanity. I feel like I lost mine the first day I woke up as a vampire; so much death and destruction at my hands. Never apologize for showing your emotions."

I closed my eyes and braced myself for seeing the back of the property and the old barn. I waved a hand. "Go up there on the right. People park there to hike sometimes. The Mercedes might raise a few eyebrows, but everyone who lives out here will just think it's someone from the city."

I dried my tears and opened my eyes when Beck parked. We were facing away from the property. I put my hair in a ponytail and drank some water. Then I got out of the car and squared my shoulders. It was like a kick to the gut when I turned and saw everything. Nothing had changed. It was like my parents were still there. Again, I was struck with this anger at how everything was different but not really.

"Get over it," I whispered.

I got a dagger and pistol from the trunk. I almost strapped on the swords, but they were hard to hide and we were supposed to look like normal people.

Beck held out his hand and I took it. He kissed my palm and raised an eyebrow, waiting for my lead.

I pointed. "That's the barn at the edge of the tree line. The house is on the other side of it, blocked from this angle."

"This is as good a time as any to see if I can teleport to a location with you."

"That would make things easier. You mean like jump right into the house?" That would be awesome. And maybe a little weird.

"No. I do not know what will happen. We are going to try simple at first. I am going to try and take us next to the barn. It is not far away and I think because we can see where we want to go it will work." Still holding my hand, Beck closed his eyes.

Nothing happened.

I didn't want to interrupt his concentration, or whatever he was doing, so I waited. And waited. And waited some more.

He growled.

"I take it it's not working," I whispered.

He opened his eyes and gave me a look that said he noticed it wasn't working and I wasn't helping.

"How does it usually work?" I asked.

"I thought of you and then I was with you. Remember, I had not done it before."

"You closed your eyes and pictured yourself with me?"

"Yes."

I closed my eyes. "So, this time you're picturing us both next to the ba—" I fell to my knees, dizzy. "What happened?"

When I'd fallen, Beck had dropped my hand. I reached out for him and I smacked a wall. Well, I smacked a barn.

My eyes shot open. Beck was standing next to me and the barn. I looked behind me to see the car parked five hundred yards away.

"What? The? Hell?"

He shrugged. "I do not believe I did that. I am sure it was you."

"The fuck you say!"

He raised an eyebrow.

"What? I can't teleport!" I threw my hands up in the air.

Beck pointed behind us and to the ground at our feet. "Yet it appears you just did."

He helped me stand. I had no desire to feel the dizziness again, but I had to know if I was the one who was responsible. I closed my eyes and pictured myself next to the car. I braced for the dizzy.

Nothing happened.

I scrunched my face in confusion. "I can't do it. You try."

He closed his eyes. And just kept standing there.

I grabbed his hand and pictured the car.

The dizziness hit. When I opened my eyes, we were standing next to the car.

"Interesting," Beck said slowly as I recovered from being lightheaded. "I can only go to where you are but together we can go wherever you think us to."

"When we get home, we can practice this more." I rubbed the side of my head.

"Agreed. Although I am worried about you being dizzy. Maybe you should try with your eyes open?"

"Sure. Why not. We've got to go back to the barn and I already feel like crap."

We clasped hands. I don't know if it was because I kept my eyes open or because we'd whipped back and forth three times now, but my head and stomach protested. I threw up as soon as we *landed*. Beck tried to hold me up but I turned away from him.

He waited a few moments while I leaned against the barn. We moved around the side so we could see the house. A minivan and a truck were parked in the driveway. Minivan made me assume they had kids. It was almost two in the afternoon on a weekday. If there were older children, they should be at school, and people with regular jobs should be at work.

We quickly went into the old barn so we could watch through the split wood and be concealed. Part of me wanted to see if I could teleport us inside but I just didn't have it in me. I reminded myself we would practice more in the safety net of home.

After ten minutes, we didn't see or hear anything.

"Can you sense their auras?" Beck asked.

I tried to concentrate, but my mind was still swirling from teleporting.

I shook my head. "Let's go. I want to be done with this. When I was growing up, people used to come by and take pictures of the barn since it's almost one hundred fifty years old. My dad always had to remind them this was private property." I enjoyed the memory for a moment. "If someone comes out, I'll tell them I was admiring the barn while you Obi-Wan their asses."

Beck laughed. "Your planning skills are going to amaze Scott and his team."

"Bite me," I said as we started toward the house. That had been one of my mom's favorite sayings. Probably wasn't one I should use with a vampire. I sent Beck that thought and he chuckled as we approached the house.

No dogs barked, no one came outside, not a curtain moved.

"Okay, I wanted this to be easy, but does this just seem a little off to you?" I asked.

Beck stopped when we were about twenty feet from the house. "Blood."

"What?"

"I smell blood."

Chapter Ten

"YOU SMELL BLOOD?" I said. "Like blood, blood?"

Beck wrinkled his forehead.

"Okay. I know. Stupid question. I'm tired of surprises, and in our world smelling blood is never a good thing."

Beck walked onto the wraparound porch and peered through the window next to the back door. My old kitchen. Were the appliances the same? Had the new owners painted? Why was I thinking about that instead of the blood?

I couldn't decide if the past or the present were going to be the worst part of this trip.

Beck met my gaze. "There is a body on the kitchen floor."

F-word. F-word. "What the hell, Beck?"

He took my hand. "Take us into the kitchen."

I thought of it and we were there. I didn't throw up and I wasn't as dizzy as before. However, when I opened my eyes, I *wanted* to throw up.

The woman was in her pajamas. The fridge hung open, a gallon of milk splattered on the floor mixing with her blood. No gunshot wound, no weapon in sight, but there was no need for one. Her throat had been ripped out.

I turned my head as the implications of that made their way

SECOND CHANCE

into my mind. Fighting the urge to vomit was nearly all-consuming. I could get through this.

Then I noticed the two highchairs at the table and blood in the cereal bowls. I made it to the sink before I threw up, at least.

Jesus. How was I going to be a Hunter if I got sick at the drop of a hat?

When I quit shaking, I rinsed out the sink and my mouth. It was difficult not to look at the bloody mess around me, but I knew I couldn't stomach seeing those highchairs again.

"Let's go upstairs, finish this, and go the fuck home." I didn't bother to wipe away my tears. The tang of copper and ammonia hung in the air to let me know there was more carnage to discover. I pulled my pistol, a small comfort in the midst of a nightmare.

Beck moved to go ahead of me.

I touched his arm. "I should go first; I know where I'm going."

He stopped. "You can wait outside if it would be easier."

"I'm not waiting outside. I'm a Shadower and I'm going to be a Hunter, I need to get my shit together and be used to seeing dead bodies."

He dipped his chin. "I meant no disrespect."

I rubbed a hand over my eyes. "I know. I'm sorry. I'm upset and angry. And upset."

I moved ahead and cleared the living room like Scott taught me. I looked to my left and the stairs. Small feet were visible halfway up.

"Body," I choked out.

He was maybe ten. We carefully stepped over what was left of him. I, of course, noticed he had bright red hair. He probably had freckles. Not that I could tell since he didn't have a face anymore.

We found pieces of the dad at the top of the stairs. A

105

shotgun lay next to his torso. Two feet away, the hand, connected to half his arm, still gripped the weapon as though he could fight off his attackers even in death.

The babies from the highchairs were my undoing. Probably twins, they had been eviscerated, their remains strewn about the secret room. No way to tell if they had been boys or girls. The only reason I knew it was both of their remains is because they were wearing different pajamas.

I turned and buried my face in Beck's shoulder, unable to stop the sobs wracking my body.

"Why? Who?" I didn't even know if he could understand me. "Why?" I sobbed out.

He held me in his embrace, stroking my neck. Then he stiffened. *"Heartbeat,"* he said in my mind.

"Where?"

"Down the hall. Stay here."

"Oh, hell no," I whispered.

I wiped away tears with the back of my hand and steadied my pistol. Three bedrooms and a bathroom were up here. My room and Dad's office were on the right, Mom and Dad's room was at the end of the hall on the left.

I cleared my old room, noting the airplane wallpaper that now covered my lavender paint. The boy from the stairs? Beck followed as I went into Dad's office. Butterflies were now the decoration of choice. It wasn't a nursery, though.

"She's in here, isn't she?"

He closed his eyes for a moment, then nodded.

"Sweetheart," I whispered. "We're here to help. The bad guys are gone. You can come out."

No one moved or came to me. I didn't hear a thing. I gave Beck a questioning glance. He nodded to the bed.

Slowly, I got on my hands and knees and peeked under the

bed. She was about six, had reddish-blonde ringlets, huge blue eyes, and blood on her face and nightgown.

As soon as she saw me, she shrank back more and silent tears ran down her cheeks.

"Oh, honey." More tears fell from my eyes. I reached out my hand, and after a heartbeat or two, she grabbed my fingers and wouldn't let go. "I've got you, baby. Come on, let's get out of here. I've got you, baby girl."

I half pulled her as she crawled to me. When she was clear of the bed I swung her up in my arms and held on like I'd never let go.

"My name is Kinsley, honey. I know you're scared and upset but I'm not going to let anything happen to you. I've got you. I'm so, so, so sorry, baby. I'll make it all better."

I was totally talking out my ass. How could I make any of this better? I was babbling and I knew it. But if it helped her, I'd promise the moon and stars. She must have felt I was trustworthy because she became a spider monkey, her arms and legs wrapped tightly around me. I could have let go and she wouldn't fall.

"We need to go back in the secret room. Even though it did not look to be much of a secret," Beck thought to me.

"What's your name, baby?"

She shook her head against my neck.

"I'm Kinsley," I said again. "This is Beck."

She kept shaking her head.

"Keep your eyes closed, okay? We're going to do something and then I promise we'll get out of here and take you wherever you want to go."

She finally quit shaking her head. I could feel her tears soaking my shoulder and it was all I could do to keep from breaking down too.

I didn't want her to see her baby siblings' remains in the

secret room, although I worried maybe she already had. I also didn't think she was going to let me pass her off to Beck. I stood to the side while Beck went in and looked at each of the already open *hidden* shelves.

"*How in the hell did someone know where those were?*" I asked through our bond.

"*I do not know, but I know who was here.*" He met my teary gaze. "*I can smell Mya and Isaac.*"

My body began to shake. I leaned against the wall and took deep breaths. "How?" I choked out.

The girl pulled back slightly and met my eyes. Her stare was of someone so much older. She'd already seen too much.

"What's your name, sweetheart?" I tried again.

"Ab—" she said then burst into tears, burying her head, once again, in my neck.

Beck ran his hands along the walls checking for more secret compartments.

"Abigail," she finally said, pulling back to watch me. "Abi."

"Abi, honey, I'm so glad I get to meet you and be with you." And then I felt like the biggest bitch in the world. "Did you see who did this, Abi?"

She froze, eyes wide and watery.

"Abi, I know this is awful. I'm going to get you out of here as soon as possible." Her little body shook in my arms. "Do you know how long you hid under the bed?"

"Forever," she whispered.

"*Pajamas and breakfast. Maybe six a.m.?*" I thought to Beck. "*I agree.*"

"*It's been eight hours, Beck. Eight fucking hours she's probably been hiding!*" My heart ached for this poor girl. What had she seen? How had she survived?

"*There is nothing here. Isaac and Mya found the journals if there were any.*" Beck moved to leave.

"Okay, Abi," I said. "We're going to go now, okay?" She nodded. "Keep your eyes closed, baby."

Carrying a child and a gun is difficult, especially down stairs and around the body of her brother. Luckily, I had run up and down these stairs my entire life. Beck led the way, my heart rate and breathing slowing the closer we got to the bottom.

We made it to the living room before shit hit the fan.

"You are so predictable," a woman's voice said.

Abi squeaked and Beck growled, blocking our bodies from the intruder at the speed of vampire. I peeked around his shoulder. Damn it.

"Oh, Beckford," Mya said, "how I've missed you."

"You bitch," I said. Abi tightened her hold.

"I waited and waited. I knew you'd be here. It made it even better the little snot-nosed brat was upstairs wetting her pants and crying. It was enough fear I could feed off it without ever breaking her skin."

I moved toward Mya before I knew what I was doing. I raised my gun. Damn it. Abi had been through enough without me firing a gun while I held her.

I noticed Mya had both her arms. That meant a vampire could completely regenerate a missing limb? Didn't seem fair or right.

"Beck, would you mind taking care of the trash while I take Abi to the car?" I turned to leave.

It felt like it happened in slow motion, but it was just too fast for me to comprehend what was really going on. One second Abi was in my arms and safe. The next, she was gone.

Isaac was in the kitchen with Abi. He held her by her hair and she was screaming. At least I think she was screaming. I could see her mouth open and I knew she had to be making noise, but all I could hear was the rushing of my own blood in my ears.

God, he was fast.

"Ah, my young Shadower."

At least we knew he hadn't changed his appearance again. He didn't look like Dr. Gabriel Finch. He was Isaac; the *man* who had seduced and tricked Marie years ago. The monster who had kept me in captivity.

"He fed from you and Marie for all those days. He is stronger than us. I do not know all he is capable of," Beck said in my mind.

"Give Abi back, Isaac. You've made your point, you have the journals, you've killed everyone else. Let me have her."

"True. I have your journals and I have this precious morsel." He licked the side of Abi's face. "Why do you want the child? She is nothing to you. I'll trade Marie for the brat. Better yet, I'll trade *you* for the brat."

He lifted her higher and now I could hear her screams. Her hair was starting to rip out. Her arms and legs windmilled wildly, trying to break his inhuman hold. How much more could she take?

Her face begged me to fix this, save her like I promised. I had to save her! That's what I got for making promises I didn't know I could keep.

I held up my hands, pistol pointing to the ceiling.

"You will never learn, will you? You have nothing. You lose again," Isaac said, smiling.

"Kinsley, no!" Beck yelled from behind me.

Beck knew I wasn't fast enough. I knew I wasn't fast enough. But I still had to try. I aimed and fired six shots in rapid succession at Isaac's head.

I hate that split-second moment when you realize something horrible is about to happen and you'd do anything to stop it or change the outcome. Back out of the room, close your eyes, pray to any entity or being who will listen.

Anything to stop the pain barreling down on you like a freight train.

I'd screwed up.

Bad.

Again.

Maybe if I had brought my swords, maybe if I hadn't been so sure of myself.

Abi's screams echoed in my ears as Isaac ripped her head off and jumped over the kitchen table. He threw her head at me and scraped my chest with claws as he flew over me to Mya and Beck.

Stupidly, I caught Abi's head in my arms, dropping my gun. Like I could save her from anything now. As I fell to the floor, I looked to her crumpled body next to her mom's. At least they were together.

I was going crazy. I had to be. They weren't together; they'd never be together again.

Isaac and Mya rushed Beck. The three of them crashed through the living room wall like a wrecking ball into the yard, wood and sheet rock splintering, glass shattering. Mya screeched as the sun scorched her skin. Beck took the momentary pause to use Mya as a weapon against Isaac. He grabbed her by the feet and swung her around, sending her flying into him as a battering ram.

Abi's voice came into my head. She told me to get my lazy, liar ass off the floor and help Beck.

I'd fired six shots at Isaac and he'd dodged every one of them. Mya couldn't. I ran to the hole in the wall, jumping through, firing at Mya. I hit the ground and rolled, pulling an extra magazine from my belt.

By the time I came to a crouch, Isaac and Beck were squaring off as Mya lay on the lawn. I'd hit her in the neck with four silver shots. Abi told me to hit her between the eyes with everything I had in my new clip. Maybe if half Mya's head was missing, I could rip it off the rest of the way.

I ran to Mya's body and stood over her. She was growling and spitting, stunned by the silver and sunlight. I fired three shots into her brain before Isaac barreled into me.

Beck flew to us. *"As soon as I touch you, think of the car."*

He reached past Isaac and touched my shoulder. Instead of the car, I pictured us in the tree. We landed on a branch. Isaac came to us and I pictured us smashing into him mid-air. We slammed into him, landing hard in the grass. I pictured us back in the tree. We did this three times before Isaac was finally stunned and lay in the yard for a few seconds.

I was dizzy and couldn't get myself to send us to the ground in time. "Jump!" I said to Beck.

We were just coming out of the tree when Isaac must have decided our teleporting was faster than his Shadower-blood-induced speed. "No!" he screamed. Then he and Mya were gone.

Beck and I landed hard. I stayed down. I was weak and light-headed and couldn't think of any reason to ever get off the ground. I'd gotten Abi killed, and Isaac and Mya had the journals.

I'd failed.

"Kinsley?" Beck said, reaching for my hand.

I pulled my hand away and stared at the blue sky.

He checked the claw marks on my chest. I didn't even feel the wound Isaac had given me when he'd killed Abi. Beck lifted me in his arms and carried me back in the house. I didn't want to be in the house.

He put me on Abi's couch.

"Is there anywhere else something would be hidden?"

I closed my eyes. I didn't care.

I heard Beck talking to someone. Maybe he could talk to Abi too. She sure as hell wouldn't get out of my head. If I let myself think about her, she kept telling me I'd promised to help her, to save her. I had to quit listening.

"Did you see anything else besides the hidden panels in the walls?" Beck paused. "You are sure?" Silence. "We were too late." Silence. "Let me talk to Scott."

The silence in the conversation was annoying me. He was obviously on the phone and not talking to Abi. Then I guess I needed to talk to her. I crawled off the couch to where her head was. I stood and limped to the kitchen and put it with her body next to her mom.

"I'm sorry," I told her.

"Sorry doesn't mean anything," she said. I think it was in my head. Or maybe she was behind me. I couldn't tell.

I knew we were going to have to burn the house. I cut a lock of Abi's beautiful hair and stuck it in my pocket. This was my reminder I wasn't perfect. My reminder I couldn't let down my guard ever again.

"We will be back as soon as possible," Beck said from behind me.

I rummaged through the drawers until I found emergency candles and a lighter. I lit two candles and put each one in the dining room windows, lighting the curtains on fire. I turned on all four gas burners of the stove.

Beck came up behind me and took my hand. I closed my eyes and thought of the car.

The explosion happened a few seconds after we landed next to the car. Beck continued to hold my hand. I thought of Scott's house.

Nothing happened.

I shook off Beck's punishing grip and climbed in the backseat of the car. After I lay down, I pulled out the lock of Abi's hair, clutching it in my hand.

My sobs rocked me to sleep.

Chapter Eleven

"KINSLEY? Kinsley? What's wrong with her?" Scott sounded panicked, his voice going higher with each syllable.

"She has not spoken a word since we left the house," Beck replied, his voice much calmer but still tinged with worry.

Though responding was impossible, I was still present enough to see and hear what was happening around me. Beck lifted me out of the back seat and carried me inside. I saw Floyd and Rachel before I scrunched my eyes shut and Beck started up the stairs to my room. I heard Marie's heartbeat monitor beeping a steady rhythm. Scott's crutches clunked as he slowly made his way up the stairs behind us. Everything seemed amplified to be bigger and louder somehow.

The world swirled as I felt my body rest gently on my bed. Everyone started talking at once, all the questions and arguing filling my head with a cacophony of pain.

After a few moments, Beth finally said, "I think everyone needs to leave."

"I'm staying," a barrage of voices said.

The auras came to me without even thinking of them. Two black orbs, hot pink, and dark blue. Beck, Beth, Rachel, and

Scott. Scott hovered over me. Then I saw Mei's yellow and Floyd's light blue by the door.

"Get the hell out of her room," Floyd said.

"I've had about enough of you, old man," Scott snarled.

"You don't understand!" Floyd yelled.

"Floyd, you don't understand either," Mei said.

Floyd's response came fast and hard. "Bullshit! The vampires and you shifters don't understand the emotions she's feeling because you're, well, you're methodical killers. Rachel can't because she's not a Hunter. Scott, you might be a Hunter, but you're a cold-hearted son of a bitch. You have to be. You've forgotten how it feels when the first innocent is lost on a kill! Get away from her and let her breathe!" Floyd was struggling to speak by the time he was done.

I wanted to yell right along with him. I wanted to jump up and hug him for knowing what I was going through when no one else seemed to.

Yet, I couldn't move. Something froze my muscles and sucked all the energy from my body.

"Please, everyone," Beth said. "Let me get her bloody clothes off, make sure she doesn't have any lasting injuries, and then you can come back."

After a few seconds, I heard them all shuffle out. Beth didn't try to get me to talk; she talked to me, letting me know everything she was doing before she did it. She cut my mangled shirt from my body, and the chilled air prickled my skin. One careful sponge bath later, I was under the sheet wearing a clean tank top and shorts. When I heard the door open, I rolled to my side so my back was to it.

"What does she have gripped in her hand?" Beth asked.

"I do not know," Beck said. I felt him gently push at my mental shields.

I could have let them all drop and shown him my anguish,

but that was too easy. I wanted to wallow in my self-pity a bit longer. I kept him locked out and shoved a mental do not disturb sign at him.

He sighed. "She will not let me in."

"Let you in?" Scott said. "What do you mean?"

"There is much for us to discuss. Just not now."

I expected them to argue. Instead, a warm hand touched my shoulder. I pulled away from the contact even though I knew it was Scott.

"Sorry, sweet thing," Scott said. "I didn't mean to scare you. I hate seeing you like this. I'll be downstairs if you need me. It was hell getting up those stairs on crutches, so you're going to need to come down to me, okay?" He tried to laugh. It was ragged and forced.

He kissed my cheek and whispered in my ear, "I guess things were pretty bad over there. I'm sorry I was too broken to back you up. I'll never let you hunt alone again if I can help it. As soon as you're ready and my leg is healed, we'll get back to training. I don't think you could have done anything differently, but I know you think you should have. I lo—" he stopped, choking on the word.

Was he going to say he loved me? Seriously? Why? I wanted to scream: "Don't you dare do this!"

"I, uh, care more about you than I've let myself care about anyone and I don't know what I'd do if you got hurt," he finally said. "Well, hurt worse than you've already been hurt. Shit. I can't imagine my life without you in it."

When Scott was gone, Beck came to me.

"We were not prepared for today. I am sorry. We should have had backup. I never expected Mya and Isaac to be there. I will find out how they knew. Find out who betrayed us."

I squeezed Abi's lock of hair tighter. Was Beck to blame for Abi? No, it was all me. He'd fought hard, and I'd been arrogant.

"Masters is correct. We will begin training again as soon as you are ready. We will hone our Monarch-Shadower abilities. I will not let you down again."

He rested his forehead against my neck and sent me soothing, loving thoughts. My clenched hand relaxed a little. Then he kissed my neck and stood.

Floyd was next.

"I know you don't know me, girl," he started in his gruff tone, "but I knew your mom and dad. I might not have been with them when they first started hunting, but I know we all made mistakes out there. It's impossible not to.

"I locked myself in my room for a damn week after my first hunt. Your dad tried to talk to me, but men aren't always the best to offer comfort. Your mom? She knew just what to say. I'm gonna tell you what she told me."

What amazing words of wisdom had my perfect mom given Floyd? I knew after I heard what she said, I would be magically better.

Floyd slapped the edge of my bed. "She said: *'Get over it! The world isn't fair and people die! Life goes on whether we're in pain or not! Our job is to save the ones we can, kill the bad guys, and live our lives until it's over. There isn't time for self-pity; the bad guys don't take breaks. Take a day, then pull your whiny ass together and get back out there.'*"

I choked on a sob and angry laugh. *My* mother never would have said that.

"I know what you're thinking! That your mother never would have said that," Floyd said, reaching over my shoulder to touch my cheek. "She used to be the most ruthless hardass I'd ever met! You know what changed her? You. You became her humanity. So, damn it, girl. Find what'll be your humanity and then balance sweet Kinsley with badass Kinsley. We got monsters to kill!"

He sniffed away some of his own tears then left.

Oh, Floyd. He was my surrogate grandpa and I'd only known him for two days. He was the godfather I hadn't been able to grow up with. He was part of our puzzle piece family now and I was so glad I had him.

When I quit being a big baby I was going to have to remember to tell him.

Rachel sat down on the edge of my bed and stroked my hair. When I didn't push her away, she lay down next to me. I thought I was all cried out, but the comfort of a best friend is something that brings down those walls we try so hard to erect.

I rolled over and showed her Abi's lock of hair. She wiped away her tears and then mine. Without saying a word, she got up and grabbed some ponytail bands from one of my drawers. She braided the lock of hair and secured the bands on each end. Then she tucked it back in my hand and wrapped me in a hug.

Best friends just know.

I cried myself to sleep for the second time that day.

AS MUCH AS I wanted to stay locked away for a week like Floyd had, the smell of bacon woke me. Something as simple as bacon reminded me my hardass mom, through Floyd, was right.

There wasn't time for pity; life goes on even when our hearts break. 'Find my humanity,' Floyd had said. Who was my humanity? Marie? Rachel? Scott? Beck? Abi?

Her braided lock of hair was still gripped in my hand.

I can't be your humanity; I'm dead, Abi whispered in my head.

"That doesn't mean you can't be my humanity," I whispered back. "Can't you be what reminds me I have to be diligent and never let my guard down? Can't you be what reminds me life and death are only separated by a millisecond?"

You need something to live for, not something to remind you death is just around the corner.

"You're six. How come you're so wise?"

Death does that. Then she was gone.

I didn't care what Abi said; she was going to be the reason I wouldn't lose. She would be what got me back to training and practicing for the next bad guy who was going to try and kill us or someone else.

I had some decisions to make. I could sit around and cry and feel sorry for myself like a little kid. Or I could become a Shadower. Since all this began, I never embraced it. I ignored things, I pretended I didn't have any responsibilities, I killed a couple vampires—more by luck than skill. I hadn't made any kind of concrete decision; one day I didn't want to be a Shadower, and the next day I ran out and acted like I was a Vampire Hunter.

Abigail's blood was on my hands and mine alone. My cockiness and laziness in training had gotten a young, sweet, innocent girl killed. This was different than when my parents died. I had just been along for the ride then; a bystander. This death was all my fault. And I could never let it happen again. The only way to do that was to become a machine. An emotionless killer who took care of business.

I didn't know if I could even do that.

My intention was to shower. However, I ended up sitting in the cold, dry bathtub crying for well over thirty minutes. My parents' rings felt heavy on the chain around my neck. What had been in those journals? What would Isaac do with them? How long would he stay powerful from the Shadower blood? What if I had taken the swords?

I replayed the moments before he had taken Abi from me. What could I have done differently?

I kept seeing her big, frightened eyes. The blood. The gut-wrenching moment I failed. The endless loop of horror and tragedy played and replayed in my brain. I had to get out of my own head.

Wiping my eyes with one hand, I turned on the water with the other and quickly washed up. It took all I had not to ruminate, to rewind the personal horror movie and watch again and again.

Concentrate on what you can control, Kinsley. After I got dressed, I opened the calendar app on my phone. I'd only slept away a day. I was so damn glad I hadn't had a dream-vision-nightmare.

Now that I knew what day it was, I could try to further process my life changes and decisions.

Time is such a strange creature.

It was exactly a week since Marie had been taken. Only seven very short and long days had passed since the first day of school.

It was like a blinking neon sign: Life Goes On. Time Waits For No Man.

Fickle Bitch.

When Raven, Rachel, and I had decided to drive to Ecstasy, I'd told myself I wasn't good at letting fate take the wheel. Time to embrace my *not quite human* status. I'd meant it then. It had backfired.

But why?

One: Rachel never should have been with us. She wasn't a Hunter. Two: I'd tried to do it without those who could help me. Three: Abi. I'd been distracted.

I needed to plan better, that was obvious. I had a lot to learn from Beck and Scott.

Stretching my arms up to the ceiling, and then bending to touch my toes, I took deep breaths and counted to ten. Time to tackle the world.

I went downstairs and as soon as I came through the kitchen door, Rachel threw herself into my arms.

"I was so worried about you!" She leaned back to look in my eyes then wrapped me in her arms again.

I let her hug me and halfheartedly tried to hug her back. It felt like we were strangers, and I'd never felt like that with Rach. We were so different now. She was a child and I felt like I'd lived a hundred lives.

She didn't appear to notice my reluctance to engage with her. She sat back at the table and picked up her coffee.

"Scott, where's Beck?" I asked.

"He had to go to the University. His secretary needed him to take care of some things." Scott looked at his watch. "He should be back any minute. I'll text him and let him know you're up. He'll be glad."

Nate was cooking. He waved the spatula at me. "Glad you're back. Lunch will be ready soon."

I walked in to check on Marie. Jared was sitting outside her plastic walls watching TV.

I held out my hand to shake. He took it and his blackened aura came to me. This was the first time I'd seen an aura with my eyes open. It lingered for a moment after we dropped hands, then it was gone.

"Has anything changed?" I asked, running my eyes over Marie's still body.

"No. Dr. Chavez set up a new IV. Her vitals are stable and there isn't a medical reason why she won't wake up."

"Can I go in?"

"Of course." He waved me by and sat back down.

She looked like she was sleeping.

"Oh, Marie. No wonder you went crazy." I laid my head on the edge of her bed. Being the captive of a sadistic vampire for twenty years would have snapped anyone's sanity. Add being a Shadower and Hunter and Marie never stood a chance.

I hoped I wouldn't lose my mind.

"You have to wake up," I said. "You're the best chance we have of finding Isaac." And then the words just tumbled from my mouth, a nonstop string of everything I needed to say. "He killed more people, Marie. He killed an innocent girl named Abi. I see her and she talks to me. Am I going crazy? Are ghosts real? Or is she just my conscience?" I wanted to pace but I didn't have the energy. "I know you don't always make sense, but at least if you were awake, I might have some answers. Would you be able to tell me about the journals hidden in the walls? And you know what? I want to talk to you about the guys. How can I possibly love them both? How can it even be love? I need you, Marie. I need you to wake up and come back to me." I closed my eyes. It was both frustrating and cathartic to say it all, but I knew I'd get no answers today.

I stayed for about twenty minutes until I heard Beck's car pull into the driveway. It was time to sit down with everyone and start making some plans. Hunting was going to be treated like a job, and we needed schedules. We also needed to set up the meeting with the employees of Masters Security. There were things to do.

I pulled myself from Marie's bed and stroked her hair. With a sigh, I left the room and met Beck at the door.

He kissed my cheek. "I am happy to see you up."

He didn't try to talk about how I was doing, which I appreciated.

We went to the kitchen. Everyone was eating lunch and visiting. Well, Rachel, Raven, and Nate were visiting. Scott sat brooding in the corner.

"Where are Floyd and Mei?" I asked.

Everyone stopped talking and stared at one another.

"Where are—"

"I locked them in the basement," Scott said.

"You what?!"

Beck said, "Kinsley, we talked through who could have possibly shared information with Isaac. The only people in the car were us, Floyd, and Mei."

I was completely floored. They'd locked an old man in the basement? "What in the holy hell is wrong with you guys? Floyd is a Hunter. Jesus! Mei is the one who had the vision about the hidden shelves! Beck you watched her have the vision! Why on Earth would they tell Isaac? And even if they did, *how* would they tell him?" I began pacing the kitchen. "No. Screw that part. Why? Why would you possibly even think Floyd and Mei had anything to do with this?"

I stalked to Scott and poked him in the chest. "This is *your* doing, isn't it?"

"Why are you blaming me?" He knocked my hand away.

"Because you're always the one who acts first and thinks later." I spun to Beck. "Or you, who thinks *everyone* is out to get us."

"Will you stop yelling and think about it?" Scott said.

"No! No, I will not stop yelling and, no, I will not think about it. Floyd and Mei have helped us!"

"Why did you find them?" Scott asked.

"What?" I spun on him again.

"Why and how did you find Floyd and Mei? Do you think it's completely coincidental you just happen to pull up to the house holding the man who is supposed to be your *godfather* and he has all the answers you need? Then Mei has a *vision* of where to find Marie. Next, Mei has a *vision* of Shadower Journals we don't even know about. Oh, that's right! *Perfect Floyd* told you about the journals and Mei told you how to find them."

Scott's snide tone and air quotes were pissing me off. Broken leg or not I was about ready to throw his condescending ass on the floor.

I think Rachel knew it, too. "Okay. You don't have to be such a jerk about it Scott," she said, pointing at him.

He glared at Rachel, and Nate growled in return. Perfect. We were back to arguing and not trusting each other. Great working relationships we were cultivating.

"Knock it the hell off," I said to Scott. "There are ways to explain things to people without being such a douche, as Rachel was trying to point out. She probably noticed I was about ready to kick your ass."

Rachel crossed her arms and nodded.

Scott looked back and forth between us. He seemed like he might actually be thinking about acting like a nice guy. The moment passed.

He stood. "It's all bullshit. I don't believe in coincidences. Floyd and Mei are liars and they work for Isaac. Hunters don't live to be in their seventies; your family is proof of that. I'm alive at thirty because I've been an untrustworthy son of a bitch since I was a teenager. Your dad reminded me of that in the years I worked with him."

Scott crutched his way out of the kitchen. I'm sure he wanted to slam a door or leave in a car, but he couldn't. His outburst made me realize I didn't know a thing about him or his life. I hadn't known how old he was, how he got into this life, how he met my dad, where his family was.

Shit. Scott was right. I'd blindly followed him and Beck without really knowing anything about either of them. I'd blindly followed Floyd and Mei. I was as young and naive as my twenty-one years. I was just as childish as I silently accused Rachel of being.

But my instincts with Scott and Beck had been spot on. Scott was a pain in the ass and Beck was a vampire, but they had protected me and taught me things.

Something had led me to Floyd. A hereditary feeling from being a Shadower or the Universe finally helping me out. Floyd was legit. He had the pictures, he knew about the monsters, and he knew about my parents.

"This is bullshit!" I yelled at Scott's back. I turned to everyone left in the kitchen. "How in the hell do I get in the basement?"

No one moved.

Rachel looked to Nate and he shook his head.

She stood. "I told you from day one I won't ever choose between you guys. You're my best friend, Nathaniel, but Kinsley is my first best friend and my woman best friend. We will *not* be pitted against each other."

Raven stood too. "I like Floyd and Mei."

Nate slid his plate over and rested his head on the table.

Beck tried to follow us as Rachel and Raven pointed to a door. I held up a hand. "Stay away from me right now. And keep Scott away from me."

The women took me to the basement. Floyd and Mei were in silver-barred jail cells with a cot and a toilet. I was beyond pissed.

"Where are the keys?" I asked Rachel and Raven.

They shrugged.

"We didn't get to come down here," Rachel said. "I think the men knew we'd take your side."

Mei had vertical burns on her face, arms, and shoulders. She'd probably slammed herself against the bars multiple times.

Her body vibrated with anger and energy. "I am going to

rip that fucking man apart when I get out of here. I'm going to tear off his broken leg and beat him to death with it. And then your sexy British vampire is next. I'm going to rip off his head and burn his body." Her voice was low and even.

I wanted to say I was sorry but it didn't seem like enough.

"I'll get you out of here as soon as possible. However, you have to *swear* to me you won't hurt either one of them."

Mei growled and threw herself on the cot. "I'm not making any promises."

Chapter Twelve

"FLOYD?" I said.

He was lying on his cot, eyes closed. He made no move to respond to my tentative voice.

"Is he asleep?" I asked Mei.

She said nothing, but her glowering gaze told me there was rage inside of her.

"I understand and I don't blame them," Floyd said, his voice just barely audible in the cold, concrete basement.

"Are you fucking kidding me?" Mei yelled. She jumped up and began pacing her cell.

"I'd have done the same thing," he said, opening his eyes. "They don't know anything about us, Mei."

"Are you trying to convince them we *are* or *are not* conniving, lying, untrustworthy assholes?" Mei demanded. "Because you're not off to a very good start for our innocence!"

"They're going to believe what they want to believe. There's no proof I am who I say I am."

"The pictures are proof," I said.

"Pictures can be doctored," he said quietly.

"Again," Mei said, "you're not helping our cause."

Floyd sat up and gave me a sad smile. "I'm sorry about Abi."

The tears flowed without warning, and that pissed me off more. Scrubbing the tears away with the backs of my hands, I yelled up the stairs, "Someone better get down here and let them out!"

It was going to get ugly if they continued to ignore me. Thankfully, I only had to yell a few more times before Nate came downstairs with the key.

"Are you the stand-in for the human and the vamp, cougar?" Mei asked Nate.

Nate growled and Mei did the same, throwing herself at the bars. Her skin sizzled and added to the burns she already had.

"Damn it, Mei, knock it off!" Floyd said. "You've hurt yourself enough. Quit being so hot-headed."

She glared at each of us, ending with a *looks could kill* on Floyd.

"Are you upset we're locked down here or upset because if Parker hadn't dumped you off, none of this ever would have happened?" Floyd asked her.

"All of the above!" Mei yelled.

I didn't blame her. I knew how it felt when it seemed your life decisions had been taken out of your hands. Not to mention the fact she had no idea where the man she loved was and now he didn't know where she was.

"Okay," I said. "I'm going to let you out and we're going to figure out what's going on. I do not, for a second, believe either one of you are in contact with Isaac."

"Why?" Floyd asked. "Mei and I sent you to your old house."

"I believe you because my parents trusted you and Marie loved you." I moved toward his cell with the key.

"Your parents trusted me and I kidnapped their daughter." He dropped his head into his hands.

I didn't turn the key.

Nate came closer. I wasn't sure what his intentions were and I tensed. "Everyone believes something different," Nate said to Floyd. "But let's look at the evidence."

"As I already pointed out, it doesn't look good for us."

"Maybe you could shut up, old man," said Mei.

Nate turned to me. "Beck and I have always trusted your instincts. But what is your evidence they didn't send Isaac after you?"

I opened my mouth, closed it, then closed my eyes. Evidence. Such a nasty word when you didn't have any.

"Exactly," Nate said.

"It's ridiculous," I said. "Why on Earth would they be working with Isaac? What do they get out of it?"

"You just met them," Nate said. "Scott was right when he asked how you ended up there. What led you to Floyd? Hell, Floyd just met Mei a couple weeks ago. Even if we believe Floyd is who he says he is, how do we know who Mei really is?"

"Because Parker loves her," Floyd said.

"And we don't know Parker," Nate said on a sigh.

"This is all very circular as you keep coming back to the fact you don't trust us," said Mei. "You know what? I don't trust you guys! I spent a few weeks with Floyd while he talked about the *wonderful* Shadowers and Hunters, who often kill shifters, and I don't think you're all so wonderful!"

Mei was right; we were talking in circles and not solving anything. I didn't know if Beck and Scott were going to let me just walk out of here with these two. At this point, I wasn't even sure what Mei would do if I let her out. Attack me? Run?

"Nate," I said, hoping to sound more confident than I felt, "I trusted you and Beck from the beginning. It was silly to start working for Beck, to move into the condo, to believe in vampires, shifters, and Shadowers. Something in me felt right. Felt like that's what I was supposed to be doing. I don't know if it's instinct, blind faith, stupid, or what. But I did it. It's the same reason I trust Floyd. Hell, Floyd has more evidence about my parents and who he is than Beck and Marie ever gave me. And Floyd trusts Mei, so that means I trust her, too."

Mei growled. Floyd sighed.

I ignored them and turned to Rachel and Raven. "What do you guys think?"

They both held up their hands in surrender.

"I don't want to get in the middle of this," Raven said. "I don't know what they would gain from communicating with Isaac and I don't think they would, but there isn't anyone else."

Rachel closed her eyes. "I trust you, Kins, but the guys had some really good arguments, and our safety has to come first. It's not hurting anyone to have them down here until we figure something out."

"Not hurting anyone?" I said pointing at the cells. "Look at them! Would you want to be locked down here?"

"It's better than dead," Rachel said, shrugging. "Scott wanted to kill them."

"Of course he did," I said, shaking my head.

Mei growled and flopped on her cot again. Watching her was giving me a headache. She never sat still for more than a few minutes. It must have killed her to be stuck in the car for so long. If Marie ever came to, it could be dangerous for these two to be together; it would be like watching hummingbirds.

Marie.

Oh no.

"Marie was in the car with us," I said quietly.

Floyd's head snapped up. "No."

"What are you talking about?" Rachel asked.

"Beck," I said in my head, searching out our ever-present connection.

"I was not sure you would be speaking to me," he said almost immediately.

"I think we have a huge problem and it's not Floyd and Mei."

"What is wrong?"

"Do you know where Scott is? We need to talk and I don't think we can do it here at the house." I sighed. Everyone was looking at me funny. "I'm talking to Beck."

"Of course you are," Mei said, hand on her hip and upper lip lifted in a sneer. "Your little connection with the vampire is another reason I don't trust any of you. Besides the obvious jail cell." She waved her arm.

"Listen, I have a horrible thought, but we can't talk here. Will you promise to be absolutely silent if I let you out?" I whispered.

"What in the hell are you talking about now?" said Mei.

"Just trust me and be silent, please."

"Kinsley?"

"Find Scott and meet us at Screamers. I think Marie is the reason Isaac and Mya knew where to find us."

"I will be there as soon as possible. Be careful."

Another great thing about Beck was I didn't have to explain myself for every little thing.

"You can't honestly believe—" Floyd started to say.

"Just wait until we're somewhere else," I whispered.

I quietly unlocked the cells and waved for everyone to go upstairs.

"Follow my lead," I said as we came through the door. I snagged the Hummer keys and tossed them to Nate.

"So, we'll just leave those two locked up and resume our normal schedules," I said a little too loudly into the living room. I opened the front door and shooed everyone out.

Raven and Rachel were looking at me like I'd lost my mind, but they were apparently getting used to my strange behavior. I wasn't sure if that was a good or bad thing.

Floyd leaned heavily on his cane and was gripping Mei's arm. It looked more like he was holding her with him rather than using her to help him walk. She didn't seem to be putting up too much of a fight. I don't know if she had caught on to what Floyd and I thought or if she was just biding her time to try and get away.

Jared stood. I put my finger to my lips and mouthed *shhh*. He cocked his head. I smiled and gave him a double thumbs up and held my hand in the universal "I'll call you" signal.

He sat back down and nodded. He didn't even know me and was also already used to my odd behaviors. Great.

As I approached the Hummer, Mei pulled away from Floyd. "Can we talk yet?"

"No," I said quickly.

We climbed in and Nate pulled out of the driveway.

Everyone started talking at once.

"What in the hell is going on?" Mei asked.

"That was really weird; even for you," said Raven.

"I don't understand what just happened," Rachel said.

Floyd gazed out the window. I knew he felt the same as me. He didn't want to believe it but nothing else made sense if it wasn't him or Mei.

"I think it's Marie," I finally said. I choked on her name. Tears threatened. I didn't want to believe my own accusations. I was going to blame Marie instead of Floyd and Mei for communicating with Isaac. An unconscious Marie who was the only family I had left.

"What?" Rachel and Raven demanded.

"That doesn't make any sense!" Rachel said. "She hasn't

woken up since we found her. She hasn't been left alone either."

Mei finally appeared calm. "The Monarch-Shadower connection."

"But Isaac isn't a Monarch," said Raven.

"He used to be," Floyd said quietly. "We don't know everything about bloodpacts. Maybe it doesn't even have to be a Monarch and a Shadower. Maybe a regular human and a regular vampire can communicate telepathically if they've shared blood."

"But she's unconscious," said Rachel. Her face held all the pain and worry I was feeling.

"Is she?" I said.

We rode in complete silence the rest of the way to Screamers. It was tense as we all mulled over our thoughts. I didn't know what everyone else was going through, but I was sick to my stomach.

The club didn't open until five so we had a few hours until the staff would show up to get ready for the evening.

Scott sat at a table in the corner by the bar and I could tell from his crossed arms and stone face, he wasn't here by choice. Beck stood a few feet from the table and the usual bouncers were flanking the men.

Why were the bouncers here already? I didn't even need to ask; Beck could read me like a book.

"I felt it was necessary to have some backup," he said.

"I don't know whether to be flattered or annoyed," said Mei. "A cougar, a wolf, and a bear for little ol' me?"

Lucas, Riley, and Kevin took a step toward her but Beck held up his hand.

"Mei, you have spent some time with me. You know my number one priority is always Kinsley's safety. I would hope your Parker would do the same if your life were possibly in danger."

At the mention of Parker, Mei lost some of her spunk. She looked away and begrudgingly nodded.

"Now," Beck said, "we must discuss the most pressing matter. We have a traitor among us. We need to know who it is and what actions to take."

"This is bullshit," Scott finally said. "We know who the traitors are. I had things under control."

I gave Beck a questioning gaze.

"I tried to explain, but he does not believe."

"Hell no, I don't believe," said Scott. "Telepathic communication while in a coma?"

"What if she's not really in a coma?" I asked. "Jared said Beth can't find a medical reason Marie won't wake up."

"You think she's faking it?" Scott said.

"No. I think Isaac is controlling her mind."

"Are you serious?"

"Beck and I have this, connection thing, and sometimes I wonder if he could make me say and do things if I didn't want to." I looked to Beck for confirmation and he wouldn't meet my eyes. "Could you?"

"Yes."

Scott grabbed one of his crutches and stood. "You mean to tell me you've been controlling her?" He grabbed the other crutch and looked like he was going to swing it at Beck.

"Stop it!" I said. "He hasn't controlled me or made me do or say anything!" I went to Scott and pushed him gently back into his chair.

"Let's try it," I said to Beck.

Scott bounced right back up. "Over my fucking dead body!"

"He reminds me of Parker," Floyd whispered to Mei.

She smiled for the first time and helped Floyd sit down. Then she went behind the bar and poured herself a drink. "This is getting interesting. I like any plan that doesn't involve me being locked in a cage," she said. "Hey, vampire, can you make the annoying human break his other leg?"

"Mei," I said. "Could you please not antagonize anyone? I'm trying to prove you and Floyd are innocent. Maybe you could zip it for just a little bit?"

She shrugged and moved back to sit with Floyd.

"You don't need to have him control you to prove your point," Floyd said, taking the water Mei handed him.

"I think I do," I said, pointing at Scott.

"You really think Marie *told* Isaac everything?" he asked, eyebrow raised. I kept expecting him to roll his eyes like a teenager.

"Yes. You all know I shared blood with Beck. He's a lower-ranking Monarch. We don't know if we've done a full blood-pact, but it's obvious we've started the bonding process. If Beck can control me, it proves Isaac could control Marie."

"Lower-ranking Monarch?" Scott said. "When were you going to share that with everyone?"

"Oh, c'mon," I said, "we all assumed he had to have power of some kind. And it doesn't even matter in the whole scheme of things. It is what it is."

Beck walked to me slowly. I took an involuntary half-step back then held my ground. I knew he wouldn't hurt me, but it was scary to offer to let someone control your mind.

"You have to let me in, first," he whispered in my ear, stroking my hair.

"Do it without touching her," Scott said. "Move to the other side of the room. Isaac isn't in the same room as Marie. Hell, last we knew, he was on the other side of the state."

Beck smiled and kissed my cheek. "You know, it has almost become a game to upset him."

In the blink of an eye, Beck was across the room, leaning against the wall with a sly smile. My body swayed toward him.

"Whoa," Mei said.

"You never get used to their speed," Floyd said. "Especially when they're trying to kill you or you're trying to kill them."

Scott grunted in agreement.

I opened my mind to Beck and felt his warmth. *"I will not do anything embarrassing, just enough to let Scott know I have control."*

"How about ballet? We all know I can't dance, so what if he makes me dance?"

Beck raised an eyebrow. "I am not sure it works that way."

"What were you going to do?" said Scott.

"Put her to sleep."

"Well, do that too." I relaxed my body and waited.

Without any control on my part, I went to plié, stood on my tiptoes en pointe, lifted one leg into an attitude, then pirouetted four times, resting back in plié.

Rachel clapped.

My mom had me take dance lessons for almost a week. I'd gotten in a fistfight with one of the other girls who had made a comment about my unmarried parents. Rachel had been amazing at the end of the season show. I'd whistled and yelled for her, secretly wishing I was on stage.

I'd never been this good or fluid at ten, so there was no way I could have done that on my own.

I tried to speak to tell Beck I wanted to go to the ballet soon to watch a performance, but nothing happened. I couldn't even make my face form a look of worry or try to get Scott's help. As my legs carried me to the table where he sat, I had a moment of panic as I pulled out the chair and settled in. I tried to relax and tell myself it was Beck and I was okay.

Then there was nothing.

When I came to, both Beck and Scott's faces swam before me.

"Wha—"

"Just give yourself a moment," Beck said quietly.

I was laying across Scott's lap.

"Don't you *ever* do that again," he said to Beck. "Jesus, Kinsley, that was the weirdest thing I've ever seen in my life. And I've seen some weird shit. It's like you were a marionette."

"How long was I out?" My mouth was dry. Where was I? I looked around. That's right; I was at Screamers and I'd let Beck control me to prove Marie was under Isaac's control and Floyd and Mei were innocent.

My head felt fuzzy.

"It was only three minutes," Rachel said from next to Beck, her face scrunched in worry.

"I'm okay. Just a little dizzy and parched. Hey, Rach, I'm better at ballet than we thought."

She smiled, all worry gone. "That was awesome!"

I closed my eyes, relishing the fact I had control over my body again.

"Maybe we can go to a professional ballet soon?" I said to Beck.

He smiled and reached out to touch my face.

Warmth spread from my feet and pooled low in my stomach; I moaned involuntarily. Scott cupped my breast and pulled me closer. Nate grabbed Rachel and threw her on top of the bar, pulling her head back for a punishing kiss. Raven and Mei walked to the three bouncers and they all began kissing.

"Stop!" Beck said, straightening and moving toward the door.

I didn't need to look to know who it was. I'd only ever felt this way once before. Well, Beck and Scott made me feel like this when I let my guard down, but I only felt like this once when I didn't have control.

She was wearing a red leather corset halter top and black leather pants with stiletto boots. And she looked absolutely delectable. I hated how she commanded the room with lust.

"Hello, darlings," Lilith purred. "Let's have some fun."

Chapter Thirteen

TIME SEEMED to move in slow motion. Scott's hand on my body felt so wonderful and so wrong at the same time. I had hoped to never see, or feel, Lilith again in my life. Her brand of seduction was addictive and dangerous.

"Let them go," Beck said.

Lilith laughed. The sound caused my body to shudder and I moaned again.

Scott moved his other hand and gripped my neck. He rubbed his nose and mouth on the sensitive skin under my ear. "What? The? Fuck?" He bit out each word as though he was fighting against himself and I knew the feeling.

"Succubus," I managed before wiggling on his lap. We both moaned in painful pleasure.

Everyone else seemed to be let out of their sex-induced trances. Everyone but us. They were all standing in place staring back and forth between Lilith and Beck and Scott and me. At least they were no longer attacking each other.

"Lilith!" Beck yelled.

"It is so much fun to watch you when I have her under my spell," Lilith said. "I have not seen you so enamored of anyone since—"

He grabbed her by the throat and lifted her off the floor.

I fell from Scott's lap, hitting my knees. The tingling continued to roll over the sensitive parts of my body but I was able to move on my own. I pulled a dagger from the ankle strap.

The bouncers pulled their guns when they saw my knife. They aimed at Lilith and Beck.

"Shoot that bitch," Scott said.

The bouncers were shifters and it meant they answered to Beck, not Scott.

Even though Beck looked like he was about ready to rip out Lilith's throat, he said, "No one will do anything."

Rachel hid behind Nate. "That's the succubus."

Nate growled, confusion on his face. "Sir, why?"

"There are matters to discuss which shall not involve violence. Or sex."

Lilith pouted, pursing her lips she ran a hand down the side of Beck's face. "How about both?" she crooned.

I moved toward them. He could boss everyone else around all he wanted; I wasn't going to listen.

Just before I could run the blade into Lilith's gut, Beck dropped her and turned to block my attack.

I felt completely betrayed. I opened and closed my mouth a few times before the words made their way out. "What the hell is wrong with you?"

Lilith blew me a kiss over Beck's shoulder. It was like consuming poison. My body tensed and I dropped the knife. Her lust poured over me again, little fingers searching and massaging. Why was Beck allowing this? Why didn't I have more control? And what the hell was she doing here in the first place? Fire lit my middle. I wanted to climb on Scott's lap again.

"Enough, Lilith," Beck said.

With a look to me I couldn't read, Beck pulled her to his

upstairs office leaving the rest of us in shock. I put a steadying hand on the back of a chair as the lust leaked from my body. I closed my eyes and took a few deep breaths to make sure I was back in control.

"Maybe someone can explain what the fuck just happened?" Scott said. "A succubus? I knew they existed, but I've never come across one. Your dad and I killed an incubus once, though."

Another reminder I had so much to learn from Scott.

"Why didn't he let you kill her?" Floyd asked.

"Yeah," said Scott. He started talking in a bad British accent: "'My number one priority is always Kinsley's safety.'"

"Sure didn't seem like it right now, did it?" Mei said.

"Nope," Scott agreed, throwing a hand up.

"He made some kind of deal with her years ago." There I went, immediately jumping to Beck's defense even though I didn't agree with him right now or even have a clue what was going on. I shook my head and opened my eyes.

"What was the deal?" Floyd asked.

I looked away and picked up my dagger.

"You don't know," said Scott.

"No! Okay. I don't know. But I trust Beck. Just like I trust all of you." Now it was my turn to throw my hands up in confusion.

Rachel came out from behind Nate. "Can we leave? I've spent enough time with her to last three lifetimes."

Nate pulled her protectively into his arms. Jealousy threatened. Shouldn't I be comforted by Beck? Instead he was protecting the Queen of Sluts. "Yes, let's leave," I said.

Scott stood, adjusting his crutches. "Are you sure?"

"Yes."

Beck had some explaining to do. I felt like the jilted lover and there was nothing I could do about it now. I'd told myself I was going to get better about compartmentalizing my emotions and getting business done. If he wasn't going to include me in whatever Lilith wanted, then I would start working with Scott without him.

"Are we good now?" I asked, waving my hand toward Mei and Floyd.

Scott looked them over. Mei stood, putting her hands on her hips. She ruined her *bad girl* vibe when she helped Floyd stand and maneuver with his cane.

"Yes, we're good," Scott said. "I can't believe how much power Beck has over you. It makes sense Isaac could be controlling Marie and even listening through her." He rubbed a hand down his face. "This is crazy. Do you know what this means? There is so much we still don't know about Monarchs and Shadowers. Damn it!"

"Speaking of that, you and I have a lot to talk about."

He raised an eyebrow.

"Is there somewhere we can go?"

"Damn skippy, sweet thing." He pulled out his phone and called for someone to come pick us up.

"I'm going to stay here," Nate said. "The club opens soon, and I need to know what the hell is going on."

Rachel sighed and kissed his cheek. "That would be nice. You might tell Beck he pulled a total dick move when he chose Lilith over Kinsley, by the way."

Rachel was awesome. I felt guilt over my earlier thought of how childish she was. Just because she was human didn't mean she didn't understand what I was going through.

"Do you want me to go with you?" Raven asked me.

"It's okay," I said. "Maybe you can finally get Mei and Floyd set up in a house. That would go a long way toward an apology."

Scott gave some quick directions and the rest of them left to go back to his house.

We stood outside waiting for the car to come get us.

"So, um, sorry about feeling you up," he said, a slight blush staining his cheeks. I didn't even know the man was capable of embarrassment.

"It's okay." I patted his shoulder. "The first time she attacked me, she *kissed* me. If I had to choose, I pick you feeling me up over kissing the Queen of Sluts." I winked.

Scott burst out laughing. "Queen of Sluts. Nice. You've grown up so much in the last few months, sweet thing. You wouldn't have been kissing women or letting me feel you up before." He leaned over so our shoulders bumped and then he winked back.

"I could get used to you being more relaxed and playful. People won't think less of you if you drop your *asshole* act. In fact, it might help."

"It's not an act, baby. I am an asshole."

"Not when it's just the two of us. Usually."

"What can I say?" he shrugged. "Everyone else pisses me off. You bring out my good side."

A new, black Hummer pulled up in front of the club. I didn't recognize the driver. He waited while I helped Scott in the front seat and I climbed in the back.

"Kinsley, this is Logan. He stepped up as my right-hand man until Oliver can return."

"Nice to finally meet you, Miss Preston," Logan said. "I'm sorry about the loss of your parents. I worked with your dad and he was amazing."

He had a surfer boy look and was, of course, tall and muscular. I suppose it helped in a private security firm that hunted supernatural creatures, but, I swear, Scott must have hired everyone from a modeling agency.

"Nice to meet you, too, Logan. But please don't call me Miss Preston, okay? And thank you. Even though I didn't know about this part of my dad's life, I'd like to think he was good at it."

He smiled at me in the rear-view mirror and nodded.

"Where are we going?" I asked.

"The downtown offices," Scott said. "You've never seen them and I didn't want to go back to the house with everyone else. Also, you can see where I work, meet a few people, and we can be alone."

I rode in silence as we went from Seattle to Bellevue. I was going to have to have the same talk with Scott I'd had with Beck. I wasn't sure if it was going to be easier or more difficult. Beck had shared his past with me and I was hoping Scott would do the same. I also hoped Scott understood my reasons for not wanting to start a relationship.

My palms started sweating so I rubbed them on my jeans. I was a big girl and I could have this conversation and hold my ground. If I'd been able to make him see reason when we'd been in a bed and his hands had been on me, I could do it fully clothed in his place of business. Of course, he'd only let go of me when he'd realized I was a virgin. In fact, he'd acted like I had the plague. Maybe I should start with reminding him again.

Logan and Scott talked about the assignments the others were on. I heard Spokane, Portland, and San Francisco.

"How many Hunters work for you?"

"Well, it gets a little tricky," Scott said, turning sideways to talk to me. "Not everyone working for me is officially a Hunter. We take on regular cases too. It's what I told you in the beginning: we work for high profile companies that have security breaches they can't explain. Nine times out of ten, it's because it's an inside job."

"Regular humans or supernatural somethings?"

"Regular humans. It's when one of my team members go in and can't find any logical explanations that I went in with your dad, Oliver, Logan, and Shawn who you'll meet when we get to the office. After your dad died, Oliver and I tried to stay in town to keep an eye on you. Except for the one big trip I had to take, we were able to. Logan and Shawn have been busy. We've had more cases in the last four months than we'd had the entire previous year before."

"Do you employ any shifters or vampires?"

"Of course not!" Scott said, narrowing his eyes at me. "Why in the hell would I employ the enemy?"

"We talked about this briefly before Oliver was hurt. You need to get over your racism."

"I am not racist!"

Logan smirked and tried to smother a laugh.

Scott turned his laser glare on Logan then back to me.

I glared back. "You know what I mean. This isn't about skin color; this is about not being one hundred percent human."

"Vampires aren't human at all!" He smacked his hand on the center console.

"They used to be," I said, shrugging.

"Used to be. As in not anymore."

"Okay, I won't argue that one with you right now. What about shifters?" I pointed behind me, in the general direction of Screamers.

"What about them? They're animals."

"No, they're not! They're humans who happen to be able to change their form to an animal. Think of the implications of that when you're fighting bad guys. Shifters are faster, stronger, have heightened senses, and are difficult to kill. How many casualties have you had?"

"I like her," Logan said.

"Shut up," Scott said to Logan. His tone wasn't mean, but it was as though this was an ongoing argument. To me he said, "I've had more casualties than I'd care to think about. I haven't lost anyone since I started working with your dad."

I smiled, even though I felt the stinging along the bridge of my nose from threatening tears. My dad was amazing.

"Probably because all the traits I just listed are the same for Shadowers. I'm sure I'm nowhere in his league but think if I was with you and we had Raven and Nate and some of the other shifters who work for Beck."

"I don't trust them," Scott said, turning to face forward.

I huffed in annoyance. "Again: Get. Over. It. Logan, why did you say you liked me? Am I bringing up something your team has tried to talk about before?"

Logan glanced at Scott.

"Don't ask for his permission to talk to me."

He pointed at me in the rear view mirror. "That's why I like you," Logan said. "It's refreshing to hear someone argue with this hard-headed ass."

Scott grunted but didn't blow up.

"How long have you guys known each other?"

"Forever," Logan said. "Our families were slaughtered the same night. It made us brothers in arms."

"Families slaughtered?" I asked, eyes widening.

Logan looked to Scott, then grimaced. "She doesn't know? How does she not know?"

"We've been a little busy with other shit," Scott said.

"Well no wonder she's pushing the shifter angle. Maybe if she knew—"

"Enough for now," Scott said.

"Knew what?" I asked.

"What happened to our fam—"

"I said enough for now!" Scott said louder.

"You've been even more jackassy than usual, boss."

Scott covered his eyes with the palms of his hands.

"Sorry if I got you in trouble, Logan," I said quietly.

"You didn't get me in trouble. I just don't understand why he hasn't told you things."

"He's right, we've been busy with other things. He's going to tell me about his past today. That's what we're doing."

"No. It's not," Scott said. "We're going to talk about the business. You don't need to know anything about my past. It's in the past and doesn't matter."

"That's bullshit and you know it," now I leaned forward to smack the center console. "Doesn't it help you understand me and talk to me because you know *everything* there is to know about me? You know things about my past I don't know since you worked with my dad. We *will* be talking about your past. We *will* be talking about everything."

"Good luck with that," Logan said, pulling in front of a two-story office building.

I didn't know Bellevue as well as parts of Seattle, but I didn't think we were too far from the salon and spa where I'd gotten ready before the Seattle Art Museum gala. Which meant Bellevue Square Mall was nearby too. It gave me a happy feeling to know I hadn't completely lost the girly part of me that got excited about the mall and salon.

After I helped Scott out, Logan saluted with two fingers and drove across the street to the parking garage.

"That's the only thing about this location I don't like," Scott said. "I wish the parking was below the building.

"I didn't know what to expect. I like it." I said. The bottom floor was glass-walled and had MASTERS SECURITY painted across it. "Are your offices on both floors?"

"Yep. Come on, I'll give you the tour."

We were greeted by an attractive, bleached-blonde secretary.

"Scott," she said, coming from behind her desk. "Why didn't you tell me you were coming? I would have had everything ready." She fussed over him, reaching out to straighten his shirt, and completely ignored me.

"I'm not having you push me around in a wheelchair anymore. I'm completely capable of moving around with crutches."

I cleared my throat as they left me standing by her desk.

She turned and, I swear, glared at me, before covering the look with one of politeness. "Yes?" she said coolly.

I looked to Scott expectantly. When he just stood there like a clueless man, I held out my hand. "Hi. I'm Kinsley Preston, Scott's new business partner."

The blonde's mouth opened as she looked back and forth between us. She was in excellent shape and wore a gray pinstriped business suit jacket and skirt with heels. Her hair was curled and fell just below her shoulders. She was classy in a way I hadn't had time to master. I put her about ten years older than me, so closer to Scott's age.

"You're Kinsley?"

"You've heard of me?"

"Sweet thing, she worked with your dad and she works with me. Everyone here knows who you are."

Which meant she was being a bitch on purpose. I still stood with my hand out. "And you are?"

She finally shook, with her fingertips instead of a real handshake, and said, "I'm Holly. Scott's *personal* secretary."

The way she said personal was more *personal* than it should have been. It was the way older women make it clear they're older, smarter, and have more experience than us dumb, young, kids. But why was she being so bitchy to me?

"Holly, can you order some takeout from the Chinese place? Double my usual order; Kins likes the same things I do. Have it brought to the private conference room. Unless it's Logan or Shawn, I don't want us disturbed." Scott turned, heading to the elevator.

Holly stared longingly for a moment then looked at me. Her face said it all. Her problem was she had the hots for Scott and he had the hots for me. Great. 'Cuz I needed more drama added to my already complicated life.

I wanted to tell her: "You can have him. It would make my life easier." But I didn't think that would go over well. I tried for polite in hopes of keeping her on my good side. I didn't need Scott's *personal* secretary hating me any more than she already seemed to.

"Thank you, Holly. It was really nice to meet you. I hope we can talk again later."

She seemed taken aback I was being so nice. She put a hand to her chest and narrowed her eyes.

"Does he ever tell you to order something for yourself from the Chinese place?" I asked.

"Of, of course not," she stammered. "We're not allowed to eat out front."

"Well, how about if today, you order something for yourself?"

"That won't be necessary," she said lowering her hand, finally recovering. "You have no idea how things work around here."

"Okay. Again, it was nice to meet you." I shrugged and followed Scott to the elevator. I watched Holly's face as the door closed. She didn't like me.

"So," I said as the elevator started moving. "What's the deal with Holly?"

"What do you mean?" Scott said.

"Are you guys, like, an item?"

"An item? You mean dating?"

I nodded.

"Hell no. I don't date. Especially coworkers. Of course, she's the only female who works here."

"Did you, *you know?*"

"Did I what? What's *wrong* with you?"

"Nothing. Never mind."

He shook his head as the elevator opened on the second floor.

I hadn't paid much attention to what was downstairs. This floor had a big open conference room and glass walled offices circling it. Restrooms were next to the elevator. There was a wet bar and a glass-doored fridge with various bottles of soda, juice, and water along with fresh fruit, vegetables, and yogurt.

"That was your mom's idea instead of vending machines with crap food in them," Scott said when he saw me looking at the unconventional arrangement. "She said it would make clients feel more at ease."

"She was right," I said numbly. My mother had been here? Had helped set up the offices?

"I know you have a million questions and I'll answer them all. While we're waiting for food, do you, ah, want to see your dad's office?"

I turned quickly. "My dad's office?"

"Yeah. I couldn't bring myself to clean it out. I should have brought you here weeks ago but it never seemed to fit in with what we were doing."

I let him lead me past the giant table to a set of offices on the far wall. One had Scott Masters Owner and CEO stenciled on the door. Through the glass I could see artwork, a beautiful view outside, and a large desk with double monitors. The office right next to Scott's had the blinds down so I couldn't see inside, but stenciled on the door was THOMAS PRESTON SENIOR CONSULTING EXECUTIVE.

"How many years?" I said, my hand on my lips.

"Well, you know we worked together for seven, but I started this business five years ago."

"I wish he would have told me," I said, tearing up. I hated the secrets.

"I know, sweet thing. I tried, I swear I did. He wanted you safe and thought this was the best way to do it."

"He was wrong." The tingle in my nose told me I was losing the crying battle.

I wiped away my tears, took a deep breath, and pushed open the door.

Chapter Fourteen

I DIDN'T KNOW what I was expecting, but my dad's office was simple and clean. Some framed pictures of Mom, Dad, and me sat on his desk.

What made me cry was a birthday card I had made for him when I was around four. I'd colored flowers and butterflies and written 'hapy bithday' in my little kid handwriting. The inside said 'to the bes dad in the hole wid worl!!!! Luv kinsley.' The 'K' was backward.

I covered my mouth, choking on a teary laugh, and dropped into my dad's desk chair. I swear the office smelled like his cologne even though the logical part of my brain knew it couldn't after all these months.

"He loved you guys more than anything," Scott said.

"I know."

I put the card back on his desk. A chewed-on pencil sat next to the computer mouse. It was almost as bad as seeing the house in Paradise. It was like Dad was supposed to walk through the door any minute.

"Maybe we could clean things up and I could use this office when I'm here?" I said.

Scott nodded. "Of course. I wanted you to be the one to go through his things."

"Thank you," I choked out. "That was really thoughtful."

My face must have shown surprise because he said, "Don't look at me like I'm growing a heart. I told you, I'm not an ass with you."

I laughed. "You're a mystery wrapped in an enigma."

"Not really." He shrugged.

After a few moments of silence, we went back to the main conference room.

"This is where we usually meet with clients. There's a smaller conference room downstairs and a small kitchen/break room," Scott said. "There are also a set of cubicles for my general employees. We started out with four and now we're up to eight. There's a private conference room through there." He pointed to the other side of the room, opposite offices for Shawn, Oliver, and Logan.

"You five have your offices up here and everyone else is downstairs?"

"Yep."

"I like the setup. It allows for privacy but doesn't seem secluded," I said, spinning in a slow circle to take everything in.

"I got lucky when this building came up for lease. I'm working on buying it, but it kind of got put on hold when your dad died."

I sniffed and blinked away tears. "A lot of things got put on hold, didn't they?"

Scott's phone buzzed. He glanced down and said, "It's Holly. Maybe food is here already."

I excused myself to the bathroom while Scott talked to her. I splashed cold water on my face, proud for not turning into a crying mess in my dad's office. A little teary, but not a sobbing mess. Maybe I was getting better at navigating my emotions. I hadn't even thought about Beck and Lilith in almost thirty whole minutes. Go me.

Abi appeared in the mirror, standing behind me. "You have too been thinking about them. But you forgot about me. How convenient."

I spun around, my heart in my throat. She wasn't behind me; I was alone. Of course I was alone; Abi was dead.

I turned back to the mirror, half afraid she'd be there again. She wasn't, thank God.

Was this going to be a thing now? Was I crazy or was I seeing ghosts? I didn't have time to deal with it, so I put Abi out of my head again. If I was crazy, it was just going to be one more thing to add to my list of issues. If it was ghosts? I cradled my head in my hands and sighed. I wasn't sure which one would be worse.

When I came out of the bathroom, Holly was putting take out containers on the table. Scott wasn't with her.

She walked to the sink and pulled a plate from the cabinet. I didn't know whether to ask for a plate, get one myself, or sit down and wait to see what she did. I continued to stand and watch. I'm sure she knew I was there. Completely ignoring me, she dished out Scott's food, put his chopsticks on the edge of his plate, then went back to the wet bar and poured him a drink.

I wondered if he made her do all this or if she thought he'd think of her as girlfriend material because of her diligence. If I were him, I'd find it annoying. What I should have done was just ask her, but I didn't get a chance.

"Why the hell did you only put out one plate?" Scott said, coming out of the elevator.

"Sorry, Scott. I wasn't sure if Ms. Preston was going to be eating as well."

Seriously? "You could have asked me," I said.

"Oh, I'm sorry, Ms. Preston," she said smoothly, "I didn't even see you there. Would you like a plate?"

"Of course she would," Scott said. "That's why I told you to order double. Jesus, Holly, what's with you this week?" He sat down at the table.

She looked hurt for a moment and I wanted to apologize on Scott's behalf, then I remembered I was working on not being so soft. She'd seen me, she was just being bitchy. I didn't need to try and smooth things over.

"Listen," I said with a sigh, "I can't control what Scott thinks or does. It would be great if you could maybe not be a bitch to me just because you want in his pants and he wants in mine."

Scott stopped mid-bite and Holly dropped the plate she was holding.

It was more fun to *not be soft* than I realized. Well, not fun, but it felt damn good to say what I was thinking instead of just having imaginary conversations in my head.

"I'm sure I don't know what you mean," she said, reaching to pick up the broken plate pieces. I think she might have had the start of tears in her eyes.

Well shit. I suppose there is a difference between not being soft and being a flat-out bitch. I went to her and tried to help pick up the pieces.

"I've got it," she said.

"So, Holly, you want in my pants?" Scott said, obviously recovered from my bold statement.

Holly closed her eyes. When she opened them and looked at me, I swear she wanted to kill me.

"He can be dense," I said, trying to be funny.

She didn't crack the hint of a smile.

When she was done picking up the broken plate pieces, she

skewered me with one last glare, smiled at Scott, and went downstairs.

"You're a moron," I said as I sat down to eat.

"What?" he said, chopsticks almost to his lips.

"Have you slept with her?"

"Why is that any of your business?"

"Because it's obvious she's pining over you and you don't give her the time of day."

"I slept with her like six months ago then realized it was a stupid mistake. She's done a great job of keeping things professional." He waved a hand in the air.

"Again: you're a moron. Two: that wasn't very professional."

"I had a moment of weakness." He ducked his head.

Holy shit. Was the unflappable Scott Masters blushing?

"I told her it was unprofessional of me to fuck an employee, a mistake like that couldn't happen again, and I gave her a small raise."

"Does she know where you live?"

He raised an eyebrow in question.

"You're lucky she hasn't killed you in your sleep. If you said our time was a *fuck*, called me a mistake, and then paid me more money, I'd probably quit and then kill you."

"I didn't call *her* a mistake, I called our liaison a mistake. We're not going to talk about this anymore. I don't know why I feel the need to explain myself to you all the time."

"All I'm saying is I can't believe she still works for you. I also can't believe she didn't sue you. You shouldn't have slept with her to begin with but you could have handled the breakup better."

"It wasn't a breakup," he huffed. "We weren't a couple so it couldn't be a *breakup*. What do you want to know about the business and your dad?"

Okay. Subject changed. His personal life wasn't my business. He was right. What did I care? Except for the fact Holly was going to continue to treat me like shit when I came to work here.

When? If? Was I going to come work here? If it would help me kill the bad guys I was.

"If we're not going to talk about you and Holly, let's talk about you and Logan. He said your families were slaughtered on the same night?"

Scott's jaw clenched. "That's your lunch topic of choice?"

I lowered my eyes. "Well, no. I'm sorry. I'm just—"

"I asked what you wanted to know about the business and your dad."

"Well, it is business," I protested. "I don't know a damn thing about you. But, you're right, it's not really a topic to discuss while we're eating."

"I need to tell you. I will tell you. I just don't know how or when." He set down his chopsticks and put his hands on his head.

Damn it. I reached toward his face and stopped.

The elevator dinged and I was afraid it was Holly back to kill Scott. I wasn't sure if I'd watch, try to stop her, or help. He really was a moron when it came to women.

The doors opened and a Greek God stepped out. Or maybe Aquaman. Again, did Scott hire everyone from a modeling agency?

"Shawn, thank you for saving me from crazy women." Scott stood and offered his hand to Aquaman.

The smile was contagious. The hair, the shoulders, the smile, *the hair*, the tattoos, the smooth, dark skin. Oh my.

I found myself moving to Shawn and holding out my hand. My smile widened. Until our hands touched.

An orange aura glowed around him and broke the spell he had on me.

He was a shifter.

Holy. Shit.

But what kind of shifter? I wanted to run my fingers through his black hair and across his caramel skin. I wanted to pet him.

As I processed Shawn was a shifter, he must have processed I wasn't human either. He dropped my hand and stepped back.

"Shawn, you finally get to meet Kinsley," Scott said, not even noticing Shawn and I were trying to keep from touching.

"Miss Preston?" Shawn's voice was strained to my ears.

I still wanted to pet him.

Damn it.

"Yes. You knew my dad?" *Code for: did my dad know what you are?*

"Yes. Tom and I worked together closely." *Translation: he knew I was a shifter and kept my secret. Will you?*

"Interesting." *Translation: I haven't decided.*

"So," Scott said, still oblivious, "let's talk about the future."

I frowned. "Shouldn't we have Beck here if we're going to talk about the future?"

"Yes. But I need to get the guys together and let them know we're bringing Alexander on board before Alexander sets foot here. I may or may not have made it clear his presence wasn't welcome." Scott shot me a crooked grin.

"You're impossible," I groaned while swiping a hand over my face. "This is going to be impossible."

Shawn laughed, a deep melodic sound that rubbed over my skin. "She sounds like her dad."

"She sure does," said Logan from the door to the stairs. "You should have heard her put Scott in his place in the car.

Best damn thirty minutes I've had since we found out Tom and Claire were dead."

I sounded like my dad? "Just start telling stories, please. I need to paint a picture of my dad as a Hunter."

And they did.

For two hours, the three men laughed and mimicked my mom and dad. Holly even popped in and added to a story or two with a fond smile.

It was wonderful and awful at the same time. Most of the stories sounded just like being with my parents growing up. How my mom would say, 'Oh, Tom!' and laugh the way she did when he did something to frustrate her. How my dad would raise one eyebrow when he didn't really agree with what you were saying, but refused to argue about it.

But then there were the monster stories. Holy hell, the monsters.

With the pictures from Floyd's house, Floyd's stories, and the Masters Security staff stories, my mom and dad were painted as bad-ass ninja, superhero, slayer, superhuman, *Underworld, Buffy, Supernatural* rock stars who couldn't lose.

Yet they did.

A collective sigh filled the room as the five of us let it fill our minds they were dead. Holly wiped a tear and stood silently. She watched me with an unreadable look, then went back downstairs.

Logan and Shawn both stretched their legs out and leaned back in their chairs, hands linked behind their heads. Scott reached for my hands, gripping both in his strong, secure grip. With the other hand, he wiped at the tears on my cheeks I didn't even realize were there.

"Thank you," I managed to choke out. I tried to pull away from Scott but he wouldn't let me.

"Damn," said Logan, "I needed that. *We* needed that."

Scott and Shawn nodded, and three sets of eyes locked on me.

"Soooooo," Shawn said slowly, "what's next?"

I turned to Scott and he squeezed my hands. "I was seventeen," he said as he looked away.

Out of the corner of my eye, I saw Logan's laid-back posture was gone and he sat forward. He flattened his palms on the table.

Shawn tried to keep his body relaxed, but I noticed the tightening of his jaw.

"At seventeen, guys tend to think they're invincible. My dad used to say things about *being careful of monsters*, but I thought he meant wild animals and the government." Scott tried to laugh but it came out more like a pained cough. "We lived in Redmond and my dad worked for Microsoft. We had money, we had security, and we had everything a person could ask for. Didn't matter."

"Monsters don't discriminate," Logan whispered.

Shawn stood slowly, met my eyes, and gave me a brief nod. "I'll give you three privacy. I've heard this story. Ms. Preston, I would enjoy talking to you later." He walked to the door and disappeared down the stairs.

Scott and Logan didn't even seem to notice.

"A fucking pack of wolves," Scott said, shaking his head. "I mean, you see coyotes and deer in the housing developments and on the outskirts of the city. But how does a fucking pack of wolves—"

"Six of them," Logan supplied.

"Fucking six of them," Scott nodded, "roam the streets of Redmond without being seen?"

"Because when they roam the streets, they're in human form. And when they break into your house, they're anything but human," said Logan.

I tried not to picture the carnage the two men painted as I learned their entire families had been slaughtered by a wolf pack of shifters. Logan lost both his parents and three younger siblings. Scott lost both his parents and a twelve-year-old sister.

The boys had gone to different schools but lived a few blocks apart. They hadn't known each other, but they'd seen each other driving around over the years. They had no idea why their houses had been targeted. After they recovered from being kidnapped, and had killed two shifters, they came up with an explanation that made sense: they were both seventeen-year-old young men who were in prime physical condition. They assumed they were meant to be changed to grow the pack.

However, instead of biting them in their homes, the wolves had held them down, slaughtered their families while they watched, and dragged them out into the night. When the guys came to, they were tied up in a factory building outside Redmond.

"Three guys, dressed like normal dudes, were playing cards when I woke up," said Logan. "I smelled like roadkill." He shook his head and rubbed one eye. "I knew I was covered in the remains of my family and I started to bawl like a little kid, until I looked over." He lifted his chin to Scott. "This scary motherfucker was sitting next to me covered in the same nasty shit I was; all that was left of his family. But he wasn't crying. No. He looked older, bigger, and badder than me and I wasn't prepared for what happened next."

I turned to Scott expecting him to pick up the story, but instead, he looked toward the kitchenette, jaw twitching from being clenched so hard.

My eyes met Logan's. He pushed a lock of hair from his forehead. "This crazy son of a bitch launched himself off the floor, screaming like a madman. They hadn't tied us to anything, just tied our hands in front of us. In *front* of us. I suppose they didn't think two teenage boys were any match for three wolves. Luckily, they were wrong.

"Scott was a force to be reckoned with. He poked his fingers into the first one's eyes and wrapped his tied hands around the dude's neck before the other two even moved. In the years since, I've never seen a human move so fast. It wasn't like a supernatural being, it was, I don't even know."

"It was someone who didn't care if they lived or died," Scott finally said. "All I could see and hear was my little sister and how they ripped her apart and feasted on her like hyenas; like the fucking monsters they are."

"Before the first one hit the ground with a broken neck, the other two were on Scott. I realized I needed to do something." Logan tried to smile. "I couldn't let him be the only hero if we actually got out of it alive, which I didn't think we would. So I used my linebacker skills, zeroed in on the bigger one, and leveled that motherfucker.

"Then he picked me up and smashed me against the wall like a wet blanket."

I had to cover a laugh, which probably wasn't the right reaction, but it still came out.

Scott tried to smile. "Been there, done that, eh, sweet thing?"

"Yes. Wet blanket is the perfect description. That's what I felt like when Isaac threw me against that tree. Made the same sounds, too."

Logan said, "I knew you'd understand. Your dad laughed at that part too."

For some reason, that brought me a measure of peace.

"Somehow, I rammed a pipe through the chest of the second one," Scott said. "I was sure Logan was dead. I yelled and ran at the bastard wolf about ready to rip Logan's throat out." Scott cleared his throat. "I hit him in the head."

Logan did laugh this time. "Hit him in the head? You pounded him so many times with that lead pipe, there wasn't a head left."

"Yeah, well, he deserved it."

"I didn't say he didn't deserve it. It was just more than 'I hit him in the head.'"

Scott shrugged and looked back at me, almost shyly.

"How many times have you told this story?" I asked.

They glanced at each other, then back at me. "Once to the local police, once to the FBI, once to your dad, and once to Oliver and Shawn. Now to you," Scott said.

"You told the police and FBI a pack of wolves killed your family and you killed two of them? And they believed you?"

"Story's not over yet, sweetheart," said Logan. "That son of a bitch with the hole in his chest from the pipe changed into a wolf in front of us. Later we found out I had five broken ribs and a punctured lung while Scott had two dislocated shoulders, a broken collarbone, a broken ankle, and three broken ribs. As much as we wanted to try and kill him, the adrenaline was gone and neither one of us could hardly move.

"The wolf was silver/gray with a black star of fur on its forehead. He laid on the floor for a few minutes until he was able to move. He could have killed us, changed us, whatever he wanted. Instead, he grabbed a cell phone in his mouth from the floor and dropped it by Scott. Then he ran and jumped through a window."

"What?" I said.

"Exactly," said Scott and Logan at the same time. Then Logan added, "We're still not sure what that was all about. We've never seen a shifter with those markings since. We don't know if he felt bad, if Scott impressed him with his killing ability, or if he just didn't think he could kill both of us since he was injured."

"He totally could have killed you," I said.

"We know that now," Logan said.

"I used the cell phone to call 911," Scott said.

"And you told the police and FBI werewolves killed your families and you killed them?"

"No," said Scott with a shake of his head. "We both knew no one would believe us. It was obvious we'd been kidnapped and hurt. It was written off as a home invasion and robbery. There were news headlines for about three weeks, then the media moved to other juicy stories.

"Our families had money and good insurance policies. We used the money to put ourselves through college with business and law degrees while we brainstormed Masters Security so we could figure out how to find and fight monsters legitimately." Scott waved his arms toward his office.

"And Shawn, Oliver, and my dad?"

"Over the years, we met Hunters. We met Oliver then Shawn. They fit what we need for humans fighting super strong monsters and they're smart. As you know, seven years ago I met your dad. With his experience and knowledge as a Shadower, we made perfect business partners." Scott shrugged. "Now you know why I hate shifters."

"But I've always tried to get him to see one wolf helped us, so maybe they're not all bad," said Logan.

Scott rolled his eyes and stood, balancing himself on his crutches.

"They're not," I said, standing as well. I put my hand on Scott's cheek.

"I'll believe it when I see it."

"What about the shifters you've met since you've been spending time with Beck and me?"

Scott stared at me until Logan cleared his throat.

"Jury is still out on them," Scott said.

I wasn't going to change his mind in just a few months, so I let it go for now.

"I'm so sorry about the loss of your families. I lost my parents, but I didn't watch them die. I can't even imagine."

Scott turned his head to kiss my palm.

"Can I kiss her, too?" Logan asked.

Scott grunted and Logan laughed.

It lightened the mood in the room, but my heart still hurt for the friends.

Chapter Fifteen

I WAS ON INFORMATION OVERLOAD. If I could get Beck and Scott to actually *talk* to each other, they'd see they had a little bit in common. There was so much knowledge they could share with the other. So much knowledge they could share with *all* of us.

I needed to get Shawn alone to find out what shifter he was and why Scott and Logan didn't know. I needed Holly to see I wasn't the enemy.

"What are you thinking?" Scott asked.

We were sitting in my dad's office. Logan had offered to drive us home but Scott said he had more to talk about.

"I'm thinking about the future. The future we can all build."

"Am I part of that future?"

"Of course." Then I realized he might mean something different than I did. "A business future," I quickly added.

He gave me one of his not-really-a-smile smiles. "I may as well keep telling you the dirty past while we're here. It's like a band-aid; we've already ripped off one, may as well rip off another."

"Ummm..."

"You're so cute when you're flustered and not sure what to say." He paused and took my hand. "Oh, cupcake."

"Cupcake?" I snarled, ripping my hand from his.

"There you are," he winked. "I was worried you'd reverted back to your teenage self."

"I haven't been a teenager in what feels like forever," I said on a sigh as I sat down.

"I wasn't a nice guy as I tried to maneuver my newly discovered world of monsters." He rubbed a hand down his face.

"You were younger than me. I can't even imagine."

"Good. Don't imagine. I was a bastard."

I waited silently. What horrible things was he going to tell me?

"There were so many women, I'm ashamed."

"Who you killed?" I squeaked.

"What?"

"What?" I asked, hand over my mouth. How many people had he killed.

"Killed?"

"What else would you do to them?"

He stared, open mouthed, for about ten full seconds then broke into hysterics. "Oh, my innocent girl," he said through his laughter.

I felt my face heat. "Slept with?"

"Yes," he said, trying to stop laughing. "Except there wasn't any sleeping."

"You're such a pig!" I said, standing.

"Yes. I was. I am."

"I don't need to hear about your conquests." I pointed a finger at him.

"I was in a bad place. I drank, I slept around, I spent my days at school being the perfect student so I could get my degrees and start a business to help me hunt monsters. At night,

I tried to drown my hate with alcohol and sex. It worked for a while.

"Then I graduated from college with a business degree, a law degree, and no idea what to do next. I'd gotten kind of a reputation for winning fights."

"Was that because the women you slept with had boyfriends or husbands?" I flopped back in the chair.

Scott looked away. "Maybe."

I waited silently.

He looked back to me. "Shawn and Oliver were bouncers at one of the bars Logan and I liked to go to. They said they got paid to do side jobs, like escort people to events and be security, stuff like that, and thought Logan and I would be interested in making extra money. They thought we were just barflies."

"They didn't know you were rich boys with college degrees?"

As though needing something to do, he stood and crutched around the office. "I think they had a hunch, but they thought we'd work well together. They were right. We started with personal security and word spread. Using our fathers' business contacts, Logan and I got some security jobs at businesses and helped them find the holes in their security.

"We hired Shawn and Oliver and things kind of snowballed, in a good way, for us. Pretty soon we had more business than we could handle. We also started seeing some of the *unexplainable* security glitches that could only be explained by things that weren't human.

"A little over seven years ago, we crossed paths with your dad. We did a couple jobs together, but he waited a few months before he revealed to me what he knew."

"And then you worked together all the time?"

Resting by a chair, Scott sat down his crutches. "Basically. Tom liked what we were doing but said we could do more if we had an established security business. He helped us invest and make legitimate business contacts.

He waved his arm around the office. "Five years ago, we officially opened our doors as a Security Firm. It let us spend more time working and less time searching for jobs. Tom liked that it let him stay at home with you guys more. He did a lot of consulting over the phone and we did most of the grunt work. It worked for all of us."

I sighed. "So, how are we going to make this work for *us*? There is so much going on now with Isaac out there and now Lilith."

"We make a plan. We have Marie, you've met the rest of the team, Beck and I have agreed to play nice. We figure out where Isaac is and kill him."

"You make it sound so easy."

"It is. Kill the monsters. It's what I've been doing for the last thirteen years."

"But what about—"

"Kins." He used the chair to move to the edged of the desk. Resting his hip on the edge, he leaned over to take my hands. "There's always going to be another *what if* or another *what about* in our worlds. I know you're not used to it yet, but this is the way it is. We go day by day, we help the people who need it, we live."

"Except I don't get to live," said Abi from behind him.

I made a sound and ripped my hands away trying to see where she was. "Did you hear that? Hear her?"

"Who?" Scott said, looking behind him.

"Abi!"

"Who? What are you talking about?" He looked back to me and sat up, glancing to the door and back to me.

My phone rang. I ignored it. I jumped up, sending the chair sliding in to the wall. I ran around the side of the desk and grabbed Scott by the shoulders. "Did you hear her?" The panic in my voice made me sound wild, crazy.

"Kinsley! Who did you hear? Was it Holly?"

"No! It was Abi!"

"There's no one here," he said, reaching for my face.

Scott's phone rang. He carefully pulled himself from my grip. He looked behind him again then nudged me back to my chair.

He pulled his phone from his pocket. "It's Beck. He was probably trying to call you first."

I still didn't care. Nothing was more important than finding out if Abi was real (a ghost?) or a figment of my imagination.

"Marie's awake," Scott said.

Except maybe that.

MARIE WAS SITTING in a chair looking out the window when Scott and I walked in his house. Floyd sat in a chair about five feet away, watching intently.

Beck stopped me before I ran to her. "Something is not right."

"I'll deal with it later. Right now I just have to touch her," I said as I pulled away.

Marie looked so small and fragile. Someone had wrapped a blanket around her shoulders. She was still wearing a hospital gown and was hooked to the IV.

I knelt in front of her and pulled her hands to my face. "Marie?"

She turned her head slowly until her eyes met mine. They seemed to almost have a black-blue ring around the dark color of her iris. She blinked a few times slowly, and it was gone.

"Oh, Claire! Finally! I asked for you and Tom. This, this,

old man tried to tell me he was Floyd." Marie glared at him. "He's not my Floyd. I don't know why he thinks he can try to trick me. Where are we?" Her voice rose and fell with her distress.

"Marie, it's me," I said, trying to keep my tears in check.

"I know it's you, Claire! Where is Tom? And who are these people? Where are we and where are the others?"

I choked on a sob. She sounded *normal*, except for the fact she thought I was my mom.

"Marie, what year is it?" I asked.

"Dear lord, Claire! I thought we were over this. I've been here long enough to show you I'm pulling myself together. It's 1980."

I plopped back onto my butt. 1980? 40+ years difference?

Floyd took a breath.

"So," Scott mumbled to Beck, "exactly how do we handle this?"

"I am not sure. I have read research about working with patients of memory loss and Alzheimer's and trying to keep routines. However, I do not know what *routine* would mean in this case."

I looked at Floyd. "Do I pretend to be my mom? Do we try to convince her it's not 1980? What do we do?"

Floyd closed his eyes.

Rachel and Mei came in with some of Floyd's pictures, one of my photo albums, and Marie's photo album.

Marie acted like she wanted to stand, but only hovered a few inches above the chair before flopping back down, almost boneless. "Who are you?" she demanded to Rachel and Mei.

Rachel sat on the floor next to me and held out her hand to Marie. "I'm Rachel. Nice to meet you. This is Mei. We have some pictures to show you."

Marie looked them up and down then held out her hand to

each woman in turn. Not a good handshake, either, a wimpy one, which surprised me. Marie taught me young to shake *like a man* because it was intimidating to some people and showed you weren't weak to others.

"How do you know Claire?" Marie asked.

Rachel turned wide eyes to me. She raised her eyebrows. I waved my hands at the photo albums and shrugged. At least this was *something*.

"Do you want to look at some pictures?" Rachel said again.

"I love pictures!" Marie said.

Rachel smiled at me.

I wasn't sure what was going to come of this. Right now, I didn't care; Marie was awake.

Rachel was amazing. For the millionth time in my life, I thanked God for giving me a best friend who always had my back no matter what.

While Marie looked at the photo albums, I sat for a moment processing what to do. She was awake.

Her eyes.

The strange ring. It was like when Beck attacked me and the Monarchs were in control.

"Beck." I opened our connection.

"*Yes?*" He seemed surprised I was communicating with him this way. "*What is wrong?*"

Part of me loved he knew me so well. Part of me was scared out of my mind.

"*You're right. Something's wrong with Marie. Did you notice her eyes?*"

"*I did not.*" He glanced to Marie and Rachel then met my gaze.

"*It's different now. But when I first sat down by her, she had a ring of blue-black fire for lack of a better explanation. It was like the night you attacked Scott and me.*"

Beck flinched.

"I'm not trying to bring up anything to argue about. I'm trying to tell you what I saw. Something is wrong with Marie. When Isaac kidnapped me, he had the same look in his eyes while he was communicating with the Sovereignty. I was right. She's under his control. What do I do?" If I had been speaking out loud, my voice would have broken. As it was, I was having trouble not throwing myself into Beck's arms and crying my eyes out.

I'd wanted to be wrong about Marie. It wasn't that I wanted Mei and Floyd to be traitors, but I didn't want Marie to be linked to Isaac.

"He will need to die in order to break the connection." Beck's voice helped calm me. "We will find him and we will kill him. I will not allow anything to happen to her or you."

I took a deep breath and reached out to squeeze Beck's hand.

"Do you recognize anyone?" Rachel asked.

Marie was looking through Floyd's pictures. She was able to point out everyone. Floyd would nod each time she got the names right. Slowly, she seemed to sit a little straighter.

"Where are they? Why aren't they here? Who are you all, again?

"Let's look at the pictures from when Tom and Claire were done hunting," said Rachel. She handed over my photo albums.

Marie turned to me and scrunched her face. "Done hunting? Why on Earth would you stop hunting, Claire? You promised to never stop until Isaac was dead so he could never hurt me again."

I looked to Floyd.

"She stopped hunting when she got pregnant, Marie." Floyd wiped at a tear.

"Oh. Oh. That's right. Pregnant. The twins."

"Not twins," I said. "Just one baby. Show her my picture, Rach."

Rachel flipped open my album and showed Marie a few baby pictures; some with just me and some with my parents and her.

"Is this Kinsley or Karly?"

"That's Kinsley as a baby." Rachel pointed at me.

Marie tilted her head. "Where's the other one?"

Floyd dropped his cane.

"What?" I looked to Marie, Rachel, Floyd, Scott, and finally Beck. "The *other one*?"

"Two babies. Kinsley and Karly."

I felt my knees weaken. What? The? Hell? A sister?

"Floyd?" I whispered.

Floyd gripped his chest and fell to the floor.

Mei screamed.

Chapter Sixteen

I HATE HOSPITALS. The smells. The sounds. The death.

Death.

I was so damn tired of death.

When would it end?

The sound of Floyd's heart monitor beeped with a reassuring cadence. Scott and Mei sat with me in the hospital room offering what little comfort they could in this situation. Beck said he couldn't handle the smell of the blood right now.

I needed Beck with me, and his immortality was keeping him away. Since when had the smell of blood bothered him?

Yet another reason I couldn't afford to get more emotionally involved with Beck. While I kept telling Scott he was prejudiced against what he considered monsters, was I now doing the same thing? Beck used to be human, but he wasn't anymore.

Of course, neither was I.

But I didn't need blood to survive.

With a huff, I shook my head and furrowed my brow. No time to worry about it now. I needed to worry about Floyd.

And what about this sister nonsense? A second baby? A

twin? I couldn't trust anything that came out of Marie's mouth. Until I could talk to Floyd, I was going to pretend Marie hadn't said a word.

The nurse came in and looked at Mei and me. "Your grandfather suffered a heart attack."

It was easier to say he was our grandpa than to try and explain our situation. So far, no one had batted an eye at the fact Mei and I didn't look related.

"Will he need surgery?" I asked.

"Just a bypass. He'll be fine."

I let out a breath I hadn't realized I'd been holding and hugged Mei. She wiped away tears and hugged me back.

"The doctor is going to need you to get us information about his current medications, allergies, primary care provider, and wishes about resuscitation if there's an issue. We also need his Medicare information and if he has supplemental insurance."

I stood frozen. I didn't know the answer to any of it. Shit.

"We'll organize all the information and get it to you as soon as possible." Scott was way better at lying than me.

"Thank you. I'll let you know as soon as surgery is scheduled." She left us alone.

"How are we going to get all that info?" Mei asked.

"I run a security firm. I've already done the background check on him. Now I'll just get his medical records."

"Or I can transfer him to Beck's medical facility. That would be easier. And safer," I said.

"Safer?"

Oh yeah. I hadn't even had a chance to tell Scott what was going on. When I was done telling him what I saw in Marie's eyes, he blinked a few times and sat down.

"Say something?"

"When the hell were you going to tell me all this? Why

does Alexander know everything before me?" Scott waved an arm in the air.

"Really? That's what you have to say?" I swear. Men's egos are way more fragile than women's.

"I'm going to get some coffee," Mei said. "Why don't we all step out of Floyd's room."

"When were you going to tell me?" Scott said.

"I'm telling you now."

"That's not enough, Kinsley. I can't keep being second in your life."

Mei pulled us both to the hall and shut Floyd's door.

Throwing my hands up, I said, "Why are you doing this right now? There are way more important things to worry about than at what moment you and Beck know things."

"You're the one who said we all have to work together."

"If you *must know right now*, because of my and Beck's connection, I realized what was going on while we were all sitting together and I couldn't say it out loud. I told him in our minds."

"I *hate* the connection you two have!"

"Sometimes so do I. And sometimes it's a great thing, like when I can't talk out loud. Or when I've been kidnapped by a lunatic vampire! Remember how our connection saved my life? I can't change it, so how about we embrace it! Quit being an asshole!" Okay. So I *was* more angry than I thought.

"Sorry," I said quickly, holding up a hand when he looked like he was ready to yell back. "I just can't keep fighting with you about the same things. We don't have the time and I don't have the energy to rehash every little thing that gets your panties in a twist about Beck." I swear his lips fought a smile. That was a good sign, so I forged on. "I will do my absolute one-thousand percent best to tell you and Beck everything equally.

But you're going to need to understand he might know things before you because of our Shadower bond."

For a moment I wondered if he'd argue with me again.

"Okay," he said. "You're right. What's done is done. You're bonded with Beck and there's not a damn thing anyone can do about it." He sighed deeply and closed his eyes.

"You should rub your temples to add to your show of distress," I almost growled at him. "This all must be so difficult for you." Hiding my sarcasm would have been impossible, so I didn't even try. "Have you even taken two seconds to think about how stressful it is for me? If you weren't on crutches, I'd probably punch you in the arm. Or maybe the face. You act like I want all this! I don't! I didn't ask for this! I don't want to sound like a victim, but could you quit treating me like a willing participant?"

Scott opened his eyes, but his face was unreadable.

I was really liking being able to speak my mind. I wasn't sure if it would *do* any good, but it *felt* good.

"You haven't acted like a victim since I met you. I don't expect you to act like one now. I've never said I'm sorry so many times in my life. You bring out my protective side."

"Well, right now, Floyd is the one who needs protecting, not me."

"That's not true. You always need protecting."

I waved a hand at his broken leg. "Last I checked, I can damn well take care of myself."

He was opening his mouth to argue when we noticed Beck coming down the hall.

"How does he always know when to show up? Did you *summon* him?" Scott asked.

"I'm about ready to shove your air quotes up your ass." I took a step forward, seriously considering punching him.

Beck chuckled as he reached us. "She did not *summon* me. I had things to take care of."

"What's more important than helping me with Floyd and Marie?"

"I *was* helping you, my dear."

"You said the smell of blood was bothering you."

"It was. I should not have told you, however we agreed to always be honest with one another. I took care of that and I took care of having Floyd moved to the medical facility." Beck looked to Scott. "I believe Dr. Chavez left you a voicemail because you did not answer. Your friend Oliver has woken up. He was asking for you."

"Shit," Scott said, pulling his phone from his pocket and stepping away.

"That's great news!" I said. I glanced around. "Where's Mei?"

"She is on her way to the medical facility. She said she was tired of listening to you fight," Beck said.

Yikes. Now I felt bad. I pulled out my phone to send her a text.

"I also set up a meeting with Lilith for us once we get Floyd and Marie moved."

I almost dropped my phone. "Lilith? Why?" The thought of being in the same room with her again made me cringe. I also didn't want her anywhere near Beck.

"She can help us find Isaac."

I had wondered if she could maybe do that when Beck told me about her being at the Inn when he was changed. I didn't want her around anyone I knew, loved, or cared about though.

"How are we going to keep her from attacking everyone?"

Beck raised an eyebrow.

"She's a damn succubus. She needs sex. How are we going

to keep her from trying to have sex with everyone she comes in contact with?"

"We will make a contract. She will have to uphold it."

"Yes, I'm sure the Queen of the Sluts will be morally obligated to uphold your contract."

"Queen of the Sluts?" Beck smiled. I forgot how damn good looking he was when he really smiled.

"It's the name I gave her when we met. I think it's fitting."

"Let us not call her names when I bring her in to negotiate. I will not let her call you names, so you will not call her names."

I supposed that was fair. Didn't mean I wasn't still going to call her Queen of the Sluts in my head or when she wasn't around. It also sounded like a parent having to keep their child in line. Maybe I was being a *tiny* bit childish. And possibly passive-aggressive.

"You take care of negotiations with her. I'm going to stop arguing about stuff and let those who are the experts take care of the things they know about. We *all* need to let the experts be in charge."

"I agree," Scott said from behind me, clearing his throat. "Alexander, thank you for setting up the move to the medical facility. While I was talking to Beth about Oliver, we talked about Floyd. She said she can get surgery scheduled as soon as she has his records. I need to get over there to be with Oliver. I think someone we know needs to transport Marie to the medical facility, too."

I appreciated Scott's *go-get-em* attitude. I was tired of making decisions.

"I am sure the hospital will need you to make the request for Floyd, Kinsley."

I had no problem letting these two take charge. This had nothing to do with men vs. women. This was about me being tired and stressed out.

We set up an ambulance for transport, and as soon as I had Floyd situated with Beth, I was going to move Marie to the medical facility, too. I had no idea if Isaac could actually control her or just listen through her. I knew Beck could control me so I had to assume Isaac could do the same. But then he'd be showing his hand. He probably didn't know I knew what he knew.

Once again, I was so tired of my complicated life. I seemed to think and say that a lot.

It wasn't safe to have Marie around us and that broke my heart. She was back with me but she wasn't *with* me. Was it safe to have her at the medical facility? Maybe it would be better to just keep her with me at all times.

Floyd was unconscious and I didn't have the energy to have small talk with the ambulance staff. I sat by Floyd's gurney and rested my head back, closing my eyes.

Scott went ahead of us to get there faster and see Oliver. I was looking forward to seeing Oliver as well.

Beck was following the ambulance so we'd have a way to get back to the house. I enjoyed the peace while I could. There probably wasn't going to be much peace in my life for a while. Again.

Once the ambulance arrived at the medical facility, things happened quickly. Floyd was taken to surgery and Beck and I went to find Scott and Oliver.

Scott sat in a chair reading a book and Oliver lay unmoving in the bed.

"I thought he was awake," I whispered.

Oliver's eyes popped open. "Kinsley! You're okay!"

His worry for me caused tears to pool in my eyes. "Of course I'm okay! You're not, though! I'm so damn sorry for getting you broken!" My voice cracked and Scott stood while Beck put a protective arm around my shoulders.

"This?" Oliver said, raising his casted arm. "I've had way worse. This wasn't your fault. Please don't cry."

I pulled away from Beck and gave Oliver a hug and wiped away my tears. "How do you feel?"

"Like I got beat up by a vampire." He laughed.

"You're really okay?"

"Yes. I wouldn't lie to you. I've got a headache and my body hurts from laying in this bed for so long, but I'm good. Dr. Chavez is setting me up with physical therapy so I can take a walk."

I let out a huge breath and fought more tears. Oliver was okay. Maybe everything else would work its way out, too.

"One step at a time. I've just got to start dealing with one thing at a time."

All three cocked their heads, and Scott raised an eyebrow.

"I can talk to myself if I want to. It's been a crazy week. Month. Life."

Scott laughed.

"Fill me in," Oliver said. "What day is it? How long have I been out? Did we lose anyone?"

"Now that I know you're okay, Scott can give you details. Call or text me if you need anything." I gave him a kiss on the cheek and his dark skin pinkened.

"What was that for?" Oliver looked to Scott and back to me, eyes wide.

"You're part of our family now buddy, whether you want to be or not. Get used to my touchy-feely ways."

"Just as long as it's not *too* touchy-feely," Scott said with a chuckle. "I've never seen Oliver blush. I wondered what it would take."

"Ha, ha. I'm going to get things figured out with Marie. I'll be with Beck and Nate. I'll talk to you later, okay?" I gave Scott a kiss on the cheek, too.

Beck nodded to both men and took my hand. An electric shiver rushed up my arm. Scott's eyes narrowed. I shook my head at him and let Beck open the door and usher me out.

"What was that all about?" I asked as soon as the door closed.

"What?" he said innocently.

I lifted our joined hands.

"After giving kisses, I found I needed to touch you."

"Territorial much?"

The electricity traveled from our fingers to my toes and back.

"Stop doing that!"

"I am not doing it. It must be you."

"What does it mean?"

"It has to do with our Bond."

"No. It did this when we first met."

He looked around and pulled me into a closet. It all happened so fast, I didn't have time to do much but stammer some incoherent words of confusion.

And then I wasn't confused.

He backed me against the door and when his whole body pressed against me, the electricity was more than I could handle. I gasped and his mouth covered mine.

The kiss was carnal and demanding. Almost punishing.

And I loved every second of it.

I was tired and stressed and I wanted to just let go. I knew it was a bad idea.

I moaned and pressed into him. "Beck."

"Just give me a moment. I will not go too far. I need this. I need you."

He pummeled my mouth with his tongue and I didn't protest. He moved his mouth to my neck and I didn't protest.

I felt his teeth.

And I still didn't protest.

If he had asked, or even broke skin without asking, I don't think I would have objected. That's how much I wanted him.

"Oh, Beck, what's happening?"

"We belong together," he said softly into my neck. "Not just because you are my Shadower, but because you are *you*."

I took a deep breath and his scent invaded my senses. With my eyes still closed, I sought out his aura and his thoughts. Both slammed into me like a freight train.

"Need her. Want her. Protect her. Need her."

His thoughts, aura, and scrape of teeth on my neck sent me over the edge.

Orgasm.

Holy Shit.

Beck breathed in deeply.

"You taste amazing."

Wait. What? He'd bitten me?

I shakily shoved him away and almost slid down the door. My damn legs didn't want to support me.

Beck looked as dazed as I felt. "Why did you push me?"

"You bit me!" I grabbed my neck.

"No, I did not!"

I hadn't heard him raise his voice in anger recently and it caught me off guard. Why was he mad? I was the one who had been bitten.

But I hadn't. I pulled my hand away and looked at it. Nothing. I checked again just to be sure.

Nope. No blood.

"The taste of your skin, Kinsley. The taste of your orgasm. I would *never* take your blood without your permission. I thought you knew that!"

How had I gone from burning hotter than a supernova, to orgasm, to being angry, to now feeling guilty?

Love is exhausting.

Wait! Love?

"What about love?" I asked before I could think better. Mental head slap.

He sighed. "I cannot offer you love; I am not capable. However, I can offer you protection, strong feelings, and amazing orgasms. All you have to do is say yes."

I closed my eyes and took a deep breath. He had to be giving off pheromones, because the air tasted like Beck and sex and I shuddered with need.

I turned and walked out the door.

Chapter Seventeen

THE RIDE to Scott's was laced with sexual and angry tension; it was not a good combination.

Beck tried once in the parking lot to talk to me, but I held up my hand and shook my head. I wasn't ready to talk about what happened in the hospital closet.

Riding in the strained silence of the car with him was physically painful. The air was so thick, it felt like I would choke on it. I couldn't get a full breath of air, and my vision had narrowed to almost comical tunnel vision.

When Beck pulled into Scott's driveway, I got out of the car before he shut off the engine. Even being out of the car didn't help. I was gasping in short breaths when Nate opened the door. I threw myself into Rachel's arms and burst into tears.

"Oh, honey," she said into my hair.

Again, the greatest thing about a best friend is you don't even have to say a word. She took me to the kitchen, pulled out ice cream and a bottle of flavored vodka, and grabbed some spoons and shot glasses.

"Spill," she said.

I heard the car screech out of the driveway and choked on a sob.

Nate poked his head in. "What in the hell happened? I haven't seen him that angry in, well, I don't know if I've ever seen him that angry. Maybe when I accidentally hurt you, Kinsley?" He shook his head. "No. I think he's even angrier."

"Grab Raven and leave, Nathaniel," Rachel said.

"No," I said, covering my face. "Grab Raven and stay, Nate. I need people to talk to." I put my arms on the table, dropped my head down, and released another sob.

"Oh, shit. I'm torn between needing to run away and needing to know what's going on. I'll be right back," Nate said.

"Honey, it can't be that bad. Did Floyd die? What's wrong?"

I picked my head up. "No! Floyd's in surgery."

"Did Oliver die?"

"Why do you think someone died?"

"Because the last time you were this much of a mess your parents died and then Abi died. What did you expect me to think?"

Huh. "That bad?"

Rachel pushed the Ben and Jerry's and the glass of vodka to me. I shot the vodka and took a big spoon of cookie dough ice cream. It really wasn't good that alcohol and sugar could make me feel slightly better, but that's a problem for another day.

"I think I'm in love with both of them," I blurted as the alcohol hit my blood then burned in my fast metabolism. The rush was great for about three seconds. I burst into tears again.

Raven and Nate walked in just as I made my admission.

"Oh. That explains everything," Nate said. "No wonder he's pissed. You told him you're in love with Scott?"

Rachel poured me another shot; not that it was going to do any good.

I slammed it anyway.

"I didn't say a word to Beck. He pulled me into a closet at

the hospital, kissed me senseless, gave me an orgasm, and I freaked out! I feel like a teenager! I don't know how to handle relationships! I can't date or sleep with Scott because it will screw everything up with Beck! I can't date or sleep with Beck because it will screw everything up with Scott! I can't date or sleep with anyone else because Beck and Scott would fucking freak out and maybe kill them!"

I looked at my friends wide-eyed and panicky. I ate another bite of ice cream and took the bottle of vodka from Rachel. Who needs shot glasses?

Raven pulled the bottle from my lips. "Kinsley, stop. Breathe. Everything is going to be fine."

"Everything. Is. Not. Going. To. Be. Fine!" I stood, took the bottle back, and threw it at the wall.

The bottle shattered and pieces embedded in the sheetrock next to the fridge, the rest tinkling to the floor in a messy puddle.

"Maybe I should leave," Nate said, backing toward the kitchen door.

"Sit down!" I bellowed at him. "I need a man's brain and perspective."

Rachel watched me like I was a caged animal. I felt like one.

"Why do I care so much about sex? Not having sex?" I clarified. "I feel like the only virgin left in the world! Who cares? Why does it even matter?" I grabbed my hair and screamed at the ceiling.

I felt like I was having an out of body experience.

"You're a virgin?" Nate said in awe.

I charged.

"Fuck," Nate said as I slammed into him.

What was wrong with me?

"Kinsley!" I heard Rachel scream.

Nate and Raven wrestled me to the ground.

I couldn't breathe or see. I couldn't think.

"Kinsley?"

"Get out of my fucking head, Beck!" I screamed at the ceiling.

"Talk to him, Kins, maybe it will help," Rachel pleaded.

"You are in pain," Beck said in my head.

"Yes!" I screamed again.

"Oh shut up," said Abi. "You don't know anything about pain."

"NOOOOO!" I yelled.

"But she is dead," Beck said.

That was probably the only thing that could bring me back from whatever breakdown I was having.

"You can see her?" I asked.

"See who?" said Rachel, Nate, and Raven together.

"No one can see me but you," said Abi.

"I cannot see her, but I can hear her. How?" said Beck.

"So, I'm not crazy?" I asked.

"Oh, you're batshit crazy," said Abi. "But I'm real. Well, as real as a ghost can be. And apparently your vampire can hear me because of you. Interesting. You were supposed to be the only one who could see or hear me."

"I will be there soon. Why did you not tell me you could see ghosts?"

I arched my back in pain. Raven and Nate each had an arm and leg pinned, but I quit fighting for the most part.

"I didn't know I could see ghosts. I thought she was a figment of my imagination. I still think I'm having a mental breakdown."

"You take on too much on your own. You do not allow anyone to help. You are still just a child."

"I'm not a fucking child!"

Warm hands cradled my face. Her aura offered comfort I was needing. Rachel's face swam into view. I hadn't realized I was crying until I pried my eyes open.

"Breathe," she said gently. Bringing a breath in through her nose and then out her mouth, she nodded at me until I started to mimic her.

My heart rate slowed, Beck's voice faded from my mind, and Abi disappeared. As long as I was looking at Rachel I was okay.

"Talk to me," she said quietly.

"Abi has been here with me since Beck and I got back from Paradise. She's not here all the time. She just shows up when I'm stressed out so I assumed it was some weird cognitive breakdown thing. But, just now, Beck could hear her through me."

"Does Beck know you're okay now?"

I looked at the shapeshifters pinning me to the floor. "I don't think I am okay," I said on a sob.

"Let her go," Rachel said.

"No," Nate argued. "I won't have you in danger, Rach."

"Kinsley would never hurt me," she said. "Let her go."

Raven let go first. Nate squeezed my shoulder and thigh in a warning before rocking back in a crouch.

"What the hell is going on, Kinsley?" he demanded.

"I wish I knew. Nothing has been right in my world for too long."

"That was a wicked panic attack," said Rachel. She moved so she could wrap her arms around me.

I laughed on a sob. "I'm so glad I have you," I said through my tears.

"I'm so glad I have you, too," she said, hugging me tighter. "How about you take a shower then eat?"

I felt her lift her head from the top of mine. She was probably giving Nate a silent message.

"Steaks?" he said.

I smiled, finally.

Okay. One thing at a time. I could do this. With the help of my friends, I could do this.

"Where is Marie?" I asked.

"She's in her room. I checked on her right before you got here. She was asleep."

"We have to figure out the best place for her. Here with us where I can keep an eye on her or at the medical facility where someone can watch her twenty-four hours a day?"

"We'll talk about it soon. Just take some time and relax for a bit. Food and important discussions as soon as you're ready." Rachel ran her hand over my hair.

She helped me to the bathroom, and after one more tight hug, she left.

I stood under the stream of water and sobbed until my nose was plugged, my throat was sore, and my eyes were so swollen I could barely see. I hadn't cried like this since my parents died.

What was I crying for? Who was I crying for?

Abi. Marie. Beck. Scott. Floyd.

Me.

A loss of innocence and being so naive to think I could have a normal life. Except, what was a normal life, really? People who didn't know about our type of monsters dealt with human monsters and loss every day. They made it. They moved on.

I actually had the means to take care of *monsters*. Time to do something about it. My breakdown had given me a little clarity. I still wanted to sleep on it, but I think I had direction.

I took care to dry my hair and get dressed, giving my eyes time to not be so puffy. It mostly worked.

The kitchen had food and all the people I needed to talk to. Rachel, Raven, Nate, Scott, and Beck. Abi stood in the corner, too, but I was ignoring her for right now. If she didn't bother me, I wasn't going to acknowledge her.

"Okay," said Rachel with a drink in her hand. "I had a few shots while Kins was in the shower. This is going to be a form of an Intervention. I will be the lead talker and I get to decide who gets to talk and when."

Nate smothered a laugh when both Beck and Scott tried to say something and Rachel silenced them with a chop of her hand and something that sounded like "pfft!"

"There are a million things to clear the air about, and Kinsley just proved we have to do it. The elephant in the room needs to be killed." She took a big swig of liquid courage. "Or something like that. I never was good with metaphors. Or analogies. Or whatever they're called."

I raised my hand.

"Kinsley?" she commanded.

"Can I eat first?"

"Yes," she said regally, lifting her chin. "We shall all eat, drink, discuss, and be merry."

"Jesus fuck," Scott said under his breath. "Who does she think she is, the Queen of England?"

"I met the Queen," Beck whispered to him. "Rachel would have given Elizabeth a run for her money. All of the Elizabeths. And the Catherines."

Scott laughed.

Maybe Rachel was onto something. We were off to a good start.

Food and drink were handed out, and we took our seats around the huge table. Surprisingly, Beck and Scott sat next to each other at one end of the table. I sat at the opposite end.

I half expected Rachel to climb on the table itself, but she grabbed a bar chair and seated herself in the middle.

"Okay, item one is business. Is everyone going to play together nicely?" She pinned her gaze to Beck and Scott.

"May I speak, your honor?" Scott asked, sarcasm dripping from his words.

Rachel played it up. She raised her eyebrows and tilted her head as though in deep thought. "I'll allow it," she finally said. I could tell she was trying to keep from laughing.

"For fuck's sake," Scott said quietly to the floor.

"I'm sorry?" Rachel said. And then she couldn't hold it together any longer. Her laughter rippled over the table until everyone was laughing. Except Scott and Beck.

"Oh c'mon, you two," Rachel wheezed between laughing breaths. "Your way hasn't been working. Let's try mine. I'm trying to be funny and you know it. Lighten up, Masters."

Finally a smile touched both men's lips. "It is entertaining, at least," Beck said to Scott. "I suppose we are in need of some humor in all of this."

Scott poured a large glass of Scotch and saluted Rachel. He drank it all, poured another, and saluted Beck. "Playing nice, it is. Kinsley and I had a long talk today. I've been prejudiced against shifters and vampires. My family was killed by shifters and so I want, wanted, to rid the world of every monster there is."

At his pause, Rachel lost all humor, and jumped off the bar stool. She threw herself at Scott and he almost spilled his drink.

"Oh, Scott! Of course you hated them! No wonder. But, you know now, there are good and bad shifters and vampires just like there are good and bad people?" She wrapped her arms around his neck.

Eyes wide, Scott tried to pull away, but Rach wouldn't let go. "It's okay," he said, awkwardly patting her back.

I found it quite entertaining he had just said his family was killed and he was trying to comfort Rach.

Scott gently pushed Rachel into Nate's waiting arms. As soon as she was clear, he downed the second shot of Scotch in his glass.

"Okay, so, um, where was I?" he said, wiping his lips with the back of his hand.

"Playing nice?" Beck prompted.

"Yes, so." Scott took a deep breath and went to pour more Scotch but changed his mind. "There is no reason why we can't keep doing what we were doing with Tom but now with Kinsley, Alexander and his crew, and you guys."

"Are you sure?" Beck asked quietly. "What will happen when there are important decisions to be made?"

Scott went ahead and poured the shot. "We'll make them together."

"As in, the three of us, right?" I finally said.

Scott drank the amber liquor slowly, set down the glass, and met my eyes. "Yes. All three of us. We are a team and we need each other. We can also do the most amount of damage together."

"It will be epic," Rachel said with a hiccup. She hugged Nate and moved to stand by me. "Okay, next. Marie."

I took a deep breath and let it out through my mouth. I had no idea what to do.

"It's not safe for you to be with Marie," Scott finally said.

"On this, Masters and I are in agreement," Beck said with a nod. "Kinsley, you know she is under Isaac's control and he can hear all we discuss and do. That is not safe for any of us."

Tears gathered in my eyes, but I knew they were right. "What do I do?"

"This isn't about what *you* have to do, sweetheart," Scott said. "You will never make any decisions alone anymore; that's what we just decided. We make the decisions together."

I thought I was all cried out, but this show of solidarity

and the fact we had all been together for over an hour and hadn't fought was going to make me weepy. More than I already was.

"We will transport her to the medical facility. Every employee is a shifter or a vampire. She will be in a room that looks like a bedroom, instead of a hospital room, and we will keep her under constant watch until we find and kill Isaac."

When Beck said it like that, it sounded so simple.

"Last," I said. "Two babies? Wouldn't someone have known if there was a twin?"

Beck nodded. "I will have one of the investigative researchers track down the birth records just to be sure, but I have never heard of such a thing until today."

"She *is* crazy, Kins," Rachel said. "And she's possessed by a crazy vampire. Maybe it was Isaac making up stupid shit to continue trying to mind-fuck you."

That made more sense than anything else that had been happening. I nodded and saluted her with my water glass.

"There's still one more thing to figure out," Rachel said.

I looked to the corner for Abi, but didn't see her. "My ghost problem?"

"No. We have to figure out which one of these men you need to have sex with first, and then everything will be solved."

I choked on my water as Beck shot to his feet and Scott got a crutch under his arm to stand as quickly as he could.

"First?" Beck echoed.

"Yes. She's going to have to have sex with both of you. It's the only way she's going to be able to make a decision and it's also how we're going to cut the sexual tension that's been floating around you all for months.

"I say she starts with Beck and then Scott, you get your turn when your leg is no longer broken. I'm sure you can't perform quite right with a cast."

"Well," said Nate, taking Rachel down the hallway, "that was interesting."

Raven excused herself from the table.

The two men and I stared at each other. I felt my cheeks heat.

"Maybe she's right?" I squeaked.

"Oh, hell no!" Scott bellowed as Beck said, "Absolutely not!"

"Just listen," I said. "I can't keep dealing with your sexual advances and innuendos! It's exhausting! Either we do what Rachel said, and find out who I'm supposed to be with, or we have a strictly friend and business relationship."

I hoped they couldn't see the trembling in my hands. I wasn't sure what scared me more: that they would agree to Rachel's absurd plan, that I didn't think I could follow through with, or that they'd try to quit getting me into bed.

"Kinsley's safety and the safety of all is more important than sex," Beck finally said. "I agree to keep a friendship and stop trying to push an intimate relationship."

I gripped my knees and looked to Scott. His eyes seemed to glitter with lust.

"I guess I can put safety above sex. For now. But as soon as Isaac is dead, I think Rachel is right. The sexual tension needs to be addressed."

Oh boy.

Scott turned to Beck. "Tomorrow we meet at Masters Security and introduce all our key players. We share information, we start actively hunting that son-of-a-bitch Isaac." He turned to me. "Then we start a training regimen so we can see how the monst—" he cleared his throat to cover his almost slip, "shifters, vampires, and humans can fight together to keep everyone safe and still cause maximum damage to the enemy. Good night, you two."

As Scott crutched down the hall, Beck met my gaze. "This is what you wanted all along, yes?"

"Yes."

"I hope you know what you are doing, Kinsley." He kissed me on the cheek.

"Me, too," I whispered.

"I will send a car to transport Marie," he said and let himself out the front door.

"You don't have a clue," said Abi. "This is going to be a clusterfuck and I can't wait to watch it all explode."

She laughed, a menacing sound that shouldn't come from a child, as I ignored her and went upstairs to Marie's room.

Chapter Eighteen

TIME IS SUCH A STRANGE BEAST. It takes forever to move forward, and at the same time it rushes by. So much was happening in such a short amount of time. There was so much to do and I needed it all done now.

The only thing I had control over was me.

How frustrating.

I watched Marie sit in a chair and stare out the window at the hospital facility. Yesterday, she hadn't said two words since I'd packed her bags and loaded her in a car. I hadn't said much either because I didn't know what to say. I figured she'd ask questions. Did she know what was going on? Did Isaac? When I was under Beck's control, I knew what was going on but couldn't do anything about it.

"Marie?" I said quietly.

She turned her blank stare to me.

"I have some meetings to take care of at the University. I'll be back tonight." I wasn't going to tell her I was really going to Masters Security; Isaac could hear things and I had to be careful.

She turned back to gaze out the window.

I left, tears gathering. I pressed my palms to my eyes and

took a deep breath. I wouldn't get her back until Isaac was dead. So that's what I was going to focus on next.

Shawn was waiting with a car.

"How's Floyd?" he asked as he helped me into the passenger seat.

"He should be awake, and he's not. But Beth assured me he came through surgery well and is healthy as can be for his age."

"That's good."

When he got in, he started the car but didn't go anywhere. He flexed his fingers on the steering wheel multiple times before finally clearing his throat. "You could tell I was a shifter when we met." It wasn't a question.

"Yes."

"Your dad knew, too. How?"

"I feel an electricity kind of thing and now I can see auras. Shifters have an orange ring. I don't know if it was the same with my dad or not. Obviously Scott doesn't know."

After a brief moment of silence, he said, "Will you help me tell him?"

"Yes, of course. Are you wanting to do it alone or with everyone else?"

"Let's see how things go with the whole group together and what other shifters are there. Then I'll decide."

"Won't the other shifters know you're a shifter?"

"Yes. But as a general rule, we don't 'tell' on each other. It's dangerous and can get you killed if the wrong people know. We try to protect each other."

He waited a beat then put the car in gear. "Don't you want to know what I am?"

I laughed and covered my face. "Yes. But I didn't want to be rude and ask. You're," I paused and looked at him out of the corner of my eyes. "You're sensual. I'm guessing you're some kind of cat, but not a cougar."

He smiled as he merged into traffic. "I've never had someone who wasn't my lover describe me as sensual." He noticed my blush and laughed. "Kinsley, you're just what we all need. You're this crazy combination of ass-kicking, innocent, leader, Shadower package."

That caught me completely off guard. "What do you mean: 'what we all need'?"

"Your dad was our glue. He understood shifters, vampires, humans. We *need* you. More than you know, obviously."

I didn't want to be anyone's glue. Did I?

"Your dad was able to diffuse the tension when we would disagree. I think you'll be able to do the same thing." He glanced at me. "You already have Scott agreeing to work with vampires and shifters. Your dad couldn't even get him to do that."

I laughed. "He's only agreeing because he wants in my pants."

"Picked up on that, did ya?"

"It's not like he's hiding it. I just want what's best for everyone. If he's going to try new things because I suggest them, I'm not going to stop him. I've also made it completely clear I won't sleep with him, so he's doing this because he wants to."

"People have controlled the world for thousands of years, on purpose and accident, with their bodies. Doesn't matter you said you won't sleep with him. In a man's mind, there's always a chance."

Wasn't that the truth.

The drive to Masters Security didn't take long. Shawn parked and walked with me to the front doors. Holly was at her desk, and her smile turned to a frown when she saw me.

Shawn immediately noticed. "What the fuck's her problem?" he whispered to me.

"I'm pretty sure she wants Scott, and Scott has made it

obvious he wants me. So, I'm competition and she doesn't like it."

"Well, she needs to get over it."

"Oh, okay." I snapped my fingers. "Did it work?"

He laughed as we got on the elevator. "Did you talk to her about it?"

"Sort of. It's not really on my list of important things right now. Maybe in a few months." I shrugged.

The office was full of people. I knew almost all of them. The only ones I didn't know were some humans who were employees of Scott's. Beck wasn't here yet.

Scott whistled to stop the conversations. "If everyone will grab any snacks and beverages, we'll meet at the big table in five. Dr. Alexander will be here in a moment." He came to us. "How's Marie?"

"Fine, I guess." My voice caught. Damn it. I thought I was over being emotional. I should have known better. "She didn't talk and she didn't put up a fight. I don't know if Isaac is there, in her mind, all the time or not. I don't know if her eyes changing color is the way to know. I just don't know enough about what the Bond means."

"We'll get through it," he said, giving me a one-armed hug.

I raised my brows.

"I'm trying to be professional but also understanding. Just friends, right?"

I smiled. "Thank you," I said, hugging him back.

A current of electricity flowed over my skin as the elevator doors opened. Lilith and Beck glided into the room and all conversation stopped again. Rachel, Raven, Mei, and I were the only women in the room but the sexual waves pulsing from Lilith didn't discriminate based on sex; she affected everyone equally.

"Turn. It. Down." I bit out. *"Beck,"* I said in my head. *"You promised she'd behave."*

Beck leaned and whispered something in Lilith's ear. She met my eyes and I swear she sent an extra wave of lust over me before she pulled it all out of the room like a physical manifestation. She was dangerous and unpredictable and I hated Beck thought we needed her.

"Gentlemen. Ladies." Lilith's accent wasn't quite British, but held the hint of something sensual all the same.

Scott leaned to me and whispered, "I tried to warn the group about her in hopes it will help. But if she throws off sex like that all the time, all the warnings in the world won't do a damn thing."

"I hate this," I said through clenched teeth. "We have *got* to get him to tell us why we need her. We can do it without her."

"No you can't," Lilith said as she moved in front of me. "But, I promised Beckford I would play nice, and I always keep my promises. And Beckford always keeps his." Her long black hair slid like silk over her shoulder as she turned to wrap her arm in Beck's.

Lilith had chosen to dress like a normal person for the meeting instead of dominatrix Barbie. I almost expected her to be in the corset outfit again just to show off. She wore a light sweater and skinny jeans with boots. Of course she looked like a damn model. I was trying not to be jealous of her looks, but it was hard. It's like it's in a woman's DNA to be critical of other women's looks. Especially when said woman is your competition. Sort of like Holly's issue with me.

But Lilith wasn't my competition. It just felt like it since she was the walking epitome of sex. And she hung on Beck like they were having sex every spare moment. Which they probably were since they had some kind of *agreement* I was supposed to learn about. I twirled Mom's ruby ring on my finger. I'd found myself doing that more and more when I was nervous or thinking.

"Please ignore her, Kinsley. We will discuss things later. I am sorry there was not time before," Beck's voice floated in my mind.

He was right. No reason to play into her fantasy of how wonderful she thought she was.

I turned my back to Lilith and gestured to the people in the room to sit. The table wouldn't hold everyone, but there were chairs against one wall for the others.

I took a deep breath and got the ball rolling. "I'd like to thank everyone for being here today. This show of solidarity makes me grateful to have all of you on our side, in this room as one team, knowing our job is to help those who can't help themselves. We fight for what's right and we stand up for the weak." I hadn't really planned on making a grand speech, but seeing all these people together in this room, made me think of Abi and her family. Of Marie. Of all the people who had received help from Masters Security for threats from the supernatural and regular threats of humans.

The room shifted from one of weariness to alertness. Everyone in here, except for Rachel and me, was a warrior. A fighter. They understood standing up for those who couldn't stand up for themselves.

"I'd really like to start by making introductions. We need to know who is who and how we are going to work together, to compliment each others' strengths.

"I know you all know who I am," the room chuckled, except for Lilith, "but I still want to say a little something. Not that long ago, I was a normal woman at college who didn't have a care in the world. Had I known about this place and all of you, I don't know what I would have done while my dad was still alive." I paused, trying to find the words to explain what I felt needed to be said.

"I'm not Tom Preston. I didn't get to see him in this setting with the members of Masters Security." I made eye contact with the employees. "But I know he trusted you or you wouldn't be here. So that means I trust you."

They nodded their thanks.

I made eye contact with everyone who worked for Beck. "You are all loyal to a fault and have already put your life on the line for me, my friends, and my family multiple times. For that alone, you have my eternal gratitude. But it's more than that. Because you are Beck's, that makes you mine. You are my family now, too."

Each shifter in the room bowed their head to me in understanding.

Feeling like I'd said too much, or maybe was grandstanding, I moved from the front of the room to see who would start with introductions. The room wasn't tense, but it held a feeling of unknown, like the beginning of a race while you waited for the starting gun to go off.

Nate stood. "I am Nathaniel. I serve Beckford Alexander and Kinsley Preston. I am a cougar."

Rachel stood next. "Rachel. I'm Kinsley's best friend and I'm only human."

Each person went through introductions. Beck's people: Raven, cougar; Gerald, wolf; Mei, leopard; Kevin, bear; Riley, wolf; Lucas, cougar. Gerald had only gotten back that morning and I was glad to see him. And while Mei wasn't really one of *Beck's people*, she was part of us now whether she wanted to be or not.

Scott's people: Logan, Shawn, Joel, and Quinn, all security specialists. They mentioned how as soon as Oliver had the all clear from Dr. Chavez, he'd be back at work. I hadn't met Joel and Quinn personally, but they nodded to me.

I made eye contact with Shawn when a few of Beck's shifters looked back and forth from Shawn to Scott wondering why Shawn hadn't said he was a shifter.

Shawn stood. "Scott, I have something to tell you."

Scott looked at me. I slid a hand into his and squeezed.

"Aw, hell," Scott said. "You're not human, are you?"

The shifters in the room growled as one, and Shawn held up a hand.

"How long have you known?" Shawn asked, trying to gauge Scott's mood and reaction.

"I didn't. Until right now. But I have to admit, I've wondered more than once if it was possible. Given my prejudice, as Kinsley not-so-nicely pointed out to me earlier, I ignored my instincts. I *like* you. I trust you. And you're a badass and one of my best men. So I figured I'd just ignore it. I'm sorry you didn't feel comfortable telling me before now."

Shawn let out a sigh. "I wasn't sure what you'd do. What either of you would do." He looked at Logan. "I know you hate shifters."

Logan addressed the shifters, who were on edge at the exchange. "Our families were slaughtered by wolf shifters. It's the reason we started this company. We never knew *good* shifters existed until all of you. I'll be honest, it's going to be tough to change years of negative thoughts and tendencies and wanting to kill shifters on sight."

Nate walked to Logan and shook his hand. "There are plenty of bad shifters, as you know. But we'll do our best to help you see we're just like you. Hell, you've been working with Shawn for years and he's your brother-in-arms. Does it change anything now you know he's a shifter?"

SECOND CHANCE

Logan looked at Shawn. "No. It doesn't change a damn thing. I'd still die for you, man."

"Same here," Shawn said.

"Same here," Scott added.

I gave Scott's hand another squeeze and moved to stand by Rachel. "This is going way better than I ever imagined."

"Agreed. Except for the Queen of the Sluts, this is awesome."

My eyes moved to Beck and Lilith. I'd been trying to ignore her. I was kind of surprised she hadn't thrown her sluttiness around the room again and she hadn't made any snarky comments. Was I being judgmental? Yes. Did I care? No.

Beck moved to the front of the group when it seemed everyone was done. Lilith stayed glued to his side. "This is Lilith. She has agreed to help us locate Isaac. I know you all know what she is. While normally we would line up to kill her, she is not to be touched. She is under my protection."

While that sank in, all eyes moved to me. I stood tall and didn't flinch.

"They're all waiting to see what you do," Abi said quietly from next to me. "They want to know why you're willing to share Beck with a demon succubus. They're picturing the three of you in bed together. Can you feel the weight of their stares and the sexual energy?"

I kept the steel in my spine. At least, I thought I did. I ignored Abi and her sing-songy voice. She moved in front of me and I tried not to look at her.

"You can't ignore me forever, Kinsley. You killed me and I'm going to stick around to see who else you kill."

I finally looked at her. Her eyes were red.

"*Beck? Can you see her? Abi is in front of me.*"

"*No. But I heard her. We will deal with this next. Do not worry.*"

I tried not to laugh. It wasn't funny. Rachel noticed my posture.

"Are you okay," she asked quietly out of the corner of her mouth. I knew the shifters could hear her even if the humans couldn't.

A few eyebrows raised around the room. I walked forward, through Abi. She hissed and disappeared.

"Lilith is under our protection. She will help us find and kill Isaac. That is the only way Marie will be safe," I said.

"And you will be safe," Nate said, moving to my side. "As Beck's menage, we follow the needs of the family. Kinsley is our Shadower. She is, and always will be, our number one priority. Sir, as long as Lilith follows the demands of the agreement and does not harm Kinsley, no harm will come to her."

Beck snarled. Fucking snarled. At Nate.

Raven, Gerald, Mei, Kevin, Riley, and Lucas moved from their seats to make a shifter cage around me. I felt protected. Loved. Shawn moved to join the group around me.

Lilith flipped her hair over her shoulder. "Interesting. Your shifters, Beckford, choose her over you."

"No." Nate's single word was an entire sentence and statement in one. The humans in the room stood. Our earlier camaraderie was ruined by Lilith's presence and words. Or was it ruined by Nate?

"In our family, Lilith, Beck and Kinsley are as one. You should know that. You will not come between them. Or us."

"Ohhh. Is that what you think, young cougar? No. No. I am only here to help. I owe Beckford." She squeezed herself closer to Beck, smashing her boobs into his arm, dropping her head to his shoulder.

How she was able to change from Queen of the Sluts to Catholic School Girl between one blink and the next was almost magic. Beck walked her to a chair, helped her sit, and came to Nate.

I wondered if Nate would kneel. I hoped we were well past that.

"Had you included me in your plans," Nate said quietly, "I wouldn't have needed to make this point. You made it look like you were on one side and we were on the other."

I glared at Beck. "You owe all of us an explanation."

Beck backed down. "Yes, I do."

"Thank you, everyone, for being here today," Scott said, taking the attention away from us. "We will begin a training schedule tomorrow. I'd like for humans and shifters to work together so we can learn each other's strengths and weaknesses and how to fight together. Dr. Alexander, Beck, has graciously offered his training facility as soon as construction is complete. Until then, we'll work here even though there isn't much room. We'll figure it out. I'd like everyone back at eight tomorrow morning."

People broke up and introduced themselves with handshakes and talking. I was happy at this part of everything.

Now to deal with Lilith.

Chapter Nineteen

"WELL," said Rachel.

The word hung in the car. As Nate drove us back to Scott's house, I went over the meeting in my head. Everything went perfectly until Beck had stood with Lilith and made it awkward.

"Did I screw things up?" Nate asked.

"Absolutely not," Rachel and I said at the same time.

"Mei?" Nate said. "As the *outsider*, what did you see? We have to look like we are together."

Mei growled. "The only thing out of place today was that damn succubus. She is the unknown and the one who doesn't fit. Having Beck seem to stand with her didn't make it look like you weren't together, per se, it was just..."

"Weird," I said.

"Yes, weird," Mei agreed with a shrug.

When we arrived at the house, Beck and Lilith were already there. How they arrived before us was a mystery, but that wasn't important right now.

"Thank you for agreeing to tell us what's going on," I said as we entered the kitchen.

Beck nodded, but didn't speak. It seemed he was gauging

my mood. I expected him to talk to me in my mind but he didn't.

Nate, Raven, and Mei flanked me in a protective triangle. Rachel trailed behind them. It was my impromptu entourage, and I kind of liked it.

Rachel waved an arm toward the ceiling. "So, um, I'll just go upstairs and leave you all to discuss business."

"Not on your life, chica," I said. "Everything going on with all of us affects you. You stay for anything that has to do with me. Without you, I don't get through things well."

Everyone sat except Beck. "Let me begin with an apology," he said.

Nate gaped at him and I looked in shocked confusion at Rachel and back to Beck.

"Yes," Beck said, "an apology. I made us look divided and weak in that meeting and it was bad strategy and planning."

"I should not have been there," Lilith chimed in.

When she wasn't oozing Queen of the Sluts, I could *almost* forget she was an enemy.

I pointed back and forth between Beck and Lilith. "Will you just get to the point and stop being so cryptic. Thank you for your apology. You're right: you made us look divided and stupid. So make it up to us and tell us what in the hell is going on."

"As Kinsley knows, Lilith was there when I was Changed," said Beck.

"Changed as in *changed*-Changed? Into a vampire?" Leave it to Rachel to be the first to recover from that bombshell.

Beck nodded. "Yes."

I did a two minute summary of Beck losing his wife and child and being *tricked* into becoming a vampire.

"Why don't I know any of this?" Nate asked. He sounded hurt.

"Nathaniel, when you joined me, it was so I could start building my power. It was not the time to share my past. When others learn our pasts, they have power over us. That was not our relationship. Now it is."

"What do you mean *building your power?*" I asked.

"This is where Lilith comes in. I'm sure you've all noticed there are not many vampires as part of my group. Just the few at the medical facility, and they were all brought in by Karlof."

I opened my mouth to say the vampires I knew and realized it was only Beth, Karlof, and now Jared. Holy shit! Why hadn't I noticed there weren't any other vampires? It was just shifters.

"Only Mya and Isaac, aka Dr. Gabriel Finch, were part of our group," said Nate. "Why?"

"I did not know until Lilith and I began exchanging information that it was all part of Gabriel/Isaac's agenda. He has been using me for years. Obviously. No one knew he was Sovereignty. He has been slowly dismantling the Monarchs for centuries. By finding Marie, he was able to kill another Monarch due to the power gained from Shadower blood."

I met Beck's troubled gaze. "How many Monarchs are left?"

"Two."

Everyone sucked in a startled breath.

"Three," Lilith said, lifting her chin to Beck. "Your status as lower-ranking is no longer."

"You're officially a full-blown Monarch?" Rachel asked.

"This is where things get more complicated. I may be a higher-ranking Monarch due to lack of numbers, but they do not consider me one of their own. Lilith knows every member of the Monarchs and the Sovereignty. The numbers are dwindling."

"In fact," Lilith cut in, "I've been working both sides and profiting lucratively. However, I think Isaac is on to me. It was a fitting stroke of luck for me when you all basically fell in my lap." She pointed at me. "You're the Silver Shadower. Your parents, you, and Marie were the last of the Shadowers. When your parents killed themselves—"

"How dare you!" I was on Lilith before I realized what I was doing. I had a hand wrapped around her throat and was lifting her from her chair when Beck grabbed me.

Lilith's eyes widened for a moment before she gained her composure. "I take it Beck didn't tell you?" She tried for innocent, but the tone in her voice proved she was trying to come between us.

Beck pried my fingers free and turned me toward him. "I will tell you later." He gripped my shoulders.

"You will tell me now!" I grabbed his arms to try and pull him off me.

Scott came into the kitchen. He took in the scene of me in Beck's hold and Lilith's chair flipped on the floor. "I suppose it would have been too much for y'all to wait for me to get here?"

"Lilith was just going to tell us about my parents *killing themselves*, which they *did not!*" I was uselessly trying to pull from Beck's concrete hold on me.

"We were going to tell her together without an audience," Scott said in a kind-of whisper to Beck.

"Someone better start talking," I said. "Tell me what?"

"I'll take this as my cue to leave," Lilith said on a laugh. "I expect to see you later, Beckford. You know where to find me." She walked out.

I didn't know where she was going or how she was going to get there, and a part of me thought I probably should, but I couldn't get the rest of my brain to catch up.

"Just say it! I'm tired of you guys keeping things from me."

"No one is keeping things from you, sweet thing. Beck just found out last night and we were going to talk to you after the meeting this morning. I didn't realize you guys were having a meeting after the meeting." Scott turned an accusatory gaze to Beck.

"Since I handled things poorly by having Lilith there, I wanted to apologize."

"And you thought that crazy bitch would keep her mouth shut?" Scott said. "You may be dumber than me when it comes to women. What's the point of living for thousands of years if you can't figure women out?"

"I have not lived for thousands of years," Beck said.

"Someone start talking!" I bellowed, finally pushing myself free from Beck.

Scott put a hand on my arm. "Lilith says the Sovereignty are the reason all the Shadower families are dead. They have slowly learned their identities over the centuries. Sovereignty take them, keep them alive for their blood for as long as possible, and eventually the Shadowers die. The Sovereignty use the temporary power to kill Monarchs. They actually approached Karlof about making synthetic blood for them like he's trying to do for Beck."

"That slimeball," I said. "I told you he couldn't be trusted!"

"He did not do it for them," Beck said.

"He also didn't tell you about it, which I find interesting," said Scott.

"I will deal with Karlof later," said Beck.

"So why on Earth would Lilith accuse my parents of killing themselves?" I asked, looking back and forth wildly between the two men.

"Lilith claims Isaac told her when your parents learned Isaac had found them, they ran their car off the road to keep from being taken captive," Beck said, moving back into my space.

I stepped back. The ringing in my ears threatened to take

me out. I didn't let it. "That's bullshit and ridiculous! My father would never drive off a cliff with my mother in the car! He also wouldn't leave me alone to deal with Isaac!"

"That's what I fucking said." Scott pulled me into a hug. He kissed the top of my head. "Someone's lying. Isaac. Lilith. Both of them. It doesn't matter because your dad would never do that."

"It makes more sense than Isaac killing them," said Beck quietly. "With the blood of two powerful Shadowers, he would have been virtually unstoppable. He would not have wasted their blood."

I understood what Beck was saying, but he was talking about my parents. "What else did your darling Lilith tell you?" I sounded as bitchy as I felt.

"My brother is a member of the Sovereignty. It is part of the reason I was Changed to begin with. The Monarchs thought I would be able to help them kill him. For whatever reason, Isaac convinced them not to tell me."

Another damn twist.

"Your brother?" I asked.

"Philip. He was just as jaded and evil as our father. I cannot imagine him as a vampire." Beck closed his eyes.

"You learned all this last night?" I asked.

"Yes," said Scott, still holding me in his arms. "I still don't know if we can believe her."

"She does not have any reason to lie," said Beck.

"She also doesn't have any reason to tell the truth," Scott countered. "You believed everything that came out of her mouth." Scott turned to Nate. "What do you know about demons? Since they're having sex, can she somehow fuck with Beck's mind along with his body? I haven't encountered enough demons to know."

"Having sex?" Mei finally said. She'd been a silent sentinel through the entire morning.

"That's my fault, too," I said. "If I hadn't gone to Ecstasy to begin with, Lilith never would have known how to find Beck."

"That is not true," Beck said. "She has known how to find me from the moment I became a vampire. It is another thing succubus are able to do. They have many, *powers*, if you will."

"Back up to your brother being *alive* and a vampire. Shit. A member of the Sovereignty. What the hell, Beck?" I said. I pulled away from Scott and moved to sit with Rachel. She linked her fingers with mine and gave me a silent nod of support. Thank God for best friends.

"He has left me alone for eight hundred years. He is not an issue right now. I cannot believe he would even care about me after all this time. Until I see him with my own eyes, I am not even going to worry about it. We have more pressing matters. Kinsley, do you want to talk about your parents?"

"There's nothing to talk about. They're dead. They didn't kill themselves. I can't change the past so let's focus on the future."

A brief silence followed. Rachel squeezed my fingers tight in hers.

"In that case," Scott said, "let's start talking about the future. After our meeting with Lilith last night, Beck and I shared some of our ideas with each other."

"You guys were busy last night," I said.

Scott shrugged. "You needed the evening with Marie and some space from us after Rachel's impromptu meeting of the minds."

I smiled. He was right; the space had been nice. It's not like Marie and I had talked or anything, but watching movies and falling asleep in her room had been just like old times.

Before she was possibly under the mind control of a crazy vampire.

"What are we going to do about Isaac?" I sighed.

"Hopefully kill him," Nate said.

"One step at a time," said Scott. "We are severely outnumbered if Isaac has the power Lilith says he has. There are now a dozen members of the Sovereignty. And as you guys know, from killing that nest in Oregon, he's randomly having vampires made. We need more people on our side so," he waved a hand at Beck.

Beck nodded and said, "I want to get the word out that Screamers is neutral territory and I am looking to grow my power in the area. Offer safe haven for any and all supernatural beings if they are willing to follow our rules."

"Smart," said Nate, nodding.

"We also need to train. Really train. Weapons, kill tactics, and how to subdue without killing," said Beck.

Scott raised an eyebrow.

"We're doing things differently now," I said, understanding what Beck was getting at. "You've always gone in to kill, no questions asked. We need beings to know we're willing to talk first, but we have the upper hand."

Beck nodded. "You also need to train mentally, Kinsley. Find out what you are capable of and what we are capable of together. That is where Lilith comes in. As a demon, she has special skills of her own and knows more about Shadowers than anyone we have met so far, except Marie. But Marie cannot share anything with us. Lilith thinks you might be able to use your Shadower abilities to break Isaac's hold."

"Really?" A sliver of hope slid through me.

"The final thing we need to talk about is blood," said Scott.

"What?" said Mei.

"Karlof and the synthetic blood," said Beck. "He has

created a formula. It is not perfect. When Dr. Chavez explained it to me in a way humans would understand, she said it was like drinking almond milk versus regular milk, whatever that means."

"How does Beth know what almond milk tastes like? How old is she?" Scott asked.

"She has only been a vampire for about ten years. She had terminal cancer and Karlof and I made the decision to show her vampires and ask her if she wanted to join us. She obviously did."

I thought through that. "What else can being a vampire *cure?*"

"What do you mean?" asked Beck.

"Floyd. Marie. Would Floyd be eternally old? Would Marie's mind be fixed?"

"Are you suggesting to turn a Hunter and a Shadower into vampires?" Scott said. "That's not possible. No!"

"Why isn't it possible?" I asked. "If it would save their lives, then it's worth talking about."

"Would you want to be turned into a vampire?" Scott countered.

Would I? I looked at Beck. "It has its perks."

"Like what?" asked Scott. "I've spent my entire adult life killing blood-suckers and shifters. I haven't seen *perks.*"

"Your prejudice is showing again," Raven said quietly.

"Shit!" Scott ran a hand through his hair and maneuvered himself to a chair. "If you asked any Hunter I know, they'd never want to be turned into one of the *monsters.*"

"Let's say, for the sake of argument," I said, "You get attacked and you're dying. Beck can change you into a vampire. Think of all the good you could accomplish with the strength of a vampire and the knowledge of a Hunter."

Scott opened his mouth to argue and paused. He ran his hand through his hair again.

"Seriously. Is there a downside?" I asked.

"Yes," said Beck. "Your soul is no longer yours. You are an abomination and will go to hell when your body is finally killed."

"Aren't I going to hell anyway? I've killed," said Scott.

"You do not understand!" said Beck. "I would not wish this on anyone."

"Would you do it if someone asked you to? Like you did for Beth? You don't get to play God," I said.

"Yes. I do," Beck said. "In that moment, it is exactly what I am doing. I get to choose whether a person lives or dies."

"But she asked for it. So how is this any different?" I asked.

Rachel said, "Marie can't make the decision. Also, I'm sorry, chica, but if it didn't fix her mind, could you even *imagine* Marie as a vampire?" She gave a full body shudder. "She already has crazy strength. We *cannot* run the risk of her being *the same* mentally *and* a vampire. We just can't."

Rachel was right about Marie. But that wasn't my point. What was my point? I couldn't even remember now.

"All I'm trying to say is people would have the choice."

Scott said, "It's not like we're going to go around building a vampire army or anything. We can't tell people about vampires and shapeshifters."

"No," I said slowly, an idea finally taking shape. "But maybe we need to have a plan for our human Hunters if they are mortally wounded, just like you make a *do not resuscitate* order at a hospital."

"What are you saying?" asked Nate.

"If a human on our team gets mortally wounded they have three choices: die, get changed into a vampire, get changed into a shifter."

Everyone stared at me like I was crazy. I looked at the two humans. "Well?"

Scott took a breath, opened his mouth, closed it.

"I'd want Nate to change me into a cougar," Rachel said.

I knew she'd get it.

"Absolutely not!" Nate said.

"You'd rather I die than be a cougar?"

Nate did his impersonation of a fish just like Scott.

"Exactly," said Rachel. She waved her hand at Beck and the shifters. "I know you guys didn't have a choice about becoming what you are. But if I *had* a choice between dying and being one of you? I'd pick being one of you, hands down."

All eyes shot to Scott.

"I have to think about it," he finally said. "Again, I've spent my whole adult life killing your kind. Oliver, Logan, and I had a pact to kill the other if there was ever a chance we would become a vampire or shifter. It *never* occurred to us to actually choose a life of being a monster. We'd die first, hands down, to use Rachel's words."

It made sense, in a weird way. Why would you become what you'd spent your life killing?

"Okay," I said. "That means we do need to know all the humans' wishes. Then we can act accordingly if someone is dying."

Raven stood. "I can't believe we're actually having these conversations. But, I guess, you're right. If we're really going to be an organized unit of vampires, shifters, and humans, we have to be a *very* organized unit."

"It's almost like the military," Mei said. "This is like some of the things Parker talked about."

"It feels good to finally be planning things," I said to Beck. "I've felt so lost since the day I met you and my parents died. I haven't had control over anything. This makes me feel like I have some control."

Scott stood. "I'll be getting this damn cast off in a couple weeks. Oliver gets to come home tomorrow and start physical therapy. We'll get Floyd doing PT as soon as he wakes up. Training starts tomorrow. We have direction and a plan. You're right, Kinsley, it does feel good. For the last month I've felt like a damn dog chasing its tail."

"The last thing I need to do," added Beck, "Is go to Greece to meet with the two remaining Monarchs. I will be taking Lilith and Nathaniel. Raven, I need you here with Kinsley. Mei, I would be grateful to have you *officially* on board, but I know you have a future that likely does not include us."

Mei shrugged then held out a hand to shake with Beck. "Until I know what's going on with Floyd and I hear from Parker, I'm not going anywhere. I am excited to train with your team."

"I think you could teach everyone a thing or two about fighting and strategy," said Scott.

"Kinsley," Beck turned to me, "as much as I want you with me at all times, I do not want you anywhere near the remaining Monarchs. I feel it would be too much of a temptation for them."

"Agreed," said Scott.

I nodded. I wasn't loving the idea of Beck being with Lilith for an extended period of time, but I didn't have a choice. I had work to do here.

"How about an evening of *normal*," said Rachel, making air quotes.

"Movies and junk food?" I asked.

"Duh," said Rachel.

Again, best friends make everything better.

Chapter Twenty

IT HAD BEEN ALMOST five months since my parents died and only four weeks since Marie had been kidnapped by Isaac.

It felt like a lifetime. Hell, two lifetimes. I was a butterfly trying to emerge from my cocoon. I didn't know what would come out, though. Was I going to be whole? Was I going to be a beautiful butterfly? A beautiful monster? Was I already a monster?

Floyd moved slowly with a walker down the hallway of the medical facility. "I'm fine, dammit, quit hovering."

I tried not to smile and failed. I was *really* glad I had this curmudgeonly old man in my life. It was crazy to me how my small circle of friends had grown into a family. I'd only known Beck, Nate, Scott, and Raven less than five months, but they were my family. Now I'd added Mei and Floyd. I wondered what other strays we would end up with as Beck spread the word about Screamers.

Beck, Nate, and Lilith had flown to Greece the day before yesterday. Floyd woke up almost the moment they were gone. I'd hoped Marie would start to be herself, too, but no such luck. In fact, she was getting worse. She took cues from the medical staff to do things like sit and stand so they could dress and bathe her and help her use the facilities, but she'd quit eating and she was a shell of herself.

Floyd and I spent the last two days with her for breakfast and dinner, but we hadn't been able to get her to eat. She wouldn't walk in the hallway with us no matter how hard we tried.

Once, I was pretty sure I'd seen the black flames in her eyes. If she wasn't possibly possessed, Floyd and I would have shown her more pictures and talked to her about the past, but we were so worried Isaac was in her head. We couldn't afford to give him any advantage over us and talking about the past would have been ammunition to hurt Marie and me more than he already had.

"I know you're fine," I soothed Floyd, patting his arm. "I was just stretching as I was walking with you; sorry it felt like I was hovering. Training and working out eight hours a day is kicking my butt. I'm sore."

"You gonna let me get in your facility and talk to you about fighting soon?"

Floyd wanted to help. I wanted his help. We just needed the all clear from Dr. Beth.

"Yes," I said. "I told you that the moment you woke up hollering about stupid hospitals and doctors."

He'd also woken up adamant there hadn't been a second baby. He said he wasn't in the delivery room, of course, but no one had said a word about twins. Plus, if there had been two of us, wouldn't he and Marie have kidnapped us both? He made a valid argument.

"How has it been the last two days without Beck?" Floyd asked.

"The first day was really weird," I admitted. "But, I've been so busy here with you and Marie, spending the days training with Scott and the team, and evenings at Screamers, I don't really have time to dwell on it."

It was the truth. I missed Beck, more than I thought I would, but I could feel him in the back of my mind, ready to talk to me if I needed him. It was equal parts creepy and comforting. I tried not to dwell on it too much.

"When I'm sparring with the team in Scott's workout room, he helps me. It's kind of cool when I completely take one of the humans off guard and pick them up and body slam them based on a push from Beck in my mind."

"Does it worry you?"

"Yes. No. I don't know."

"Yes you do." Floyd side-eyed me.

"Okay, fine!" I threw my hands up in the air. "It doesn't worry me and that's what worries me. It's like I know I should be completely freaked out there's a vampire in my head all the time. But I trust him and I care about him. And I can't change it, so I may as well learn to live with it and use it to find and kill Isaac."

Floyd made the turn to head back down the hall to Marie's room. His was across from hers.

"Good," he said.

"You're not going to tell me I'm stupid?"

"Hell no! When Abi was killed, I told you to come to terms with all this. Life's too damn short, Kinsley. Look at me!" Now it was Floyd's turn to throw a hand in the air. "I'm a damned old man I should have done things differently. I could have had a life with your parents. A life with Tyler. A better life with Parker. I can't change the past but I sure as hell hope I can help you build a future."

He was exhausted, but wouldn't admit it. We had been doing a walk before and after breakfast and dinner. The nurses did it with him at lunch since I wasn't there. Our super exciting routine the last two days.

"You going to Screamers again tonight?"

I wasn't sure if it was disapproval in his voice or not.

"Yes. Mei, Raven, Rachel, and I have been *working* there. We make and serve drinks and keep track of who's been coming and going. Kevin, Riley, and Lucas are all there and everyone knows them since they're the regular bouncers. No one bothers us. In fact, it's kind of fun. I've met some cool people. No vampires, yet. Last night, Logan and Shawn showed up. At first, I thought maybe they were there because Scott sent them, but they were kind of flirting with Mei and Raven, so I think it was personal."

"Flirting with Mei! Ha! I'd pay money to see that. It was the panther, wasn't it? Did she kick his ass?" Floyd smiled.

I laughed. "Yes, it was Shawn. She politely let him know she thought he was great but had a boyfriend. He took it all in stride and found someone to go dance with."

We made it to Marie's room. It didn't look like she'd moved.

"Kinsley, try something for me?" Floyd sat in the chair across from Marie.

I raised my brows. He wrote on a piece of paper: *Make her come back to us. Force her with your mind.*

Make her? Could I do that?

"Beck?"

"Yes, my dear?"

As always he was right there. I smiled. Then out of curiosity I asked, *"What will happen if you're busy? Do you have mind voicemail?"*

He laughed in my head, and it gave me goosebumps. I missed his face and the feel of his hand in mine. Something to ponder for another day.

"I also miss the feel of your skin, my darling Kinsley. And,

no. There is no voicemail. *I know you jest. However, I will never be too busy. I am at your beck and call. What do you need? You are done visiting Floyd and Marie and ready to go to Screamers, are you not?"*

"Yes. But Floyd just gave me an idea. Do you think it would be possible for me to take control of Marie's mind? Or force Isaac out?"

"*You can try. If it does not work, Isaac may see us as weak.*"

"He already thinks we're weak. If it works, he'll realize we're not as weak as he thinks. So, what do I do? Just yell at him to get out of her head?"

Beck laughed again. "*I miss your sense of humor. Let me confer with Lilith.*"

For the last two nights, when Beck and I spoke in our minds, he let me know how wonderful Lilith had been as they bargained with the Monarchs. I still didn't know what they were *bargaining* for or why Lilith was so helpful, but I trusted Beck. I supposed even vampires were scared of demons. I didn't know what Lilith was capable of besides sex, but maybe there was more she was able to do. When they were home I would know what was going on.

"*You are not going to like her idea,*" Beck said.

"No, probably not. But, tell me anyway."

"*Take Marie outside and strike her with lightning.*"

I sat down slowly next to Floyd. I wrote Lilith's suggestion on the paper.

Floyd's eyes widened. "Are you crazy?"

"Apparently. Because I'm considering it."

"Jesus Christ." Floyd closed his eyes and held his head in his hands.

"Marie," I said quietly. She didn't move. Enough of this. It was time to do something. "Isaac. I know you're in there."

Marie's eyes met mine but they were black.

Floyd opened his eyes to watch our interaction.

"We're on to you. Beck and Lilith are in Greece negotiating with the remaining Monarchs. You've been a busy little beaver, haven't you? Killing Monarchs."

It may have been Marie's voice, but I knew I was talking to Isaac. "You bitch," he snarled. The barb drove home. Having Marie call me names hurt even if it wasn't her.

"Come back to me, Marie. You're stronger than him."

"No she's not and you know it," Isaac said through her. "She's never been strong. She'll always be mine."

I watched her eyes closely, looking for any sign my Marie was in there. I didn't see anything to give me any hope. What would me calling down the lightning do to her physical body? Could it kill her? Would I rather be dead than controlled by Isaac?

Yes.

I stood and pulled Marie to her feet. I put my hands on each side of her head and used every ounce of power I thought I had. Meeting her eyes, I didn't flinch when her face contorted in rage of Isaac's doing.

"GET! OUT! OF! MY! AUNT!"

Nothing happened. I'd really thought it would work.

Maniacal laughter ripped from Marie's mouth. It seemed to fill the room. I felt a pressure on my mental shields.

"Beck?"

"*Not me. We must keep him out of your head. Let us try together.*"

Isaac trying to get in my head was the link we needed to blow him out of Marie.

I used the image of lightning to direct my rage. It flowed from my brain in silvery ropes into my arms, out my fingertips, into Marie's mind. I could see and feel the energy crackle and burn along the connection Isaac had with her. His laughter turned to screams and then it was silent.

Marie and I both fell to the floor. I smelled smoke and then heard the fire alarm going off. Had I started a fire?

Beck pushed into my brain. I felt him do a mental medical exam of my body. Nothing really hurt. Well, my hands. But I hadn't actually thrown lightning, I'd just sent it through my mind. Hadn't I? My head hurt. The connection with Beck throbbed in time with the pain in my hands.

"Jeez, girl. That was the strangest thing I've ever seen! Are you okay?" Floyd's face swam into view.

"I'm fine," I answered both men.

"Your eyes," Floyd said. "You really are the Silver Shadower."

"It would appear that way," said Beck.

I echoed that to Floyd. Then, "How is Marie? Why is the fire alarm going off?"

"You burned the chair to a crisp."

"Shit. Beck, did you hear that?"

"Yes. Do not fret. Lilith will teach you to control the lightning when we return."

Yay.

"Is Marie okay?" I asked Floyd.

"She hasn't moved yet."

Nurses came running into the room.

Gerald moved over me next to Floyd. "Are you okay, Miss Kinsley?"

"Sure am." I tried to sit up and couldn't. No, really. I'm fine. Maybe if I said it to myself enough, it would be true.

The wailing fire alarm was shut off. I could still smell smoke, but it wasn't filling the room. I rolled to my side. The chair was a white pile of ash. The floor didn't seem to be charred. Holy shit. I sent a mental snapshot of the chair to Beck.

Gerald helped me to my feet.

"Thanks for being here," I told him. He'd been driving me around since Nate was gone. "I'm not sure I'm going to Screamers tonight. Can you text the group and let them know?"

He nodded and left me with Dr. Beth.

"Well," she said. "I'm not sure if I'm supposed to be amazed, quizzical, or scared. What did this?"

I wasn't sure how to answer. Did I need people knowing I could shoot lightning from my hands? Lightning I thought was a metaphor.

I looked to Floyd. "Does she know about the Prophecy?"

"Everyone knows about the Prophecy," said Beth. Then realization dawned. "Kinsley? You did this? Were you trying to kill her?"

"No! I thought I was sending metaphorical lightning to burn the connection between Marie and Isaac. I did that, too, I think. But obviously it wasn't just mental fire." I sighed.

"I'll take Marie for new brain scans. Dr. Karlof and I thought maybe we saw a small blur in a portion of Marie's brain while she's under the mental influence of Isaac. We'll see what it looks like now." Beth put a hand on my shoulder. "How are you? Do you need me to look you over?"

I shook my head. "I'm fine. I have a little headache and hand ache, but both are already going away."

I stared at the ashes. What if I had accidentally done that to Marie? Why *didn't* I do that to Marie since the lightning had been directed at her?

Twenty minutes later, I was sitting in the waiting room outside the CT scan room. I was drinking water and pondering my life when Scott crutched in with Shawn close behind.

"Thank God!" Scott said as he came to me and pulled me up into his arms.

It felt good to be comforted. I rested my head on his chest as he kissed the top of my head. Tears gathered in my eyes. I hadn't felt like crying once since everything had happened. Why now?

"Are you okay?" Scott mumbled into my hair.

"Yes. I didn't kill anything except a chair. And I think I blew Isaac out of Marie's head, but I don't know for sure."

"You're amazing and a little scary," said Shawn. He patted my arm.

"I've had almost five months to get used to my new amazing-scary and you *don't* get used to it. Also, every time I start to think I have a handle on things, I realize I don't."

"It's like the first Ironman movie when Tony is figuring out how to use his suit," said Shawn.

I stared at him. Was that supposed to be helpful?

Scott shook his head. "You were ordered to no longer use Avengers references."

"Ordered?" I asked.

Scott smiled. "We tried using a jar he had to put money in, but he didn't care about paying up. So I threatened to fire him."

"You did not!" I said, slapping his chest.

"I didn't really mean it, but it has helped. He only makes a reference once a day now."

I was really glad Scott hadn't thrown away this friendship because Shawn was a shifter.

"You guys, I swear." I laughed and it helped take away the tears gathering in the corners of my eyes.

"Kind of like your life," Scott said. "We're learning to roll with the punches and laugh when we can."

"There hadn't been much laughter since your dad died," said Shawn. "I told you we needed you, Kinsley."

I nodded and my throat tightened with emotion. "As soon as we know the results of Marie's brain scan, I really want to go home."

"You bet," said Scott. "Also, Rachel, Mei, and Raven weren't sure if you needed them or if you wanted them to go to Screamers."

Shit. I pulled my phone out. Rachel had texted me and I hadn't even noticed. It said: don't want to smother you. If you want us there, we'll come with Scott. If you need some time, we'll go to Screamers.

Then another text: you probably don't even know Scott is on his way. (laugh emoji)

I wrote back: I'm good. Marie's good. . . I think. I just need some quiet and rest. You're more than welcome at the house but I'm not going to do anything but sleep. And you're right, I had no idea Scott was coming. (kissy face emoji)

Beth came out with Karlof. "Brain scans look normal. The small mass we noticed last week is gone. So that may have been something Isaac was doing to her brain."

"Can I see her?" I asked.

"Yep. She's being taken back to her room now. I'd really like her to stay overnight and possibly longer. It will depend on what you think and how she's acting. She's lost weight since she hasn't been eating, and her lack of food and exercise may cause her to have limited mobility for a bit."

"Or because it's Marie," Scott said, "she may be just fine."

"Right?" I said. "After learning about Shadowers and the Shadower Bonds over the last months, I don't know what is normal and what's not. For all I know, I'll be as bat-shit crazy as Marie after being bonded to a vampire for too long."

"Unlikely," Dr. Karlof finally said. "After Beckford explained Marie's previous captivity to me, I'm sure Isaac's physical and mental abuse is to blame. You will be perfectly safe bonded to Beckford."

I really hated that Karlof called Beck *Beckford* just like Lilith did.

"Good to know, Dr. Karlof. Thank you for your input," I said. Shawn noticed my forced sincerity and raised an eyebrow. I gave a tiny head shake hoping he'd know I'd tell him later.

"Whelp," I pulled away from Scott. "Let's go see what we're dealing with."

We walked back to the room side of the medical facility.

Marie wasn't there.

Chapter Twenty-One

"SHE SHOULD BE BACK BY NOW," Beth said, pulling her cell out and dialing.

I took a chance and headed across the hall to Floyd's room. Marie was devouring a sandwich, sitting cross-legged in the chair, watching Floyd.

He was laying in bed, watching her. He wasn't scared, but he was wary. He met my eyes and it looked like he'd been crying.

"Marie?" I said slowly.

She shoved the last of the sandwich in her mouth and bounded toward me. "Kwinslwy," she said. She tried to laugh, covered her lips with one hand, and held up the other in a wait gesture. She chugged some water and threw herself in my arms.

"Oh my goodness! You did it! Claire could do that, too! I can't believe you saved me from him!"

"Do you need to sit down?" I asked. This wasn't what I expected. Although, it was Marie, so I never knew what to expect.

"Kins, baby, we can't really trust Lilith. I mean, for some things, maybe, but not for much."

She sounded so much like a combination of my mom and dad and so much *not* like Marie I wasn't sure what to do or say.

"What do you mean, Marie?" Scott asked.

"Masters. Tom trusted you. At least enough to work with you but never to bring you home. Well, I guess that wasn't trust. It was a safety issue, wasn't it?"

Scott met my eyes and I shrugged.

"And Shawn," Marie continued. "Tom kept your secret, but Scott knows now. See? You could have told him sooner. Or, maybe not. I suppose he wouldn't have taken your birthright well before. What should we call it? *Before Kinsley* sounds good."

Birthright? Wait a second. He was born a shifter, not changed into one? "Are there more of you?" I blurted. "Wait. Sorry. Not the time or place. Marie, how do you know all this?"

"Oh honey. It was amazing and awful. I knew what was going on but I couldn't do anything about it. I was so glad when you figured out he was in my head."

"So what was amazing about it?" I asked.

"I was in Isaac's head, too. He thought I was crazy but he didn't realize him being in my head for so many years is *what* made me crazy."

"He's been in your head this whole time?" Floyd asked. "Since when? Since Tom and Claire rescued you?"

"Yes and no," Marie said.

The weird part about all this was Marie was back but she was different. She finished sentences and stood in one place while she spoke to us, meeting our eyes. It was like she was still possessed but it was by her *non-crazy* counterpart. Or maybe this was all Isaac. How would I know? She wasn't acting the way I knew her to be the whole time I was growing up.

"Your mother did it, too," Marie said.

"What?"

"Blasted Isaac out of my head. She never caught anything on fire, though." Marie laughed. "That part was kind of cool."

I looked to Floyd, and he shrugged. "It never happened while I was around."

"Claire didn't figure it out until after we kidnapped Kinsley."

I didn't want to ask, but I knew I had to. "Was there another baby? A twin?"

"Yes. But she was stillborn."

I sucked in a breath. Why hadn't my parents ever said anything?

"There had never been Shadower twins born before. Could you imagine what a bad-ass pair you would have made? Running all over, killing everything." Marie started to spin in the room like she had a sword. This was the Marie I was used to. She bounced to the chair and landed nimbly in a crouch, feet on the cushion. "We're starting your training first thing tomorrow. There's so much I have to teach you."

She dropped her pretend sword and met my eyes. "*This* is what I was meant to do. And because you're strong enough and *finally* know what's going on, I can teach you!"

"How do we know it's really you?" Scott said, suspicion barely masked behind a cautious tone.

Marie turned to him. "Great question. I was wondering when someone was going to ask. Let's go home and I'll let Kinsley into my head and she can see for herself."

"Beck, you're here right?" I could feel him *listening in* but I needed to talk to him.

"Of course."

"Now what?"

"Lilith says it is possible for you to determine if Isaac still has a hold on her. You just need to do what you did earlier, without lightning."

"Marie said we can't trust Lilith."

"We can trust Lilith as much as she can trust us."

It was such a Beck answer, I chuckled. Everyone turned to me.

"She's talking to Beck," Marie said. "Let's do it here, Kins. You can't take me home until you know it's safe."

By this time Beth and Karlof were standing in the door watching our exchange.

"I'll bring another chair," Beth said.

"A few chairs." I lifted my chin to Scott. "He should be sitting."

Beth smiled and put her hand on Scott's. "I know you want me to take that cast off early. Why don't you come back tomorrow and we'll do x-rays and see about a walking cast. You'll be moving slowly, but you'd be able to get rid of at least one of the crutches."

"That would be amazing, Doc. Thank you." He squeezed her hand.

My heart did a little somersault. Beck was sleeping with Lilith, because he had to, and I was jealous. Scott and Beth were flirting with each other, it seemed to me, and I was jealous.

I swear to God. Emotions sucked. Why couldn't I control my feelings?

"Feelings weren't meant to be controlled," said Abi from the corner of the room. "They were meant to wash over you like drowning ocean waves. To whip in and out of your soul like the hurricane winds. Without feelings, how do you know you're alive?" She looked sad.

I wanted to ask her if she still had feelings now that she was dead. She sure seemed like she'd been feeling rage every time she reminded me I'd gotten her killed. I ignored her. I had to. After I knew if Marie was really herself, I'd ask Abi some questions.

Some nurses brought in chairs. Marie and I sat down facing each other, knee to knee, and the others made a little semicircle behind us. I tried to ignore our audience and focus on my inner feelings.

"Do you stay or go, Beck?"

"Lilith suggests I stay so you can use the visual of our bond to look for whatever you need to see in Marie."

"Here goes," I said to everyone.

I closed my eyes and did the *float above map* I had done with Beck at the Vampire house in Oregon. I slowly picked out everyone's auras and used Marie and me as the focal point. I let everyone else fade away and moved *in* to my head. Beck was there, it was like a mercury rope connecting us, strong and pulsing. The bond was growing stronger. Off the end of his rope, there was a faint gray string. That hadn't been there before.

"*Focus on you and Marie,*" Beck said.

I moved closer to Marie. She was glowing pink. Fresh and strong, compared to when she'd been bleeding out. It gave my soul a burst of strength. There was nothing around her or connected to her.

"I don't see anything connecting Marie to anyone else."

"Could Isaac somehow hide the connection?" Scott asked.

"I don't know."

"Can Alexander hide your connection?" Scott prompted quietly.

"Not since I know what to look for."

"So look for something like that," said Beth. "It would be the same connection, wouldn't it? A Shadower/Monarch or, in this case, Shadower/Sovereignty connection? Since you know what it looks like, you should be able to see it."

I cleared my mind again and *floated* above all of us. When I really concentrated, I could see thin spider-webby connections between Scott and me, Marie and Floyd, Scott and Shawn, and Beth and Karlof. The only thing Marie was connected to was me and Floyd. That was a good sign, right?

Beck came to look with me. "Interesting. I wonder what makes a connection?"

"It must be emotions."

"Everyone is connected somehow," Abi said quietly. "You just have to know how and where to look."

"Why are you being so helpful all of a sudden?"

"Who?" Scott asked.

Oh, ya. He didn't know about Abi. I was going to have to tell him about her.

I opened my eyes. "For now, there doesn't seem to be any connection to Marie besides Floyd and me."

Marie dropped my hands and stood. "Floyd?"

I looked at Floyd. He raised his shoulders and pursed his lips. That's why he'd been crying. She didn't know it was him.

"Oh Floyd," I said sadly.

Marie moved to him. "Floyd? What happened to you? I'm so sorry." She climbed up in the bed and curled into him like a child.

His face took on the fear of a caged animal.

"C'mon, Marie," Shawn said, pulling her from the bed and toward the door.

Beth moved over to Floyd. "How about a light sedative to help you relax and sleep?"

I hoped he would be okay. It had to break his heart to have Marie back and know he couldn't have her. I didn't want him to suffer another heart attack.

"Do you want me to stay? Or Mei to come over?"

Floyd wiped away tears and shook his head. "I just want to be alone."

"Okay," I said.

Some nurses took the chairs out of the room and Scott waited by the door while I stood with Floyd for a few minutes, holding his hand.

"I love you, you know," I said.

He looked startled for a moment then smiled. "I love you too, girly. I'm glad you brought Marie back even if she isn't mine anymore."

I kissed his forehead and left with Scott. Shawn was waiting with the SUV at the entrance and helped Scott and me in. I sat in back with Marie and waited to see what she was going to say or do.

"It's been a long time since I've seen Floyd. I should have known it was him. He loved me, you know?" She stared out the window.

"Did you love him?" I asked.

"I think so? I don't know what real love is, Kins. I only ever had Isaac as an example, and that's not real love. That was manipulation and control and one-sided. I guess I had your parents as an example. But seeing and watching love is different than feeling it. What about you?" She turned sideways and took my hands. "Have you found love?"

I laughed as Scott turned to watch us. "Yes, Kinsley," he said smiling, "tell Marie if you've found love."

I rolled my eyes. No point in waiting to tell her later. I'd already said it all to Scott. "Well, it's like this," and I went on to explain how I had feelings for both Scott and Beck but couldn't pick one over the other, let alone have a relationship with someone other than one of them for fear of ruining our relationships and bonds.

"Don't worry," Marie said as Shawn pulled in to Scott's house, "things have a way of working themselves out." She kissed my cheek and hopped out of the vehicle.

Scott laughed. "It's like it's the regular Marie, but not."

"That's exactly what I've been thinking."

"Do you really think Isaac's hold is broken?"

"I couldn't sense or see any connection, but in all honesty, that doesn't mean a damn thing because I'm new to all this and don't know how it works. Time will tell." I shrugged. "I guess we move forward. It's not like it's been a secret we're looking for Isaac; he knows that."

"I'll head out now, bossman, unless you need me to stay," Shawn said, helping Scott out of the vehicle.

"I'd kind of like you to stay," I said. "But first, can you go pick up at least Rachel? I need her to help me talk to Marie and process things. If Mei and Raven want to come, they're more than welcome."

"I texted Rachel from the medical facility," Scott said. "I gave her a brief rundown. She's already here."

I kissed Scott's cheek. "Thank you!"

The squeals of delight reached me as the front door flew open and Rachel and Marie reunited like two kids.

"Why do I need to stay?" Shawn asked, rubbing his ears.

Scott patted him on the back. "Because I'm kind of useless in the muscle department and if Marie is a problem, Kinsley is going to need your help. She might be crazy and out of practice, and look like an innocent high school girl, but she is a Shadower, which means she's super fast and super strong."

"What he said," I said nodding. I loved that Scott was starting to get me. "See? We don't need a mental connection. You're figuring out how I think."

"Scary," Scott said with a smile.

It was a three hour carpet picnic with snacks, giggles, and story telling. Raven and Mei had trouble keeping up with Rachel, Marie, and my conversations. They mostly laughed and ate.

"It's like listening to The Chipmunks, but on fast forward,"

I heard Mei say to Scott who had moved as far away from us as he could.

"I heard that!" I hollered. "You're right, but you don't have to pick on us!"

Finally Marie started telling us about the night her family was murdered by Isaac and his vampires. By the time she was done, she was crying and so was I. I looked up and saw everyone in the room was in various stages of tears.

"I'm sorry," Marie said as she wiped her eyes and blew her nose. "I haven't told that story in a long time."

We gave her a moment to pull herself together. "My whole reason for sharing is to tell you what came after."

I jumped in and told everyone about the scars on her legs, being Isaac's prisoner, and her rescue by my parents, Floyd, and the other Hunters.

"We need to create and execute a plan to get Isaac," said Marie. "The original Hunters are all dead and gone, except Floyd, and he's too old to be any help physically. Scott, your team hasn't really been hunting, you just kill when you come across a threat."

"How is hunting different?" asked Rachel.

"Using a sports analogy," Scott said, "we'd be on the offensive instead of the defensive."

"It would feel good to actually be doing something instead of just hanging out," I said.

"Oh, c'mon," said Raven, "you haven't just been hanging out. You've been working out, practicing weapons, using your mind powers, and we're learning how to work together as a team."

"We need more than a few days, though," said Shawn.

"And we've got it," said Scott. "Alexander won't be back for maybe another week. We keep working together, learning weapons and the best kill tactics."

"I can help with that," said Marie. "So can Floyd. He might not be physically able to do it, but I'm sure he can remember how we used to train and pass along that information."

"So we need to know the most efficient way to kill a Vampire," said Scott.

"Decapitation," I said at the same time as Marie, Mei, Rachel, and Raven.

"Pretty sure decapitation is the way to go for any creature," said Shawn. "Shifter, vampire, or human."

"And burn the body, just to be sure," said Mei. "In China, we even burn human bodies so vampires can't possibly change them."

I shuddered. Would they make zombie vampires or just regular vampires? Were vampires a type of zombie anyway? Sometimes I hated the way my mind took off on its own tangents.

"We can't kill him," said Marie.

The room went so silent, you could hear our breathing.

"What was that?" said Scott.

"We can't kill him on sight. We're going to need to catch him."

"Catch him?" said Shawn. "He's not a rodent. He's one of the most powerful vampires in the world. He's the head of the Sovereignty, has been killing Monarchs, and may or may not still be drinking Shadower blood. We can't just try to *catch him*."

Marie pursed her lips. "Well, this is the part I've been putting off telling you. Because of the bond, if you kill him, you kill me."

Chapter Twenty-Two

"FOR FUCK'S SAKE. Well, of course that's how it works. Nothing can be *easy*, can it?" Scott said.

I stared in shocked silence at Marie.

"Beck. When were you going to mention death of a Shadower or bonded vampire kills the other?"

"Soon."

I took a huge breath and Scott looked at me.

"Fuck, shit, damn it all to hell!" He levered out of his chair and began to crutch back and forth in the living room. Every once in a while, he'd stop and drag his hands over his face and through his hair.

It took a few moments for the implication of this new bombshell to sink in to the others.

"That means. . ." Rachel said.

"Yeah," I said.

"Don't worry," said Marie, "this is good."

Scott stopped mid step and slammed the crutches down. "Good news? How is having Kinsley's life directly tied to Beck and your life directly tied to Isaac *good* news?"

"Isaac won't kill Beck for fear of losing the power Kinsley can give him. He also won't kill me or have me killed for the same reason. It means he'll want to capture us, too, instead of kill us. Duh."

Scott met my eyes. "You are *not* to be alone. *Ever.*"

I sighed. Yay. We were back to this.

"She's never alone anyway," said Rachel.

"I've already been kidnapped once. I don't want it to ever happen again." I looked at Raven. "Don't worry, I know you were ordered to keep an eye on me."

"*She was not ordered,*" Beck said. "*She volunteered.*"

"I offered," Raven said. "I consider you a friend."

"So did Nathaniel," said Rachel.

They waited to see what I'd say or do.

I held up my hands. "It's okay everyone. I'm not going to freak out. A few months ago, hell maybe even a few weeks ago, I would have. But, this isn't just about me anymore. I can't change being a Shadower and I'm finally admitting it to myself. This is my life now."

"That means we need to be prepared. Scott, your house just isn't going to cut it," said Marie. "We need more room."

"The rebuild of Beck's building should be complete in a month," I said.

"We should move back to Paradise," Marie said.

"No we shouldn't," said Rachel.

I knew her reason was emotional. She didn't want to be in the same town as her parents.

Scott quit pacing and sat back down, propping his foot up. "Beck and I talked about it. Part of us thought maybe we could just hide out like your parents did. The problem is, things are too big now. We need to stay in the city and build Beck's followers. It would be way too obvious in a small town if we were training and recruiting."

"I suppose you're right," said Marie. "I like Paradise. Except for Rachel's parents."

Rachel laughed. "You and me both, chica. Well, I have gotten used to being in the city. I like it since I never have to be the one to drive anywhere. It might be a different story if I had to drive in this traffic." She laughed.

"Beck," I said aloud, "can you come home sooner?"

Everyone waited.

"I will try. Negotiations are not going well. The Monarchs still act as though they are in charge. They are not acknowledging their lessened power. They seem to think you and I coming to Greece would solve everything."

"I am *not* going to Greece to be Monarch food!"

All eyes widened.

"Fuck no, you're not," said Scott.

"Assure everyone that is not even an option. I will convince the Monarchs to join us or suffer the consequences."

I wasn't sure what that meant. Was he saying he'd kill them?

"He should just kill them and be through with it," Marie said.

"I will be back in two days."

I wasn't going to ask if killing Monarchs was on the table. "He said two days," I told the group.

"I vote some more movies and sleep. It's been a long-ass day," said Rachel.

"Yes," I said. "But before that, I really need Marie to tell me about how my mom got Isaac out of her head. Can he come back? How will we know? What happened when you figured out he was doing it?"

"It's in the journals. Don't you have them?"

I gave her the quick story of finding out about the journals and where they were hidden and Isaac beating us to the house since he had been in her mind.

Marie paced the living room. "We moved around

constantly. About every year, your mom would notice I was acting strange."

Rachel and I laughed.

"Oh girls. You saw the *me* who wasn't *me*. I guess none of us know who the real *me* is supposed to be anymore. It doesn't matter though, we'll move forward from here. It took almost thirty years for your mom to put together I'd go *crazy* on the anniversary of them finding me and rescuing me from Isaac. We thought maybe it was PTSD. Isaac was just playing with us. He was coming to wherever we were and taking my blood while I slept and messing with my mind."

"I suppose when you're a vampire, you play games for entertainment. It was almost like a long con," said Scott.

"That's all we could come up with. He was *waiting* for something."

"*You.*"

I closed my eyes. "Beck said he was waiting for me."

Marie stopped pacing. "Yep. When you were born, I couldn't figure out why I would have wanted to take you. Isaac made me. Poor Floyd. He was just another innocent pawn."

I opened my eyes and went to Marie, pulling her in for a hug.

She rested her head on my shoulder. "Your mom found the fang marks after we'd kidnapped you and put it all together. She put her hands on my head like you did and it felt like being electrocuted."

"What did she do? Scramble your brain? Kinsley and I grew up with a version of you that is not," Rachel motioned her hand from Marie's head to her feet, "this."

Marie laughed. "I guess so. I was also broken. I'd lost Isaac, who my brain and body was convinced I needed, and I lost Floyd, the man I thought I could maybe love. Then we moved to the Middle of Nowhere, Washington State from Maine. It was all a shock to the system."

"Well, I'm glad I didn't scramble your brain," I said.

"Or burn her to a crisp like that chair," added Shawn, his deadpan humor defusing the tension in the room.

"Food, movies, and sleep," Marie said heading to the kitchen.

"This is going to take a little time to wrap my brain around," said Rachel. "She's different but I like it."

I nodded.

"And I'm scared it's not her," Rachel said in a whisper.

I told her about my *mapping* of our connections at the hospital.

"Ohhh! Do me! Do me!" She clapped and bounced on her toes.

I laughed and had her sit so I could hold her hand. "I have to admit, my first thought when I saw the little spiderwebs connecting everyone was what our connection would look like! But that's only if it's based on emotions."

I closed my eyes and looked at Rachel's and my connection. It was thicker than the spiderwebs I'd seen at the hospital. I followed my connection to Marie. It was thicker than I'd realized, too. Now that I knew what I was looking for, I could see everything better. The connection let me know they were alive, and I almost thought I could tell moods. Rachel was lonely because Nate was gone but happy because I was happy Marie was back.

Marie was tired, a little scared, but overall happy.

"I wonder if I can show you." I lightly pushed into Rachel's mind.

"Oh! That's tingly!" she said. "Like the start of a headache. And my nose feels like when you need to sneeze."

But that was all I could do. Either I couldn't get in a human's head or I didn't know how to do it.

"Okay, you have to stop," Rachel said. "I don't like how it feels. It was worth a try, though." She let go of my hands and pulled me in for a hug. "We'll get through this. Just like we always do."

She kissed my cheek and went to the kitchen with Marie and the others. Scott still sat in his chair.

"So?" he asked. "You want to try with me?"

"I already saw our connection. It's not like the Shadower bond, but we're definitely connected."

"I meant do you want to try and get in my head."

It felt like an intimate request. One I wasn't ready for. "Honestly? No. Not right now. I've had enough of an emotional day."

"Sweet thing, I don't know if you've noticed? But *every* day of your life is an emotional day. If you're planning to wait until there's the possibility of not having a crazy day, we're going to be waiting forever."

"Why would you want me to try and get in your head?"

"Jealousy."

"What?" I shook my head.

"You get this, look, on your face when you and Beck communicate. It drives me crazy."

I opened my mouth to remind him I couldn't change it and he cut me off.

"Wait. I'm getting better at not being so territorial about you, but I can't change my feelings. I want you all to myself, and that's not possible. Then, damn Rachel got me thinking about sex. With you. And you having sex with Beck. I don't know if I could do it."

I put a hand to my throat. "Do what?"

"Share you. Use you like that. Make you choose. It's not

good for a man's ego or his emotional state to be in a contest like that."

"Rachel was drunk. I would *never* do what she suggested. I'll say it again: I'm not sleeping with either of you. I need both of you for my physical survival and my emotional well-being. No. Sex. But obviously, a lot of emotions." I rubbed my eyes and sighed.

"Do you want to get in my head so you know how I feel about you?"

"Do you care about me enough to know I'm not going to pit you and Beck against each other or sleep with either of you?"

"Yes. I love you, Kinsley. I always will." He stated it so easily; like I should have already known.

My breath caught.

"I love you as well."

"Don't make this a competition," I said to Beck.

"I am not trying to."

I blew out a breath and then jumped off the cliff. "I realized over the last few weeks I love you both."

My connection with Beck hummed with shock and need. Scott was so still, I would have thought him a statue.

"But?" Scott said.

"There isn't a *but*. This is just the way it is. We need each other. We're connected in a way that goes deeper and is more important than physical."

Rachel chose that moment to come back in the room. "Says the virgin." Then she busted into laughter.

Scott joined her, and in my head, so did Beck.

"And on that note, I'll let you know Beck is laughing with you. PFFFFFT!" I stuck my tongue out at them. "Whatever."

Rachel put her arm around me. "I wasn't trying to make it seem like your emotions aren't important. I just had to raz you. You're right. There's more to relationships than the physical.

The last few days away from Nathaniel really cemented my feelings for him. You know how I am. All my relationships have always been about sex and having a good time. I'm in love with him, but I really *like* him. I miss our conversations, making meals together, playing video games. I haven't had that connection with anyone else, besides you of course, so I get what you mean."

Scott smiled at us and nodded.

"So can we finally call an end to this day?" I begged.

Rachel laughed. "After we eat. Raven and Shawn are cooking and Marie is trying to help, but she has absolutely no culinary skills."

We ate, had dessert, and visited like normal people while movies played in the background.

Slowly, everyone retired to their beds. It had been another four hours but I didn't think I could sleep. I needed to try. The sun was going to be coming up and I wanted to go have breakfast with Floyd.

I brushed my teeth, put on pajamas, and crawled into bed. Marie was asleep and it looked like a drunk octopus had been in bed with her; blankets and pillows were everywhere. I smiled. Sometimes normal is just what we make it. This was my normal.

My mind wouldn't shut off. I did some breathing exercises and tried to empty my head of all thoughts.

The dream came to me in shades of gray in the beginning. I saw a couple making love in a gauze canopy bed with candles illuminating their sweaty bodies. The woman, long dark hair, rode the man in wild abandon.

I blushed and tried to look away. Was I dreaming about sex since we'd talked about it before bed? At least this time it wasn't me in the dream/vision.

The man sat up and wrapped his arms around the woman. It was Beck.

But it wasn't me with him. It was Lilith.

He drove his fangs into her throat and fed as she thrashed and moaned. But it wasn't in pain. Oh no. Her trashing was in ecstasy.

I tried to wake up, close my eyes. Anything.

"Damn it, Kinsley. I am sorry."

Beck pulled his face from Lilith's throat and met my eyes across the room. Lilith turned and met my eyes as well. Then she moved Beck's face and placed her lips a fraction of an inch from his. I watched as she sucked out his aura and her skin shimmered.

I felt a mental shove and I was back in bed. I looked at my phone. It had been ten minutes. I hadn't been dreaming. I'd gone to where Beck and Lilith were.

In bed together.

I wasn't completely stupid. Beck had had to sleep with her the day I met her as *payment*. I'd wondered if part of their agreement was for her to feed off him while she was here. I hadn't wanted her to feed off anyone else, so I'd practically handed Beck to her on a silver platter.

"Kinsley?"

"It's okay."

"No. You were not supposed to see that. Lilith—"

"For real, Beck. It's okay. *I didn't want her to feed off anyone else. It's either you or me, and I haven't been feeding her.*"

"You could," Abi said from the foot of my bed.

"How about a little time apart, Beck? I'm not mad. But you have other things to do and I don't need to watch that again."

"Kinsley, please."

"We'll talk when you get back. We need a break." I severed our connection.

"Can we talk in my head so we don't wake up Marie?" I whispered to Abi.

She sat by my feet. Of course the bed didn't dent and I couldn't feel her physically, but I did get a chill from my toes to about my knees.

"She can't hear me and you won't wake her. She sleeps like the dead, she always has."

"What? How do you know that?"

"You won't wake her up. What do you want to know?"

I shook my head. "Who are you? *What* are you?"

Abi shrugged. "You don't think I'm the ghost of the six-year-old girl you killed?"

I wrinkled my nose. "You're way too old and worldly to be the girl I met and lost."

She smiled and it wasn't the face of a little girl. "I told her you'd figure it out. Now she owes *me* a favor."

"Told who?" But I was pretty sure I already knew.

"You tell me." Abi shrugged.

"It's Lilith, isn't it?"

She smiled and clapped. "You are *so* much smarter than she thinks you are."

"This has something to do with her being a demon, doesn't it?"

"DingDingDing!" Abi chimed.

"So, who are you really?"

"I'm a demon, too. I just don't have the power the succubus does. Not many demons do. If the conditions are right, demons can be pulled from hell and put into host bodies. In this case, I didn't get a body, I got a ghost."

"Where is Abi? Abi's soul?" I asked, tears in my eyes. It was almost like her dying all over again.

"Well, if there's a hell, there must be a heaven, right? I didn't get to meet the kid. I just got thrown into her dying body.

I'm kind of stuck for now until I can find the power to either gain corporeal form or go back to hell."

Now that I knew for sure this wasn't a six-year-old, it was so obvious. There had been something off about having a ghost following me around. I think I'd realized this wasn't really Abi's ghost when I thought I'd been going crazy but Beck had heard her in my mind. This had to do with the connections we all had.

I snapped my fingers. "Lilith has a connection to Beck, Beck has a connection to me, so I have an off-hand connection to Lilith. She's been using you to make my fears a reality. All the things I've stressed and worried about, you came and reinforced!"

Abi lifted her little arms and shrugged. "Just doing my job. I got out of hell and got a *body* for doing what Lilith wanted. Then I got here, and I kind of like you guys. Loophole. She didn't give me a real body so maybe I won't do all the things she wanted me to do."

I flopped back on the bed. So, I had a demon ghost as part of my entourage. I wasn't really sure much else could surprise me at this point in the game.

You know Murphy's Law? Also, how people say: Don't ask what else can go wrong.

Murphy and those people are assholes. And they're right.

Chapter Twenty-Three

RACHEL WAS A BAD-ASS AT SHOOTING. It shouldn't have surprised me; she grew up on a farm. Her dad may be an abusive bastard, but he'd taught his daughter to hunt deer, kill coyotes, protect the farm animals from any predator, and to hunt rabbits for dinners.

She was impressing Scott's men as well.

"You shoot great for a—"

"If you say *girl*, I may accidentally shoot you," Rachel said, cutting off Logan.

"For someone I thought was untrained," Logan said, hands up. "Swear. I wasn't going to say for a girl. Now that we know you're adept with a rifle and pistol, let's move on to the knives and swords."

Oliver sat off to the side and instructed Rachel the same way he had me months ago with my dad's daggers. Having done yoga and dance for many years, Rachel's balance was better than mine had been when I'd first started, so she was adjusting to the movements faster than I had.

"We'll keep working with her," said Scott.

"She's the only one I worry about. She couldn't protect herself when Mya took her."

"That won't happen again." He pulled me in for a one-arm hug.

We turned to watch Marie in a speed fight with Shawn, Joel, and Quinn. Since Joel and Quinn were human, they were no match for her. Shawn was able to keep up. It was like the movie scenes with the good guy in the middle and the bad guys surrounding them. She had two curved-blade, short swords and she was magnificent in her movements. Poetry in motion.

I hadn't wanted her to fight with anyone until we knew her mental state. She'd blown through Scott's small obstacle course training room in minutes, destroying his practice dummies.

He'd brought Holly in to take an order for new training equipment times ten and rush delivery. Holly'd pursed her lips at Marie and me, as though it was our fault full-blown training was going on. I mean, I guess it kind of was, but this was a security firm for heaven's sake. They were supposed to be training.

"This seems a little excessive, Scott," she said, hand on his arm.

"What?" The clip in his voice made it clear she'd overstepped.

"Nothing. I'm sorry. I'll get this right in."

"Order some more chairs for the conference room, too; we'll be having a few more people than usual around, and I want everyone comfortable."

With one last notation on her iPad and a glare at me, Holly left to go do whatever it was she did. Torture children, pull the wings off butterflies, poke pins in my voodoo doll.

I rolled my eyes and looked back to Marie. She would explain her moves as she made them so the men could watch her muscle movement, arm and leg stances, and sword swings.

"Every supernatural creature I've ever met telegraphs their intentions somehow. Only the really old vampires don't do it.

They're still, and then they're gone. So, not counting them, watch your targets' stances."

She went on to show what she meant. In just a few minutes she had an audience of shifters and humans who were nodding along, ducking and weaving with each strike and explanation she made. Shawn would add things he knew about shifters and their movements. How cat shifters were different than some of the bigger bodied shifters. He reminded the humans that animal shifters were going to move the same way as their regular animal counterparts, but maybe a little slyer because their human brain was also driving them. Things that would scare away an animal in nature wouldn't scare a shifter.

Scott looked at his phone. "Beth said I can come in for those x-rays. Do you want to go with me?"

I waved Rachel over. "Would you be okay for a few hours while Scott and I go get his leg checked out?"

"You bet. And, holy shit, chica! Marie's a rockstar! The two of you together are going to be unstoppable." She gave me a quick hug and went back over to Marie's lesson.

"She's right, you know," said Scott.

"I'll never be as smooth as Marie. She has training and age on her side."

"She was also crazy for a huge chunk of that, so it might make you even."

I hadn't gotten much sleep and Scott noticed. I hadn't told him about Beck and Lilith's extracurricular activities or Abi the demon. I needed to.

It was kind of weird to be the driver after five months of being chauffeured around. I flexed my fingers on the steering wheel in the traditional ten and two position. "I have a couple things to tell you," I said as I pulled out of the parking lot.

"Uh oh."

"It's not *awful*, just informational. First, until Beck gets back physically, I closed our mental connection."

"Any particular reason?"

"When I tried to sleep last night, I'm pretty sure Lilith opened the connection so I'd see them having sex."

He didn't say anything.

"You already knew they were having sex, didn't you?" I sighed.

He turned toward me and raised an eyebrow. "Well, ya, everyone does. You didn't want her feeding off anyone and Beck has been using stored blood and now the synthetic blood, so it's kind of the obvious decision. It helps both of them. She gets more power feeding from a vampire and I'm sure he gets his rocks off double since she's a succubus."

I gripped the steering wheel. I didn't want or need to think about Beck getting his *rocks off*.

I sighed again. "I realized this morning that was more than likely the case, but seeing it with my own eyes was more than I wanted or needed."

"I get that," he said. "I wouldn't want to watch someone I cared about have sex."

"I want to trust Lilith because Beck does, but I can't figure out what she's getting out of this."

He laughed. "Oh, c'mon, Kins. What's she getting out of it? What's she *not* getting out of it? She gets to feed off a vampire whenever she wants, have sex whenever she wants with a partner who can't be injured, and she gets to annoy you. It's all a powerplay. Can you imagine how she felt showing up to the remaining Monarchs with Beck, being able to put down demands instead of the other way around?"

"Okay. That does make sense. But she's a damn *DE-MON*, as in undead, Satan following, from hell, *demon* and is who knows how many years old. Doesn't she have, like magical powers?" I waved a hand toward him. "Have you ever come across any demons in your hunting days? Can she be killed? What would it take for her to kill us?"

"I get what you're saying. Apparently for thousands of years she's just been feeding off vampire leftovers when according to lore, as a demon, she should be able to snap her fingers and kill everyone."

I hit the steering wheel. "Exactly!"

"Yes, she's a demon, but she's a succubus. No, I never came across a demon in my hunting days, but as far as I know, they have to be summoned. I haven't done that." He smiled. "I thought about a deal with the devil a time or two but I never followed through. Also, most of my clients aren't the demon summoning types. When your dad and I came across the incubus, he'd been summoned on accident by a lonely housewife, drunk on too much wine."

"Okay," I said, finally smiling, as he'd wanted me to.

"A succubus gets power from sex. She can live forever, unless decapitated with silver and burned, she's eternally beautiful, and she feeds off and enjoys sensuality and sexuality. I don't think she's the type of demon we're used to from movies, books, and TV shows. That being said, I'd still try to talk to Beck without her around to see if he knows anything else about what's she's capable of. If we're going to work with her, we deserve to know that much." He reached over the console to squeeze my thigh.

I put my hand over his and squeezed. "Thank you. I feel better already. But this next part might make you upset with me and question Lilith's powers."

He pulled his hand away.

I went on to tell him about seeing Abi's ghost, thinking I was going crazy, Beck hearing Abi in my mind, and ending with Abi sitting at the foot of my bed.

"Holy shit," he said as I pulled up to the medical facility. "Have you slept at all?"

It wasn't what I expected. "You're not mad at me?"

"Why in the hell would I be mad at you?"

"For not telling you sooner."

"You know how last night you said you were done freaking out over things?"

I nodded.

"Well, me too. I was being an asshole to you when I thought I was finding out things too late. You've got a lot going on. Plus, you didn't even know if Abi was real. You're telling me now." He unbuckled his seatbelt.

"Well. Um. Thank you?"

He laughed. "I really was an asshole to you for quite a few months, wasn't I?"

I nodded and held up five fingers.

"So, the issue now is, if Lilith is *just* a succubus, how did she get the power to put a demon into a ghost."

"Exactly."

He pursed his lips. "As soon as Beck's back, we'll sit down with him."

"Thank you. I'll park while you go meet Beth. Speaking of that," I said, wiggling my eyebrows at him, "I think I've seen you flirt with our beautiful Dr. Chavez a few times."

He blushed! Actually blushed. "It's instinct. And then I remember she's a vampire."

"So? You told me you weren't going to be prejudiced anymore."

"That was against shifters and Alexander, not all vampires. Besides," he waved a hand back and forth between us, then dropped it. "I guess there is no *us* is there?"

I swallowed. "Nope. Just super close friends."

He looked thoughtful for a second then shook his head.

"Naw. I don't need the trouble of a relationship right now. Quit bringing up impossible things and park."

It only took me a few minutes to get in the building. Scott was already in a room, on a table, and both Beth and Karlof were with him.

"Kinsley," Beth said. "Dr. Karlof and I have been working on something we'd like to share with you and Scott. I haven't even had a chance to talk to Beck about it."

Scott shrugged at me.

"Okay," I said.

"Do you know how I became a vampire?" Beth asked.

"Beck said you were dying of cancer and he and Karloff changed you."

"Yes. But we did it scientifically. Dr. Karlof had already been experimenting with blood since he'd been trying to create a synthetic for Beck. Long, gross story short, they hooked me up to a high-powered transfusion machine. The cancer was in almost my whole body and Dr. Karlof didn't think me ingesting blood orally would do the job."

Made sense, I supposed, if you were looking at it scientifically and medically.

Beth continued. "My *sick* blood was removed and it was replaced with a combination of the incomplete synthetic blood mixed with enzymes from Dr. Karlof and Beck, since vampires don't create their own blood, but do hold a store in their bodies for a short period of time."

Scott said, "Okay. What does this have to do with us? Or anything for that matter."

Beth turned a screen so Scott and I could see it. She pointed to her microscope and the slide under it. "This is human blood." She held up a different slide. "This is cancerous blood." She showed us the differences in the red and white blood cells so we could tell healthy blood from unhealthy. She held up another syringe. "Don't get mad."

I looked from her to Scott to Karlof. "You son of a bitch," I said to Karlof.

He leaned toward me and pointed a finger. "You and Beckford would not listen. I knew you were special. That your blood was special."

"What's going on?" Scott asked moving to get off the table. I wasn't sure if he was going to grab me or Karlof.

"That's my blood, isn't it?" I said.

"What?" asked Scott.

"Yes," said Beth quickly. "But watch."

Before I pummeled both her and Karlof, she injected one drop of my blood onto the cancer cells. It looked like insects fighting under the microscope. The cells slowly took the shape and color of healthy cells.

"What the hell is happening?" asked Scott.

"Her blood heals the bad blood. Look." Beth put the two slides side by side. You couldn't tell a difference between them.

Oh. My. God.

"This is how you finally created the synthetic, isn't it?" I asked.

Karlof tuned away and then spun back. "No one has ever had access to Shadower blood with the technology we have today. But you wouldn't even let me look at it! You wouldn't even listen!"

"I'm not a science experiment!" I yelled at him.

Beth stepped in front of me. "Your blood can heal Scott's leg. Oliver's arm. If any other humans got hurt, you could save them with your blood."

I stopped mid swing, chest heaving as I tried to breathe and process what she was saying.

"No," said Scott. "You blindsided us with this bullshit

while Beck is out of the country and using my leg as a carrot. No." He moved to get off the table. "We're leaving. Go find Floyd. We'll bring him home and take care of him ourselves."

Scott was pissed. Pissed on my behalf. And I was considering the implications of having all-healing super-blood and what that meant for my friends and family.

I held a hand up for Scott to stop. Then I looked at Beth and Karlof. "What are the side effects?"

Karlof smiled and crossed his arms. I hauled off and punched him. Since he wasn't expecting it, he careened into the TV screen and ripped it off the wall as he went down.

"That's for tricking me, lying to me, and now being a pompous ass about it." I turned to Beth. "I trusted you, Dr. Chavez." I looked at Karlof as he tried to pull himself from the floor with some dignity. "If either of you *ever* lie to me again: I. Will. End. You. Are we clear?"

Both looked at me with new eyes.

Now it was my turn to point a finger. "I am *not* completely unreasonable. It's been a fucking rough five months. I didn't even understand what I was. All I knew was vampires wanted my blood. If someone had put together some science and come to me, come to Beck and me, I would have heard you out."

Beth nodded. "I'm sorry, Kinsley. You're absolutely right. I got so caught up in the science and the implications of what this meant, I lost my head. I had to become undead in order to survive cancer." She laughed without humor. "Survive. Such a misleading word. Your blood could have cured me. That's all I could think about." Her voice broke. If vampires could cry, there would have been tears. "Then I thought about Scott's broken leg and Oliver's broken arm. Hell, even Floyd's weak heart. One drop of your blood fixed those cancer cells." She waved her hand at the microscope.

"First, how long have you had my blood?" I looked at Karlof.

"You are an impetuous child!" he spat at me. "You are no different than the human Beck tried to bring in with us two hundred years ago. And just like her, you're going to get people killed. You can't think beyond your own needs instead of the greater good."

"What greater good, huh, Karlof? Yours? Vampires?"

He hissed at me like a cat and strode from the room. Now who was the impetuous child?

I wanted to go after him. I also wanted to know about whoever he was talking about who Beck had *brought in* two hundred years ago. But not the time.

Beth held out her hand to stop me from chasing after Karlof. "We've had your blood since the night of the SAM Gala. I took it as standard procedure when someone is brought in. I didn't take it to be sneaky. Then we saw how fast you were healing and I just went to work on you. Later that night I remembered I'd taken the vial. I kept thinking: she healed so fast. I wonder what her blood looks like under the microscope."

Beth ducked her head. "I didn't even know until weeks later when I told Karlof I thought your blood could heal humans like it did Beck, that Karlof had already asked and you and Beck said no. I like you. I think you liked me. It just kind of snowballed. Then I thought: well, if it does what I think it can, she'll understand and she'll be happy. I was wrong."

Scott was watching Beth and me closely. "I don't think you're wrong. I just think she's overwhelmed and felt she'd been tricked."

"Life is kind of tricky right now," I said. I really liked Beth. I hoped she wasn't lying to me. "Okay," I said on a sigh. "Side effects."

Beth moved into doctor mode. "It's only for short term. Even though it appeared to heal those cancer cells on the slides, it's more like it gave them a boost to fight for the moment, but in the regular blood stream, there are too many sick cells. I think a cancer patient would feel better for a bit, but then the effect of your blood wears off, or gets overwhelmed by the cancer, and the blood of the sick patient eventually goes back to their normal."

"So I can't cure cancer."

"No. It would have to be like what Beck and Dr. Karlof did to me; complete removal of the sick blood replaced with new blood *infected* with the vampire virus. One death sentence for another. At least I'll live forever." She smiled sadly. Ignoring the sympathy in my eyes, she continued. "Your blood can heal broken bones and non-mortal wounds. The cells regenerate in a targeted, localized spot."

"You didn't experiment on humans, did you?" Scott asked. It was right on the tip of my tongue to say the same thing.

"Yes and no," Beth said. "I work nights at the county morgue. It's a way to keep track of strange deaths and use cadavers of unclaimed bodies."

I almost asked what she used the cadavers for. Instead I said, "Is this all sanctioned through Beck or is this just Karlof?"

"Beck knows," said Beth. "It's how we get blood for consumption and it's how we've been working to create the synthetic."

She pulled some pictures up on her phone. "I'd show these on the screen, but," she waved at the broken screen Karlof had ripped off the wall.

"Sorry," I mumbled.

"This person had been stabbed multiple times and died at the scene of the crime." She showed us a stab wound. "I was on scene with the Coroner Van. It had been maybe an hour since his time of death. I injected some of your blood into the area around the wound." She swiped to the next picture. The wound was closed and we could see where the skin had stitched itself together without real stitches.

"Holy hell," Scott said, leaning in closer.

I swallowed. "But this person is dead. Just because the outside of a wound healed doesn't mean it would work on living tissue for any period of time or that there wouldn't be some kind of side effect."

"You are correct. But I've never had a living test subject." She looked at Scott.

"No!" I said.

"Why not?" asked Scott. "Alexander had your blood. Why can't I?"

He was trying to joke with me, but it wasn't funny. What if my blood killed him? Turned him into. . . into what? It couldn't turn him into a vampire could it? No. Because I wasn't a vampire.

I threw a hand in the air. "We have to ask Beck. Or Marie. Or, or, Lilith!"

"You're really grasping at straws if you want to ask the Queen of Sluts for help," Scott said.

Beth smothered a laugh.

He reached out and took one of my hands. "Kinsley, it's my decision. It's just a blood transfusion or an injection? What would it be Doc?"

"Well, since it needs to be localized, we need to do it like a bone marrow transplant or harvest. I'll need to inject it directly into your bone."

I grimaced. "Isn't that excruciating?"

"Yes," Beth said.

"Let's try it," Scott said.

I threw both hands in the air and turned my

"Sweet thing," he soothed, "can you imagine what this means if it works?"

I turned to face him again. "Yes! I continue to be a damn blood bank for everyone! That's a scary thought."

"No," said Scott. "You decide when and what your blood is used for. You. No one takes it without your permission and you could save people. Humans. Shifters. Didn't it help Nate when you were kidnapped?"

It had. And that had saved my life and Nate's.

"We won't tell anyone," Beth said.

"If this works, he'll have a healed broken leg weeks early." I waved at Scott's cast.

"We'll just say it was from the synthetic blood. Lock who we hang out with. I bet no one even questions it," Scott said.

"You really want to do this?" I asked.

"Hell yes. Why don't you want me to?"

"What if I *infect* you?" I waved an arm between us.

"With what?"

"I don't know! It's unknown. It's never been done!" I rubbed my eyes with my palms. "You're doing this? No matter what?"

"Yep." He nodded.

Okay then. "I'm still going to ask Beck."

"That's fine," said Scott. "We'll go get set up in the surgery room. Doc, if Kins is gloved and gowned, can she be in with me?"

Beth smiled. "Yes. And, Kinsley, I know you're angry, but I'd really like Dr. Karlof with us."

I looked to Scott. "That's up to him."

Scott nodded at Beth. "Whatever you want, Doc."

"If you die, I'm going to kill you," I said.

He laughed. "If I die, you finally get to say *I told you so*."

"Not. Funny."

He shrugged. "It kind of is."

Chapter Twenty-Four

"BECK?"

"*I am here.*"

I moved to the hallway and sat, head in hands. Rather than trying to talk, I did what Beck did in the car when we were going to Paradise. I opened my mind and sent the whole morning to him, including Marie's training techniques.

"*My. I did not think it was possible, but you continue to find more and more unknown situations.*"

I went back to talking out loud. I wasn't sure what made me feel crazier: having a conversation in my head or having a one-sided out loud discussion. "I didn't even do anything. I'm just along for the ride."

"*I want to begin with an apology of you seeing Lilith and me.*"

"It's fine. You need her, she needs you."

"*I do not need her.*"

I sighed. "You know what I mean. I won't bring it up if you don't. I do want to say, just to get the last word in, whatever she's doing for us better be a pretty damn big deal. Now, to Scott. Will my blood kill him?"

"If Beth and Karlof say he will be okay, what is your hesitation?"

"If I kill him, it will destroy me." A tear slid down my cheek and I wiped it away.

"You are not doing anything. A medical procedure is being conducted. Scott wants to do it and a top blood specialist and surgeon are going to complete the operation. As far as we know, your blood does nothing out of the ordinary except regenerate at an extreme rate which allows it to have healing properties. It is not like vampire enzymes which we know to mutate and adjust the host."

"Why couldn't Beth just say that to me?"

"I know how your mind works. I said what you needed to hear to ease your heart, but it is all true."

"Thank you."

"Would you like to keep our connection open until I am home?"

"Yes."

"Thank you for trusting me."

I stood, but stayed in the hallway. "None of this is going to work if we don't trust each other."

"You are absolutely right. We are on a plane tonight. There are still things to do, but I will be right here if you need me."

"Where will Lilith stay when you get back?"

"As soon as we have captured Isaac and Mya, Lilith gets Mya and she will leave."

"What do you mean, Lilith *gets* Mya?"

"Lilith's payment has been essence from me and her other payment is a vampire or shifter to keep and use. Since I am not willing to give up anyone, I decided Mya was the perfect choice. We would kill her anyway."

I slid back into the chair. "So Mya will be her what? Sex

slave? What if she gets away? She'll want to kill us even more than she already does."

"She will not get away. And if she does, we kill her."

I had to remember I was now part of a universe that didn't operate like the human world I was used to. I was going to have to get rid of my preconceived notions of right and wrong, black and white, life and death. We were going to continue to take risks with our lives and the lives of people we loved and cared about.

Scott was right. He had to do this. If my blood could heal the people I cared about, that was all that mattered.

Shaking my head, I stood again on wobbly legs. "If this works, do you think we could kill Isaac and still be able to save Marie? She should have the same healing I have and we could like, double it, with my blood?"

"Maybe. You will have to allow Karlof to take both your and Marie's blood and continue more experiments."

"Whatever. At this point, it doesn't matter. If it will save lives, save Marie's life, then I will give him whatever he wants."

"He will be pleased."

I huffed out a breath. "I'm not doing it for him."

"Noted."

I waved my arm, even though Beck couldn't see me. "Go do your stuff. I'm going to either watch a medical miracle or the death of my friend."

"As I am sure Masters will say to you: quit being so melodramatic. Everything will be fine." He laughed.

I laughed, too. Everything would be fine. It had to be. I wasn't accepting anything other than that. Back straight, legs steady once again, I marched back to Scott's room.

It took three hours to get everything set up. Scott's cast was removed and his leg put in traction to keep it set during the procedure. Beth took a fresh vial of blood from me.

The surgical room was all white sheets and stainless steel. I looked like an extra in a medical TV show with a set of light blue scrubs, matching cap, surgical mask, gloves, and paper booties over my shoes. I wasn't going to take any risks with *normal* germs and Scott's health even though he wasn't technically being cut open.

Scott was given a local anesthetic on his leg since he'd be awake. They were going to inject my blood directly into his bone marrow. We had two screen views, one was regular and one was magnified so we could see exactly what my blood did to Scott's bone.

Science geek that I was, I was super excited to see what would happen. Emotional mess that I was, I wished it was someone else we were watching it happen to.

"Here we go," said Beth.

I moved by Scott's shoulder and took his hand. He gripped me tight as the giant needle pierced skin and then moved to the bone.

"Take some relaxing breaths," said Beth.

Scott tensed. It had to be excruciating, but he didn't say a word.

The sci-fi factor did not disappoint.

Beth pulled the bone needle free and we watched the screen as my blood moved in like little worker bees and the bone began to stitch itself up.

Scott inhaled and threw his head back, jaw clenched.

"What's wrong? What's happening?" I stroked his face with my gloved hands.

"It's okay, sweet thing, just hurts like a son of a bitch. It feels like it did when it broke."

I looked to Beth. "Is that normal?"

"Honey," Scott said, pulling my hand to his face, "how in

the hell would she know? No one's ever done this before, remember?"

I closed my eyes and lowered my forehead down to his. It was awkward with the masks, but I didn't care. Pulling back enough to meet his eyes, I sent calming thoughts to him. Our minds connected in that moment and I let Scott feel all the love and respect I had for him. The fear of losing his friendship. The fear of letting down all the people who were counting on me.

His eyes widened. "Holy shit, sweet thing."

"Sleep," I whispered.

He closed his eyes and his breathing evened out. The heart monitor went from the painful, speedy beeps to an even, rhythmic cadence.

"Did she just do what I think she did?" I heard Karlof ask from behind me. "She's too powerful. I've never heard of a Shadower having vampire mind control."

I looked over my shoulder. Eyes wide, he gaped. Fear, awe, and a glimmer of need flashed over his face. He wanted to taste my blood.

I looked away. I wasn't scared of Karlof anymore. I wasn't scared of anything. And that wasn't good. There was so much I was capable of. That made me necessary and dangerous. It was going to take time to process.

"This is amazing," Beth said.

We watched as the small hole for the bone needle closed itself.

I kissed Scott's forehead and moved the hand I'd been gripping carefully on his stomach. Turning to Beth I said, "How long will you keep him here?"

"It all depends. The break is completely healed. As long as he can walk and doesn't have any pain, he can go home when he wakes up." She tilted her head toward Scott. "How long will he be asleep?" she asked.

"I don't know. Not long, I don't think." I shook my head. "I've never done that before so I don't know."

Beth nodded. "I'll have him moved to a recovery room where we'll continue to monitor his vitals."

"I'm not letting him out of my sight. Let's go." I waved an arm toward the door.

Twenty minutes later, Scott's vitals were stable and he was starting to wake.

I had just finished texting Rachel and Shawn letting them know Scott's doctor's appointment was over but we wouldn't be coming back to the office. I asked if Marie was still doing okay and what time they thought they'd be home. Scott opened his eyes just as I hit send.

"Hey," I said quietly, moving to take his hand and touch his cheek. "How do you feel?"

He took a moment to close his eyes and stretch. When he opened his eyes again, he smiled. "I feel fucking fabulous." He moved to get out of bed.

"Slow down there, tiger." I chuckled. "We don't know how you're going to do. Does your leg hurt?"

He lifted his leg off the bed. "Not at all. This is amazing. I also feel full of energy. Like super full of energy. Like I could run a marathon."

He stood slowly, testing how the leg would take his weight. When he looked steady, he started doing jumping jacks and then jogging in place. He looked ridiculous since he was wearing a hospital gown. I stifled a laugh.

"Seriously, Kins, holy shit."

I raised my eyebrows. "You've been saying that a lot."

"I can't come up with anything better." He picked me up and spun me around. "Your blood has, like, supercharged me."

Laughing, I wrapped my arms around his neck. "That's a scary thought. I'm not sure what a supercharged version of you would be."

He gave me a quick kiss and set me on my feet. "Scary is how you were in my head. Is that how it is with Beck? All intimate and open? No secrets?"

I shrugged. "Basically. I'm learning how to block some of it when I need to."

He shook his head. "I don't think I'd like that all the time. I owe you an apology for accusing you of telling him things before me. You didn't really have a choice, did you? I know you tried to tell me, but a normal person can't know what that whole mind-meld thing is like." He stopped pacing, and turned to me, eyes wide. "I wonder if you could get into a complete stranger's head?"

I'd been wondering the same thing. What an invasion of privacy. I almost didn't want to try. No one should have their mind looked into against their will.

My phone chimed. Rachel. She said Marie was great and had been doing training exercises all day with a break for lunch and they'd be home by five. It was two o'clock

"Let's walk in the hallway. You're obviously fine since you can do jumping jacks, but I'd like to go see Floyd."

"Can I put on pants?"

I laughed. "I guess so. Although, the staff probably wouldn't mind seeing your ass."

He punched me on the shoulder and moved to the bathroom to get dressed. The normalcy of our teasing made me think things were looking up.

We headed to the other side of the facility with the rooms.

Floyd was eating Jell-O and watching TV. When he saw Scott, he raised his eyebrows. "Where are your crutches? And your cast?"

I lifted my hands. "So, apparently my blood heals. Want some injected into you?"

Floyd barked a laugh. "Things are never dull around you guys."

"I thought we weren't going to tell anyone," said Scott.

"It's Floyd. Of course I'm going to tell him. Besides, he knows everything else, so why not?"

"I don't know everything," Floyd said.

I waved a hand at Scott's leg. "Ever heard of anything like this? Did my parents ever give anyone their blood after a fight to help heal them?"

Floyd scrunched his face in thought. "Not that I know of. The only people who ever healed quickly were your parents and Marie. The rest of us had to nurse our wounds and be normal."

I moved to the edge of Floyd's bed. "Why did you actively hunt? I've been thinking about it. Scott and his team just happen to stumble across supernatural beings and if needed, kill them. He runs a legit business and has more regular security cases than paranormal ones."

"Good point," said Scott, dropping into the chair. "I tried looking for monsters and rarely found huge groups."

"You have pictures of Hunters looking like paramilitary groups from South American jungles. How did you guys travel all over and kill things and no one noticed?" I asked.

Floyd took another bite of Jell-O and set down his spoon. "It was a different time. I fought with your parents from the early sixties to the mid-nineties. It was a time of free love, communes, and lots and lots of sex and drugs. If people saw or experienced anything weird and tried to tell someone, it was usually attributed to drugs. We realized many of the communes popping up all over the country were really run by vampires and shifters. They didn't work together, but they had factions.

The East Coast was mostly vampires. The West Coast mostly shifters; easier for animals to blend in, I guess." Floyd fumbled with the bed remote, pushing buttons until he adjusted his bed so he was sitting up straighter.

"The communes would bring people in. The vampires brainwashed people into giving them their money and cutting ties with their families. Then they fed off them until they died. Sometimes they'd turn people, but we learned later most of the people they tried to turn died."

I sat on the foot of Floyd's bed. "Beck had said Monarchs were the best at turning people. There's more to it than just a bite and giving the human vampire enzymes."

"Yep," said Floyd. "And it appears vampires are more about having food sources than having more vampires."

"Competition?" Scott pondered. "The more vampires, the more food you need? You start having too many vampires and it draws unwanted attention because you have more vampires to feed."

"Could be," said Floyd. "We never took time to ask."

"What about shifters?" I asked.

Floyd shrugged. "Most people attacked by a shifter die. And from what I learned from Mei, only two blood born shifters can have offspring, and even that is rare. The female can't shift while she's pregnant or the offspring die from the internal trauma caused from a shift."

"That makes sense, now that you say it," I said.

"Yeah," said Floyd. "We never knew that when we were hunting. Again, never took the time to look into it."

I looked to Scott and then back at Floyd. "I get vampires having communes and brainwashing people; it's easier to write-off a disappearance or strange behavior. So you guys showed up at these communes and killed everyone?"

Floyd nodded. "Basically. Your mom and sometimes Marie

would go in as bait. They'd have a story of running away from an abusive relationship and needing a place to stay. Within a day or two your mom would know if there were any vampires. She'd recon, get us our info, and then the rest of us would come in, kill the vamps, and get the humans out. Or sometimes we'd kill the vamps and the humans would stay and keep living in the communes. It wasn't a bad way to live if you liked that sort of thing."

"Shifters?" Scott said, an edge to his voice. "Did you ever have cases of shifters slaughtering families like mine?"

Floyd shook his head. "Sometimes. But it was rare. For the most part, our experience with shifters was they tried to live normal lives, maybe they hunted wild animals to tamp down that instinct, but they kept to themselves."

Scott rubbed his forehead. "So when would they kill innocent people?"

Floyd shrugged. "All your dad could come up with was just like normal people, there are good and bad. Maybe a person with questionable moral qualities had been turned and they realized they had free rein to kill now. Or maybe they couldn't keep the chase and kill instinct held at bay by killing wild animals and wanted the thrill of hunting people."

"Now that we're working with shifters, it's time to ask," I said. "Off the top of my head, my thought is they don't *need* to kill and feed like vampires because shifters can eat regular food. So, the only reason to kill a person is for sport."

"And to maybe try and change them, but it doesn't work out," said Scott. "I guess I'd never taken the time to think about it. I didn't care because I just wanted to kill them all."

"Of course you did," I said, moving off the bed to stand by him. "Your only experience was death. The death of people you loved. You wouldn't have known *good* shifters existed." I put my hand on his shoulder.

He shrugged, but unclenched his jaw. He'd spent his whole adult life killing what he thought were monsters. It was a lot to wrap the brain around that not *all* of them were bad.

"So going back to the beginning," said Floyd, "I don't know as much about Shadowers as I do Hunters and being a Hunter. And being a Hunter isn't really a thing anymore. Technology has changed a lot. Vampires can hide, and get money and blood different ways. I'd think shifters would be having a harder time, too, with the fact more and more areas are being developed. Vampires have more food, more people, and shifters have less food, less wild game."

"But shifters don't have to hunt. They can eat regular food," said Scott.

Floyd lifted his hands. "But they're still a *wild* animal. There will be an instinct to hunt, to chase, to kill."

We all let that sink in for a moment. "Are we safe around all Beck's shifters?" Scott finally said quietly. "I mean *really* safe. I know you've been around them for five months but that's only been a few of them. What kind of danger are we potentially bringing into our house by actively recruiting vampires and shifters into our city, Beck's club, and my business?"

I didn't know what to say. Scott was right. When he said it out loud, it seemed like a really bad idea. Beck was inviting vampires and shifters to come to the Seattle area. How would we police any of them who were bad?

I looked helplessly at Scott.

"How about this," Floyd said. "I lived half my life with Tom and Claire. We never did have any shifters or vampires as part of our hunting group. But, Scott, was Tom trying to get you to add some?"

Scott nodded. "He said maybe it was time to join forces. I said: 'the enemy of my enemy is my friend?' and he said it was more than that. That we needed to know what was coming so we could protect the people we loved."

"Needed to know what was *coming?*" I said. "What the hell does that mean? That sounds ominous. Especially since mom and dad were killed."

"If Tom thought it was time to join forces, then maybe it's time," said Floyd. "What you've done the last few months seems to be working. I say you keep doing what you're doing until it doesn't work. What else can you do?"

"*You going to contribute to this conversation?*" I asked Beck.

"*You are trying to justify the means to understand the end. Because you are all human, you need human explanations. Why does a shark hunt? Because it can and because it is hungry. Vampires are the top of the food chain with shifters just below. We follow your human rules only to keep from drawing attention to ourselves. We will be here when you are dead.*"

His matter of fact and cold tone was true. But it still scared me.

Chapter Twenty-Five

WHEN SCOTT WALKED into the kitchen, Rachel almost dropped a jar of pickles. "Didn't you have two more weeks of a cast?" she asked.

"Yep," he said, going to the fridge. "Seems having vampire doctors and synthetic blood is a benefit."

"Eww," said Mei. She covered her neck with her hands. "Does that mean you're going to want to suck someone's blood? Are you going to turn into a vampire?"

"Guess we'll see," he said, winking at me. "I'm starving."

"For regular food, right?" asked Mei, stepping away from him.

"Yes." He rolled his eyes. "For regular food."

"The energy it took your body to heal makes your metabolism work overtime. You'll be eating like Nate and me for a bit. I wonder how long?" I said.

"I'm a science experiment," Scott said as he constructed two giant roast beef and cheese sandwiches.

"Those better be for me," I said, crossing my arms.

He paused and grabbed the loaf of bread. "Sorry. I forgot you needed to eat too."

"How is Floyd?" Mei asked. "I should have gone to see him, but training with Marie was awesome."

I gave Mei's shoulder a quick squeeze. "He's good. Beth said I can bring him home tomorrow. He said he might want to go back to Newport soon. Being around Marie is going to be tough for him." I looked around the kitchen. "Speaking of, where is she?"

Mei set a pan of leftover spaghetti on the table for us. "Upstairs taking a shower."

We were in the middle of devouring sandwiches and spaghetti when my cell phone rang.

"No one ever calls you," Rachel said, looking at my phone like it was going to bite her.

Glancing at the screen, I grunted. "I don't recognize the number." I answered, switched to speaker, and set the phone on the table. "Hello?"

"Kinsley," said a voice I didn't recognize, "this is Riley. We met a few times at Screamers and again yesterday at the staff meeting. Beck hired me last year as a bouncer."

"Riley, yes." I did a quick glance at Rachel.

She nodded and whispered, "Short, beefy, hot."

"Thank you," Riley said, "but I didn't call for a dating bio. Raven told me to call you because she wasn't sure what to do."

I stood from the table, food forgotten. "What's wrong? Why didn't she call me? Is she okay?"

Riley cleared his throat. "Nutshell: unknown wolves showed up about ten minutes ago and wanted to talk to Gerald. Gerald said it was part of his pack and everything would be fine. They went out back to the alley. Things are getting heated. Raven, Kevin, and Lucas are working on getting the humans out. Told them we have a gas leak in the kitchen and they have to go home. Luckily there aren't too many people here since it's still early evening. Raven said we need you down here and to bring Mei. This could get ugly."

Shit.

I did some quick mental planning then said, "Rachel, stay here with Marie; we'll send Oliver over. Even with a broken arm, he's a force to be reckoned with."

Scott was already calling Oliver as I went back to Riley on the phone. "Try to keep damage to a minimum. We need to be diplomatic if Beck wants to bring in shifters and vampires as allies. The last thing we need is word getting out wolves were killed at Screamers."

"Or a supernatural fight ending up all over social media," said Rachel, eyes wide.

Shit. I hadn't thought of that.

Riley cleared his throat again. "That's why Raven had me call you now. Gerald may have everything under control, but wolf packs can be territorial. I was shocked when I got here last year and met Ian and Gerald. They never did tell me why they left their pack and joined Beck. Maybe it's just about that."

At the sound of Ian's name, my heart squeezed. He'd died to protect me and it still hurt. "We'll be there as soon as we can." I ended the call.

I sprinted upstairs behind Scott and we entered the tactical room for gear. I didn't want to go in visually carrying and add to the tension, but we also had to make sure we were safe and could keep our people safe.

We both did shoulder holsters with two pistols and extra clips. I added the sword sheath to my back. My hair mostly hid the top, and a jacket would cover the rest.

"Boss?" Oliver yelled from downstairs.

"Coming," Scott called.

Marie appeared in the doorway, wrapped in a towel. "I can help." She grabbed my arm.

Scott looked at me and held up his hands. My choice.

I shook my head. "I just got you back, Marie, and I don't know exactly what's going on. Stay here and keep Rachel safe, please." The pleading in my voice was obvious. Marie was still a wild card.

She tilted her head and pursed her lips, but she let go of my arm. "You watched me this morning. You know what I'm capable of. You need my help."

"Please? Next time." I pushed past her and took the stairs two at a time, Scott on my heels.

Oliver pulled back when he saw Scott practically running. "Um, didn't you have a broken leg this morning?" he said, holding out the fob to the Hummer.

Snatching it, Scott nodded. "Yes. I'll tell you about it later. Is the Hummer loaded up?"

Oliver pointed out the window. "Yep, regular tac gear in the lockbox. You're loaded for bear if you need it."

"I hope we don't," I said.

"Be careful!" Rachel called to our backs. "Call or text me as soon as you can!"

Scott, Mei, and I were in the Hummer headed out of the driveway, weapons ready, three minutes after Riley called. Not bad.

"What do you know about wolves?" I asked Mei and Scott.

"They hunt in packs," Scott said.

"They don't play well with others outside their pack," Mei added.

"Why?" I asked. Every shifter I'd met so far treated other shifters and humans the same.

Mei shrugged. "Because wolves are pack animals, their pack always comes first. If you betray your pack, it's usually a death sentence. They don't act much different than dogs and real wolves when it comes to dominance. There will be a pack leader, the alpha. The wolves in his pack will be submissive to him. As outsiders and not being wolves, we have some choices. Making eye contact is a show of equality and/or dominance. You can exert your dominance by keeping eye contact.

"Cat shifters are about family, whether it's family like mine, blood and born, or family they create like what Beck has with your cougars. We're fine alone, but we like the interaction when it suits us."

She paused and huffed out a breath. "I've been thinking about the dynamics of what Beck is trying to build. You've got a random bear and a couple lone wolves, but the rest are cougars. Maybe because they blend in since this is the Pacific Northwest?" She shrugged. "If I stay and Shawn throws in, a leopard and a panther don't blend. We'll have to be really careful when hunting animals."

I'd been thinking about that, too.

She cocked her head. "Does Beck know why Gerald and Riley aren't with their packs? It's strange for wolves to be packless."

"*Riley did not want to join a pack. Ian and Gerald did not like how their pack was being run. That is why they came to me years ago,*" Beck said.

I tossed my hands in the air in frustration. "It's about time! Where have you been?"

Scott could tell I was talking to Beck, so he told Mei.

"*Finishing with the Monarchs took all my concentration; I am sorry. We are boarding the plane. I will stay with you during the confrontation in case you need my power. The leader of Gerald's pack can be tricky. Watch your backs.*"

"Apparently our wolves didn't like how the local pack was operating," I told Scott and Mei.

"Local is relative," Beck said. "*They are part of the Okanogan National Forest in Washington and Canada. There is* more than one pack in that area since it is over two million acres of land."

I shared this with Scott and Mei.

"So what's the agenda, do you think?" Scott asked.

"I assume they want Gerald back and there may be retaliation over Ian's death. I am sorry I am not there."

I laughed without humor. "I'm guessing their timing is orchestrated. Someone told them you left the country and they showed up thinking the rest of us couldn't protect ourselves without you."

"They will be sadly mistaken."

I agreed.

Scott took a corner at break-neck speed. "I had Oliver put Joel, Quinn, and Logan on standby. Shawn will meet us there. We're going with a *no human* policy tonight if we can help it."

"Last I checked, you were human," Mei quipped from the backseat.

He smirked at her in the rear-view mirror. "I got a little super boost today. This pack of wolves isn't going to know what hit them."

I put my hand on his arm. "I don't want any deaths if we can help it. Let's hear them out and go from there. Again, Scott, you've always gone into all situations in elimination mode. That's not the case this time."

"I remember," he said, pulling up to Screamers. "But if anyone tries to hurt you, they die."

"I love a take charge man," Mei said, choosing a pistol from the lockbox. "I know how to shoot, but it's never been my weapon of choice."

"What is?" Scott asked.

Mei held up her hand and the ends of her fingers became two-inch curved claws. It felt like a trick of the light. Or magic.

"How the hell did you do that? That was Wolverine shit!" Scott said, eyes wide. "I've never seen a shifter do that!"

"Is shape shifting magic?" I asked. "Because it looks like magic. That's magic." I reached out a hand to touch Mei's claws and stopped about an inch away.

She laughed, and pulled the claws back into her body, and her hands were hands again. She turned her hands palm up and then palm down. "Born shifters have the ability to change parts of them as needed if they're old and have practiced. I am and I have." She shrugged. "The gun will be more for show. They'll be able to smell I'm a shifter, but they'll have no idea I'm capable of shifting that way."

Shawn stepped from the shadow of the building. Damn it. I should have known he was there; I needed to do a better job of paying attention to my surroundings using the auras.

"Think you can teach me to do that?" Shawn asked Mei.

She tilted her head. "Maybe. You said you were blood-born. Where is your kin?"

"Dead," he said, matter of fact.

"Do you want a weapon?" Scott asked him.

"I'll take the Smith and Wesson M&P 15," he said, grabbing a short barreled semi-automatic rifle from the lockbox. He strapped on extra magazines like I had at the house.

"Nice choice," said Scott. "I'll do the same so we can share magazines if it comes to that. We haven't gotten all the silver rounds from production yet, so we're short on silver ammo. Let's start with lead and switch to silver if things turn deadly. I really hope it doesn't. As Kins reminded me on the way over, we're being *diplomatic*." He made air quotes.

Shawn laughed. "I don't think I've seen you be diplomatic in a tactical situation. This should be interesting. And, didn't you have a broken leg this morning?"

Scott nodded. "Sure did."

I watched the men gear up and lock up the Hummer.

Scott slipped an earpiece in, so did Shawn. "Check," said Scott. "Logan, Joel, Quinn, check?" He paused. "Hold the perimeter; do not engage unless I request. Keep civilians out of the area."

"This is all about a show of force," I said. "The wolves didn't feel strong enough to exert their power with Beck here. They obviously didn't know about us. So whoever told them Beck was gone didn't know we were working together or they don't know I'm a Shadower."

"Or they're hoping we all kill each other," Scott said with a shrug.

"Or that," I agreed.

"They'll know we're here," said Shawn. "They'll smell us. I don't know if adding me and Mei will make it worse."

"At this point, it probably doesn't matter," said Mei. "They'll think their pack together will be stronger than our ragtag band of cats and a bear. If they attack, they'll go for Scott first since he's human. They'll also be expecting Gerald and maybe Riley to side with them since they're pack. "

"She is correct," said Beck. "*Except Riley was never pack. He chose not to stay with them. Follow your heart and brain when you talk to them, as you did at the meeting at Masters Security. I will stay out of the way so I do not distract you. Draw from me if you need my power.*"

"I don't know how to do that."

"*You will know when you need to.*" He moved to the back of my mind, as promised, and our group headed to the door.

"Kinsley, pull your pistol," Scott said.

"Nope. I'm going in like this. They'll smell the gunpowder and know I'm carrying. I want to show them I just want to talk."

He clenched his jaw. "Again, anyone goes for you, I'm shooting first and asking questions later."

I patted his cheek and pulled open the door to Screamers wondering what we'd find inside.

Kevin lay just inside the door, not moving but no obvious wounds. "I can hear his heartbeat," Mei said. "So he's alive."

They had knocked out a bear shifter instead of killing him. That had to be something in our favor.

Scott and Shawn shouldered their rifles, visually sweeping the room, and Mei did the same with her pistol.

"I won't kill anyone unless you make me," said a deep voice from the shadow of the bar.

Shawn did another visual sweep and then took a deep breath. "I've got six hostiles, four friendlies. Scratch that. Ten hostiles. Mei, you get a whiff of four more?"

"Yes," she whispered. "No visual."

I took a moment to send out my feelers and make an aura map. I didn't have time to concentrate the way I needed, but I was at least able to tell there weren't any humans, except Scott, anywhere.

"They're at the door to the alley," I said. I had to close my mental map so I could concentrate on the people in front of me.

"With Gerald," the unknown voice supplied. "Either he comes with us or he dies."

I stepped forward to get a better look at what was going on.

The stranger continued, "I haven't decided what to do with Riley. He came to the pack years ago but never joined. Technically he's not mine. But I should kill him for being a prick."

Riley growled.

The apparent leader of the wolves punched him and Riley fell to the floor. I didn't have a lot of experience with shifters in human form, but for this guy to punch another shifter and knock him out seemed like a pretty big deal. I wondered if that's what had been done to Kevin.

Six wolves, all in human form stood about twenty feet in

front of us. Two wolves held Raven and two more held Lucas. Another stood between them, just behind the wolf who had been speaking to me; the leader. The alpha?

He tilted his head at me as I examined the situation and him. He had shoulder length, dark brown hair, golden skin, and yellow eyes. Those were wolf eyes, not human. Were they always like that?

"Bring Gerald," he yelled to the back of the club.

The four wolves came from the door to the alley with Gerald hanging limply between them, feet dragging as they brought him into the room.

The leader of the wolves titled his head to me. "Who are you?" he asked, waving a hand. "What gives *you* the right to come in here with weapons, getting in the middle of pack business? You're not a vampire." He sniffed the air, nose high. "But you smell different. Not shifter, not quite human." His forehead wrinkled in confusion.

I held out my arms and projected my voice through the room. "I am Kinsley Preston. You are in *my* territory, in *my* club, in *my* city. You don't get to show up here and hurt *my* people."

The wolf laughed. "*Your* territory, city, and club? Last I checked, you weren't the infamous vampire, Beckford Alexander."

I paused and then said in a lowered voice, "I'm his Shadower."

The wolves sucked in a collective breath. I could feel the fear from some of them.

"No," the alpha wolf whispered. "The Shadowers are all dead. It isn't possible. That son of a bitch lied to me!" He said the last part almost to himself.

"Let me guess," said Scott, moving to my side, rifle still up and ready. "Isaac told you Beck was in Greece submitting to the Monarchs and his territory and people were up for grabs."

The alpha wolf recovered from the momentary shock and squared his shoulders. "I am Dagan of the Pacific Pack. I am here to take what is mine. According to Pack law, I have that right."

I shrugged. "I am not Pack, so we do not recognize your Pack law. If you would like to release my people, my friends, we can talk like civilized humans and come to an agreement."

"I am neither civilized nor human," Dagan said with a throaty growl. "However, I am intrigued by your offer and why you seem to think you and your cats can stand against me and survive." Dagan waved his hand and his wolves dropped Gerald to the floor and stopped restraining Raven and Lucas.

I was getting really tired of this arrogant asshole. Luckily, I'd had months to learn how to handle arrogant assholes. I tilted my head to Scott, Shawn, and Mei. As though we were walking in a pit of vipers, we carefully moved around and situated ourselves until Dagan and his nine wolves were on one side of the dance floor at the tables and the rest of us were on the other side of the dance floor. Raven moved to Riley, and Lucas went to Gerald.

I heard Kevin groan from behind us, so he was coming around from being knocked out. Riley twitched, groaned, and then held a hand to his head. Gerald had been beat to shit in the alley, and I expressed my displeasure by kneeling and putting a hand on his shoulder and then glaring at Dagan.

"He wouldn't listen to reason," Dagan said.

I squeezed Gerald's shoulder and gave him a nod to let him know I had his back. Then I stood and took a few steps toward the pack of wolves. "What do you consider reason? You have no right to hurt my people," I said slowly, letting him see my anger.

"You want to talk about hurt?" Dagan yelled, grabbing a

chair and sliding it across the room with a screech. "You got Ian killed! You stole Gerald! Pack is family! You killed and kidnapped my family."

From his point of view, he wasn't wrong. But that wasn't the point. I looked at Gerald. "Did you come to Beck and his territory by your choice?"

Gerald nodded.

I lifted my chin in Dagan's direction. "Tell Dagan who got Ian killed."

Gerald lowered his head so he wasn't looking Dagan in the eyes, a sign of respect to acknowledge Dagan's dominance. "The vampire Isaac is the reason Ian is dead."

Dagan narrowed his eyes. "Explain."

Gerald looked to me.

Another chair flew across the room. "She is not your pack! Do not ask for her permission!"

Gerald put his head down more and whimpered. When he didn't speak, Dagan marched toward us, reached down, and picked Gerald up by the throat one handed, lifting him off the ground. Gerald thrashed and struggled to breathe.

"Stop!" I yelled. My voice carried power through the room like when Beck had been in Floyd's house. The shifters all whimpered, as if in pain, and moved to kneel on the ground, except for Dagan. He did drop Gerald, though.

He turned and moved to charge me. I held up a hand and energy flew from my fingers, slamming into Dagan, throwing him into the tables and chairs.

"That is how you draw on my power."

I didn't even know how I'd done it or *that* I'd done it until it was all over.

"What just happened?" asked Scott from behind me. He was trying to sight the rifle on Dagan but the power had knocked him to his knees as well.

"Don't shoot him," I said to Scott. "I want to see if he's ready to discuss terms now that he knows I can kick his ass."

Dagan slowly pulled himself from the floor. "You will regret that, human."

He pulled off his shirt, revealing corded muscles and more golden skin. He was going to shift to wolf and I wouldn't have any way to talk to him.

Damn it, I didn't want a fight.

Chapter Twenty-Six

"KINSLEY ISN'T HUMAN, as she just demonstrated, sir," Gerald finally said. "Please listen to her so she doesn't kill everyone in this room. Not only is she a Shadower, she is the Silver Shadower. How do you think she just did that?" Gerald stayed kneeling. "I believe all this has been orchestrated by the vampire Isaac."

"How have I been manipulated?" Dagan growled. He paced in short steps, back and forth, rotating his shoulders. He shook his head, and I saw the bones in his jaw shift, as though to start elongating to form his muzzle.

"Jesus," Scott said from behind me, rifle still sighted on Dagan and his men. "If he shifts, all bets are off."

"Agreed," said Shawn.

Mei moved next to me, knelt, and set her pistol at her feet. "You have much to learn about shifters, young Shadower." She winked at me but the others didn't see.

To Dagan she said, looking at the floor, "Dagan of the Pacific Pack, I am Mei Ling Xiu of the Qinghai Province. You have heard of my father, Chun-Chieh, leader of the Qinghai Province and surrounding areas?"

"Your father is Chun-Chieh?" Dagan finally stopped pacing. He cocked his head to the side, listening intently.

Mei stood and turned, pulling her hair up in a pony tail. A raised scar-brand of a Chinese symbol covered a one-inch section on the back of her neck.

"You are here why?" Dagan asked. His face was returning to normal. A man next to him handed over his shirt without moving from the floor.

Mei held out a hand toward me. "I offered assistance to the Silver Shadower and the Puget Sound Vampire to find their family member who was kidnapped by Isaac, the Sovereignty leader. As you have pledged, the Sovereignty is the sworn enemy of all who wish to stay hidden from the humans. If you attack the Shadower, you attack me. Which means you attack Chun-Chieh. I do not think that wise."

Beck's presence floated into my awareness. *"Two things: this is not the leader of the wolf pack I dealt with years ago, and I had no idea Mei's father was Chun-Chieh."*

Since I couldn't hold a conversation with Beck and pay attention to what was going on in front of me, I ignored Beck for now.

"Isaac is Sovereignty?" Dagan said, jaw clenched. A small spasm by his eye telegraphed his anger.

I nodded. "He has been passing himself off as a Monarch. He switched sides long ago. I'm making it my mission to kill him. He has taken much from me and many others. He is the reason Ian is dead."

Everything depended on Dagan's next move. Either he believed me and we were good or he didn't and it was going to be a bloodbath.

I held out my hands in what I hoped Dagan would take as a peaceful gesture. "Has word made it to your pack that Beckford

Alexander would like to offer Screamers as neutral ground? A place to network, feel safe, relax?"

Dagan bristled and bit out between his clenched teeth, "He wishes to steal more of my pack."

"No," I said quickly. "He wishes, *we* wish, to find more of our kind. Give hope to those who have been having to hide and feel alone. If you prove yourself an ally and show your pack will allow some freedoms, maybe more wolves will join you."

Dagan bared his teeth. "Pack does not get freedoms."

Mei stepped closer to Dagan. "Although he is a leopard, you know how my father has united the remaining shifters in Europe and Asia. You also know how he did that. By making changes from some of the old ways. Maybe it is time to change things."

Gerald stood slowly, still keeping his head down. "Dagan, you were powerful when Ian and I were in the pack, but you were not in charge. Warner was."

A collective shudder moved through the wolves. Gerald shook his head, lifted his eyes, then looked back to the floor. "It is true, then? That monster no longer leads our pack?"

Dagan sucked in a breath. "It is not *your* pack anymore; you left."

"And you know why!" Gerald yelled, raising his eyes. He clenched his fists at his sides. I'd never seen him like this. He no longer kept his head down. "That *monster* was demanding the defilement of the women of our pack! Of my sister! Of human women! He wanted pups and didn't care what that meant! He was poisoning the heritage of our pack!"

"I know!" Dagan roared. It turned to a mournful howl and the other wolves joined in, even Gerald and Riley. It was the sound of loss and death. Goosebumps covered my skin and a shiver ran over my body.

"Yes!" Dagan said, slamming his fist onto a table. The legs

buckled under his anger, and splinters of wood and metal littered the floor. "Warner is dead. I killed him. After the death of your sister and when you left, a small group of us knew change needed to come. You could have stayed and helped us. You *should* have stayed. It took years of planning and fight challenges and many more deaths. But I killed him and am the new pack leader. Me!" Dagan lifted his arms and made a full circle turn. His gaze landed on Gerald. "And now I am bringing our pack back together. You will come home."

"I have a new life," said Gerald, dropping his head again.

"I mean no disrespect," Mei said quietly, nodding her head down and then back up to meet Dagan's eyes, "but this would be a good time for me to once again remind you of my father and what he has accomplished over the last hundred years. I will get you in contact with him. He can help you."

Beck offered his thoughts. *"As a new pack leader, this Dagan will be looking to heal his pack and show his strength. Isaac took advantage of that. Let him know as my Shadower, you can offer them an alliance. This is another show of strength for him and us. Wolf packs do not usually align with a vampire due to power struggles. I am not interested in controlling his pack."*

Dagan turned his golden gaze to me." You are aligned with Chun-Chieh?" He pointed from me to Mei.

Ummm. I didn't even know who Chun-Chieh was or why he was apparently so damn important.

"Chun-Chieh controls and leads all of Asia and Europe's shifters; a king for lack of a better explanation. He is the strongest leader anyone has ever seen except for the Monarchs. And now he is the strongest since the Monarchs are no longer."

I sucked in a breath that I hoped no one around me heard. But they all had super hearing, so probably not as sneaky as I wanted. *"What do you mean the Monarchs are no longer? And do I admit to this aligning? Does it help or hurt us?"*

Mei tilted her head at me and raised her eyebrows. Covering for my too long pause of answering Dagan, Mei offered a small bow to him. "We are in the process of beginning discussions."

A lie but not?

"Monarchs are for the discussion when I am home. Let Mei handle any talk of her father so you are not to be made a liar."

I stood tall and held out my hand. "As Beckford Alexander's Shadower, I offer you, Dagan of the Pacific Pack, a truce and alliance." I tried to use Mei's formal wording so maybe I'd sound like I knew what I was doing. "Beckford Alexander, Monarch, does not want any control of your pack. He wishes for shifters and vampires to work together to continue hiding in plain sight. Everyone's numbers are dwindling. You can work together to stay safe and grow without the unnecessary deaths of humans, shifters, or vampires." I dropped my hand and linked my fingers behind my back to hide the tremor starting in my arms. I felt like I was walking a tightrope.

Dagan tilted his head. "I will discuss matters with my council and be in touch. It is a tempting offer, but it's not always wise to trust a vampire."

I couldn't disagree with him, so I offered what I could. "Then talk to your council about Shadowers and *our* history of strength and keeping the peace. I am Beck's Shadower, I am the Silver Shadower, and I'm not going anywhere. We need to work together and be able to trust each other. Go back to your pack and your council, learn about Isaac and his history of death and destruction and lies, now that you know who he is."

Dagan nodded. "I would like to offer my appreciation for the fact you came in here to talk, not just attack and try to kill. That shows me much of your character and trust." He turned to Mei and dipped his head. "I would also like to speak with your father, if he will hear from me."

Mei sighed, looking at me. "This is going to mean Blade and Blaze will show up. I'm sorry."

I wasn't sure why she was apologizing and the confusion must have crossed my face.

She raised her upper lip in disgust. "You'll understand when they get here." Mei bowed to Dagan. "I agree to act as an intermediary between you and my father. I will also do so for the Shadower and vampire, if you all wish." She turned back to me. "This was kind of my job when I was in China with my father. I'm good at it." She was more relaxed, and Dagan was too.

I waved a hand. "Yes, you are. Not a shot fired, no one shifted, and no one hurt. Thank you, Mei, I accept your offer to be our intermediary."

"As do I," said Dagan, "for both."

The collective feel of the room dropped from DEFCON 1 and thinking everyone was going to die, to DEFCON 5 and let's have drinks. I laughed and shook my head as Scott moved to my side.

"You did good, sweet thing." He put his arm around my shoulder. "Maybe there's something to your plan of diplomacy."

I laughed. "Did you just maybe admit shoot first isn't always the best plan?"

He shrugged, "Don't go putting words in my mouth. I will deny everything." He kissed my temple and used his coms to call in the others.

Logan, Joel, and Quinn joined us and for almost an hour, Mei shared contacts and suggestions with Dagan of how to interact with her father and a few thoughts on how to organize his broken wolf pack. Dagan also shared his story. He had only killed Warner a week ago and was figuring out how to be, not only a pack leader, but a better pack leader. I didn't envy him the job; it looked and sounded exhausting.

"*Not much different than being a Shadower,*" Beck said.

I chuckled and sent a text to Rachel to let her know all was good, no deaths, but now we were playing the game of *how to be nice to each other* and I didn't know what time we would be home.

"Speaking of home, when will you be home?" I asked Beck.

"*It is a twelve hour flight. Another ten hours.*"

"Good. While I like having a constant connection to you, having you back with us physically is better."

"*I agree, my dear. If I was not so drained from the confrontation, I would just pop myself to your location. I do not have the energy, though. I am sorry.*"

I shrugged even though he couldn't see me. "It's okay. It is what it is and everything worked out. I'll see you soon."

Beck sent me a zinger of need and love before closing our connection, and I shivered in full body technicolor with how he made me feel. If he had been in the room, I would have wanted to climb him like a tree. But he wasn't here with me, he was on an airplane with the Queen of Sluts. I growled as my brain tried to give me a picture of Lilith sex and blood because I knew he needed to feed, but I shut off the images before they could take over.

I needed my full attention on the here and now and what I could control.

Dagan was going to stay for a few days so he could meet Beck in person. He also wanted to see what Screamers was like and how the humans and shifters interacted. He needed to talk to other shifters to see what they said about Beck and me and what it was like to live in the city.

The wolves had cleaned up all the broken furniture and the plan was to open the club back up so everything appeared business as usual. Mei was going to stay to make sure that when the doors to Screamers opened, Dagan and his wolves could blend in. Raven offered to stay with her. Mei said she'd meet me in the morning to get Floyd.

After exchanging cellphone numbers, I reminded Dagan no killing on my way out the door and to call or text me if he needed anything or had any questions Mei couldn't answer. He gave me a cheeky finger wave.

Scott and I loaded up to head home and enjoyed a comfortable silence on our drive. I rode the whole way with my head back and my eyes closed thanking whatever God watching over us that things had gone smoothly and that Beck would be back by my side soon.

Considering it was still early, I was surprised when we pulled up to the house and everything was dark.

"Huh," Scott said. "Did Rachel ever text you back?"

I shook my head and looked at my phone. "No, now that you ask. We were so busy talking and I was soaking in all Mei's advice, I didn't really think about it."

The lights were on at Oliver's. "Did Oliver text you to say they were going to his house?" I asked.

Scott checked his phone. "Yes, he did. He said Marie wanted to practice with the daggers in his back yard using the human shaped targets."

I laughed and shook my head. "She spent the whole day fighting and practicing. You'd think she'd be tired."

"She's a machine," Scott said, laughing with me.

He pulled the Hummer into the garage and we agreed we'd take care of stowing the weapons upstairs after we checked on Marie, Rachel, and Oliver.

We walked over to Oliver's house, going through the side gate to get in the back yard.

It took my brain a moment to process what my eyes were

seeing. Rachel and Oliver were standing in front of two of the practice dummies, heads down, arms behind them. What were they doing? Wait. They weren't standing in front of the practice dummies, they were *tied* to the dummies. Blood coated the fronts of their shirts.

"I don't know how you got here so quickly, but you're messing with my fun."

Damn it. Isaac. How?

"The wolves were a distraction. Beck, what do I do? Scott and I are no match for Isaac, Mya, and a dozen other vampires! Oliver and Rachel are alive, but barely."

I was getting better at my mental mapping. I could pick out the auras faster every time I tried.

Isaac stood with Marie cradled to him. Her eyes were glazed again.

I stepped farther into the yard. "Your plan with the wolves didn't work," I said to Isaac, sounding more sure of myself than I felt. "They know who you are now and are siding with us."

He laughed and crushed Marie closer to him. "I could give a shit about a little pack of wolves. I just hoped they'd kill your humans and shifters and you'd kill them. I needed you away for a few hours to get my Marie back and feed my newly changed followers."

"You know you're no match for me, Isaac." I pulled the swords, glad I hadn't locked them in the lock box with the guns. That meant Scott only had one pistol on his hip, though. No sliver ammo and probably just one clip. We were outnumbered and outgunned.

Isaac lifted his chin to Oliver and Rachel and a half dozen of the vampires swarmed toward them. "I don't need to be a match for you. Do you want your friends to live?"

"Sword," Scott said to me as he took off at a run.

I tossed one sword to him as he zoomed by, straight to the

vampires around Oliver and Rachel. If circumstances had been different, if Scott hadn't had my blood and the vampires hadn't been newly turned, it never would have worked.

It took five seconds, six swipes of the sword, for Scott to cut the heads off the vampires where they stood. He stopped in a crouch by Rachel and Oliver. It was fantastic poetry in motion just like Marie had been during training.

Isaac sniffed the air and screamed at the sky in confusion and anger. "How? How do you move and smell of Shadower? You can't be. This can't be happening." Marie didn't move or acknowledge Isaac's temper tantrum.

Electricity moved over my skin and a popping sound came in my right ear.

Beck teleported in next to me.

Isaac screamed at the sky again and moved like he was going to fly away with Marie. I was not going to have a repeat of the last time he took her.

I grabbed Beck's hand and teleported us right on top of Isaac. I slammed him to the ground, sliding the short sword into his right shoulder, pinning him to the grass. He screamed in pain as the silver burned through skin and muscle. Marie finally reacted, but it was not the one I wanted. She screamed in pain along with Isaac.

Beck was holding her locked in his arms. Blood oozed from her shoulder, a wound inflicted from an invisible sword. She really was that connected to him. He bled, she bled. Part of me had hoped it wasn't true.

I let go of the sword and put my hands on Isaac's head. "SLEEP!" I sent power flooding into him. His body bowed off the ground, but he didn't sleep or pass out.

"He is too powerful due to Marie's blood," Beck said, trying to soothe Marie.

I heard a rush of air and turned my head just as Mya

jumped at me. I held up my hands to try and grab her so I could throw her. She used the distraction to pull the sword from Isaac's shoulder and swipe it at Beck and Marie.

As the sword sliced Beck's arm, searing pain shot through mine. I fell to my knees, gripping my bleeding arm as Beck released Marie to come to me.

Scott grunted from behind us. I chanced a look. The six remaining vampires were more careful than the first. Scott was holding them off and getting a good slice in here and there. Two of the vampires were missing arms.

Knowing he was holding his own for now, I put my attention back to Isaac. He hadn't moved from the ground. Marie crawled to him, touching his face and crying.

I stood, squared my shoulders, and raised both hands to the sky. "Marie," I commanded, "come back to me!"

Mya moved to Isaac and Marie, my sword in her lowered hands. "Let's go," she begged, Isaac. "This isn't what was supposed to happen. The Shadower can kill us."

"Not yet," Isaac said. "This needs to end."

I agreed with him.

I could feel the slice in my arm healing and I assumed Beck's was healing too.

"Marie," Isaac said, slowly moving from the ground. "Kill them." He took the sword from Mya and handed it to Marie.

Beck moved to protect me.

Marie stood slowly, eyes black orbs. Her and Isaac's shoulder wounds were healing as well.

"What do you wish me to do?" Beck said, glancing over his shoulder at me then back to Marie.

I put my hands on his arms. "We can't kill her or Isaac. We *can't*. We have to do something. Anything but that." But I had no idea what.

I looked from behind Beck and made eye contact with

Marie. *"Marie,"* I sent the mental message to her. *"Please, Marie. You're stronger than him. Fight it."* My body vibrated with tension and I tried to break the bond between Marie and Isaac.

Howls filled the air. A dozen wolves, two cougars, one with a purple tuft of hair, a brown bear, a leopard, and a panther scrambled over the security fence like a colony of ants. Growling and howling, they made a circle around the vampires trying to kill Scott.

All eyes moved to Beck and me, waiting for a sign of what to do next.

"Please, Marie, come back to me!"

Arms dropped to her sides, one hand gripping the sword, Marie said, "We will all be free, Kinsley." Her voice was monotone, devoid of any emotion.

Isaac laughed manically. "Yes," he said. "Yes! Do it, Marie! Kill the vampire. He won't hurt you because Kinsley will always choose *you* over *him*!"

Beck's body tightened under my hands.

Marie's eyes finally met mine. She was her again; there was no confusion or black. Yes! We were going to make it through this.

Then she said, "I love you, Kinsley. This is the only way I know to protect you. Please forgive me. I love you."

"What?" Why was she asking me for forgiveness?

Marie lifted the sword, ready to take Beck down.

"Marie! No!" I screamed as I tried to get around Beck to block the sword. She *knew* if she killed Beck I'd die too. This was how she wanted to protect me? I thought she was herself again.

"Do it, Marie!" Isaac chortled. "We will live forever!"

"The moment she attacks me, Kinsley, you have to get to Beth. Maybe she can save you."

"No!" I yelled at him. "I won't leave you!"

"Masters!" Beck yelled without taking his eyes from Marie. "Get Kinsley to Beth! Keep Kinsley alive until Lilith arrives! Remind Lilith she owes me! Do you understand?"

"Fuck! I understand!" Scott said, running toward us. He dropped the sword and picked me up in a fireman carry. Before I could protest, we were running the opposite direction.

"Put me down, you son of a bitch! I can't just leave him!" I pounded on Scott's back and he grunted and stumbled.

"Kinsley, stop," Beck said quietly in my mind. *"It is okay. When I am dead you will be free."*

The fight went out of me and I sobbed. "You can't die, Beck! I need you! I need us. I'm not whole without you!" Scott stumbled again, but this time it wasn't because I hurt him physically. I'd driven the metaphorical knife into his chest as we all realized I'd made my choice.

"God *damn* it," Scott said as he stopped and put me on my feet. "I knew I didn't stand a chance against him." He slammed his mouth onto mine in a brutal mating that hurt but left me breathless.

I pulled away. "What are you doing?" I wanted to slap him. I wanted to sink into him and disappear from the hell going on behind us.

He rested his forehead on mine in a half-second touch. "Well, if we all die today, I needed to kiss you one last time. And if we all live, I needed to kiss you one last time. It's obvious you don't love me the way you love him." He kissed me one more time and turned to the fight.

Beck stood there, waiting for Marie to kill him. Scott pulled his pistol from his hip holster. He didn't have silver, but it would slow them down while I tried to figure out what to do. He ran, firing alternating shots at Marie's and Isaac's torsos.

Their bodies moved from the impact but it didn't do a damn bit of good.

Marie lifted her arms to swing the sword, but shifted her feet at the last second and swiped the blade across Isaac's throat.

The sword tumbled from Marie's slack hand as they both fell to the ground.

Isaac's head was barely connected to his body.

Which meant Marie would die too.

Chapter Twenty-Seven

SEARING pain ripped through my heart. I screamed at the sky. The wolves howled with me, a hollow mourning song to echo the pain in my soul. Lightning flashed.

"Kill the vampires," I said waving my hand at the group Scott had been fighting.

The wolves mourning howl changed to a hunting song. I barely registered the carnage behind me as I gathered energy from the sky.

My whole body felt electric as I pulled the energy into my hands. I wanted to blow things up; I *needed* to kill and make my pain felt by all.

"Kinsley. Come back to me. Stop."

Suddenly Lilith popped in next to Beck.

"Finally," he said.

I pushed Beck's voice from me. He couldn't stop this pain. No one could.

The lightning hit all of them: Beck, Lilith, Marie, Isaac, and Mya. Their bodies flew through the air, scattering around the back yard like rag dolls dropped from a toy box. I fell to the ground, hands flat on the grass. The pulsing of the earth worked its way from my palms to my wrists to my elbows. It was thicker and softer than the energy I'd taken from the sky.

Abi appeared next to me. "What exactly do you think you're doing? Maybe you could see if Marie's dead before you kill her some more? Temper tantrum much?"

I closed my eyes to stop the dizziness threatening to make me pass out. "What do you know?"

Abi laughed and it almost sounded like a kid even though I knew she wasn't. Her giggle made my skin crawl. "Demon here, remember? I know a little about death and destruction. If you hadn't just blown Lilith around, she could have saved Marie for you."

I felt Scott at my side. "Kinsley? Are you okay? Did you do that on purpose?" He paused. "Where did this damn kid come from?"

My eyes shot open. "You can see her?"

Abi put her hands on her hips. "Seriously. You have got to be one of the dumbest humans I've dealt with in a long time. Your priorities are messed up. Gotta be honest here; I'm going to take advantage of your emotions." Abi did a finger wave at Scott.

"You're the ghost demon," he said.

"He's a little quicker on the uptake than you," Abi said.

I shook my head and looked around. It had taken less than thirty seconds for my shifters to tear the vampires to shreds. Body parts I didn't even want to try and identify littered the yard.

"Beck? Marie?" I said, trying to make my voice carry to where I could see them on the ground.

Nothing.

What had I been thinking? Why did I bring the lightning? I hadn't been thinking, that was the problem. Once again, I was letting my emotions get in the way. I hadn't even tried to see if

Marie was still alive, I'd just assumed she was dead because Isaac looked dead.

I sent out my mental map. Everyone in the yard was alive. I could still save Marie.

I moved to where I'd blown them down. The ground had a three-foot round by one-foot deep charred crater.

Raven moved to me and bumped my legs.

"How did you know?" I asked, even though she couldn't answer. "Thank God you guys showed up."

"God didn't have anything to do with it," Abi said. "It was more like a vision by your leopard I may or may not have pushed into her mind."

"You can do that?" I took a step away from her.

She shrugged. "I wasn't sure if I could, but I thought I'd try."

"Thank you?" I said slowly.

"I didn't do it for you," Abi said with a dangerous smile.

Damn demon ghost girl was too cryptic for my current state of mind. "What do you want?" I sighed, hands up.

"If Marie isn't already dead after the near decapitation and you trying to roast her, I'll save her life while you kill Isaac."

"What's the catch?" asked Scott.

"Who cares!" I said. "Yes." I turned to the shifters. "As soon as you can, get shifted back to human. We need the medical crew here! Someone call Dr. Chavez and someone else procure a clean-up crew."

I found Marie's body. She wasn't moving and she looked dead. Her head was attached, but her neck was bleeding out. Her aura was weak.

Scott rubbed a hand down his face when he came to us." What about using your blood?" he asked. "Maybe you could cut yourself and drip blood on Marie's neck? Or in her mouth?"

"I'll do it for you and you won't have to injure yourself," said Abi. "Tick tock, times'awasting. Let's get this over with."

"What's your hurry and what's the catch?" Scott said again.

"What's my hurry?" Abi said, waving an arm at the bodies. "It's already been a few minutes while your silly girl here threw a temper tantrum with lightning. Isaac's head is barely attached to his body which means he's still alive but won't be for long. That means Marie won't be alive for long."

"What do I need to do?" I cried.

"I'll keep Marie alive while you incinerate Isaac. Use the lightning, completely destroy his body, and I'll make sure Marie doesn't die with him. You have like ten seconds to decide. You'll just owe me a favor some time down the road. No biggie." She put her hands behind her back and kicked at the dirt, the perfect picture of an innocent six-year-old. Who wasn't innocent. Or six.

"I'm not super religious," Scott said, putting his hand on my arm, "but I'm pretty sure owing a demon a favor *is* a big deal."

"*Beck?*" I tried again. I needed his advice and probably Lilith's, but did it really matter? Abi said she'd save Marie.

I stood and pulled on the lightning like I did before.

"Make sure your aim is better than last time," Abi said, putting one hand on Marie's forehead and one on her chest. "You need to make sure you hit and destroy only Isaac and not the rest of us."

"Kinsley," Scott said, reaching for me again.

"Stay back so I don't hurt you. It will be fine." I think.

"Ready?" said Abi. When I nodded she said, "Three, two,"

"No!" Lilith screamed at the same time Abi said, "One!" and Scott said, "Holy Shit! Your eyes. Your hair."

I threw all the energy I'd been holding from my hands into Isaac's body.

The strike was so bright, I couldn't see anything but a

white-hot ball of light. I heard groans, growls, and yells from all around me.

"Damn you!" I heard Lilith say.

"What have you done?" Beck asked.

Sure, now he was awake.

Abi laughed, the creepy combination of small child and demon. "Don't forget," she said, "you owe me a favor." And she disappeared.

"Beckford!" Lilith screeched.

"Kinsley, what have you done?" Beck repeated, sounding sad and angry.

I moved to Marie and used my mental mapping. Her aura was bright and healthy.

"I saved Marie and killed Isaac. That's all I've ever wanted to do."

I knew she was alive even if she wasn't awake, it was all I needed to know right now.

"So," Scott said slowly, looking around the destroyed back yard, "we're going to need to talk about your abilities. Your hair was flying around your head and you were glowing; your eyes and your skin."

I shrugged and held up my hands.

Scott moved to where Isaac had been. It looked a little like the chair in Marie's room at the medical facility. There was a pile of ash where Isaac used to be.

I let out a huge sigh. Tears gathered in my eyes. "It's finally over," I whispered.

Scott came to me, acted like he was going to pull me in for a hug, but stopped. "What now?"

Such a loaded question.

People in different stages of shifting and clothing moved around the yard. Gerald was getting Rachel untied from the practice dummy and Raven and Mei were working on Oliver.

Shit. I'd forgotten about Rachel in my need to save Marie. Once again, the humans were hurt. I shook my head and rubbed my eyes.

Sighing, I turned and put my hands on Scott's face. He didn't move away from me, but he shifted his eyes. "I'll take care of organizing all these guys. You go make sure Beck's okay. I'll have Raven stay by Marie until Beth gets here," he said.

I held his face and pulled his forehead down to mine so he'd have to look at me. "I'm sorry," I said. "I wasn't trying to choose one of you over the other."

He kissed my forehead and pulled my hands away. "I know, sweet thing. I also knew I never stood a chance. You're a Shadower. You're *his* Shadower." He kissed me on the cheek, dropped my hands, and backed away.

My heart clenched. I *was* Beck's Shadower. We were puzzle pieces that fit together perfectly. Which meant I needed to get rid of Lilith. We didn't need her anymore now that Isaac was dead.

Beck was trying to placate an enraged Lilith when I went to them.

"I should unleash my lust on this back yard and make them all fuck until their hearts explode!" she screamed at me.

Ewww. What?

"*Beck?*"

"Take Mya, as agreed, and go. We will make good on the rest when the time is needed."

"No!" Lilith yelled. "I refuse to be indebted to you!"

"You mean as I was indebted to you for so many years? It is not a good feeling is it? Take Mya and leave. We will be in touch." The steel in his voice left no room for argument.

Lilith threw a scorching gaze at me. Expecting her to *unleash her lust*, as she had said, I threw a barrier up to try and stop her from getting in my head. It worked.

She stomped her foot like a pouting child, put a hand on Mya's arm, and the two of them disappeared in a pop of air.

Beck turned to me, eyes bright.

"We did it," I whispered, tears falling onto my cheeks.

"You did it," he said, opening his arms.

"I'm so sorry I kind of blew you up." I put my head on his chest.

He kissed the top of my head. "We need to work on your control. Your emotions must have something to do with the amount of power you throw around. I feel weak as a kitten."

I stayed in the circle of his arms, but pulled back enough to look up at him. "You were really going to sacrifice yourself for me?"

He raised an eyebrow and shook his head like I was silly. "Of course. I could not kill Marie; you would never forgive me."

I closed my eyes, put my head back on his chest, and let him hold me. For a moment, I had been put in the situation of having to choose between Beck and Marie. I hadn't wanted either of them to die. But what had really been going through my mind when I thought Marie was going to try and kill him?

That I couldn't live without Beck.

I stood on tiptoes and pulled Beck down for a kiss. I sent a mental message to him of how much he meant to me. We were going to need some alone time once things were cleaned up and I knew Rachel and Marie were okay. We had a lot to figure out. He kissed me back and a calm came over me. Everything was going to work out; I could feel it.

He pulled back from the kiss, his face relaxed. I smacked him on the chest. "So, you can teleport from a moving jet? And so can Lilith? You better call Nate. He's probably pissed you *popped out* without a word."

Beck put both hands in my hair and massaged the back of

my head and neck. "He will know you needed help. I will let him know we are okay, Isaac is dead, and Rachel is safe."

Beck pulled his phone from his pocket and I went to Rachel.

The wolves were laughing and congratulating themselves on the kills and the fact not a single shifter was hurt.

"Vampires taste gross," one of them said.

"You've never killed a vampire?" another asked.

"Enough," said Dagan.

"I recognized you," Scott said slowly. "You have black hair that looks like a star on your wolf's head. You were there that night."

I froze. Dagan was the wolf who had left Scott and Logan alone that horrible night? The one who'd left them a cell phone and not killed them?

"Yes," said Dagan.

"Why?"

"Exactly what I said at Screamers. Warner was a horrible man, wolf, and pack leader. He sent us out to kill families and bring back people to change. You boys fighting back let me get away with not bringing you in."

I waited to see what Scott would do. He turned to me then back to Dagan. "Before Kinsley, I'd probably just kill you. But she's taught me things aren't always black and white. Plus, you saved us that night."

Dagan dipped his chin. "I will never allow the pack to be as it was when Warner was in charge," he said. "I can't change the past, but I can build a future. Forgive me for the deaths and the pain you suffered."

Dagan held out his hand and Scott didn't even hesitate. They shook, nodded to each other and sealed some kind of invisible pact to let the past go.

Scott patted me on the shoulder and walked to Oliver.

Dagan moved to me. He lowered his head in a brief show of submission. I tried to make sure the surprise wasn't on my face.

He lifted his head and met my eyes. "Silver Shadower, I underestimated you and your power. I am glad the vampire Isaac is dead. My pack and I are indebted to you for helping us see his deception and for destroying him."

I nodded. "You're welcome. I'd like for us to work together as much as possible. There is power and safety in numbers."

"Agreed," Dagan said. "I promise to be in touch after I talk to Chun-Chieh."

"Thank you," I said. I offered my hand for a shake just as Scott had. Dagan accepted. "Now I'm going to go check on my human friends."

Even though I knew Oliver and Rachel weren't dead because of my aura reading, I didn't know how badly they were hurt.

Raven looked up when I got to where Rachel and Oliver lay on the ground. She said, "I healed the bite marks at their necks. Their heartbeats are slow. There's no telling how much blood they lost from the feedings. We need to get them to the medical facility for blood transfusions and I'm pretty sure Oliver's arm has been rebroken."

"Damn it, I think you're right," Scott said from the ground by Oliver.

"Do you think he'd object to my blood?" I asked.

Scott snapped his head up. "You'd do that?"

"Of course."

"Do what?" Raven asked.

Karlof, Beth, Jared, and two other vampires from the medical facility came through the gate into the backyard. Beth searched me out in the mess and moved briskly toward us. "What do we have?"

Raven explained how Rachel and Oliver had been fed on

by probably a dozen new vampires and we didn't know for how long.

I put my hand on Beth's arm. "Beth? Would it be possible to inject them both with my blood as a short term fix?"

She opened her eyes wide and nodded. "Yes. But do you want me to do it in front of everyone?"

I shrugged. "If it will fix them, I don't care."

Karlof grunted his approval. "There's hope for you yet, child."

"Do not push your luck, Karlof," Beck said.

Karlof seemed taken aback Beck was there. As far as everyone knew, he was still in Greece. "I am sorry, sir," Karlof mumbled.

The wolves brought some chairs to us and Beth used a syringe to withdraw my blood and inject it into Rachel and Oliver. They started to come around almost immediately.

"We'll do the bone thing with Oliver's arm if he wants," I said. "Also, I need you to check on Marie."

"Never a dull moment since you joined us, Kinsley," Beth said with a smile. "At least this time no one from our side is dead and no one's been kidnapped."

Scott laughed. "If we keep setting the bar that low, it should be smooth sailing from here on out."

Chapter Twenty-Eight

THE SUN WAS COMING up when Nate burst through the doors of the medical facility.

Beck took him to Rachel's room since I had just finished in the OR for Oliver's bone injection of my blood. Scott and I sat side by side outside the room waiting for Beth to finish up.

"In a million years, I never could have pictured this future," Scott said. His eyes were closed and he was slouched down so his head was rested on the wall and the back of the chair. "I had no idea what was going to happen when Tom and Claire died. When I approached you at the cemetery I thought: she has to know *something* even though Tom said you didn't."

I rubbed my eyes. "Can you imagine if he just would have done it? Trained me? They wouldn't be dead."

Scott's eyes popped open. He sat up and took my hands. "Don't do this, sweet thing. You can't change the past. You can't play *what if*."

I gripped his hands. "Why would Isaac kill them?" I asked. "I hate to admit it, but Lilith and Beck were right about that. Isaac wouldn't have wasted their blood."

"He didn't need their blood. I think his goal was to get Marie back, then get you. He knew you hadn't been trained.

He figured you were just a kid and he'd have you both as captives, maybe even convince you both you needed him and loved him." Scott reached up to wipe tears from my cheeks. "Tom and Claire were in the way. Had always been in the way. He had a chance to kill them and took it."

I took a deep breath and nodded, pulling my hands back, wiping more tears away. "You're probably right. So, now what?"

He shrugged. "Everything we had planned before this shitstorm hit us. We work together, we train, we take out the bad guys, and we recruit the good guys. None of that changes. The world goes on. Just now, Isaac isn't in it, thanks to you."

I broke eye contact. "What about us? Did I ruin everything?"

Scott gently took my chin and turned my head so I had to look at him. "Of course not. We already proved we can work together. None of that changes, either."

I stood and pulled Scott up with me. "Thank you for taking care of our people."

He shrugged. "We had a lot of help. It was a sight to behold, watching the shifters kill those vampires."

"What about you? Six vampires? Impressive." I bumped his shoulder with mine.

He shrugged again, but looked away embarrassed." They were newly turned and I had Shadower blood."

"Don't be so modest. You kicked ass. Speaking of that, how do you feel? I don't know if we should have waited to see if you had side effects before we gave my blood to Rachel and Oliver."

He stretched his arms to the ceiling, then dropped them down and rolled his shoulders. "I'm tired, as I should be, considering I haven't slept for over thirty hours, but I'm not dead on my feet. I also still feel stronger than a *regular* day."

Beth came around the corner, catching the end of our

conversation. "I'm really curious to know how long you're going to feel the effects." She turned to me. "Rachel is completely healed; Oliver is feeling no pain and should be completely healed soon; Marie is awake, all vitals look good. Beck went to her room and asked for you to join him. Karlof is there."

I took Scott's hand and squeezed. "Scott, really. Thank you. I wouldn't have survived without you."

He pulled me in for a side hug. "Yes, you would have. But you're welcome. Go be with Marie."

As I went down the hall I heard Scott say, "So, Doc, how about dinner tonight or tomorrow? Wait. You don't eat food. How about a movie?"

I shook my head with a chuckle. The man was incorrigible. And I obviously hadn't broken his heart.

Marie sat in the hospital bed, arguing with Beck and Karlof. "I'm fine. Unhook all this crap and take me to Kinsley."

"I'm here. What were you thinking?" I threw myself into her arms and started to sob. "You were going to kill yourself? What were you thinking?" I wasn't even sure if she could understand me. All the fear and loss I'd kept held in since I'd seen her slice Isaac's throat flowed over me.

"Oh, honey," she said, awkwardly pulling me so she could hold me in her arms on the bed. "I couldn't think of any other way. As long as Isaac is alive, neither of us will ever be safe. I'm sorry I tried it. I didn't know what else to do. We'll come up with something."

I let her hold me a little longer, then her words sank in. I pulled back and wiped at my eyes and nose with the back of my hand. "We'll come up with something for what?"

"To kill Isaac," she said sadly, shaking her head. "I don't know how, but we will."

I looked back and forth from Beck to Karlof. They

shrugged. I put my hands on Marie's face. "Isaac is dead. I burned him to ash with lightning."

She pulled her head away. "You what? How?"

"I used the Silver Shadower Powers."

"No," she said slowly, "how am I not dead too? Is the lore wrong? Can a vampire die and its Shadower doesn't?"

I scrunched my face and held up my hands. "I kind of made a deal with a demon. She kept you alive while I killed Isaac."

Marie whipped her head to Beck. "You let her make a deal with a demon? What's wrong with you?" She pushed me aside to get out of the bed, like she was going to attack him.

He held out a hand. "I did not let her do anything. I was knocked out."

Karlof grunted and left the room mumbling about me having too much power.

Marie turned back to me, fear in her eyes. "Oh, Kinsley, what were you thinking?" She covered her face with her hands. "Demon deals never turn out the way you hope."

I gripped her shoulder. "We can't change it. It's done. You're alive and Isaac is dead. I'll deal with the consequences of owing Abi a favor when the time comes."

"Abi?" Marie said, moving her hands. "Who's Abi? It wasn't Lilith to make the deal?"

"No. Lilith was knocked out, too. The demon is stuck in the ghost of the little girl Isaac killed at the old house. The girl's name was Abi, so now that's the demon's name to me."

Marie laughed. "I thought I caused problems! You're worse than me!"

I swatted at her hands and laughed too. "I am not!" I felt better. Isaac was dead. Marie was free. Everything was going to be okay; I could feel it. "How do you really feel?"

She closed an eye and cocked her head. "I thought you

blasted Isaac out of my mind again and that was why I couldn't feel the connection. I feel *so* good, Kins. My mind is clear, my body feels young and strong. I haven't felt like this, well, since my parents and siblings were alive." She closed her other eye. "Am I really finally free?"

"Yes," I said and hugged her. "Let's go home."

She opened her eyes and sat up straight. "Where is home?"

"Good news," Beck said. "While we were in Greece, Nathaniel received the call that construction is done on the building. The inspection is tomorrow and we can move in."

I looked at Beck. "Since we're on the outskirts of town now, with the hunting property, I was thinking maybe you can build some small cabins for when we have visiting shifters and vampires."

Beck nodded and smiled. "That is a wonderful idea. I will have Nathaniel talk to the contractor."

"Marie, you're going to love it," I said. "Beck designed the new living quarters for all of us to have privacy but still together. It will be a little like the condo Isaac blew up, but only two levels and a basement along with a parking structure."

"Will the basement still have training facilities and the armory?" Marie asked.

"You know it," I said. "And the pool and hot tub in a UV filtering glass enclosure that can be blacked out if we have vampires who can't be in sun at all."

Beck smiled. "You sound like a real estate agent."

I shrugged. "Ever since you told me about it at dinner that night and then all the issues of living at Scott's, I've been thinking about it a lot."

Beck dipped his head. "That makes me more happy than you know."

I hugged Marie one more time and climbed off the bed. I took one of Beck's hands. "Originally, there were going to be the two studio apartments on the first floor for Gerald and Ian. I wonder what Floyd and Mei's plans are? If they stay, they can't live in a studio together. I wonder if they'll want to stay at the house on Scott's property?"

"Finish telling me about the new digs and then we can talk to Floyd," Marie said.

I leaned into Beck's side and told Marie, "The bedrooms will all be in a horseshoe around the perimeter with removable panels in the closets to let us into the room next door in case of emergencies. We have our own rooms, bathrooms, and sitting areas. It's almost like a little apartment so we can have privacy when we feel the need. Beck even made sure there's a gaming room so you and Nate can play video games whenever you want."

Marie clapped her hands and offered Beck one of her radiant smiles. "What a wonderful design. I can't wait."

"Me either," I said.

Beck pulled my hand to his lips and kissed the inside of my wrist. "Nor I."

"Enough you two," Marie said. "Get a room." But then she laughed. "Oh to be young and in love." She hopped out of bed, removing the monitor stickers on her chest. "Let's go check on Floyd."

Mei was in Floyd's room on the phone.

"Parker finally called," Floyd whispered.

I shot my attention to Mei. I couldn't gauge her mood. She was pacing and listening to whatever Parker was saying. She wasn't contributing much to the conversation except to occasionally agree or disagree.

"Marie, you look just like I remember you," Floyd said shyly, then looked away.

"Floyd," Marie said, "I'm so sorry for the pain I caused you all those years ago."

He shrugged and wiped a tear quickly. "It's the past. Can't be changed so no point in dwelling on it."

She stepped toward him but stopped. "The parts I remember, you were always so good to me. You deserved a life."

He smiled sadly, "Hunters don't have lives, love, you know that. I did have a son. A son I didn't really get to know. But now I have a chance with a grandson." He lifted his chin to Mei. "I'm going to do my best to help Parker understand what Mei is and that he can still love her."

"Will you stay with us, Floyd, or go back to Newport?" I asked.

"It all depends what Parker has to say and what Mei wants me to do. She said she agreed to be a mediator for the new group of wolves, or something like that. Her brothers will be coming, and she said she may have to go to China once her father found out she was here and working with the Silver Shadower."

"You are always welcome with us," I said. "You're our family."

"Thank you, girl, that means a lot. It's just really hard, you know?" He gestured to Marie.

I nodded. "I do know. Which is why I'll leave the decision to you. But I'm not going to let you disappear, just so you're warned."

He smiled. "Okay."

"We'll give you some privacy," Marie said. She reached out like she was going to try to hug him, but at the last minute gave his shoulder a squeeze and pulled me from the room.

"Can I go back to Scott's?" Tears ran down her cheeks.

I hugged her to me. "Life's going to be a little different now that you know what's going on around you."

"I guess I better start new Shadower Journals for us," she mumbled into my hair.

I pulled back to look at her. "What was in the ones Isaac took? Do you think he destroyed them or maybe Mya knows where they are?"

Marie let out a sigh. "The Journals were where each Shadower kept a record of what they went through, what happened during their lives, the creatures they came in contact with, and who were friends and foe. Also the time spent with Monarchs and how the bond grew, changed, and developed. Since your parents never bonded, their journals were just their hunting and observations."

I sighed in frustration. "So it probably doesn't even matter and Abi and her family died for nothing." I think that hurt more than not having the journals. Death in vain.

"Wait, Mya is alive?" Marie said. "You didn't kill her when you killed Isaac?"

"Lilith got to keep Mya as a payment of sorts."

Marie laughed. "They deserve each other. Maybe Beck can get Lilith to make Mya tell her where the Journals are."

"Beck and I have a lot to talk about and figure out." I felt my cheeks heat.

Marie finally smiled. "Yes. Yes, you do. So how about if you get Raven and Nate to take Rachel and me back to Scott's. Go figure out your Monarch, baby girl. Life is about to change again." With those prophetic words, she wandered down the hallway.

"Beck?"

He popped in next to me. "Shall we go?" He held out his hand.

"That's really convenient," I said through a laugh. "But you were literally ten feet away in the other room. Now you're just showing off. Are we going to *pop* somewhere else?"

He shook his head. "Not this time. I wish to take you on small trip."

We drove out of Bellevue, got on I-90, and headed toward Issaquah.

Beck pointed to the trees as we drove. "The property borders the Cougar Mountain Wildland Park. That park is next to Squak Mountain State Park and Tiger Mountain State Forest. Acres upon acres for shifters to run when they need. Even though people hike there, lots of people actually, at night it is a safe place for the shifters to hunt wild game. I had never built out here before because the commute to the University would have been horrible."

I laughed. "A vampire complaining about commuting is probably one of the weirdest things I've ever had to ponder."

He shrugged but laughed with me. "It always seemed ironic to me as well. Top of the food chain, as I like to remind myself and others, yet something as simple as traffic still has an impact."

I turned to watch his expression. "Is your resignation at the University official?"

He nodded and reached over to take my hand. "Yes. And it is okay. You were right at the beginning of all this. We cannot be on campus putting humans in danger. Also, there is much to do in other areas of our lives. Screamers is going to be busy. I am putting Nathaniel in charge of Screamers. I also have the antiquities business." He squeezed my hand. "If Marie really does have no ill effects from the loss of bonding from Isaac, I thought of having her run the antiquities and art side of things. Having lived many years, she would be great at it. It will also give her something to do."

I gawked, eyes wide. "When did you have time to come up with all this?"

"While flying to Greece," he said with a shrug as he parked in front of a hotel not far from Lake Sammamish. He turned sideways in his seat and took both my hands. "With nothing sexual attached to the offer, I wish for you to stay the night with me in a multi-bed suite, have dinner, discuss the future, and just be alone and relax."

I squeezed his hands in mine. "I would like that very much."

Beck looked at the hotel front, then back to me. "There are fancier hotels in the city, but I wanted to take you with me tomorrow for the inspection of the new complex and this puts us just a few miles away."

I looked at our joined hands and back to him. "I don't need fancy, Beck. I just need you."

His eyes dilated slightly, taking on the golden ring. I felt our bond pulse.

"And I need you. But talking first," he said.

As we got out of the car, a thought hit me. "I don't have an overnight bag. Maybe we can go shopping?"

He smiled and pointed to the trunk of the car. "I had Raven put together a small bag for you. If there is something missing, we will get it."

I wasn't sure how I felt about Raven knowing I was spending the night with Beck. I brushed it off. It didn't matter what anyone else thought. I was his Shadower and no matter what happened in our relationship, there wasn't time to worry about modesty or other people's opinions. There wasn't going to be much privacy ever again. Especially when we were all back living together, even if we had our own rooms. There wasn't anything conventional in a world of shifters, Shadowers, and vampires.

For the next few hours, we spent time together like any new couple on a first date. Brunch, a leisurely walk around the paths of Lake Sammamish, and coffee before heading back to the hotel. We held hands, we laughed, and I told stories of growing up. It was like before I'd found out I was a Shadower.

There was no threat, I wasn't responsible for anyone but me, and I could act like any other twenty-one-year-old for a little bit.

"Age is relative," Beck said as we entered the hotel lobby. "I was not trying to read your mind, but I find we are even more connected than usual."

"Age is just a number, isn't it?" I sighed. "Sometimes I feel young and inexperienced and sometimes I feel I've lived multiple lifetimes. Do you know how long I'll live?"

He shrugged as he led me down the hallway. "I do not know for sure. The Monarchs were evasive in the questioning Lilith and I performed. I do not think even they know since the last of the Shadowers are you and Marie. The Journals of all Shadowers are lost and the Sovereignty did not care about anything but their own survival. Had the Sovereignty been smarter, they would have tried to work with Shadowers instead of kill them."

We entered our room and I slipped off my shoes. I sipped my coffee and moved to the small couch. "So," I said slowly. "What kinds of numbers are we dealing with? How many Sovereignty are there? Counting you, there are three Monarchs, right?"

He moved to the couch, but didn't sit. "At last count, Lilith knows of one hundred seven Sovereignty, all different levels of power. There were one hundred eight, but you killed the oldest and most powerful. Apparently my brother, Philip, is now the leader of the Sovereignty, because he was next oldest after Isaac. What we thought were only twelve members of the Sovereignty are actually twelve Cardinals who are their governing board."

I set down my coffee and held out my hand. Beck sat down next to me. I asked, "Do you know where Philip is?"

He sighed. "No. But Lilith does. She was supposed to stay

here and share what she knew. But when you made the deal with Abi, she was upset."

I raised an eyebrow. "Why was that?"

"I think, now, Lilith planned all along to offer the same deal Abi did. We have spent centuries trading favors. Two hundred years ago she helped me kill the Sovereignty who killed my human lover. I have owed her since." He paused and leaned over to give me a small kiss. "Yesterday, I killed the last of the Monarchs, setting her free of her debt to them, so now she owes me."

I pulled my hand away and put it to my now clammy face. "You killed the Monarchs? You're all that's left? Why would you do that?"

He shrugged like it was no big deal. "Simple. Power and your safety. I no longer answer to anyone, and you and Marie will always be safe. Except from the Sovereignty who will, undoubtedly at some point, come for you. But with all the power I gained from the last of the Monarchs and our combined Shadower bond power, we will be impossible to stop."

Black dots danced in my vision. I closed my eyes and took deep breaths. I had no idea how to respond to the news he'd killed the Monarchs. A small part of me felt relief; they wanted me and my blood. A small part of me was appalled. And while he gained from it, he was right, it made Marie and me safe from one less threat.

He touched my cheek. "Are you angry with me?"

When I felt like the need to pass out was gone, I met his gaze. "I'm just trying to wrap my brain around it. I know our world is different than the expectations and laws of the *normal* world. What kind of power did you gain?"

Beck took my hands again. "When a vampire kills another by biting them, they gain their memories. I have the memories of thousands of years of Monarchs passed down through other deaths. That means there are huge holes in the history because many Monarchs were killed by beheading or by Sovereignty instead of other Monarchs. My plan was to kill Isaac by biting him, draining him, and then beheading him."

I shivered.

"Then I would have had his memories and knowledge. But when we all realized the bond he still had with Marie and killing him would kill her, I was trying to come up with another way. Lilith said she could do it, but she would not share how."

I sighed. "So you kept Lilith around, once again, for me. To protect me."

He nodded. "Yes. As I have tried to explain, everything I do is always for you."

"Why didn't you just tell me from the beginning?" I pleaded. "I've felt threatened by Lilith and her sexuality since I met her."

He looked away, but didn't let go of my hands. "I wanted you to trust me. I needed to know how far you would go for *us*. It was a silly human emotion I did not even know I could still feel. Jealousy. Need. I think I wanted you to be just as jealous of Lilith as I was of Masters. Stupid and dangerous, I know."

I moved closer to him on the couch and made him look at me. "Emotions suck sometimes, don't they?"

"And sometimes they are perfect." He leaned down and nuzzled my neck, nipping at the skin. "You control everything, Kinsley. How fast or slow this new relationship progresses. The future. It is all in your hands."

I sucked in a breath, heart beating faster, and let myself go for the first time in months. I tried to push everything from my mind except Beck, our connection, and all he had done to keep me safe. I hadn't known it at the time, but he was my safe harbor and the anchor that held me there.

Chapter Twenty-Nine

HOURS LATER, I lay on the bed naked and satiated, heart completely full, mind completely blank.

"Holy cow," I said.

Beck chuckled and nuzzled my throat. "You have said that four times. Should I take it as a good sign?"

"I can't even move. Or think. Rachel was right when she said I'd finally understand when the deed was done."

"She cannot fully understand the bliss you felt," Beck whispered, causing goosebumps to erupt over every inch of my skin. "The bloodpact and our bonding makes the physical joining of our bodies that much better. A million times better. Even for me." He nipped the skin where my neck and shoulder met. "Hundreds of years of lovers. A succubus. The ecstasy of our lovemaking beats all of them."

The pride I felt disappeared and foolishness replaced it. It wasn't like the lovemaking was so amazing for him because it was me, but because of our bond.

"No," Beck said, meeting my eyes. "It *is* because it is you, my love." The gold of his eyes was stronger than I'd ever seen because I'd also let him feed from me.

I couldn't put into words, the way my body and heart felt.

"Complete," I said to him, trying to give some kind of explanation to the feeling.

"Yes. Complete," Beck echoed, putting his head back on my shoulder.

I stretched my arms over my head, the delicious ache of my body making me greedy. "How many days can we stay here?"

Beck moved back on top of me and kissed me deeply. He pulled back and smoothed the hair away from my forehead. "If you would not object, we will stay until it is time to move into the new house."

"That sounds like heaven," I said, pulling his lips back to mine.

He spent more hours loving me, loving my body, giving me bliss I'd never known was possible. I knew in my heart, mind, and soul this was what I was supposed to feel. This was where I was supposed to be. He was my *home*.

Evening arrived and I couldn't hold off my hunger any longer. We sat in the living room area, Beck on the couch, me on the floor using the coffee table as my dinner table. We chose to forgo regular clothes for the comfort of the luxurious hotel robes.

Despite my satisfying and mind-blowing intimacy with Beck, something had been bothering me. Since my sex-addled brain finally decided to work properly, it raced with new questions. After knowing the feeling of being Beck's completely, I didn't understand why my mom had chosen to be with another Shadower.

I reached out and touched Beck's knee. "Why do you think my parents chose each other instead of a Monarch?"

He shrugged. "We will never know, my darling. Maybe they never met a Monarch. Your father did an amazing job of staying hidden." After a brief pause, he added, "They had also seen the after effects of Marie and Isaac."

I shivered. "That makes sense. It was enough to scare me away from you. Isaac was supposed to love and protect Marie."

Beck reached out and trailed his fingers lightly over my cheek. "In the beginning, he may have thought he was. The power can go to your head. The rush is addictive."

I regarded him carefully, having another bite of soup and then pasta, giving myself time to form my question. I took time to eat slowly, wiped my lips with my napkin, had a drink of water, then finally asked, "How will we keep balance in our relationship?"

Beck carefully pushed the coffee table a few more feet from the couch and slid to the floor next to me. Pulling me into his lap so I straddled his hips, he locked his arms behind my back. He kissed my lips. "By mutual respect." He kissed each of my eyelids. "I believe I have fallen in love with you even though I tried to tell you I could not offer you love." He kissed each side of my neck then put his forehead to mine. "Your actions over the last day have reminded me there is unconditional love. The feelings and emotions I have when I slide into your body and feed from you is unlike anything I have ever had in eight hundred years."

My breath caught. Hearing him say the words made me happier than I thought possible. I'd felt the love from him even if he hadn't said it out loud. I felt more connected to him than any other person in my life, and that was saying something for all the love I had for my parents, Rachel, and Marie.

But friend and family love is different than romantic love. No less or more, just different. And Beck felt like the other half of my soul now that we'd surrendered to each other completely.

He slid his hands from the small of my back, over my shoulders, to my cheeks. "I love you, Kinsley," he said, as though testing the words.

"I love you too, Beck," I said without hesitation.

"Then we will survive anything together."

Yes, we would. I kissed him deeply, then offered my neck, sending him the feelings of love, hope, and passion that were zinging through my body. As his fangs gently slid into my skin, the same feelings echoed back to me like an invisible infinity ribbon, twisting and turning back and forth between us. Connecting us for eternity.

The evening was perfect. No phone calls or texts, no threats from psychotic vampires. We watched movies, explored each other's bodies more, and shared about our pasts. I snacked on food and drank wine until finally I couldn't keep my eyes open.

While I had dozed off and on during our lovemaking marathon, I hadn't allowed myself to fall asleep because I didn't want to miss a moment of my time with Beck. I finally admitted I was exhausted around midnight, my body deliciously sore and my heart full.

"Do you sleep?" I asked as I climbed into bed. I'd just dried my hair from a shower that had less to do with getting clean and more to do with mutual body exploring.

Climbing in next to me, he said, "I do not sleep the way you do, especially when I have fed so well and so much." He waggled his eyebrows and I blushed, hitting him with a pillow. I loved this playful side of him. "However, I do have to rest sometimes," he admitted.

I turned to him, propping my head on my hand. "I feel weird going to sleep when you can't."

He pulled me into his solid body, warm from our activities. "I will stay next to you and just hold you in my arms. I will rest. It will be glorious to be with you and watch you sleep. I will protect you."

I kissed him again, because I could, and gave myself over to the exhaustion I'd been keeping at bay.

SUNLIGHT WAS PEEKING through the curtains when my phone chimed with a text. I opened my eyes slowly as I stretched and adjusted my head on Beck's shoulder. I was in the same position I'd been when I'd fallen asleep.

"I didn't drool on you, did I?" Please don't let my first night with a guy be embarrassing. I wiped at my cheek and his shoulder.

He laughed. "Even if you did, I would find it adorable. But no. You did not." He kissed my temple and moved from the bed. "I will go get you breakfast and coffee. The text is Rachel. Nathaniel was able to keep her from contacting you until now. Her exact words to him were: 'If Kinsley doesn't call me this morning with the sexy deets, she may lose her best friend status.'" He handed me my phone with a laugh. "So please call her while I am gone so she is happy."

I giggled as I tapped my phone screen. "You sound exactly like her!" The text had a line of emojis: a peach, an eggplant, six hearts, another peach and eggplant, and the wide-eye face.

I covered my eyes and fell back on the bed laughing.

I sent her back the monkey covering his eyes, a heart, a peach, and an eggplant then typed that I'd call in ten minutes.

When Beck left, I brushed my teeth and hair, washed my face, and got dressed. As much as I wanted to pull the man back into bed, we had things to do today.

"Oh! My! God!" Rachel screamed through the phone when she answered. "How was it? No, wait, I know it was amazing. It has to be like sex with a shifter. But better. Does he drink your blood while you do it? Wait. Don't tell me. I don't want to know. Wait. Yes I do. OMG! How was it? How much will you tell me?"

I don't think she took a breath.

"How am I supposed to answer if you don't shut up?" I said through my laughter.

She shrieked, "It's not funny! Nathaniel wouldn't let me text you! He even took away my phone! I think Beck told him to! So? Tell me!"

As haughtily as I could, I said, "All you're going to get is that it was the most wonderful experience of my life. I refuse to share details the way you have for our entire friendship since you first had sex." I switched back to my normal voice. "But I will say, he told me he loves me!"

Rachel whooped, then asked, "So is Scott next?"

I pulled the phone away from my ear to stare at it. If Rachel had been here, I would have smacked her.

"No!" I shouted. Then I remembered to put the phone back to my face. "Beck and I are connected and bonded and he's it for me! Your stupid idea is not happening and Scott knows it! So don't bring it up ever again!" My chest was heaving and I felt like I might throw up. There was no way I'd be with anyone else. And I hoped Beck knew there was no one else for him, either.

Jealousy was my best friend and I'd kill anyone who tried to touch my man. Including Lilith. Queen of the Sluts would die a slow painful death if she thought they were just going to go back to their original arrangement.

Whoa. Finishing the bonding process with Beck had turned me into a crazy woman apparently. I'd felt jealously before, but not this soul-searing desire to eviscerate someone who tried to come between us.

Rachel laughed, pulling me from my mental murder scene. "I never wanted you to go through with it," she said. "I only said it to make you all think about it. Scott had to know you were always going to end up with Beck. You had to realize it, too. The rest of us knew it."

I froze, almost dropping my phone. "You did?"

"Well, yeesss," she said, like I was stupid, drawing the word out. "How could you possibly be bonded to a vampire and not be in a relationship with him?"

"Huh." I knew I probably looked like I'd taken a bat to the temple. "I was so busy trying to stay out of a relationship with either of them, I never really thought about what a relationship would or could be like. You're right."

"Well, yes, I'm right. I'm your best friend. I know these things." I could picture Rachel flipping her hair and rolling her eyes at me.

I moved to the couch. "So why didn't you sit down and tell me this months ago?"

She sighed. "You had to figure it out on your own so you and your silly heart would be on board. If I told you you *had* to be with Beck because you were bonded, you would have felt like it wasn't your choice. Every other choice about your life has been taken away. You had to make this choice so you'd know it was real."

Rachel was right. Looking back, I probably did know the only choice *was* Beck. I'd said it myself. I couldn't be in a relationship with someone else because it would rip Beck and me apart. For our Shadower bond to work the way it's supposed to, we couldn't have anything between us.

In that moment, in Oliver's yard, when I thought Beck was going to die and he was willing to sacrifice himself instead of killing Marie. *That* was when I'd known we were meant to be together.

I face palmed. "Took me long enough," I said at the exact same time Rachel said, "Took you long enough." We both broke into giggles.

She screeched through my phone again. "And, holy cow, chica! Your blood makes me feel like a whole new person! I can't believe how much energy I have and how good I feel. And my stamina in bed with Nathaniel almost matches his. It's like a drug. You could be addicting."

I blushed thinking of her and Nate because it also made me think of Beck and all the things we'd done together. Even though no one could see me or know what I was thinking, I was still embarrassed at the thoughts going through my head.

"*I know what you are thinking,*" Beck said. "*And I will be back in five minutes. You may eat and then we are going to do more of those wonderful things.*"

"Rachel, I have to go," I said breathlessly.

"Ooohh! You're going to go at it some more."

I huffed. "No, I am not. But Beck went to get me breakfast and when he gets back we're going to go to the new house for the inspection. Then we need to get furniture picked out and delivered so we can all move in." I hoped I sounded calm. I felt like I was on fire.

She blew a raspberry, the buzzing sound making me smile. "Whatever. You're going to spend the day doing the horizontal mambo, bumping uglies, and living your best life."

I scrunched my face in horror, even though she couldn't see me. "Bumping uglies? What are you? A twelve-year-old-boy? You're disgusting!" But I was laughing again. She was forever my bestie, for good and bad.

"Fine. I've been replaced," she fake whined. "I'll never see you again because Beck is going to keep you locked up as his sex slave for all eternity. And you're going to let him because now you know how amazing sex is." She sighed dramatically. "I'm going to miss you. I love you. Goodbye!" She was laughing as I hung up on her silly speech.

When Beck got back with food, he pulled me in for a kiss. "I have to tell you. In all the time we have been connected, I have never felt the joy and contentment you have in these moments."

I rested my head on his chest. "I didn't realize how much stress everything was causing. You, Scott, Marie, Isaac, and then Abi. It was eating me up. Now I finally feel free. Isaac is dead, Marie is not. You and I are completely bonded. Everything is as it should be."

"Yes, it is." He kissed me slowly. "Eat. So I can ravish you some more."

WE WERE late to the inspection meeting. Beck had turned me into an insatiable hussy. I loved it.

He squeezed my hand as I sent that thought to him. Then he became all business as the inspector went room to room with his clipboard.

The new condo was even better than I imagined. Seeing it complete after dreaming about it for weeks was a dream come true.

An hour later the inspector said, "I've never seen a project go up so fast. Did they work around the clock?"

"Yes," Beck said smoothly as they signed the papers.

The inspector tapped the clipboard to his palm. "Well, everything is in order. You can officially take occupancy."

"Thank you," I said shaking his hand.

When the inspector left, Beck called Nate and let him know the furniture could be delivered.

"You already have things ready?" I asked. Then I shook my head. "Wait, of course you do."

He smiled. "I needed you out of Scott's house and back with me as soon as possible."

"I feel like I should apologize," I started, trying to look away, but Beck cut me off with a finger to my lips.

"There is no apology necessary. The night Scott and I talked about your parents we also talked about you."

I put my hands on my hips. "Really?"

Beck smiled and took my hands, pulling my palms to his chest. "Nothing bad. Scott admitted he knew you and I were always supposed to be together. He said there would be no way for you to have a relationship with another person with the Shadower bond in the way. I told him I needed you to figure that out on your own."

I pulled away and tossed my hands in the air. "Did everyone know but me?" I covered my face.

Beck pulled me back to him. "Thank you for choosing me," he said quietly, kissing me in our new kitchen.

I wrapped my arms around him. "I think I knew it was you from the beginning. But it scared me."

He kissed the top of my head. "I know. And now that all is right in our worlds, it is time to decide what to do about Philip and the Sovereignty."

We drove back to Bellevue so we could meet with Scott, Floyd, and Mei. I wanted to know what Parker had said to Mei and I wanted to see what would happen when Scott, Beck, and I were in a room together.

I looked at my text messages as we came into Bellevue. "I texted Scott to see if we could meet at Masters Security, but he said Floyd was pretty tired. So let's go to the house." I turned to look at Beck. "I wonder if Floyd should have stayed in the medical facility longer?"

Beck reached across the console to rub my thigh. "If Beth said he could leave, then he is fine. He is frail and weak. A lot has happened in a short amount of time for him. The heart attack was inevitable."

I sucked in a breath. "You act like he's going to die soon. Do you know something I don't?"

Beck parked in front of Scott's house and turned to look at me, taking both my hands in his. "As we discussed last night: age is a number for people like us. Age is a ticking clock for humans. He will die, Kinsley. Many of the people in your life are going to age and die. It is the way of life. You are no longer part of that cycle, but it will be difficult in the beginning as you lose the humans you love."

I had a vision of funerals: Floyd, Scott, Rachel, Oliver, Logan.

"Stop, please," Beck said, taking my face in his hands. "I am sorry for bringing it up. Please do not cry."

I moved my hands to his and felt my tears. I hadn't even realized I was crying.

Beck put his forehead to mine. *"I am sorry, my love. I ruined our wonderful time."*

"You didn't ruin it," I said, giving him a brief kiss and wiping at my eyes. "I just haven't really had any time to wrap my brain around all the things being a Shadower means. They cross my mind and I start to think about dealing with one aspect, and something always happens. There's another emergency to deal with and I have to push my questions away." I rubbed my face. "You didn't ruin anything, I promise. I just have to take things as they come."

Rachel came bounding out of the house.

"Hurricane Rachel incoming," I said as I got out of the car, wiping away more tears.

As soon as she saw my face, Rachel went for Beck. "What did you do? She was happier than happy when I talked to her on the phone this morning!" She poked him. "Ow! What are you, made of steel?"

"Rach, he didn't do anything. I'm worried about Floyd and how frail he is. It got me emotional."

Rachel made a beeline for me and pulled me in for a hug. "Floyd'll be okay. He's too stubborn to die. He's just tired. We're all tired. It's been a crazy couple weeks."

Once inside, Nate was getting lunch together and we all congregated to the kitchen.

"Furniture will be delivered to the new house tomorrow," Nate said putting the makings for tacos on the table.

"Thank you," said Beck.

Mei, Floyd, Marie, and Rachel were at the table with Beck and me. "Where's Scott?" I asked.

"Right here," he said from behind me.

I stood and gave him a hug he didn't return. He stood stiff as he looked at Beck.

"Hey," I said, drawing his attention back to me. "It's okay. You're my friend and business partner, remember?"

Finally, he hugged me back. "You're glowing," he whispered in my ear. "Happiness looks good on you." He kissed my temple and moved to the table. My body relaxed and I released a breath I didn't realize I'd been holding.

Everything was going to be okay.

After everyone had made their tacos and eaten at least one, Scott pointed at Mei. "As usual, we have a problem."

The food sat like a rock in my gut. "What now?"

Mei finished a second taco before speaking. "Parker finally called yesterday, as you know. He wanted Floyd and I to know he was okay and things are progressing *great* with his clandestine *monster* hunting unit." She used air quotes when she said *great* and *monster*. She rolled her eyes, but I could see the stiffness of her shoulders and her controlled words were almost rehearsed.

"Just tell them," Floyd said, smacking a hand on the table.

Mei pushed her chair back. "Parker is going to meet Floyd and me at Floyd's house tomorrow. He said he needs to tell us some things about his new mission. In China." She closed her eyes briefly, then met my gaze.

I dropped my taco on my plate, no longer hungry. "Aw, hell," I said. "You have to tell him, show him, who you are. You have to keep him from going to China. Do you think the mission is your father?"

Mei sighed. "I can't think of any other reason for a military secret monster hunting unit to go except for my family."

"I'm going to drive them back tonight and be there when Parker gets there tomorrow," Scott said. "I'm going to take Logan and Oliver with me. We're going to sit down and tell him about my and Logan's families, what we've been doing as far as security and hunting, and then be backup when Mei confesses she's a shifter."

I looked back and forth from Scott and Mei. "Beck and I will go with you. Help explain things."

Mei was shaking her head. "Scott, Floyd, and I talked about it. We think it would be better if it's just humans. Parker's been ordered to kill anything not human and we're hoping he won't try and kill me." She wiped away a tear and waved her hand at us. "I don't want to put him in the position where he would have to try and kill any of you. Because Beck will protect you, Kinsley. If anything happens to Parker, I don't know what I'd do. I can't put anyone in this situation."

"I won't let him hurt Mei," Floyd said quietly. "We'll get him to listen to reason, leave that damn military unit, and come work with you guys."

I didn't know Parker, but I didn't think it was going to be as easy as Floyd thought it would be. Of course, what did I know?

I was the queen of making things harder than they needed to be.

Maybe Parker's love for Mei would be enough.

Chapter Thirty

"I LOVE THIS!" Rachel said the next morning as we supervised the furniture delivery. "I can't believe we get to live here!"

"It's amazing, isn't it?" I said, my attention drifting to my phone. I kept expecting a call or text from Scott.

"Stop," Rachel said. "Parker won't be there for hours, and then it may take hours of talking. They've got it under control. Enjoy this moment."

She was right, as always. Moving into our new home was a big deal and a huge step in my and Beck's new relationship. I owed it to the people here with me now to be present in the moment and help set up our new home. I couldn't help Mei and Floyd with Parker; Parker didn't know me. If Scott couldn't help, no one could. Scott had similar experiences as Parker. When and if they needed me, they would let me know.

It took a few hours for all the furniture to be unloaded from the delivery truck, unpacked and unboxed, and set up where we wanted it. Slowly our condo/apartment/house (I was going to have to pick a name) took on Beck's personality as the dark wood furniture was placed and colorful artwork hung on the walls.

It still amazed me all money could accomplish. For *normal* people, this would have taken eight to twelve months.

Beck came to stand in the living room with me. He took my hand. "I am sorry I did not ask you to help pick out the furniture."

I shook my head. "It's all beautiful. It reminds me of your old condo; sleek, modern, and you."

He kissed me on the cheek. "You still have your room but I would like it very much if you would consider sleeping in my bed. I do not spend much time in it myself, but I like the idea of the room, the sheets, smelling like you."

I blushed and looked around to make sure no one heard him.

"Still so innocent," he chided.

"It's just new to me."

"We will navigate the newness of this together."

And I knew we would. I had Marie and Rachel with me. Life was different, but we would handle it together. I was a Shadower and I could handle anything with my people.

Beck's phone rang. He showed me the screen: UNKNOWN CALLER, USA.

A tingle of unease worked its way up my spine. "It wouldn't be Floyd, would it? He'd call me, not you if he needed something, wouldn't he?"

Beck answered on speaker. "Yes?"

"Hello, Beckford," a man with a British accent said. "I hope you do not mind Lilith told me how to contact you. In fact, Lilith had all sorts of things to share."

I narrowed my eyes. I didn't know who was on the phone but I knew we wouldn't be able to trust Lilith.

"Beck!" Lilith screamed. "He has a witch! I never would have talked!"

A witch?

"Philip," Beck said slowly, "had I known you were not dead, we could have been together this whole time."

"Liar!" Philip yelled. "You betrayed me! And now I have your succubus and soon I will have your Shadower."

The line went dead.

A surge of anger and fear came from Beck through the bond. Fear? Why would he be scared of Philip with all the power we now had? I was the Silver Shadower and had destroyed Isaac. Philip was no match for us.

Was he?

Rachel stuttered, "A-a witch? Like bubbling cauldrons and magic wands?"

Nate pulled Rachel into his side and looked to Beck for guidance.

"No bubbling cauldrons or wands," Beck said. "But magic, yes."

"What does this mean?" I asked. "I'm the Silver Shadower. I destroyed Isaac. I can destroy Philip if that's what you want me to do, Beck."

Abi appeared in front of us, all bouncing curls and glowing red eyes, wrapped in a nightgown and holding a teddy bear. Seriously? Now she was just screwing with me.

Rachel screamed and Nate pushed her behind him, ready to attack.

That answered the question of whether or not everyone could see her now.

"You might have stood a chance if they hadn't found the witch," Abi said with a laugh. She pointed at me. "About that favor you owe me. Time to pay up before the witch gets here and kills you all."

A Note From The Author

Thank you so much for picking up your copy of *Second Chance*. I want you to know that without you, this adventure would not exist and I appreciate you more than I can say. You matter to me as a reader! As an independent author, your reviews of my stories matter too. I depend on the honest reviews readers like you leave on Amazon (just scan the QR code below) and Goodreads. Other readers use your insights when choosing what to read and will appreciate hearing your opinions of my book. I, of course, would love to hear from you as well. Please leave a review to let me know what you think.

Wishing you all the best,
Kyona

Acknowledgments

Everyone you meet is fighting a battle; be kind.

To my readers: I'm SORRY it took me so long to write the sequel. Life got in the way. Thank you for the emails and words of encouragement while I was writing FOR TWELVE YEARS. I love these characters and want to share their lives with you.

While this story is about love, loss, and family, it's also about friendship. I couldn't survive without the people who have always been there when I needed them.

Charity....I never have the words to thank you for your love, friendship, and business expertise. Thank you, Obi-wan.

Erin, thank you for always being a sounding board and friend.

Kelly, you are always there and know just what to say and do when I need you.

About the Author

As a teacher, Kyona is always writing stories and reading books for work and fun. Reading gives people an opportunity to relax and escape the pressures of everyday life. She lives in Eastern Washington with her loving husband and crazy dogs.

Life is short; enjoy it any way you can.

Also by Kyona Giles

RUNNING SERIES
Outrunning The Hunter
Running Out of Time

VAMPIRE SHADOWER SERIES
First Death
Second Chance

Made in the USA
Middletown, DE
21 May 2024